HARRIET'S DAUGHTER

Sarah Turner

Published in 2009 by Heron Books

Copyright © Sarah Turner 2009

First Edition

Sarah Turner has asserted her rights under the Copyright, Design and Patents Act 1988 to be identified as the author of this work.

This book is a work of fiction. Names, characters places and incidents are either a product of the author's imagination or are used fictitiously. Any resemblance to actual persons, living or dead, events or locales is entirely coincidental.

Printed and bound in Great Britain by
CPI Antony Rowe, Chippenham and Eastbourne

HARRIET'S DAUGHTER

Sarah Turner

Heron Books

Also by Sarah Turner

Cruel Legacy
Still Waters
Waste of Shame
Act of Love

For My Husband

About the Author

Sarah Turner was born in Co Durham and lived in London and France before settling in Warwickshire. She is married and has three children, three step-children and a horde of grandchildren.

Acknowledgements

I wish to thank Tom Williams for the cover design, Sue Clark for layout, Derek Turner and Angela Harris for editing and the rest of my family and friends for their encouragement and support.

PART ONE

Chapter One

March 1999

Laura was running, her Doc Martens pounding the pavement.

Without slowing down she glanced over her shoulder. He seemed to be gaining on her.

It hadn't been the smartest idea to leave the flat via the bathroom window and down the fire escape, but then she hadn't expected him to be in the yard, talking to Mr Patel who owned the shop below. It was so obvious she was doing a runner that he had immediately tried to stop her, but she had been too quick for him and now she was heading down the Foleshill Road, with him chasing her and not very far behind.

Terror sent a chill down her spine as she weaved her way through the crowded busy street, trying to lose him. She dreaded to think what he would do if he caught her, he was a mean bastard.

It wasn't her fault that they owed him three months rent, it was her stupid brother, but he was well out of it locked up in prison, not that she didn't feel sorry for him, but he had landed her in the shit.

Dodging down a side street she reached the edge of a building site. Ignoring the Private Property No Trespassing sign, she climbed through a hole in the wire fencing and crossed a stretch of litter-strewn wasteland, splashing through muddy puddles on the uneven ground. Her auburn hair worked loose from under the grey hooded tracksuit and fell across her face, so that she had to push it aside constantly. She skirted mounds of excavated earth and stacks of bricks in protective polythene until she finally reached the other side.

Without breaking her stride she crossed the ring road, dodging traffic, and headed towards the city centre. Her lungs felt as if they were on fire and she could hardly breathe. *God, she was unfit.*

She slipped down a narrow alleyway in the shadows of the cathedral and sat on a wall to catch her breath. Turning her head, she peered nervously through the darkness but the street was empty. She'd lost him.

It wouldn't be for long though, she knew that. She had to get out of town. Where to go was the question utmost in her mind. In her jeans pocket she had a crumpled ten-pound note and some change. She closed her eyes, seeing again Terry's anxious face last night. 'Go home, go back to Mum,' he had said.

'Never!' She had been shocked that he could suggest it.

'Laura, you're fifteen for fuck's sake, you can't stay here on your own.'

Then he confessed about the rent and that the landlord had threatened to break his legs if he didn't pay up. She had felt defiant because she was scared. 'He won't touch me, I can look after myself,' she had boasted.

Now, today, her brave words didn't sound so clever. But last night she hadn't really believed he would get sent down, certainly not for *three fucking years!*

She hadn't expected to be left on her own.

She was already missing him. Even though he was never big on conversation she missed his company. Despite what he had done, he was her brother and she idolized him.

She had returned from the courtroom this morning, back to the flat they had shared. Knowing she could no longer stay there didn't bother her. She hated it with its stained mustard-coloured walls; threadbare carpet and a sofa that must have come from the local tip. The permanent smell of curry wafting up from the Indian take-away below did nothing to endear the place to her.

She had stuffed her few possessions into her rucksack, there was very little to take; she didn't own much; two pairs of jeans, a few worn out tee-shirts and some faded underwear. The furniture belonged to the landlord; apart from the stolen telly and stereo.

Now as she sat alone in the darkness she thought about her options. There didn't seem to be any. Maybe going home was the best thing after all, but the moment Terry was released, she would be back. No question.

The phone box had been vandalised and stunk of urine, but at least the phone worked. She dialled home.

'Hello, who is this?' The voice was shrill. Not her mother. Laura was thrown. 'Sorry I must have the wrong number. I wanted Tina Armstrong.'

'Don't live 'ere no more.'

'What!' Laura was shocked. 'Where's she gone?'

'No idea. She buggered off without saying where she were going. Sorry can't 'elp yer.' The line went dead.

Leaving the phone box, Laura wondered whether to go to London anyway. Perhaps a neighbour would know where her mum had gone, or Linda, her mum's friend. She felt hurt, although not really surprised that her mum had disappeared without telling them. She had always been a crap mother. Even before her dad had walked out, her mother had shown little interest in them, preferring to spend her time at bingo, or clubbing with Linda.

Four years ago she and Terry had left and not been back. She supposed it was too much to hope for that her mother would be pleased to see her, especially as she had a new bloke. Nevertheless she was going to try and find her.

With a resigned shrug of her thin shoulders she headed for the bus station.

Chapter Two

Harriet Malin heard her husband insert his key into the lock of the front door and braced herself. She was on a short fuse and had been since Tuesday when the letter from the building society arrived. It was now Friday and Jeremy was home.

He kissed her cheek. She steeled herself to be polite. 'Had a good week?' she asked.

'Very good, excellent in fact. Signed up two good company pension schemes. Shall we eat out tonight to celebrate?'

Harriet forced a smile. She didn't believe him. Jeremy hadn't made a sale for several weeks. He was unaware that she knew that he lied about his job. He was a financial adviser for Northern Equity Insurance, based at their Warrington branch. There had been a lot of bad press lately about pensions in general, and Northern Equity in particular had been slated; consequently he had found it hard to sell pensions and investments. Everyone was naturally nervous. Whilst she understood it was a difficult time, she was angry at his continued façade and his failure to curb his spending. 'I've already cooked,' Harriet said snappily, 'and anyway we need to talk.'

Jeremy groaned. 'That's a recipe for disaster,' he quipped.

Harriet turned away. 'Dinner in half an hour,' she told him.

Jeremy retreated upstairs to have a shower. She poured them both a dry Martini and sat and waited. She sipped her drink, twisting a strand of hair round her finger, an unconscious habit she had when agitated, and tried to curb her growing irritation.

She wondered how her marriage had gone so wrong in such a short time.

She had met Jeremy when she was twenty-three and had just graduated. His easy charm, his winning personality, had captivated her. She could be forgiven for assuming he was rich. He drove a BMW, wore Ralph Lauren suits and a Cartier watch. He took her to restaurants in the West End and bought her presents from Harrods. The size of the diamond engagement ring when he proposed took her breath away.

She remembered how happy they had been then. He had let her choose and buy everything for their semi-detached house in Charlton Kings because he said she had such good taste. She hadn't minded; she could well afford it; her salary at Sunrise Cosmetics more than covered her expenditure. Debt was something she abhorred. She didn't even own a credit card.

Although she didn't know his exact salary, she assumed it was substantial. His wardrobe was full of designer clothes; he upgraded his BMW to the latest model and had put a deposit on a villa in Spain, yet to be built.

Soon after their marriage she discovered it was all a façade. Everything he owned had been bought on credit. His debts were huge and escalating rapidly.

It terrified her just how bad things were. It had rocked her world to discover just how unconcerned Jeremy was about it all. He laughed it off, telling her it was no big deal, and that she worried too much.

She wished there had been someone to confide in. She felt out of her depth in dealing with it. There was no-one, even her parents lived in Canada and besides, her pride would not allow her to ask them for help. Jeremy's parents were both dead and his only sister, Abigail, disliked her intensely, making no secret of the fact that she was mortified that her brother had married outside their Catholic faith. Harriet thought her strange and far too possessive of her brother, and would rather die than seek her help.

She had pleaded with Jeremy to return the car to the hire

purchase company, sell the house and buy a flat, anything to ease the burden of their debts. Unconcerned, he shrugged it off, insisting that he needed an affluent image.

She had been horrified the day he had asked her to sign a document for a second charge on the house. 'Why do you need a loan of fifty thousand pounds?' she asked puzzled.

He explained diffidently that he was behind with the payments on the car and his credit cards were up to the limit, and also the second payment was due on the villa in Spain. This loan would clear his debts and the arrears on the car finance, and leave a sum over for an investment.

'An investment in what?' she had asked.

Jeremy had looked pleased with himself. 'A franchise in the overseas property market. For just a small investment of twenty grand we can make an annual profit in excess of over a hundred and thirty grand,' he said excitedly.

An intense argument followed, and in the end she had agreed to raise enough capital on the house to clear his debts, but she refused to allow him to invest in any speculative scheme. She also insisted that he cancel the contract on the villa in Spain, even though it meant losing his deposit.

She knew her attitude angered him; nevertheless, she was adamant there would be no more debts.

Two years into their marriage Jeremy was transferred to the north-east area. There was no question of them moving. Harriet refused to leave her job, so Jeremy lived away during the week.

For the next year she lived in blissful ignorance, assuming they were out of debt, until a final threatening demand had come from the Inland Revenue.

'Jesus Christ!' she had screamed at him, 'what do you do with your money?'

He had bought a stake in a racehorse. A sure-fire winner he had been assured, but it had lost every race.

She gave up. She lent him the money for the tax bill and told him, no more. No more or she would leave him.

It didn't stop him though and she didn't leave. In the four years of their marriage she had lost count of how many times he had lied and cheated. As always when there was an issue to discuss, she had to tread carefully. Jeremy hated being criticised. He hated being wrong-footed and never admitted that he was ever to blame.

She waited until after dinner before she spoke. She let him tell her about his week, about his successes. He gloated that the commission earned from the two pension schemes he had just written would clear his latest debts. His hazel eyes were alive as he relayed his achievement.

'How much commission?' Harriet asked tight-lipped.

'Not sure yet, but it will be substantial.' Jeremy smoothed back his neat brown hair. His hair was receding, making his elongated face more pronounced.

'Enough to clear this?' She handed him the letter from the Stroud and Swindon Building Society.

He glanced casually over the letter. 'Couldn't this wait until tomorrow? I've been away all week and you greet me with this.'

'Jeremy, we are three months late with the mortgage. This letter is telling us to call in to see the manager. There is a serious threat here that they will repossess. No it can't wait.'

'I'll sort it out in the morning.' Jeremy looked sullen.

'I pay my share of the mortgage into your account, why hasn't it been paid? What have you done with the money?' she spat, forgetting their agreement never to question each other regarding their separate personal bank accounts.

'I needed the cash on a temporary basis,' Jeremy said. 'It's no big deal.'

'No big deal!' she screamed, feeling herself losing control and hating it. 'We are going to lose the house.'

'Stop being hysterical, it's a measly two grand, this commission will soon clear it,' Jeremy said confidently, 'unless of course . . . .'

'No, Jerry, I'm not bailing you out again.' She always called him Jerry when she was annoyed with him; she knew how much he hated his name being shortened.

'No problem, just a thought.' Jeremy's confidence wavered slightly.

'What did you need the cash for this time?' she asked scathingly.

He brightened immediately, thinking she was interested and missing completely her sarcasm.

For the next few minutes she had to listen to his latest get-rich-quick scheme. Apparently it involved selling health products on a network marketing basis.

'It sounds like pyramid selling to me,' Harriet said doubtfully. 'And that's illegal.'

'Not the same at all,' Jeremy insisted.

'So how much have you invested this time?' It was hard to stay calm, she wanted to scream.

'Not much, four grand. I'll recuperate that in no time. I promise you, Harriet this one can't lose.'

He really believes it, she thought. She watched him move to the sofa and switch on the TV. She wondered when she had stopped loving him. It had not been a single defining moment, more a gradual realisation, an emptiness, a lack of any real connection between them. She stopped her thoughts and returned to the immediate problem. Although still angry, she spoke calmly. 'I've been thinking this over. I'll take over the mortgage payments on one condition.'

'What?' His attention was on the programme.

'You sign over the deeds of the house to me.'

Jeremy's head jerked round, he looked shocked. 'Are you asking me to leave?'

'Don't be silly, of course not. I just want the house to be in my name. I can't live with the threat of losing it. I need the security.'

'And you will pay the mortgage?'

'Yes.'

'That seems a bit unfair on you.'

'You can pay me rent.'

'*Pay you rent!* You're my wife.' Jeremy looked furious.

She shrugged her shoulders and said nothing.

'I'll think about it.' He turned back to the screen, dismissing her.

Harriet felt riled. 'We have an appointment with the building society tomorrow at ten. I need a decision before we go.'

Jeremy turned off the T.V. set. 'Do whatever you fucking want, I'm going to bed.'

As she watched him leave the room, she knew she had won. The victory left a sour taste. She suspected this was the beginning of the end of their marriage.

The following morning's visit to the building society was painful. Jeremy was brash to the point of rudeness. He kept repeating that changing the mortgage to her name was only a temporary arrangement. There was an awkward silence when the manager suggested that Harriet see a solicitor to get Jeremy's name taken off the deeds, and she thought he was going to change his mind. Eventually he nodded in agreement.

Jeremy was morose on the way home. 'Did you really have to humiliate me?' he said.

'I'm sorry. I'm not enjoying this.'

'You could have just lent me the money.'

Harriet said nothing. They had been over this so many times. She was tired of it.

Jeremy pulled into the driveway. 'I have an appointment at two, this has made me late.'

Harriet got out of the car without replying. She leaned back in through the window. 'See you Friday.'

'Okay, I'll ring during the week.'

'I won't be here. I'm going to Bath on a computer course, remember.'

'Right. See you Friday then.'

She watched him reverse the car out of the drive and roar away. Letting herself into the house she relaxed, revelling in the fact that she had the rest of the week-end free to pamper herself.

On Monday she would drive to Bath.

Chapter Three

It started to rain as Laura walked towards the A45, a thin drizzle that had her soaked in no time. There had been no coaches to London until the morning, and she couldn't hang around that long. Besides she hadn't enough money for the fare.

Hungry, because she hadn't eaten all day, she'd bought fish and chips, eating them as she hurried along. She stood for an hour, trying to thumb a lift, just beyond the roundabout, as the evening grew rapidly darker. No one stopped. She was frozen; her thin tracksuit wasn't much protection against the cold wind and rain. Just when she was beginning to think this was a bad idea, a lorry pulled up.

The driver leaned out of the cab window. 'Where yer headin', luv?'

'Anywhere you are,' she said shivering. She was fed up standing here. Sod looking for her mum, she just wanted to get out of the rain and away from Coventry.

'Cheltenham any good?'

'It'll do,' Laura said.

The driver opened the door and she climbed up. It was warm in the cab. 'What's your name?' the driver asked as he pulled out into the traffic.

'Laura.'

'Running away from home?'

Laura laughed. 'No. Going home,' she said.

He looked sceptical but didn't pursue the conversation. He handed her a thermos flask and she drank the hot tea gratefully.

They reached Cheltenham at eight o'clock. Laura thanked the driver. Arnold had been almost fatherly as he talked during the journey, telling her about his teenage daughter. There had been pride and love in his voice that had made Laura ache yet again for her dad.

Arnold wished her good luck and she watched his rear lights disappear with a feeling of panic. It was dark now as she headed for the town centre. She wished, too late, she'd asked Arnold if he knew of somewhere she could spend the night.

She walked through the deserted streets until she reached the doorway of Cavendish House in the Promenade. The store was closed; however, there was a girl huddled in the doorway. Wrapped in an army greatcoat that reached her feet and a grey woollen hat pulled down over her ears, she was counting money, a handful of coppers. A small terrier was asleep at her feet. The girl raised her head as Laura approached and her eyes were instantly wary.

Laura gave her a friendly smile. 'Is there anywhere I can doss down for the night?'

The girl gave her a scornful look. 'Do I look like a bleedin' charity?'

'I guess not. Sorry.'

Laura walked away.

'Wait.'

The girl was slipping the money into her pocket and rolling up a brown blanket. 'Follow me.' Tying a piece of string to the dog's collar she set off down the street.

They walked past the Municipal Office and then left into Imperial Square, past the Town Hall and left again, so that they were now at the rear of the shops. The girl stopped at a narrow alleyway between the buildings, the ground uneven and littered with rubbish. Behind iron railings stood a neglected building of crumbling grey stone with boarded-up windows. Glancing

21

around to make sure no one was about, the girl climbed over the railings and down worn steps to a boarded-up basement door. Laura watched as she prised at the board and was amazed at how easily it came away. She clambered inside. Laura followed her.

The place smelt rank. It was pitch black, and she waited for a few moments until her eyes got accustomed to the dark. Eventually she made out the shape of the room, and as she moved further inside she stumbled against a mattress on the floor.

A match flared; a small candle was lit.

Beyond the mattress was an old sofa. The girl indicated that she could sleep there. She didn't fancy it but she was in no position to be choosy.

'I'm Laura,' she said, trying to be friendly.

'Lisa.' The answer was no more than a grunt.

Laura watched Lisa as she moved about. She had opened her coat, and underneath she was dressed in several jumpers of various colours and lengths, khaki combat trousers, and what looked like brand new Nike trainers.

Laura was envious. 'Like your trainers.'

Lisa nodded. 'Struck lucky. Got them from the homeless centre. Got small feet you see, only take a size three.'

'Cool.'

Lisa glanced at her. 'You should go there. Looks like you could do with some decent gear.'

'Ta, I will.' Laura had no intention of going. They might report her to the social. Anyway she was bound to get a lift to London tomorrow.

The mongrel had settled down in a corner, his head on his paws, his mournful eyes flicking backwards and forwards between them. 'What's his name?'

'Spirit.'

'Cool.'

Lisa unfolded the brown blanket and laid it on the mattress. She sat down and from the depths of her coat pocket produced a bottle of beer. She took a long swig and handed it to Laura.

Not wishing to appear rude, yet not really wanting it, Laura took a small sip.

'Got any fags?' Lisa asked.

'Sorry, don't smoke.'

Lisa muttered and pulled out a squashed packet of Marlboro Lights. After lighting the last cigarette, she threw the empty packet into the corner of the room.

'Don't suppose you do smack either,' Lisa said after inhaling deeply.

'No.'

More muttering.

Laura wondered if the girl was regretting having invited her here. Certainly she was regretting coming as smoke filled her nostrils. She tried not to cough.

'You homeless then?' Lisa said, the beer obviously mellowing her slightly.

'Yeah.'

'How come? You got no folks?'

Laura shrugged. 'Me brother's just been banged up.' No point in explaining about her parents.

'No way!' Lisa looked impressed. 'What did he do, kill someone?'

'No,' Laura laughed. 'He were done for car ringing.'

'Right,' Lisa sounded disappointed.

Laura was silent as she remembered how shocked she had felt when the charge was read out in court; she had thought they'd got the wrong person. Terry, part of a gang involved in car ringing? No bleeding way! She thought he was up for receiving stolen goods. When he pleaded guilty she had felt a deep unease. Her unease had escalated when she heard how much he had received. If he had been paid that much money how come they were always broke? She couldn't work it out. It didn't make any sense. She didn't think he did drugs, she knew him better than that. Or did she? After today's hearing she wasn't so sure she knew him at all.

It had been a revelation to listen to the lawyer explaining to the judge that the garage owner, Clive Mason, had been the ringleader. She had met Clive on several occasions and thought he was really nice. He was always polite and charming to her. To know that he had got Terry to steal cars, fix the milometers and sometimes even weld together smashed-up vehicles, horrified her. That Terry had no part in the number plate switching or the falsifying of documents went slightly in his favour, but not much.

The outcome today had been awful. Three years, and a court order to pay five thousand pounds compensation. She knew Terry had not expected such a harsh sentence. His legal aid solicitor had promised he would get a reduced sentence, maybe even get off with a caution if he pleaded guilty. It hadn't worked.

She hadn't even been able to talk to him today before he was carted off to Winson Green prison. And she wouldn't be able to visit him either without an adult.

Lisa, obviously bored that the crime wasn't anything sensational, finished the beer and stubbed out the cigarette. Without another word she blew out the candle and, pulling the blanket over her, lay down and closed her eyes.

Laura bent to ease off her Doc Martens, then decided it might be better to keep them on, just in case she needed to beat a hasty exit. Using her rucksack as a pillow she lay down. Despite her exhaustion sleep didn't come easily. The girl snored, the dog made whimpering noises and the sound of traffic filtered in from outside.

Chapter Four

Laura woke cold and hungry the following morning. She rubbed her eyes, feeling surprised that she had actually slept. She lay for a moment, wishing she was back in the flat. As bad as it was, at least it had been warm, with a proper bed. It was hard not to blame Terry, difficult not to feel resentful for the mess she was in. If only he hadn't been so stupid.

Her limbs were stiff with cramp from lying in an uncomfortable position; she had curled up tight, wanting the least contact with the flea-ridden sofa.

A chink of light filtering in through the uneven boards allowed her to see the room better. The sofa was covered in faded brown velour. She tried not to imagine what the stains were.

She glanced across to the mattress, grey-striped and filthy. There was no sign of the girl or the dog. She was alone. She wondered, briefly if Lisa had gone to fetch food.

It took a minute or two to realise that her rucksack was missing. A moment of awful realization: everything she owned was gone. It was incredible that the girl had managed to get it from under her head without waking her.

The bitch had robbed her!

Determined not to give way to despair she headed through the town towards the London Road in the hope of getting a lift. Several passers-by gave her directions, telling her that was the best place to try. It was warmer than the previous day and the sun was shining. Passing a bakery, where the delicious aroma of fresh baked bread wafted into the street, her stomach rumbled. She stared hungrily through the window for a few moments before moving away. Lisa had robbed her of her last penny.

Laura continued through the fashionable avenue of the Promenade, awestruck by the lovely shops. The town was bustling, so she didn't notice the woman immediately. She was standing alone beneath one of the many trees that lined the street, and it was her stillness that attracted her attention. She found it odd that anyone could stand so perfectly still, so strangely motionless.

She was not young, Laura guessed her to be in her early thirties, but her face had a calm, nun-like quality. She was also very thin, almost anorexic, Laura noticed. A long black coat hung unopened, and underneath it she wore a pale blue dress.

Suddenly the woman started singing, taking Laura completely by surprise. Her voice was clear and haunting as she sang, *Let It Be*. Laura was fascinated.

Passers-by were also obviously taken with the singing, because several threw coins into a man's cap that was at her feet. Spellbound, Laura continued to watch her, moving nearer. It was only as she got closer to the singer that Laura realised she was blind.

Laura wished she had some money to give her. She also wished she had the nerve to earn money by singing. She would probably get arrested if she tried, her voice was so awful, she thought with a grin.

Despite the urgency to get to London she couldn't tear herself away, the singing was so beautiful. The woman finished the song and picked up the cap. Laura watched her walk a few steps to a nearby restaurant, marvelling that she didn't use a white stick.

There were about ten tables spread across the pavement and several customers were seated, enjoying the weak sunshine. The woman sat down. Laura was surprised. The restaurant, *Le Fleur* bistro, looked really expensive; she wondered if the woman realised this.

She debated whether to warn her, but as she approached a waiter came out carrying a tray that held a single mug. He placed it before the woman, who was now busy counting the money from the cap, her fingers deftly feeling each coin.

'Well, Nancy how did you do today?'

A smile appeared on Nancy's face. 'Pretty good,' she said. Nancy placed the money inside a bag strapped across her chest.

'You take care, darling,' he said as he went back inside. Carefully, Nancy reached out for the mug, found it, and lifted it to her lips.

On the table next to Nancy the customers had gone, leaving their lunch half eaten. Laura saw the meat pie and her mouth watered. No one seemed to notice as she sat at the table. She ate the pie quickly and stuffed a handful of cold chips into her mouth. On the periphery of her vision she saw Nancy walk away. The waiter returned to serve another customer. She got up to leave and stumbled, sending the chair crashing to the ground. Anxious in case she was questioned she quickly righted the chair and hurried away.

Laura reached the London Road at last. She had stopped at a ladies toilet and washed her face and ran her hands through her tangled hair. It felt matted and greasy but she had no comb to tidy it. If she didn't get a lift today she really was in the shit.

She found a good position to thumb a lift. Only two cars stopped and neither had been heading for London. As darkness descended she felt tired and scared as she headed back to the squat. Much as she hated the place there was nowhere else to go.

* * *

A grey dawn broke over the town as Laura uncurled her body from the concrete floor. She had hardly slept. The makeshift bed made from a discarded cardboard box found in the alleyway had not prevented the cold from penetrating her body. She had abandoned the sofa and had no wish to sleep on the putrid mattress. She tried to rise, but her knees buckled and she swayed. It took a few moments to regain her balance.

Despite all her efforts she couldn't get a lift to London. She had now been here a week, sleeping each night in the squat, dreading being discovered. There had been no sign of Lisa, not that she had really expected to see her.

She was tired and hungry and her limbs ached. She'd not eaten for days, drinking water from a tap in the ladies toilet; ignoring the warning that read, **This Is Not Drinking Water.**

Leaving the squat she wandered through the maze of back streets. The smell of fried food from a greasy spoon café drifted in her direction. Nausea made her feel light-headed. The rear door of the café opened and a fat man in a grubby apron lifted the lid of a large dustbin. The stench filled her nose and mouth. She doubled over and heaved. Bile splattered her shoes. The fat man swore at her and called her a filthy pig. He returned to the café, slamming the door.

She lurched her way towards the town centre, her vision blurred. She wanted to find the ladies toilet to rinse her mouth and wash her face, but the road was unfamiliar, she felt disorientated.

Reaching a public garden of lush green grass and shrubs she knew she had come the wrong way. There was a bench; she lay down and closed her eyes.

It was dusk when she was prodded awake. The policeman was looking stern. 'Have you no home to go to?'

It took a moment to remember.

'Yeah,' she muttered.

'Then I suggest you go home. This is no place to spend the night.'

He waited as she staggered to her feet. She walked, trying to pretend she knew where she was heading. She turned a corner out of his sight. It took half-an-hour until she finally recognised her surroundings. She never thought she'd be pleased to see the squat.

She felt better the next day and found her way with ease to the Promenade. In the public toilets she washed her face and drank some water. A cleaner, a large black woman, half-heartedly mopping the floor, scolded her. 'It will make you sick,' she said. Laura hurried away.

She was sick again that night, vomiting in the corner of the squat, making the place smell even worse. She lay down on her bed and for the first time gave way to tears. Great choking sobs, filling her throat, and stinging her eyes with salty tears. It was hopeless; there was no chance of ever getting to London to find her mother.

Another day dawned. She tried to rise but the effort proved too much and she sank back down. Her head ached unbearably and the single shaft of light, penetrating through the wooden boards, hurt her eyes. A bluebottle buzzed above her head. Her body was soaked with sweat, her tee-shirt drenched. Despite this she was shivering. What the hell was wrong with her? She tried to keep her eyes open but lost the battle as her vision blurred. Her eyes closed as she drifted off into blackness.

When she woke again it was daylight. She had no idea of the time or the day. Her mouth was parched, her throat sore. She managed to sit up, but when she tried to stand her legs gave way. She rested an hour, maybe two, and tried again. This time she managed to crawl to the opening. She desperately needed a pee, and she squatted in the alleyway, not caring if she was seen.

She couldn't remember getting back to her makeshift bed but when she woke again it was night. Tears of helpless frustration ran down her cheeks, soaking her hair. Her neck was stiff and sore. She drifted off again.

Days passed. She had no idea how many. Two, maybe three. She woke one morning and managed to stand up. Clinging to the walls she propelled herself outside. In the street a few people were hurrying to work, to their warm offices or shops or wherever they worked. No-one paid her any attention. She was not surprised; they probably thought she was a tramp or a druggie. She envied them. They had somewhere to go. She had no destination, except a vague idea to find a mother who didn't really want her. It all seemed pretty pointless.

Her head still felt hot as she wandered aimlessly into the town centre, asking people for some change to buy a cup of tea. No one stopped, everyone walked past her as if she was invisible. Slumping down on a bench, she stared blankly into the distance.

She had no friends, no money, nowhere to live. She had been worried about Terry, but at least he had a roof over his head, food and someone to talk to. She was completely on her own. Now she was sick.

She closed her eyes, too weary to move.

Nancy's voice woke her. She must have dozed off. Nancy was standing outside Cavendish House, singing *Jerusalem*.

Once more Laura was curious about her. Why didn't she have a guide dog or a least a white stick, how did she manage to get around? And was the waiter her boyfriend?

There was no time to sit here wondering. She must try again to get a lift to London. She turned to walk away as four boys, no more than eleven or twelve years old, pushed past her and moved towards Nancy. They circled around her, jeering and making rude comments. One of them poked Nancy in the chest. 'Oi you a spazz?' he said.

Nancy stopped singing. Her hands moved protectively to grasp her shoulder bag closer to her body. One of the boys saw this gesture and tried to pull it from her. Nancy held on tightly as they jostled her, trying to grab it.

Laura began to move towards them when she saw one of them pick up the cap. He peered into it and his face broke into a grin. 'Leave the bag this'll do,' he said to his mates.

Laura grabbed the boy by the arm. 'Give that back.' She shook him. It was feeble attempt because she felt so weak.

Startled the boy grunted. 'What's your problem?'

'Give it back or I'll call the police,' Laura snapped.

The boy stood his ground. 'You can't make me,' he sneered. 'You're just a girl.' He yanked his arm away, dropping the cap, spilling the money. He swore, and nodding to his mates, started to walk away with studied nonchalance. The other three followed, smirking at Laura. She was tempted to go after them but she was feeling ill again.

'They've gone now.' Laura said.

'Thank you. Thank you for helping me.' Nancy was trembling.

As Laura bent to retrieve the money a wave of dizziness halted her. Before she could take another step she felt herself falling.

Blackness descended as she crumpled into a heap, sprawled at Nancy's feet.

Sunlight warmed her face. She stirred and opened her eyes. Curtains fluttered from an open window. It took a moment to realise she was no longer in the squat. She was in a room with eggshell blue walls that smelled fresh and clean. The bed felt soft. Lifting the duvet she saw she was wearing a white nightdress.

There was no time to wonder before a light tap on the door startled her.

'Come in.'

Her mouth gaped to see the waiter from the café. 'How are you feeling?' he asked, coming into the room with a tray.

'Where am I? What happened?'

He laughed softly and handed her a cup of tea. 'Drink this and then I'll explain. It's so good to see you looking better.'

She drank the tea gratefully.

'My name is Brett. You collapsed in the Promenade, do you remember?'

'Vaguely, some boys were trying to steal from the singer.'

'Nancy yes, she's my sister. She told me what you did. You were very brave standing up to them.'

Laura smiled weakly. She hadn't felt brave, only useless because she had felt so unwell.

'We brought you here, to our home in Upper Wyre. It's a small village ten miles north of Cheltenham,' Brett explained, 'you have been quite ill, with a virus, the doctor said.'

'You're the waiter from the restaurant, right?'

'Not exactly,' Brett grinned. 'I own *Le Fleur.*'

'Oh, sorry,' she flushed.

There was another soft tap on the door and Nancy entered. 'Hi,' she put out her hand.

Laura took it. It felt soft, the skin white and smooth. Laura noticed the contrast to her own rough hands, the nails bitten and ragged. Embarrassed, she pulled away before she remembered Nancy couldn't see them.

'Can you tell us who you are?' Nancy asked.

Laura hesitated; she was anxious in case they had called the police. She was homeless and underage; they might contact the social services.

'You're not in trouble.' Brett saw her hesitation. 'We only want to help you. We are so grateful for what you did.'

Brett had a nice face; she liked his thick brown curly hair and gentle brown eyes. She saw only kindness in his face and instantly trusted him.

'I've been trying for ages to get home, but I've no money. I - I've been living in a squat.'

'And where is home. Is it London?' Nancy asked.

'Yes, Lewisham, how did you know?'

Nancy smiled. 'You have a slight accent.'

'Oh, right. There's a bit of a problem, see, me mum's moved.' Laura was surprised at herself for confiding in them, she never gave anyone details about her life. 'She didn't leave an address. I was going to try and find her.'

'What about your dad?' Nancy asked.

'He died when I was little.' She always told people this; it sounded better than saying he had left them. He had fallen in love with another woman apparently. She hadn't blamed him for that, considering how awful Mum had been to him, but she didn't understand why he no longer cared about her and Terry.

'I'm sorry, I shouldn't have asked.'

'That's okay.'

'Do you feel strong enough to have a bath? I sponged you down, but I couldn't wash your hair,' Nancy said.

'Yeah, that'd be great.'

Her legs felt so weak she had to lean on Brett as he walked her to the bathroom. From an airing cupboard he pulled out a large white towel. Steam rose from the bath water.

'There's no hurry, take your time.'

Thanking him, she waited until he had closed the door. The bathroom was spotless. She curled her toes into the deep cream shag pile carpet and thought, what joy it would be to live in a house like this.

Taking off the nightdress she sank into the fragrant hot

bubbles.

A knock made her jump.

'I've left some clean clothes here,' Brett called out.

'Ta.'

Half an hour later, dressed in one of Nancy's shirts – the unfamiliar feel of soft silk – she wandered downstairs and entered the kitchen. The wool skirt was long and covered her feet. Brett looked up and grinned at the sight of her. It was a friendly smile. She smiled back. The clothes were old-fashioned, not her style, yet she was still glad of them.

'I'm afraid your clothes had to be discarded,' Nancy apologised. 'When you are well enough we'll get you some new ones.'

Laura felt a choking lump in her throat at their kindness.

'Are you in a hurry to get to London?' Brett asked later when they were alone. It was Sunday and Nancy had gone to church.

'Not really, but I don't know what else to do. I've no money.'

'How old are?' Brett asked gently.

'Fif - sixteen.'

'I don't suppose you want a job,' he asked.

'Doing what?'

'Only washing dishes I'm afraid.'

'At *Le Fleur*?'

'No, at *Flamingo,* my café here in Upper Wyre. My regular girl gave her notice in this morning and I'm desperate.'

A restaurant and a café. Not poor then, and yet Nancy had to beg. She was filled with curiosity. She hesitated. It sounded okay and she badly needed the money. Even so she felt nervous.

'Only when you're strong enough,' Brett said, misunderstanding her hesitation.

'I've nowhere to live.'

'You can stay here. Nancy would be delighted to have some female company and if you want, you can help with the housework to earn your keep.'

'Wow, you must be desperate,' Laura laughed.

They sat in companionable silence for a few moments until

Laura blurted out. 'Why does Nancy have to beg?'

Brett looked startled at the bluntness of her question. 'She doesn't consider it begging, she enjoys it. Busking is a respectable occupation. It's her bit of independence.'

'Don't you mind?'

'No, why should I? It's usually quite safe. I keep an eye on her from the restaurant. Those boys, well that has never happened before. She doesn't do it for the money. I earn enough to keep us. Nancy just loves to sing. I would never make her give it up. She's brilliant.'

Laura heard the pride in Brett's voice as he spoke. She thought of Terry. Why couldn't her brother be a successful businessman instead of a thief?

'Why are you doing this?' She was suddenly suspicious of her good fortune.

'What?'

'Being kind to me, you don't know me.'

'What you did to help Nancy was brave, foolish, but brave. They could have harmed you. I can't thank you enough.'

'It was nothing,' Laura flushed, embarrassed.

For the rest of the morning Brett chatted amiably, not asking her awkward questions, for which she was grateful. She would have hated to confess that she had run away from her landlord because she owed the rent and that her brother was in prison.

That night she found a clean, cotton nightdress and a new toothbrush on her bed. Once again their generosity made her eyes fill with tears.

Laura walked through the village, skirting a pond, towards the café. A week had passed and she felt ready to start work. She stared around curiously; she had never been in a village. She liked the quaint cottages with tiny leaded windows. *Flamingo* was between a perfumery and a gift shop. Once inside, Laura looked around at the white-washed walls and low exposed oak beams; the inglenook fireplace, the tables with vases of real flowers, and knew she would like it here. The waitresses wore black skirts with white blouses and tiny laced-edged aprons.

Laura was shown to the kitchen and an enormous stack of dirty crockery. She put on a huge navy apron and started work.

Chapter Five

At least, thank God, she wasn't the last to arrive. Harriet hated being late, but the traffic had been awful, she'd had difficulty finding the hotel, and then the car park was full, and had only managed to get a space because someone was leaving.

There had been no time to freshen up. In the hotel lobby she was directed to the conference room where the course was being held, and slid quietly into a vacant chair. There was still one place not taken.

Ten minutes later he strode into the room without an apology, knee length navy overcoat and yellow cashmere scarf hanging loose. He sat down at the computer next to her. She turned to smile politely and felt a sudden extraordinary jolt as she stared into steel blue eyes, and immediately thought, sexy, very sexy.

The sensation shook her. She was not usually prone to such impulsive thoughts.

He returned her smile. A smile that reached his eyes and his gaze mirrored her attraction to him. 'Have I missed much?' he whispered.

She shook her head and turned back to her screen.

He introduced himself. 'Daniel, Daniel Pembroke, Danny to my friends.'

'Harriet Malin,' she said coolly.

'You're beautiful,' he said and, despite herself, she smiled.

She was very conscious of his nearness as she tried to concentrate. It soon became apparent that he knew even less than she did about database systems. Feeling superior, she helped him with the basics when the tutor's attention was elsewhere. His presence unnerved her a little; it was not his manner, because he was relaxed and whispered witty comments, even flirted a little, it was more the powerful sexual aura that surrounded him. She thought he was a man that always got what he wanted, especially with women. He was immensely attractive; tall, nearly six foot, his suit hung perfectly on broad shoulders. As he leaned towards her, she was aware of the woody fragrance of an aftershave she didn't recognise. His hands on the keyboards were big, with neat square-nailed fingers. On his left hand he wore a wide gold wedding ring.

When the session ended at four o'clock, Danny gave an audible sigh of relief. 'I need a drink. Will you join me?'

She had managed to avoid him at lunchtime but now she agreed. 'Okay,' she said, 'but first I must change for dinner.'

She showered, taking her time, letting the hot jets of water revive her tiredness. She thought about Danny waiting downstairs.

Looking at her face in the mirror, she leaned closer to the glass, inspecting her skin with a critical eye, searching for wrinkles. There were none. Her complexion was perfect. Her blue eyes clear as a mountain stream. Danny had said she was beautiful. And she was, but for how much longer? She was fast approaching thirty. Soon there would be deterioration.

God, she needed some excitement. She was bored with her life, with her marriage. Despite Jeremy's lack of attention she had never been unfaithful. Not that she was contemplating it now, unless . . .

Tonight, she decided, with a shiver of sexual anticipation, she would flirt with Danny. She needed some fun.

She took her time drying herself with the hotel's soft white towel and blow-drying her long black hair. She loved her hair, luxuriating in the feel of it; loved its sheen. Checking that it was lying smoothly to her shoulders, she dressed in Dior black trousers, and a cream silk blouse, and sprayed on Joy perfume. Then with a last look at her herself in the mirror she went downstairs.

It was gratifying to find Danny already waiting when she entered the lounge bar. He rose as soon as he saw her and waited until she was seated in one of the large leather armchairs before signalling to a waiter to order champagne.

'Champagne?' she raised her eyebrows in surprise.

'I always drink champagne at the start of an affair,' he said seriously.

Her eyes widened and she pretended to be shocked. 'We are having a drink. We are *not* having an affair.' Secretly she was thrilled.

'Not yet.' He held her gaze, challenging.

She laughed. 'That's the worst chat-up line I've ever heard.'

He chuckled deeply, obviously amused by her, and she let herself relax.

As the evening progressed she discreetly studied him, liking what she saw. She liked the way his dark brown hair was thick and wavy and his mouth wide and sensuous, and those wonderful eyes were fringed with the longest lashes. She wondered what he would be like in bed. She suspected he would be good . . . very good. She felt a shiver of desire. Sipping her champagne she found the idea of sleeping with Danny, a man she hardly knew, exciting.

'Why are you on the course?' she asked. 'I mean what line of business are you in?'

'I'm a perfumer, I have my own perfumery.'

'How exciting.'

'I guess so.'

'You don't sound very enthusiastic.'

Danny shrugged. 'It wasn't my choice of career. I inherited the business from my father. He was originally a pharmacist, and the perfume thing was simply a hobby because he had what he referred to as "the nose" for it. Then my father's circumstances changed when he inherited some money. He turned the perfumery into a thriving business. I grew up with his constant quest for new fragrances, new blends, but I wasn't really interested. I wanted to be a photographer.'

'What happened?' Harriet prompted.

'He died suddenly of a heart attack. There was no one to run the business. My mother, she's dead now, God bless her, had never worked since she'd married. She pleaded with me to take it over otherwise we wouldn't have had any source of income. So I went to Bath University and studied organic chemistry.'

'Do you enjoy it now?'

Danny shrugged again. 'I would have preferred to be a photographer, but yes it's an enjoyable occupation.'

'Are you wearing one of your own creations?'

Danny looked pleased. 'Yes. It's called Woodland.'

'It's very sensuous.'

'Thank you.'

'I'd be interested to see your place.'

'You're welcome any day. I might even blend a perfume especially for you,' Danny said.

'I'd like that. Is your perfumery local?'

'Not far away. Upper Wyre in the Cotswolds, my home is there too.'

'Oh, that's a charming village. I envy you. We have a house in Charlton Kings . . .' her voice tailed off as Danny lifted her hand from where it was resting on the chair arm. He lightly touched her wedding ring, nestling against the large square diamond of her engagement ring. 'Tell me, Harriet, are you happily married?' he asked softly.

'That's a very personal question,' she said, discomforted. She didn't want to spoil the evening thinking about Jeremy. 'Why do you want to know?'

'Because I'm intrigued by you.'

She laughed lightly. 'I'm not sure I should tell you.'

'Then the answer must be that you are not,' he smiled.

She shrugged, not wanting to divulge the intimacies of her marriage, the disappointments and the sense of failure.

'Tell me about yourself,' Danny said as if sensing her unease. 'I want to know everything about you. What do you do?'

'I'm in research and development at Sunrise Cosmetics.'

'And where did you study?'

'London. Four years at St Martins, left with a Cosmetic

39

Science honours degree.'

He looked impressed. A warm flush of pleasure spread over her skin.

She dined with Danny that night, although not alone. The rest of the course students joined them. Throughout the meal she felt his eyes on her and she suspected that afterwards he would seek her out and want to go to bed with her. She wanted that too. But she wanted more. A one-night stand was so unsatisfactory and that's all it would be if she let him into her bed tonight, even though Danny said they were on the brink of an affair. She wanted the thrill and danger of that. However she didn't want him to think she was easy, she would make him wait.

They said goodbye the following afternoon after the course had ended. They'd had lunch together in the hotel, the conversation light and only slightly flirtatious. She felt she could almost have imagined last night's intimacy.

Then he kissed her very briefly on the mouth and she knew she hadn't imagined it. The contact was very fleeting, yet enough to create the most wonderful sensation. She had the most extraordinary impulse to take his face in her hands and kiss him and keep on kissing him.

She pulled away with difficulty. All her senses were alive. His gaze was deep and unfathomable, yet she knew he wanted her.

She hardly remembered getting into her Peugeot and driving away.

She was both surprised and disappointed that he hadn't arranged for them to meet again. She began to doubt her instincts. Perhaps she had just been a distraction, a little flirtatious diversion, and now he would go back to his wife, chaste and faithful. Somehow she thought not. They would meet again, she was certain of it.

She thought about Danny throughout the following week. She wasn't sure why he'd had such an effect on her. Perhaps it was because she had never met anyone like him. She thought about everything he had told her. About his wife, Christine, and how he had said that although he loved her, he was not *in love* with her any more. 'In fact we no longer have sex,' he had confessed. 'We are more like brother and sister. We stay together mainly because of the business.'

She longed to believe him; however, she doubted that what he said was true. No woman could live with such a sexual man and stay unaffected.

Her relationship with Jeremy grew more strained. She thought of Danny every day. She was tempted to visit his perfumery to prove to herself that she had not imagined what had gone on between them, but she didn't go. Just suppose she was wrong and he had forgotten her already.

She was in her laboratory two weeks later when the receptionist buzzed through to tell her she had a visitor.

She frowned in surprise; visitors were rare at work. Still wearing her white lab coat she went through to the reception. Danny was sprawled on one of the brown leather reception chairs reading a newspaper. He looked up and grinned as she approached.

'What on earth are you doing here?'

He leaned towards her and kissed her. That sensation again leaving her breathless. 'I've come to take you to lunch.'

She wanted to refuse. He was taking far too much for granted. She was annoyed with him. Not a word for two weeks and then turning up out of the blue. She was the one to make the rules. She was the one in control.

She changed out of her white coat and into her navy jacket and short straight skirt.

'Nice legs,' he said as he helped her into his Audi.

'What!'

'I never saw them before, you were wearing trousers.'

She couldn't help but laugh.

'That's better, you're scary when you're cross.'

They chatted over lunch about the computer course, friendly small talk, nothing intimate. He told her they were blending a special perfume for a member of the royal family.

As the coffee was placed on the table Danny said. 'I haven't stopped thinking about you.'

'Me neither,' she confessed, relaxing with him.

'I have a room booked, spend the afternoon with me.'

She swallowed hard. God she wanted that so much. 'I can't,' she said.

'Why not?'

'I'm scared.'

'Of me?' he sounded hurt.

'Of getting involved.'

He smiled. 'I think we already are,' he said.

She shook her head. 'I have to go,' she said.

'I won't give up. I'll call you again next week,' he said as he dropped her outside Sunrise Cosmetics.

She shrugged. That was better. Now she had his interest.

Chapter Six

A huge bouquet of flowers arrived for her at work the following Monday.

'Wow,' Dee, her assistant said, 'Jeremy must be missing you.'

Harriet smiled weakly. She knew they wouldn't be from Jeremy. It wasn't something he ever did.

She put them in water. There was no note.

He called her later that day. 'Did you like the flowers?' he asked.

'They're gorgeous.'

'Like you.'

'Please Danny, this must stop.'

'Only if you have dinner with me.'

'I can't.'

Flowers arrived over the following four days. Her office was looking like the Chelsea flower show. It was embarrassing because she couldn't take them home.

He rang again on Friday. It was fortunate she was in the lab by herself. 'I've booked a table for next Tuesday at a wonderful little restaurant called *Le Fleur* in Cheltenham. I know the owner. I've said you are a client. I have a proposition for you.'

'Danny . . . '

'I promise I won't try to seduce you. There is something really important I want to talk to you about.'

'All right, what time?'

'Eight o'clock. Do you know where it is?'

'Yes.'

She spent the week-end buying new clothes, shoes, silk underwear. She felt alive for the first time in years.

She arrived at five to eight. He was already there; standing at the small bar talking to a man who she presumed was the owner. Her first thought when she saw him was, thank God she was wearing the new sexy underwear. Her heart pounded. He looked so wonderful. His clothes were obviously designer label, light grey suit, black shirt and silver-grey tie. As soon as he spotted her, he came over, grinning hugely. He took her hands and kissed her cheek.

'Hello.'

'Hi.'

The owner had followed him. 'Good evening,' he said, 'I'm Brett. Follow me, your table is ready.'

The table was secluded in a cosy alcove.

'Can I get you a drink?' Brett said when she was seated and he had taken her coat.

'Martini and soda please.'

She studied the menu, uncomfortably aware that Brett must know she was not a client. She wondered what he thought of her having dinner with a married man. She wished suddenly she hadn't come.

'Brett thinks we are discussing a fragrance for your husband for his birthday,' Danny whispered when Brett had left to organise their drinks. 'I told him you were very rich and wanted a blend specially made.'

Harriet buried her head in her menu, trying hard not to laugh. He was outrageous.

A waitress came and took their order; another brought a bottle of wine. She relaxed; the food was delicious, Danny entertaining. He talked a lot about the perfumery, the places abroad he had visited. Muscat in India and the perfume museum in Grasse. He had travelled to Italy and Thailand; to Provence for French lavender; to Bulgaria for roses, and sandalwood from India. He went to source the raw materials, to get the best price and delivery. It all sounded very glamorous. Her life seemed very dull by comparison.

'I would love to visit those places,' she said wistfully. 'I've never been abroad.'

'You could go if you accepted my proposition,' Danny said, suddenly serious.

She frowned slightly. 'What proposition?' She had forgotten he had mentioned the reason she was here was to discuss some proposal he had.

'Come and work for me.'

She was thrown into confusion. 'Why?' she asked.

'My company is expanding. I can't do all the work myself anymore, I need an assistant, someone with your experience and qualifications. Someone to help in the research and development of new products. And because I can't stop thinking about you.'

His gaze was deep and intense. She swallowed hard. *I can't stop thinking about you.* This was more than a job offer; much more. This was dangerous ground. 'Can I think about it?'

'By all means. Are you just a bit tempted?'

'Of course I am.'

The evening was late and dark as they strolled back to her car. As they walked down a deserted side street she shivered and he put his arm around her, drawing her close. His mouth found hers, his tongue probing, and for a moment she clung, frozen in his embrace, then waves of intense pleasure surged through her, erupting from the very core of her and drowning her with such an ache of longing that she would have fallen had he not held her so tightly.

She was hungry for sex. It had been months since Jeremy had made love to her. Her mouth opened to his searching tongue, her body pressed so hard against his ribcage that she could feel his heart beating. He pulled away for a second, gazing into her eyes. The silence between them filled with unspoken need, then with a stifling gasp she reached up and grasped his hair, pulling his face closer. Her body moulded to his with alarming naturalness. He unfastened her blouse and she felt the cool night air on her breasts. He kissed her erect nipples. She felt the warm wetness of desire.

He pulled her into a darkened doorway. She leaned against the wall, her head back staring at the night sky. He kissed her throat. 'My God you are beautiful. I want you so much.'

His fingers slipped into her wetness. She reached her hand down to guide him into her. 'Not here,' he whispered against her mouth.

'What?'

'I have a flat near here. Montpellier Villas. Will you come, will you stay the night?'

'Your wife?'

'Christine's abroad.'

And Jeremy was in Warrington.

They hurried now, crossing Imperial Square, through Montpellier gardens until, breathless, they reached the villas, a crescent of Regency apartments.

A small flight of steps led to an outer door and once inside he ushered her up to the first floor. She waited, aching with wanting him as he unlocked the flat door and kicked it shut behind them. Within seconds they were naked on the bed.

'Now, please,' she implored as he kissed her body with slow lingering kisses, yet still he teased her, his tongue probing, caressing, bringing her closer and closer to the brink. Then just when she thought she couldn't last another minute he was inside her, pulsing, pushing deeper and deeper into her body.

She cried out. Her orgasm was amazing. Jeremy had never managed to do that for her. Exhausted she fell asleep in his arms, happiness lapping over her.

He was an accomplished lover and several times during the night their lovemaking reached new heights.

She woke early, and slipped out of bed leaving Danny sleeping. The bathroom boasted a Jacuzzi and she luxuriated in the hot bubbling water, feeling alive and vibrant. She thought about the previous night and smiled to herself. There was no sense of shame, no feeling of guilt; she felt only a joyous exhilaration. She had never experienced anything like this with Jeremy. Danny was something special.

She dressed. Danny was still sleeping, so she looked around

the apartment. It was large and beautifully furnished in light oak with soft cream furnishings. The kitchen was modern stainless steel and oak. She wondered if he brought all of his women here. She was determined not to ask.

The cupboards were well stocked. She made coffee and toast.

Danny joined her at the breakfast table. He wore a thick white dressing gown, his hair tousled; he looked very sexy. Something stirred inside her, something more than sex. It was a dangerous feeling. She should be sensible and walk away before she got hurt.

Danny buttered a slice of toast. 'Have you thought about my offer?'

She nodded. 'I'll have to give a month's notice.'

He took her hand and kissed the palm. 'You won't regret it.'

'I already have,' she said, smiling.

'Come back to bed.'

Later as she lay beside him she said. 'What about your wife, won't it be awkward having me working for you?'

'Not if we're discreet. Christine looks after the retail sales side of the business and the accounts. She has nothing to do with the laboratory. However, we must be *very* discreet. I don't want to hurt her. She must never suspect anything, otherwise she will divorce me. She invested quite a lot of money into my business and she might want it back if I betrayed her. Infidelity is not something Christine would tolerate. I can offer you great sex and a good time. I can't offer you marriage. You must understand I'll never leave Christine.'

She admired his honesty. She didn't want a messy divorce either. A discreet affair would be much more fun.

Chapter Seven

Laura waited nervously for the first customer to arrive. Today was her first day as a waitress. She had turned sixteen the previous month, and Brett had decided she was too good to continue washing dishes. She was so wound up she could hardly concentrate. Earlier she had placed the cutlery on the table the wrong way round and only just managed to correct it before it was noticed. She hoped she didn't mess up on her first day.

The bell over the café door tinkled, signalling her first customer, giving her no time to dwell on her feelings of inadequacy. She smiled a greeting. 'Good morning, Danny.'

She was glad that he was her first customer. She liked Daniel Pembroke. He was great, really friendly, asked her to call him Danny, and told her interesting stories about his perfumery, which was adjacent to the café. She also got to know some of his staff, who usually came in at lunchtime. Pauline, Clair, and Janet, and Zoe, who had become her friend.

The only person who didn't frequent the café was Danny's wife, Christine, although she had seen her coming and going to and from the perfumery.

Danny glanced at her now, commenting on her neat black skirt and white blouse. 'You look good, Laura. Brett has promoted you at last, I see.'

'Yeah, great isn't it,' she said shyly.

The first time she had met Danny had been a disaster. She had come out to clear tables because the waitresses were so busy. She had accidentally knocked over his cup of coffee, spilling it all over him. Mortified, she had apologised, brought him another and prayed he wouldn't tell Brett. She was sure she would get the sack. But Danny had been great, even telling her that it was his fault, that he had placed it too near the edge. He then told her that she was the prettiest girl in the café, and he was shocked that she was washing dishes. She should be out where the customers could see her. He said he would speak to Brett about it. When Brett had offered her the waitress job she had wondered if it had anything to do with Danny's influence, but either way she was thrilled.

He had asked her about her life, about her education, and she confessed she had never been to school properly. She told him a little about her life, her mother who had disappeared, and her brother, Terry, in prison. Somehow he seemed to elicit information from her without her realising she was giving it.

'Don't you have any ambitions, Laura?' he had asked.

'Not really,' Laura shrugged.

'Surely you want more from life than being a waitress? You could be anything with your looks, you're a stunner.'

'Yeah, right,' Laura giggled, not believing him.

'I'm serious.'

'Anyway what's wrong with being a waitress?' Laura said indignantly.

'Nothing, but it's not much of an ambition,' Danny said seriously.

'I'd love to get married one day, have kids, but that's only a dream. Doubt it'll 'appen.'

'Why do you say that?'

'Get real. Who'd marry *me*?'

Danny had given her a gentle look. 'Don't put yourself down. Trust me, you'll have loads of proposals, but first you should think about having a career,' he said. 'You're still young. You should finish your education.'

She didn't agree with him. Anyway, she had Terry to think about. He would come for her once he was out. Terry needed her. Realising she was daydreaming she said quickly. 'What can I get for you?' She poised her pencil over the order pad.

'A large Cappuccino and a Danish pastry,' Danny said without hesitation.

As she moved away to get his order the door opened again. She smiled when she saw it was Danny's friend, Robert Lloyd. He was a Detective Chief Inspector based in Cheltenham, but he lived in Upper Wyre and occasionally came into the café. Laura remembered her nervousness when Danny had first introduced him. He was not in uniform, so she hadn't realised he was the police. Robert Lloyd was okay though.

'You've made it to waitress at last,' Robert said giving her a wide smile. 'It won't be long before you're running your own café.'

'As if,' she returned the smile, enjoying his friendly teasing. She liked his blue eyes which, despite his obvious middle-age, still had a sparkle.

Laura returned with Danny's coffee and cake and took Robert's order. The men were deep in conversation.

Zoe came in at lunch-time looking cross.

'What the matter?' Laura asked.

Zoe had befriended her from the first week, and the two girls seemed to click. She'd never had a friend before, not a real friend. Zoe was seventeen, had olive skin and dark hair and lived with her parents and two younger brothers, but couldn't wait for the day she could afford to leave home. 'I want to go and live in a big city,' Zoe had said, 'there's nothing to do here in the village.' Zoe had taken her home to meet her parents. They welcomed her so warmly that Laura felt envious of their happy family life, and couldn't understand why Zoe was so anxious to leave.

'Got a new woman started today. She's a right bitch. Hadn't been there an hour and she told me off. Bloody cheek! I complained to Danny, but he said I had to take notice of what she said, because she knew what she was doing. I nearly told him where to stick his job.'

'That would have been a shame you really like working there.'

'I know,' Zoe grinned ruefully. 'Get us a coffee and a cheese omelette. If I keep you talking much longer you'll lose your job.'

The café was filling up, and Laura scurried about taking orders. The other girls from the perfumery came in and joined

Zoe, and she could hear them gossiping about the new woman, who apparently was called Harriet and was too far up her own arse for her own good. It made Laura laugh.

Laura walked home at six, pleased that her first day had gone so well. She enjoyed walking through the village, over the quaint little bridge, and even though it was dusk, she stopped to throw bread to the swans as they glided towards her along the river.

It was so lovely here, a far cry from the Foleshill Road, or her home on the council estate in Lewisham.

Home. She pictured the little terraced house with the garish red door, the tiny front garden full of weeds and the grey net curtains. Only now, living in Nancy and Brett's fantastic house, did she realise just how bad her home had been. And yet, when she was little, she had thought it perfect. It had felt safe and warm. That was before her father had left, when she had no idea that her father had been so unhappy. She had assumed that because she was happy, so was the rest of her family. Her dad, Ron, was a taxi driver and he worked long hours, often not coming home until the morning, just as she was about to go to school. She would make him tea and toast and they would chat and he would tell her funny stories about his passengers. Then he would ask if her mother was up yet and she would laugh and say, 'Dad it's only eight o'clock,' and he would sigh and look around the house, neat and tidy, because she had been up since six cleaning, and he would ruffle her hair and tell her she was a star.

She wished he had loved her enough to have stayed.

She entered the house and found Nancy already there preparing the dinner.

'Hi,' Nancy said, 'how was your first day as a waitress?'

'Brilliant.' Laura said hanging up her coat tidily on the hall stand. 'I didn't make one mistake.'

'Good for you,' Nancy laughed.

'I've been thinking about home,' Laura confided as she switched on the kettle. She talked to Nancy a lot, confided some of her feelings to her. Nancy was aware now that Terry was in prison and that her father had not died. When she had finally admitted the truth to them she had expected them to be horrified and ask her to leave, but they hadn't. Once again she was thankful for their kindness. Only one thing jarred. Nancy was deeply religious and tried to get her to go to church. It made her feel awkward, because her belief in a God was very unclear. She was ashamed of her past, of the things she had done, but religion played no part in her contrition.

She had to admit though that Nancy always gave her good advice, and listened to her as if she really cared. Despite her disability, Nancy was warm and friendly. She admired the way she coped with her blindness. She had been blind since the age of three, after an attack of measles, yet she never seemed to let her disability hinder her. Laura had never known anyone like her. She thought Nancy was a truly good person. She had no idea such people existed. Not only had they shared their home with her, a complete stranger, they never made her feel uncomfortable in any way.

Nancy sat down on at the kitchen table. 'You must miss your mother. Do you still plan to go to London?'

'I'm not sure. What if I can't find her, what will I do then?'

'Maybe you should go to London just for the day. See what you can find out.'

'Yeah, that's a good idea.'

'And if you find her, will you go home?'

'I don't know. Do you want me to leave?' Laura said anxiously, putting a mug of tea in front of Nancy and sitting down at the table.

'No of course not, that's not what I'm saying,' Nancy assured her. 'It's for your own peace of mind. You can stay here as long as you want.'

'Can I really?' Laura was overwhelmed.

Later that evening in her room, after she had washed up, she wrote to Terry. She told him of her plan to go on the train to see if she could find Mum. After she had sealed the envelope, she lay on the bed and thought of the future, and wondered if Terry would like living here in this lovely village.

Chapter Eight

Laura entered the house and rushed up to her room to change. There wasn't much time; she was meeting Zoe at the bus stop in half-an-hour. Today was her half day and they were going shopping in Cheltenham.

Zoe was taking her to a nightclub on Friday, and she needed some new clothes. Zoe had said she could get them past the doorman with no problem so long as they wore the right gear and put on loads of make-up. Laura wasn't bothered about going. It would mean spending some of her precious savings, however, Zoe had been uppity, so she had relented - she hadn't wanted to upset her.

Pulling off her white blouse and black skirt she wriggled into her skin-tight white hipsters and slipped a skimpy top over her head. The top didn't quite reach her waistband, exposing an inch or so of skin. Zoe had tried to persuade her to have her belly button pierced, but she was having none of that. Mutilating your body did nothing for her.

Grinning at herself in the mirror, she pulled self-consciously at the top. Her breasts had developed over the past months, and the low-necked top showed off her cleavage. She had to admit she did look and feel good. She fastened a gold chain belt around her waist, pushed on a pair of sunglasses, grabbed her bag, and headed for the bus stop.

'We need a plan,' Zoe said when they were seated on the bus.

'For what?'

Zoe looked fantastic, in a red halter top that suited her dark colouring. She wished she could wear red, but it clashed with her auburn hair.

'To decide which shops to target,' Zoe said impatiently.

Laura frowned, not understanding.

'We'll start with the smaller shops like Dorothy Perkins and Gap, maybe Next. If they have security guards on, we need to be extra careful.'

Laura felt her stomach lurch. *Shoplifting.*

She had done a bit in Coventry of course, but only, in desperation, for food when they were really broke or maybe a bar of chocolate from the Pakistani corner shop, but Zoe seemed to be planning to nick a whole load of gear.

She baulked at that.

She had enough money in her purse to buy what she wanted; there was no need to nick anything. Even though she hated spending money she didn't want to go back to her old ways. She wanted a new start for her and Terry and she squirreled away her savings for when he was released. She wanted them to have a decent place to live, where she could keep an eye on him, make sure he didn't do anything stupid again. She wrote to him every week, and she understood when his replies were very few and very short. Life in prison must be terrible for him, and she couldn't wait until he was free.

'Are you listening?' Zoe nudged her arm.

'Sorry.'

'Have you heard a word I've said?'

'Yeah, course.'

'So!'

'So what?' Laura suspected she had missed something important while she had been daydreaming about Terry.

Zoe sighed theatrically. 'So which shop will we go at first. What do you need?'

'Just about everything,' Laura said, thinking of her sparse wardrobe. Now that she was earning she refused to allow Nancy to buy her anything more. She wasn't a charity case.

Neither was she prepared to steal. The thought of going to prison like Terry made her feel physically sick. How could she tell Zoe though without her kicking off? She was obviously well into it. She didn't want to be thought of as a loser, but there was no way she was getting involved.

Another nudge, harder this time, made her gasp. 'Really Laura, what's up with you today, you keep going off on one.'

'Sorry. It's just well – I'd rather not, you know *steal* anything.'

Zoe shrugged. 'Suit yourself.' She turned her head away and looked out of the window, clearly annoyed.

Laura bit down on her lip. She didn't want to fall out with her. 'Sorry Zoe, I'll come with you, look out for you.'

'That's better,' Zoe grinned. 'Let's start off at Dotty P's, I need underwear.'

The sun was shining as they walked along the High Street in Cheltenham town centre. Not a cloud in the clear blue sky, and the August sun felt warm on her bare arms.

She had to admit Zoe was good, not once had she seen her lift anything and slip it into the Gap store bag she had brought in readiness. After Dorothy Perkins they had been in Monsoon and River Island and Oasis, working the shops in Regency Arcade and the Promenade. Laura was exhausted, mostly from tension.

She had followed her into each shop, browsing through the clothes while watching Zoe nip in and out of the changing rooms. Each time they left the store she was convinced Zoe would be stopped.

'Just one more shop,' Zoe said and then we'll have lunch.

'What!' Laura gasped. 'I thought you'd finished.'

'I need some jeans.'

'Which shop then?' Laura sighed, knowing it would be useless to try and dissuade her.

'Cavendish House.'

'No way!'

'Why not?'

'They have security guards.'

'So?'

They rode the escalator to women's wear, pretending they didn't know each other. Zoe headed for jeans while she browsed through the tops and skirts trying not to look conspicuous.

The sales girl had gone to attend to a customer. Zoe took six items into the changing rooms unchallenged.

Laura wandered around, the clothes were gorgeous. She slipped on a cashmere wool jacket and admired herself in the mirror, running her hands over the soft fabric. The pale blue suited her colouring. She turned up the collar. It looked well cool. She took it off and tried on a designer labelled knee length coat. She looked about twenty-five in it. She sighed and hung it back on the rail.

She turned and looked straight into the eyes of a security guard.

He nodded to her and she held her breath as he moved between the rails of clothes. She glanced nervously towards the changing room praying that Zoe wouldn't choose this moment to come out.

The guard turned and stared at her again and she flushed guiltily. She turned away. Now she'd done it, brought attention to herself. She could feel his eyes still on her. On the edge of her vision she could see him coming towards her. She tried not to panic. Zoe had left her holding the Gap bag full of stolen gear.

Just as she was sure he was going to question her, his mobile phone rang. He turned away.

Laura fled into the ladies toilet. Locking herself in a cubicle she rang Zoe on her mobile.

'There's a guard hovering,' she whispered. 'Be careful.'

'Okay.'

She stayed in the toilets for five minutes before she felt brave enough to come out. Her heart was beating so fast she felt as if she had been the one stealing.

Back down the escalator, through the perfume department towards the door. Zoe was ahead of her.

She was sure she must look suspicious, but no one took any notice of her.

Zoe was almost at the door.

'Excuse me, miss.' The sales assistant looked serious.

Laura turned away. She had no idea what to do. She pretended to be looking at perfume while staying within earshot. *If Zoe got arrested she would just die!*

The store assistant was speaking to Zoe. 'Can I interest you in a having one of our store cards?'

Laura felt faint with relief. She hurried out of the door and took a gulp of fresh air. Zoe followed her out. 'Okay?' she asked worriedly.

'Yeah,' Laura nodded

'Only you look as white as a sheet.'

Laura laughed nervously. 'Never do that to me again,' she said weakly.

'First time's always the worst,' Zoe said, linking her arm.

As they emerged into Pittville Street they almost fell over a huddled figure sitting cross-legged against the wall. Laura immediately searched in her purse and threw a pound coin into the waiting bowl.

'You know he's probably a con man,' Zoe commented as they walked away, 'or on hard drugs.'

'Probably, or he might not be,' Laura shrugged.

'You're such a soft touch,' Zoe laughed.

Laura didn't reply. She was remembering the time when she had begged, desperate for a few coppers for a cup of tea. She had been ignored. She dreaded to think what would have happened to her if she had not met Brett and Nancy. She was so grateful that someone had cared. Whenever she passed someone begging, she always gave them money, thinking how different her life was now to when she had first arrived in Cheltenham and that awful squat. She would never forget the feeling of despair at being homeless.

They bought burgers and chips from MacDonald's and sat on a bench.

'Do you want some of this gear?' Zoe said, 'only we are about the same size.' She rummaged in the bag and pulled out a couple of tops. 'You can have these if you want.'

Laura flushed. She didn't want them; there was no way she would feel comfortable wearing knocked off gear. She thought back to the flat and the stolen telly and stereo. She hadn't been so choosy then. Must be Nancy's influence, she decided.

'Thanks,' she said, 'but they're not really my colour.' She hoped Zoe wouldn't take offence.

Zoe looked at her. 'Yeah suppose you're right.' She stuffed the clothes back into the bag.

'Sorry,' Laura said sensing Zoe's irritation.

'No problem, your loss.'

Before she could say anything further, she glanced across the road and saw Danny pull up in his new sports car.

The two-seater E-type Jaguar coupe was a classic. Laura knew he had only picked it up yesterday. He had come into the café to show it off to Brett.

'Now that's what I call a set of wheels,' Zoe said following her gaze. 'He could take me to bed any day in exchange for a ride in that.'

'What!' Laura gasped.

'I said I wouldn't mind having sex with him.'

Laura tried not to be shocked. 'You're kidding, right?'

Zoe laughed. 'Maybe.'

'I know he's nice and all that, but he's well – far too old for you.' Laura frowned.

'Not really, he's only thirty-nine and he's well fit. I like my men experienced. He'd be better than the geeks we meet at the disco. They don't know what to do with it.'

'With what?'

'Laura!'

Laura blushed.

Zoe's eyes widened. 'Don't tell me you're still a *virgin*?'

Laura lowered her gaze, her face crimson.

'Wow! Awesome.' Then seeing her crestfallen face, she said more gently. 'Sorry, me and my big gob.'

'It's okay.'

'Have you ever, you know, had a boyfriend?'

'Of course.'

'Liar. I can tell you haven't. Wicked!'

'Shut up!' Laura was mortified.

'Talk about something else, Danny's coming over,' Zoe

whispered.

'Hello Zoe, what have you been buying?' Danny nodded towards her bag and Zoe nudged it further under the table with her foot.

'Just stuff, you know,' Zoe shrugged. 'I'll probably take it all back next week when I realise how much I've spent.'

Danny laughed. He turned and smiled at Laura. She could feel his eyes on her body. 'You look fantastic, Laura,' he said.

'Ta.' Laura couldn't meet his gaze, her face felt as if it was burning. She was glad when he turned and walked away. She watched him cross the road and enter Ernest Jones jewellers.

Zoe was spluttering with laughter. '*You look fantastic, Laura,*' she mimicked and Laura was surprised to hear a touch of jealousy in her tone.

Feeling discomforted Laura said. 'What's Danny's wife like? I've only ever seen her in the street, she never speaks.'

'She's not that friendly. Christine puts up with a lot from him though. Everyone said she married beneath her because she comes from a very posh family. She's okay to work for, kind and fair. I don't think she's happy, but she would never let it show.'

Danny emerged from the jewellers. 'I wonder what he's buying her,' Laura said curiously.

Zoe gave her a knowing look. 'What makes you think he is buying for his wife?' she said with a grin.

'What do you mean?'

Zoe leaned across the table. 'If he's buying jewellery, I bet this week's wages it's not for Christine.'

'Who then?' Laura was intrigued.

Zoe winked conspiratorially. 'It'll be for Harriet.'

Chapter Nine

Laura felt nervous as she got off the train at St John's station in Lewisham. She had, at last, decided to come to London for the day. Now that she was here though, she wondered if it was such a good idea after all. How was she going to feel if she couldn't find anything about her mother's whereabouts? Nancy had said it was a chance she had to take, that she had to at least try, but now she wasn't so sure. Why was she bothering to look for her? She had been a crap mother and she doubted anything would have changed. And yet a small part of her wanted to see her. She was, after all, her mum, however bad she had been.

She emerged from the station and shivered as she remembered stories that her dad had told her about a terrible train crash that had happened here, long before she was born. Apparently the ghostly cries of those trapped could be heard every December the fourth, and today was December the fourth. What a day to choose to come here.

Hurrying along Loampit Hill, she reached Lewisham High Street some twenty minutes later. Passing the shops, she remembered hanging out here when she should have been at school. She remembered nicking a bag of sweets from Woolworths and scoffing them down so fast she was nearly sick.

She turned right passed her old primary school and peered through the railings at the deserted playground. Her first day here had been terrifying; her mother leaving her at the school gate to face a sea of rowdy children. She had turned, wanting to go home, but her mother was already hurrying away. She had hated crowds ever since, loathed being in a group. She had never made any real friends and school had been a lonely place.

Finally she reached the council estate and stopped outside her old home. The door was now painted white and the curtains had been replaced by Venetian blinds. The garden was paved too.

She moved on to the house next door and rapped sharply with the tarnished brass knocker.

Linda McCarthy hadn't changed a bit. She still looked slovenly, her bleached blonde hair unwashed and straggly. A cigarette hung from her bottom lip.

'Hi,' Laura said, 'remember me?'

Linda glared suspiciously. 'Nah,' she said, 'and if this is a trick to get me to do one of yer fecking surveys yer wasting yer breath.' Her broad Irish accent was just as she remembered it.

'I'm Laura. Me mum was Tina, your best friend,' Laura insisted. 'We lived next door.'

Linda took a drag of the cigarette and squinted through the smoke. 'Little Laura that run off and broke her mother's heart. Is that you?'

Laura tried not to laugh. Broke her mother's heart indeed! Was that what Mum had been telling everyone?

'Do you know where mum is?' Laura asked, desperately wanting to get to the point.

'Nah. She buggered off ages ago. Left in the middle of the night they did without so much as a goodbye. Some friend she turned out to be – and she owed me. Five quid it were. Don't suppose I'll ever see that now.' She gazed at Laura hopefully.

Laura opened her purse and took out a five pound note. 'Here,' she said.

Linda grabbed it greedily. 'Ta.'

'Does anyone around here have any idea what happened to her?'

Linda pursed her lips and pretended to consider it. 'You could try down at the Legion. We used to drink there most Fridays. I don't go there any more so I've no idea if anyone there even remembers her.'

'Okay, thanks anyway.'

Laura turned away and decided to try Mick Logan, three doors away. He was a taxi driver like her dad. She liked Mick; he had been really kind to her after her dad had left them. He had never married, said he preferred his freedom.

Mick looked as if he had just got out of bed when he finally answered the door. Unshaven, hair tousled and wearing only a vest and trousers with red braces dangling, he looked at her in annoyance.

'Hey it's me,' Laura stammered nervously.

He stared blankly.

Shit, didn't anyone remember her?

'Laura Armstrong, Ron's daughter.'

'Blimey didn't recognise yer. It's bin a long time. What yer doing back 'ere?'

'Looking for me mum.'

Mick shifted, looking uncomfortable. 'Come on inside a minute.' He opened the door wider.

Mick took her through to the kitchen, a replica of her old home but much cleaner and tidier.

'Want a cuppa?'

'Love one.'

'Sit yerself down,' he indicated a chair against a pine table.

As he made the tea, Laura looked around at the bright yellow painted walls and the cheerful blue and yellow print curtains, the china plates on the welsh dresser, and thought of how often she had sat here, crying her eyes out, after dad had left. 'Don't blame him,' Mick had said, 'he couldn't help it. He loved you and Terry. Never forget that.'

She had blamed him though. Mick was wrong. Her dad hadn't loved her. She was only eight when he had left. She had seen him twice since then. Once on her ninth birthday when he had taken her to McDonalds and then the last time when he had told her he was emigrating to New Zealand. How could Mick say her dad had loved her when he had gone to the other side of the world where there was no hope of her ever seeing him again?

Mick sat down opposite her. 'Your mum left under - well - a bit of a situation. That new bloke of hers, Nigel, he were a right rum un, not 'alf the man yer dad were,' Mick said shaking his head.

'Where did they go?' Laura interrupted, not wanting to discuss Nigel. He was one of the reasons her and Terry had left home.

'No idea. They said they were going to his family, only they never said where that was. They were in a lot of debt. I took them to the station. They had no money, didn't even have enough to pay the cab fare.'

Sighing, Laura opened her purse. 'How much was the fare, I'll pay it,' she said.

'No you won't, don't be silly.' Mick looked offended and she flushed.

'Sorry,' she mumbled.

'So you don't know what train they caught.'

'Sorry love. If they told me, I don't remember.'

'Do you ever hear from Dad?'

Mick shook his head.

The spark of hope that he may have returned flickered and died. Laura sighed.

Mick patted her hand. 'How yer doing anyway? You look lovely.' He smiled.

She told him about Terry being in prison and Nancy and Brett and her new life. He made more tea and gave her a chunk of fruit cake and it was two hours before she left.

On the train home she felt glad that she had come; she was no wiser to her mother's whereabouts, but suddenly it didn't matter anymore. Mick had told her to get on with her life and not to look back and she decided that was exactly what she would do.

Chapter Ten

Harriet was late. It was frustrating when they had so little time. The few hours that Christine, Danny's wife, was at her Friday night women's institute meeting, were precious, not to be wasted.

Arriving at the apartment on this crisp December evening, she found Danny waiting.

'Bloody traffic,' she said breathlessly as she slipped off her wool coat and threw it over a chair.

He kissed her briefly. 'Your face is cold.'

'I need warming up,' she acknowledged, giving him a sexy smile.

He had already poured two glasses of Merlot and she accepted hers gratefully as she sank into the soft comfort of the cream sofa, peeling off her knee-length suede boots and curling her legs under her.

She almost purred with pleasure. She loved this apartment, had enjoyed every minute of making it personal, buying special things; pictures, rugs, adding her own impeccable taste to the rooms. And, of course, filling the wardrobe with clothes and shoes to change into for when they dined out; clandestine dinners as far away as Gloucester or Bath.

Danny had also moved some of his stuff in, shaving gear, toothbrush; the aromatic cologne he used. Gradually, suits, shirts and shoes took up space in the wardrobe. His dressing gown hung on the bedroom door next to hers as the pattern of their lives evolved.

They met two or sometimes three times a week. Sometimes in the afternoon, sometimes in the evening, like now. On the rare occasion when Christine was away they spent all night together. They had been lovers now for seven months. She was ecstatically happy. She couldn't help but compare him to Jeremy. Danny was sensitive to her mood in a way that Jeremy had never been. With Danny she was perfectly at ease; she had a strong sense of belonging. She had driven home after that first night feeling on cloud nine until she reached the house, when a sudden pang of guilt made her stop and catch her breath, and left her wondering if she had made a big mistake.

The phone had rung the minute she had walked into the house. He had told her he loved her. 'You hardly know me,' she had protested weakly.

'Don't you feel the same?' he had questioned her.

And she did. She knew she did. It was amazing, incredible but true. She had given her notice in the next day. There was no going back.

She had been nervous facing Jeremy in case he sensed a change in her. However, he was so full of his health products scheme that he hardly listened to a word when she explained that she had a new job, better pay, more interesting. 'Good for you,' was his only comment.

Her first day at the perfumery, meeting Danny's wife, had been nerve-racking. Christine had greeted her coolly and said that she really must be something special because she usually did the hiring of staff. Harriet was certain that she suspected something. Even when Christine had said that her references were glowing and they were lucky to have her, she felt that Christine was paying lip service. She didn't believe for one moment that she was pleased Harriet was there.

Over the ensuing weeks Christine was polite, though not exactly friendly. Harriet learned to live with her guilt, to suppress her conscience that she was hurting Christine. Even though she hated the lies and the secrecy of their affair, her feelings for Danny were too strong. She simply couldn't help herself. Despite her earlier scepticism, she began to believe that Danny really did love her. He seemed to need her as much as she needed him.

She lived for the precious hours she and Danny spent at their apartment, cherishing and savouring every moment. Her love for him grew stronger with every passing week.

That she was also deceiving Jeremy somehow didn't seem quite as important as what she was doing to Christine. Jeremy irritated her more and more. She couldn't bring herself to have sex with him – not that he seemed to mind, which made her think he also had someone else. It eased her conscience a little.

She enjoyed working at the perfumery; the job was interesting and demanding. She worked in the compound room, extracting and blending. She liked the clean white walls and the cold stainless steel table, and the sense of precision and order. She delighted in the knowledge that Danny was in the adjoining laboratory, creating and designing perfumes. *Her secret lover.*

She didn't socialise with the other girls, they weren't really her sort. Pauline was middle-aged, divorced, constantly complaining about her ex-husband, and the other girls were far too young and empty-headed to be interesting. So she kept to herself and ignored the snide comments that she was stuck-up.

She often wondered if Danny, despite his denial, slept with his wife, but she didn't torture herself with those images. She didn't delve too deeply into that particular emotion.

When Danny came into the compound room it was hard to remember not to exchange even the remotest personal glance; she knew that if anyone even slightly suspected, Danny would end it. He was paranoid in case Christine found out.

'Is there something wrong?' Danny asked, breaking into her thoughts and bringing her back to the present.

'No, sorry, I was just remembering the very first time I saw you.'

He smiled and leaned to kiss her. 'I wanted you the first moment I set eyes on you and I want you now.'

Putting down her wine glass, she snuggled closer and began to unbutton his shirt. Sex with Danny was fantastic. Just as it had been that very first time.

'I have to go to Milan next week,' Danny said later as they were dressing.

'How long for?'

'A few days, a week at the most, depends.'

She felt deflated. 'Right,' she said trying not to sound possessive or needy.

Danny laughed.

'What's funny?'

'The look on your face.' He reached across and kissed her. 'I want you to come with me,' he said softly. 'We can spend whole days together, and more important, whole nights.'

Her heart soared. 'Danny I love you.' She kissed him passionately.

PART TWO

Chapter Eleven

2001

Harriet woke on Saturday morning feeling the now familiar rush of nausea and hurried to the downstairs toilet to throw up. She didn't use the bathroom because Jeremy might hear and guess that she was pregnant.

She had been sick every morning this week. It was becoming a pain. Hiding her condition from Jeremy wasn't going to be easy either. She didn't want him to know. Not yet, not until she had worked out what to do. There was not the remotest possibility that Jeremy was the father.

Jeremy came downstairs an hour later. 'I fancy a fry up this morning,' he said, 'do you want some?'

'No thanks.'

'I'll cook it.'

'I've already eaten.'

'Oh.' He looked around the spotless kitchen, 'what did you have?'

'Cereal, I washed up the bowl.'

Jeremy laughed. 'You know you're getting obsessively house proud. You need to get out more.'

'Don't be stupid,' she snapped.

He looked at her strangely. 'It was only a joke, my goodness you are tetchy this morning. Are you okay?'

'I'm fine. Stop fussing. Are you going to Abigail's today?'

'Yes. Actually she wants me to decorate her living room. It will mean I'll be there most of the day and probably tomorrow as well.'

'That's fine.'

'You don't mind?' Jeremy said perfunctorily. It would be all the same if she had.

'No of course not,' she said, filled with relief not to have to spend the week-end with him.

On Monday evening she waited nervously for Danny, pacing the room. She couldn't tell him at work and the day had seemed endless. She was the first to arrive at the flat and she poured drinks. He was late, over half an hour, and by then she was on her second gin and tonic.

He sensed at once there was something wrong. She had intended to tell him gently, perhaps after they had made love, but she was too distraught.

'I'm pregnant,' she blurted out.

She watched the colour drain from his face. 'Christ, Harriet you can't be.'

'I've been to the doctor, he confirmed it.'

'You stupid woman, didn't you take your pill?'

'Of course I did,' she retaliated angrily, 'and stop acting as if it's my fault.'

'Then how has this happened?'

'I've no idea. I'm just as shocked as you are.'

He ran his hand distractedly through his hair. 'This is a disaster, a fucking disaster.'

It was not what she wanted to hear. She wanted comfort, his arms around her, telling her that he loved her, that he would take care of her. 'What are we going to do?'

He swallowed a gin and tonic in one go. 'I'll pay for an abortion.'

'No.' She felt a stab of panic. 'I can't do that.'

'You must.'

She sat down, feeling scared. 'Please, Danny don't do this to us. We love each other, this is our baby.'

A look of fear shadowed his face. 'You don't understand,' he said quietly. 'This will kill Christine. If she finds out I'm the father of your baby . . .'

'You told me neither of you wanted children.'

'No, I never said that. I said *I* never wanted any. Christine has always longed for a child.'

'So you don't want mine?' she said bleakly.

'Harriet sweetheart, it's not that I don't *want* it, it's just . . .'

'Just a bit inconvenient,' Harriet said sarcastically.

'Don't be like that. You must see the problems it will cause.'

'I'm keeping the baby. It's your choice as to whether you want to be involved.' She shrugged, pretending indifference even though her heart was racing in case he totally rejected her.

'What does Jeremy say about your pregnancy?'

'I haven't told him yet. He'll know it's not his because we don't sleep together.'

The barb hit home when she saw him frown. She no longer asked if he had sex with Christine. She knew the answer and had pushed it to the back of her mind.

'How far are you gone?'

'Two months.'

'Sleep with your husband then. Tell him the child is his, it will save a lot of trouble.'

Harriet stared at him, unable to believe he could ask this of her.

At last he took her in his arms. She remained stiff, unyielding. 'Come on, darling this is the answer. No one will suspect.' He nuzzled her neck as his hand moved to her breast.

She pushed him away. Sex was suddenly abhorrent to her. 'Don't Danny, I'm not in the mood.'

He took a step back, his face surprised. 'What do you want me to do?'

'We could get married.'

'You know that's not possible.'

'Why isn't it? I love you. I thought you loved me. I don't want to hurt Christine but people divorce every day. The baby changes everything. I need you Danny. I want us to be together.'

He took her in his arms again. 'I adore you, Harriet, I don't want to lose you, but I won't divorce Christine. I told you that right at the beginning.'

73

She knew it was no use pleading with him. The idea that he did not want their baby made her feel utterly desolate.

Jeremy arrived home on Friday evening. She had worried all week about telling him, knowing she couldn't do as Danny asked and sleep with him. Ever since Jeremy had signed over the house to her he had not approached her in bed. If she slept with him now it would be too obvious.

They ate dinner in silence. Her nerves were stretched to the limit. She passed him a cup of coffee and said. 'I'm pregnant.'

His face drained of colour. 'Obviously not mine.'

'Obviously.'

'You cheating bitch. Who's the father?'

'You don't need to know that.'

'Presumably he's also married.'

Harriet shrugged.

Jeremy left the table and began to pace the room. 'How long – how long has it been going on?'

'Does it matter?'

'*How long?*' he shouted.

'Two years.'

'Jesus! How could you? I've never been unfaithful to you, not once.'

'Oh stop playing the sanctimonious martyr. You have done far worse to me,' Harriet snapped.

Jeremy's face was like thunder. He took a step towards her, his hand raised, and she thought he was going to strike her.

He lowered his hand. 'Do you love him?' he said quietly.

'Yes.'

He seemed to slump. 'Do you want a divorce? Are you going to marry him?'

'No.'

'Why not?'

She shrugged.

'Ah. He doesn't want you now that you're pregnant.'

His smug glance was more than she could bear. 'Piss off,' she said irritably.

'I intend to. You're on your own. I'm leaving you,' he said.

'Whatever.' She was too tired and dispirited to care.

Jeremy turned and walked out of the room. She heard him go upstairs. Exhausted, she crumpled on the sofa. She felt drained and too tired to think straight. She heard Jeremy come back downstairs. He was carrying a large holdall. 'I'll be at Abigail's,' his tone was bitter. 'I'll send for the rest of my things later.'

She didn't answer. She knew his sister would be delighted to have him.

The silence after he had gone was unsettling. She didn't blame Jeremy, she was glad he had gone.

Now that painful scene was over she needed to concentrate on what to do. It was not too late to have an abortion, but as much as the thought of raising this child on her own terrified her, she couldn't kill Danny's baby.

Maybe, just maybe, Danny might change his mind and want the child once it was born. It was a thin, tentative thread of hope, yet she clung to it.

For the first time since she was eighteen she longed for her mother. Of course that wasn't possible. She had not spoken to her since they had emigrated. An incident involving her uncle had caused a rift. There would be no reconciliation, not now. Apart from the fact they now lived in Canada, they were devout Presbyterians and her mother, especially, would not understand or condone her relationship with a married man, let alone being pregnant by him.

If Danny abandoned her she really was on her own.

Chapter Twelve

Laura sipped a vodka and coke as she sat on a stool at the bar, feeling anxious. She didn't really like vodka, but she thought it might relax her a bit. Today was her eighteenth birthday and Zoe had insisted they come to the disco with the other girls from the perfumery.

She didn't want to be here and had only come to please Zoe. She wasn't very good at dancing; she was clumsy because her co-ordination was rubbish.

She watched the girls enjoying themselves and wished she felt more comfortable in a crowd, but she had always been a loner and she guessed that would never change. Even at school – the few times she attended – she always hovered on the periphery of her group of classmates, never quite joining in.

Her anxiety wasn't totally because of the disco. There had been too many shocks today for her to feel relaxed and happy. First Nancy had announced that she was getting married. Nancy had met Angus six months earlier at a charity event where Nancy was singing. Angus was a charming man and genuinely in love with Nancy. He organised and managed gigs for her so she no longer sang in the streets. She was a great success.

She had been so happy with Nancy's news, but selfishly she had also been worried. Brett had made it clear that she couldn't stay once Nancy had left; apparently it wouldn't be appropriate. Nancy had told her not to fret, she wasn't leaving until September, and she was sure to find somewhere before then, but there wasn't much rented accommodation in the village, certainly none she could afford.   Once again it looked like she was homeless.

Next was the letter she had received from Terry with her birthday card. She hadn't heard from him for months and she was sure he wouldn't remember her birthday. But he had. She had torn open the envelope eagerly, recognising his handwriting but not the postmark. It had puzzled her. It certainly wasn't from the prison. Inside the card was a cheque for a hundred pounds. She had been overwhelmed until she read the letter.

Dear Laura,

Good news, I have been released early. I shared a cell with a fellow prisoner, Kevin Richardson. He offered me a job in his new garage. Kevin is a good bloke, so don't worry. I am now in Sidmouth, Devon, working for him and sharing a flat. I hope you are well. Write to me please. Love Terry.

How could he have left prison without telling her? And why was there was no mention of her going to live with him? She had worked and saved and waited for the day when she could be with him and he had buggered off to Devon, miles away, without a thought of her. He didn't need her. The hurt turned to anger and she screwed up the letter and threw it in the bin. *Sod him!*

'Hi, want to dance?' She looked up, her vision blurred, to see a young lad standing over her.

She squinted at him, noticing he had blond hair, long and curly like a girl's and he looked vaguely familiar.

'No thanks, I'm rubbish at it,' she confessed shaking her head.

'Ah come on, it's easy. I'll show you. My name's Mark.' He grabbed her hand and hauled her to her feet.

'Have I seen you before?' Laura asked as they stepped onto the crowded dance floor.

'Yeah I'm Debbie's brother. I've been in the café.'

Debbie was a waitress at *Le Fleur* but came over to *Flamingo's* occasionally when they were short staffed. She vaguely remembered Mark coming in.

She wriggled about a bit trying to copy the other girls but she felt stupid and clumsy.

'I'm going to sit down,' she said after about ten minutes.

'I'll get you a drink,' Mark offered, 'Vodka and coke?'

'Yeah, cheers.'

On the perimeter of the dance floor she found a free table on a raised balcony and sat down. It was dimly lit and smoky. Mark brought the drinks over and slid along the leather sofa, sitting really close to her. She was glad she had someone to talk to. She was comfortable with him and when he put his arm across her shoulder she didn't object, it felt nice. It took the edge of her worries.

Zoe and the girls were still on the dance floor, shrieking to the music. It was dark beyond the disco lights and nobody seemed to take any notice of them.

Mark kissed her tentatively at first and when she didn't object he got bolder. She returned his kisses, liking the taste and feel of his mouth.

'I need the loo.' She stood up and swayed. The room spun.

Mark laughed. 'Hey, I'd better help you.'

She clung to him as they staggered towards the ladies.

'Will you be okay,' he said outside the toilet.

'Yeah,' she giggled, 'you can hardly come in.'

Inside the ladies cloakroom she splashed her face and tried to sober up but the room was still spinning. Oh God, she must be really drunk.

Mark was waiting. 'Come and get some fresh air,' he said, 'you'll feel better.'

The May evening was cool and dark, making her feel even more light-headed. She was glad of his arms around her; she felt so unsteady she thought she would fall over. She wanted to lie down and sleep, but Mark was pulling her towards the rear of the building. Leaning against the wall for support she closed her eyes.

His kisses were more urgent this time, his tongue darting in and out of her mouth, hungrily. Mark pressed himself closer to her; his breathing was heavy as his hands moved down her spine and caressed her buttocks.

'I really should go back in,' Laura murmured dreamily. 'Zoe will be wondering where I am.'

'Just a bit longer,' Mark pleaded. 'You're so sexy.'

Laura opened her eyes and gazed up at the dark sky, her eyes following the stars. She was so tired and yet she didn't really want to go back in, it was great being kissed and cuddled.

Snuggling up to him she allowed him to slip his hand inside her bra. She liked the feel of her breasts being stroked and she moaned softly.

'Let's go and sit in my car for a bit.' Mark licked her ear lobe.

It would be good to sit down, her legs felt like jelly.

The car park was pitch-black. They climbed into the back seat of his Volvo.

He kissed her again and stroked her hair. 'I've fancied you for ages,' Mark whispered against her neck. 'Do you like me?'

She thought it was a silly question when she hardly knew him, but she didn't want to hurt his feelings so she murmured that she did.

He bent his head and sucked her nipples. Her breasts had slipped out of the top of her dress without her realising it. She didn't object; it would have taken too much effort. She closed her eyes again and gave herself up to the warm languid feeling.

She felt his hand on her leg and then her thigh and then inside her knickers. She really should stop him.

'Maybe we should go back now,' she murmured half-heartedly.

'You can't stop now,' Mark groaned, 'you can't leave me like this.'

'Like what?' She opened her eyes and saw his trousers were undone.

'Jesus!' she gasped in surprise. She had never seen a man naked before. She was too stunned to protest as he took her hand and placed it over his erection, moving it slowly up and down.

Sobering up a bit, she was about to say she must go back to the disco, but then she thought of Zoe laughing at her because she was still a virgin.

She shivered a little in fright.

'Hey, it'll be all right,' Mark said soothingly. 'I've got a jonnie.'

She turned her head away embarrassed as he pulled on a condom. He kissed her again, his fingers working their way inside her.

'Is this your first time,' he whispered in her ear.

'Yeah.'

He was encouraging her to come but however hard she tried she couldn't seem to get aroused. She closed her eyes and moaned a bit, pretending she was enjoying it.

She cried out as he entered her, it was so painful, but Mark seemed to think she was having a climax.

She wanted it to be over, she wanted him to stop but he was thumping away so hard he was beyond reason.

At last he came with a shuddering jerk and then collapsed with his head against her breast.

'You were fantastic,' he murmured. 'Did you enjoy it?'

'Yeah sure,' she lied, wishing suddenly she had said no. She felt nothing for Mark, she hardly knew him. She had wanted someone to love her. Sex was not enough.

Chapter Thirteen

Harriet felt the week drag by as she struggled to cope with her pregnancy. She hated the sight of her large swollen body. She shopped at Mothercare; bought a pram, cot and baby clothes. She did it all without any real enthusiasm. She couldn't envisage the child being born. She didn't hear from Jeremy at all, but Abigail visited her just once, a week after he had left. Abigail called her a whore and a deceitful bitch and said if she had anything to do with it Jeremy would divorce her. Harriet told her to go ahead, she wouldn't contest it. 'You know he can't,' Abigail screamed. 'You know it's against his faith.'

Harriet remembered then that Jeremy was a Catholic, a lapsed one, but he still adhered to their beliefs when it suited him.

Danny was distant with her at work, clearly made nervous by her pregnancy. They no longer met at the flat; she couldn't bring herself to have sex with him, and each visit had ended in an argument. Now he didn't bother to arrange anything.

At eight months she took maternity leave. Sitting in the garden on a sunny August day she thought of the future.

Since she had left the perfumery she had not even spoken to him. The days were long and lonely and she thought back to the start of their affair and how wonderful it had been. She longed for his presence, for the touch of his hands on her body and his warm sexual kisses. The way his wonderful eyes sparkled when they met, the loving look that sent shivers of pleasure down her spine. How long ago that seemed. She wondered if after the birth, Danny would want her again. Could she juggle a job, a baby and an affair? It might be difficult but not impossible. The idea of never seeing Danny again didn't bear thinking about. She had thought she had lost the ability to love him, so great was the distress he had caused her, but as the weeks went by and her hurt subsided she knew she would always love him. Nothing he did could ever erase her feelings for him.

She missed him so much, and although he had hurt her deeply she began to dream of a future. Even though marriage was out of the question they could still have a life together, a secret life. She could accept that. It would be better than not having him at all. Maybe she would move away from Cheltenham to a place where they were not known. She would buy a house and Danny would visit. In time she was sure he would grow to love their child. The idea was so appealing she began to feel better.

Harriet's labour pains started late one Monday afternoon in September. She phoned the perfumery, wanting Danny at her side when she gave birth to his child, and was shocked to hear that he had taken Christine to Italy on holiday.

When her contractions were twenty minutes apart she took a taxi to the hospital. She fought the need to scream when the pain became unbearable; her pride would not allow her to make a fuss.

Eight agonising hours later, a small scrawny infant was placed in her arms. The child seemed alien. Surely she should feel something, some connection, a certain measure of love, but all she wanted to do was to sleep. Handing the baby back to the nurse she closed her eyes.

It seemed she had hardly slept when someone was gently shaking her shoulder. 'Baby needs a feed,' the nurse said.

'Can't you give her a bottle?' Harriet grumbled. She tried to sit up and winced as the stitches pulled. 'Christ,' she said. It hurt like hell.

The nurse lifted the baby from the Perspex cot. 'It's better for baby if you breast feed her.'

Harriet gave her glare. 'Take her away, I'm too tired,' she turned her head away and buried her face in the pillow.

When she woke again Jeremy was at her bedside. He looked ill; pale and unshaven. She hadn't seen him since he walked out.

'How did you get in?' She was not pleased to see him.

'I'm your husband. They assumed I'm the father.' He sat on the plastic chair twisting his hands together. 'You had a girl then?'

'Yes.' Harriet glanced at the cot where the baby was asleep.

'She's pretty.'

'What are you doing here?'

'I want to come back home. I'll look after you, and the baby of course.'

'Why?'

Jeremy shrugged. 'Because I love you.'

She stared at him, trying to work out the real reason. 'Has Abigail thrown you out?' she asked.

He looked sullen. 'No, but I can't stand living with her. She preaches to me every bloody hour. It's getting on my nerves.'

Harriet laughed. 'Poor Jeremy.'

'So that's settled then.'

'Hang on a minute, I haven't agreed. I need to think about it.'

'You need me. You won't manage on your own,' Jeremy said belligerently.

'What about your job?'

'I've been allowed some time off.'

'Why would they do that when we're no longer together?' Harriet looked doubtful.

'I never told them.'

She was surprised. 'Why not?'

'I didn't want the office to gossip about me. I've seen what they do to colleagues whose partners cheat on them. They have no sympathy, they just ridicule you because you can't keep your wife. How would it make me look if they knew you'd had a kid by another man?'

Harriet sighed. As always it was about him, about his image and what people would think.

'Actually I've not been well. Had a bit of a breakdown,' Jeremy was clearly uncomfortable with his confession.

Harriet groaned. She hoped he wasn't going to blame her for that.

'I got depressed. It was the shock. But I'm okay now. I realised you made a mistake and no doubt you're sorry. It probably wasn't your fault entirely. Anyway I've forgiven you.'

'How generous of you.'

Completely missing her sarcastic tone Jeremy rambled on. 'We can pretend the child is mine. I'll get a job closer to home, be there every night. I've a mate that's offered me a share in -'

Harriet held up her hand. 'Jeremy stop, wait. It won't work. I don't want you back.'

'Why not? I thought you'd be pleased seeing as how Pembroke doesn't want you.'

'What!'

Jeremy snorted. 'Did you imagine I didn't know who the father was?'

Harriet frowned. 'How did you find out?'

'I made it my business to. I wondered if it was your boss, there was always something in your tone whenever you mentioned him. I came home early one Friday and went to the perfumery to meet you. You'd already left, Pembroke wasn't in either. I rang your mobile but it was switched off. I began to think my suspicions were right.'

'Why did it matter to you who the father was?' Harriet interrupted.

'It didn't, not really. I was just curious, and angry of course, angry that you were cheating on me.'

'Go on,' Harriet sighed heavily.

'A couple of weeks later I was in Cheltenham, at our head office. I saw you drive by in your car. I followed you, saw you enter that flat in Montpellier just before Pembroke arrived.' Jeremy smirked, obviously pleased with his detective work.

'Why haven't you said anything before?'

'I have to admit I was tempted to go and see Pembroke's wife. I guessed she had no idea what you were up to with her husband. But then I decided to wait to see what happened after you'd had the baby. I suspected Pembroke wouldn't want to know.'

'He does. He's going to ask his wife for a divorce. It's just a matter of waiting for the right time.'

Jeremy guffawed. 'If you believe that shit, then you're stupid.'

'Get out Jeremy, just *get out*,' Harriet yelled furiously.

Harriet left the hospital three days later. The baby, whom she named Amy, had turned from a red wizened creature into a human being. Her skin was pale and smooth and her hair thick and black. Harriet thought she could see Danny's eyes and her own shaped mouth. Even so, the child didn't seem to be part of her and she dreaded being alone with her.

The house was cold and the kitchen full of unwashed dishes. There had been no time to clear up before she left. She turned the central heating on full and laid Amy down in the new pram. Amy immediately started to cry.

The next few days passed in a haze of tired confusion. Exhausted, she staggered through days and nights that seemed to be filled with making bottles and changing nappies. She couldn't stomach the thought of breast feeding and she took tablets to take away her milk. Amy cried constantly.

She heard that Danny and Christine had returned from Italy and she tried to talk to him, but he never took her calls or returned her messages. She wanted him to see his child, to talk about their future.

A week became a month and then two. Danny never came to visit. No one called, not even Jeremy. The health visitor gave advice which she ignored. Amy was not a contented child and since her birth she hadn't known it was possible to feel such exhaustion. The child never seemed to sleep long enough for her to organise a routine. The house was a mess; she had neither the time nor the energy to tidy up. Her wonderful neat and perfect home became a tip of dirty pots, plates encrusted with half-eaten meals and unwashed floors. The house stank. She couldn't believe that this tiny scrap of humanity was having such a devastating effect on her life. She wished, despondently, she could love her.

One afternoon when Amy refused to settle she took her out in the car to get her to sleep. It seemed the car was the only place Amy liked to be. She drove to the perfumery and parked outside. She wanted to go in, to show Danny his daughter, but she was afraid to face him in the state she was in. She knew she looked terrible; her unwashed hair hung lank and greasy, her clothes were stained and her face ravaged with tiredness and tears.

'Danny, Danny, I need you so much. Help me.'

It was useless. She couldn't go and beg him. She remembered her plans of how they would be together, a family, a secret family, but she knew now that would never happen. Danny had abandoned her.

She ached to see him, but not like this. She longed for the time before Amy was born, when she felt attractive, sexy and in control. Now she felt a failure.

She drove home. The minute she entered the house Amy woke and started screaming. In a rage she lifted her up and shook her. 'I hate you,' she screamed, 'I hate you. I wish you'd never been born.'

There was a moment of shocked silence, when the child seemed not to breathe, then she howled louder. For a split second she was tempted to smother her, but then she laid her in her cot and left the room. As she closed the door she was terrified at how close she had come to harming her. Utterly miserable, she lay on her bed and sobbed.

Chapter Fourteen

The storm was unexpected. Gale-force winds had blown in from the Atlantic, sweeping across the country and, as the squall heightened in its intensity, blinding rain fell from the dark sky. Seventy mile-an-hour gusts whipped fiercely through the trees, violently battering everything in the wind's path. Thunder rumbled with a deep resounding crash. Lightning crackled across the sky.

The forked lightning struck the gnarled old oak in Hunters Lane, fracturing the heart of it. For a split second the tree stood suspended, illuminated in the blackness of the night; then it tilted and swayed until falling with a deafening thud of splintering wood. It lay across the lane, scattering the wet road with branches and leaves and clumps of mud, as its roots were torn from the ground.

No one saw it fall or heard the noise. A tawny owl screeched in terror as it flew across the dark moonless sky. The tree finally stopped shuddering and lay silent in the darkness, unseen and dangerous, on the unlit narrow country lane.

Chapter Fifteen

Laura was excited. Today, Friday, was her last day here. At long last she was going to Devon to see Terry.

She was over the disappointment of him not contacting her when he had left prison and had forgiven him. No longer needing her savings for them to be together she had splashed out on a car, a Ford Fiesta, with seventy-eight thousand miles on the clock and a dented rear bumper, but it was cheap, and the engine was sound according to Brett. He had taught her to drive and she had passed her test first time.

The previous month she had written to Terry telling him she had to move out because Nancy had got married and she and Angus were moving to Scotland. Obviously she couldn't stay in the house with Brett, so she would have to find new lodgings.

Terry had replied immediately, invited her to Devon and giving her another shock. He had moved into a house with Alison, a girl he had fallen in love with.

Stay as long as you want, he had written. She had thought it over carefully and decided she would go. Although she was sad at leaving her friends, she was also thrilled at the prospect of seeing Terry and meeting Alison.

So much had happened here since her birthday in May.

First there had been Nancy's wedding in September. She had looked so beautiful and so much in love. It was wonderful to see her happy. The day had been perfect and watching her exchange her vows with Angus made her cry. She had been the only bridesmaid, and Nancy had given her a tiny silver cross on a fine chain. 'I know you don't believe,' Nancy had said, 'but I hope you will wear it and maybe one day you will find God's love.'

She wore it for Nancy's sake. She still didn't believe.

Nancy and Angus honeymooned in Greece and then returned to the house. The purchase of their new home in Scotland had taken longer than they'd thought but they had finally moved last week.

Now it was her turn move on. An exciting new phase in her life. In Devon there would be new people to meet, new challenges.

Last night she had said goodbye to Zoe. It had been hard. Zoe had been her first real friend and she would miss her. Zoe had been gutted when she had told her she was leaving to go to Devon.

'What about our plans for London? What about finding your Mum, you were always banging on about?' Zoe had moaned.

They had talked incessantly about going to London together, sharing a flat, having a laugh.

'Yeah maybe I will go one day but it doesn't seem so important now. I really want to see Terry. I'm not planning to stay with them for ever. Don't suppose they want me hanging around anyway. Give me a few weeks and I'll ring you and we'll decide what to do. I mean we'd have to get jobs and everything. It won't be easy.'

Zoe shrugged. 'Yeah, whatever. Just don't forget, all right?'

'As if,' Laura grinned.

She was running late. She had intended to leave this morning but somehow the time had flown by and now it was two o'clock and she was only just packed and ready.

She had been to *Flamingo's* to say a final goodbye to Brett and collect her wages, but he had gone to the bank to arrange finance for yet another café. She had gone across to the perfumery to say goodbye to Danny, but he had not been there either.

An hour later she began to fret. Brett still hadn't returned and she didn't want to leave without seeing him. She loaded her possessions into the boot of the car and returned inside just as the telephone rang.

'Laura.'

'Brett, where are you?'

'At the hospital, I've had an accident.'

'My God! Are you okay?'

'I've broken my ankle. I'm getting a taxi. I'll be home in half-an-hour.'

'Okay.'

'Put the radio on and listen to the weather forecast, apparently there's a storm brewing.'

'Will do.'

She turned on the little transistor radio but all she got was static crackling. She went to the window and looked out. The sky was heavy and black but no rain had started yet. If Brett hurried up she might miss the worst of it.

A moment later a low rumble of thunder started in the distant and the first large drop of rain hit the window.

She paced the room undecided. Maybe she should go anyway, let Brett send her wages. Then again it didn't seem right. After all he had done for her she could hardly just sneak off.

Brett had been right about the storm, it was raining heavily now and the thunder getting nearer. She needed to wait until the worst of the storm was over.

The sound of a taxi pulling up had her rushing to the door, and she flung it open. A sudden flash of lightening made her jump.

His foot in plaster, Brett hobbled up the path.

'How did this happen?' she asked when he was settled in the kitchen and she had made him a coffee.

'Fell off a ladder.'

'What, at the bank?'

'No silly, at the new property. I was checking the roof space to see if I could convert it.'

Laura headed towards Hunters Lane and the A429. It was now early evening and she had been tempted to wait until the morning, but it wasn't raining quite as hard as earlier and the wind was less fierce. Anyway she was anxious to see Terry.

She had left Brett hobbling around the house on crutches. She had offered to stay but he had refused, knowing how much she wanted to get to Devon. He had given her a fifty pound bonus with her wages.

She glanced anxiously out at the dark night and prayed her car would get her to Sidmouth without breaking down.

It was eerie down Hunters Lane, there were no street lights. She'd be glad when she reached the end and a properly-lit road. Nervously she stared out at the tall majestic chestnut trees, so large and heavy with water that they reached across the road forming a dark leafy tunnel. Their threshing limbs seemed almost menacing. She switched on the radio. Radio One was playing an old track from Blondie, 'Tide is High', one of her favourite songs, she relaxed.

Chapter Sixteen

Harriet drew back the curtains and looked out of the bedroom window. Although it was still raining the storm was easing, the lightning and thunder moving away into the distance. The garden trees, battered by the wind and rain, swayed, scattering the last of their brown autumn leaves onto the overgrown lawn. Turning back into the room, she glanced in the dressing table mirror. Her eyes were swollen and puffy from lack of sleep. She couldn't go on like this.

Going downstairs, she turned on the radio and made a coffee. The newscaster talked about the damage the storm was causing. She hardly listened, her mind foggy, her thoughts scrambled. She needed help. She couldn't hack the endless crying any more.

Resentment filled her as she stared down into the dregs of the coffee mug. It wasn't fair that she had to cope on her own. Well she wouldn't, not any longer, not when she didn't have to. There was a way out of this.

She glanced at her watch: six-thirty. She would go now, before she lost her nerve. She remembered that every Friday Christine went to her WI meeting. It was an ideal time to call and see Danny.

She hurriedly packed a small holdall with necessities for Amy. Bottles, nappies, change of clothing. The rest she could send round later.

She bundled Amy into the carrycot and strapped her into the rear of her Peugeot. She already felt a sense of freedom, of release. Soon she would get her life back; her independence. It wasn't much to ask for.

The journey to Upper Wyre was slow, the evening traffic on the main road heavy, but at last she reached the village. She pulled up outside Danny's house. The gates were closed, but his car was in the driveway, thank God. She sat for a moment planning what she was going to say to him. She had to make him see that Amy was ruining her life. *He had to help her.*

She opened the car door and, swinging her long legs, stepped out onto the road. The rain pitted against her face and the fierce wind nearly took the door from her hand as she struggled to close it. Her thin designer coat was no protection against the weather and she wished she'd dressed more appropriately.

Her shoes squelched into the grass verge. Looking down at her expensive black suede high heels, she swore. Hurriedly crossing the pavement she pushed at the wrought iron gates; they swung open easily. Returning to the car she drove through the gateway, along the block-paved driveway, and pulled to a stop.

The house was built in mellow Cotswold stone; partially covered in ivy, with a grey slate roof and leaded windows; it was far bigger than her home. She felt a burst of confidence. She was doing the right thing. Danny could easily afford to raise their child.

Once more she got out, opened the rear car door, and leaned inside. Amy gazed at her with large, serious blue eyes.

Harriet felt unnerved by the stare. She wanted to tell Amy that she would be happier with two parents instead of one. Parents that had plenty of money and would give her a good life. She wanted to justify her actions but she felt silly talking to a baby.

She lifted out the carrycot, raising the hood over the child, and struggled purposefully up the few steps to the front door. The carrycot was cumbersome and bumped against her legs.

Stepping into the comparative shelter of the porch she banged on the brass knocker of the black oak-studded door. As she waited she knew exactly what she would say.

The door opened after several impatient minutes. Danny looked tanned from his recent trip abroad, and so handsome and relaxed that she felt a rush of desire for him. Then resentment flooded through her as she remembered he had abandoned her and their child.

For a split second they stared at each other in silence. Harriet held his gaze, her heart hardening, although her stomach was fluttering with nerves. Danny's face changed in an instant from a look of welcome to fear at the sight of her. His eyes registered incredulity at her presence. 'What in God's name are you doing here?'

'Why haven't you been to see me?'

Danny looked puzzled. 'I didn't think it was wise.'

Harriet placed the carrycot carefully on the doorstep. 'This is Amy, your daughter.'

'Harriet!' He sounded exasperated.

'I want you to have her.'

'What!'

'I want you and Christine to bring her up.'

'Are you mad?'

'You told me Christine always wanted a child.' She stared at him, determined not to weaken, not to let the tears filling her eyes spill out. If he saw her crying she would be lost.

'Hang on a minute,' Danny snapped angrily, 'you can't do this.'

'Why not? She's your child, *you* take care of her. I can't hack it any more. I'm exhausted.'

'What about your husband?'

The wind caught tendrils of her sodden hair and blew it across her face. Impatiently she pushed them away. 'Jeremy left me ages ago. As soon as he found out I was pregnant.'

'I thought you'd . . .'

Harriet stared at him in disgust. He was only bothered about not getting caught, making sure Christine never found out. He didn't care about her or his daughter.

'No I didn't pretend it was his. I couldn't do that. He knows you're the father, he found out.' Harriet felt a great rush of satisfaction at the look of horror of Danny's face. Why should he have it so easy, after all she'd had to put up with? 'Your name's on her birth certificate.'

'Jesus!' Danny was visibly shaken.

'Did you think I'd deny her the right to know who her father is, even if that father doesn't want her?'

'We need to talk about this,' Danny growled.

'There's nothing to talk about.' She spun round and ran back down the steps. Anxious to be gone, before he could stop her, she slid into the front seat and switched on the engine, no time for the seat belt. Without a backward glance she drove away.

Danny stared after her in disbelief.

'Harriet, come back you stupid woman,' he shouted. What on earth was she thinking of, she must have gone mental.

He ran a hand distractedly through his hair. Thank God Christine was out. He glanced down at the carrycot, where only the baby's head was visible, and closed his eyes briefly in despair. *Think, think, what to do now.* He couldn't have the child here when Christine returned.

He grabbed his raincoat from the hall stand and, picking up the carrycot, ran to his car. He wasn't having this.

The sports car was not designed for transporting children. Unceremoniously he dumped the carrycot on the passenger seat. Reversing the car out of the drive, with a screech of tyres, he swore loudly. 'Damn the woman, damn and blast her.' Bloody hell, if Christine found out he's fathered a child . . . if she'd even suspected he'd been having an affair – it didn't bear thinking about. He nearly choked in his fear and rage. If the stupid bitch didn't want the child then she should have it adopted. Why involve him?

A few moments later he saw her car tail lights in the darkness of Hunters Lane.

Harriet heard the long blast of a car horn; saw the headlights flashing in her rear mirror and knew it had to be Danny. Pressing her foot harder on the accelerator she increased her speed. The rain was lashing so hard that even with the screen wipers going full pelt it was almost impossible to see. She drove by instinct, leaning forward over the steering wheel, hoping and praying that there would be no oncoming traffic. Her headlights shone on the wet road, reflecting the uneven surface, where deep pools of water sent sprays, like ocean waves, splashing across her windscreen. She glanced briefly in her rear-view mirror; the white glare of his headlights seemed to be closer; he was gaining on her.

She could feel the tension in her neck and shoulders as she returned her gaze to the road. No matter what happened, she would not take Amy back.

The road widened and the Jaguar drew level. She turned her head and saw Danny gesticulating frantically for her to stop but she ignored him. The road narrowed again and she swerved, narrowly missing a ditch, to avoid hitting the Jaguar. Danny pulled back but stayed close, constantly flashing his headlights and blasting his horn.

Bloody maniac! If he wasn't careful he would kill them all. Danny's car nudged her rear bumper and she gasped in fright. Struggling to regain control as the car slewed across the road she managed to accelerate away from him.

In her mirror she saw Danny slow down. Taken by surprise she wondered what he was up to.

A sharp bend in the road loomed but she didn't slow down. Her whole concentration was on getting away from him.

Too late, she saw the tree felled by the storm.

Frantically she slammed on the brakes and yanked at the steering wheel. Jesus Christ!

In a split second of realisation she knew she was going to hit the tree. She struggled for control but it was impossible, she was going much too fast to stop.

She felt the tyres lose their grip as the wheels locked, sending the car hurtling across the wet surface. Her eyes were wide with fear and her breath ragged as she frantically wrestled with the wheel, but the car rocketed forward. She felt the thump as it struck the fallen tree.

She heard a scream, hardly aware that it was coming from her own mouth.

From then on everything happened in slow motion. The Peugeot was flung in the air, it somersaulted, landed upright, and skidded across the slippery verge before crashing through the undergrowth. It plunged down the embankment with a resounding crash of grinding metal and breaking glass. A half-hidden boulder finally halted its descent and she shot forward. A sharp, searing pain tore through her head, and then blackness.

Chapter Seventeen

Danny watched the Peugeot disappear from view. He was frozen in shock. He passed a trembling hand over his face. Bloody hell! He had slowed down, aware of the sharp bend ahead, and he had expected Harriet to do the same.

Switching off the engine he climbed unsteadily from the car, and walked to the edge of the embankment. He stared down, but he could see nothing through the darkness. 'Harriet, Harriet!' he shouted.

Nothing.

He needed help. He looked down the road but it was empty. He glanced back to the car where the baby was sleeping. The rain had stopped, but the eerie howling of the wind in the trees made him shiver. He was alone.

Pulling himself together, he located a torch in the boot of the car, switched it on and began to make his way down through the torn and crushed bushes. At last he saw the Peugeot. It was tilted, nose down, its lights broken and the driver's door hanging crookedly open.

The rear window was shattered, making it impossible to see if Harriet was still inside. In the dip, sheltered from the wind, only the drip, drip of water from the trees disturbed the darkness.

'Harriet!' He called out again, but the only answer was a rustle in the undergrowth and the sharp snap of a twig underneath his foot.

With a renewed sense of urgency he began to inch forward, when suddenly the car started to rock. He smelt petrol and saw smoke seeping out from under the bonnet. Jesus Christ!

Sheer terror sent adrenalin churning through his veins. He stopped walking and stood still. His heart was racing in panic.

He didn't want to get any closer; he wasn't brave enough to risk his life. Harriet was probably dead anyway. There was nothing he could do. He tried to convince himself as he began to back away. He took a deep breath to steady his nerves, but his heart was still pounding. Breathing heavily he turned and scrambled as fast as he could until he was far enough away.

Shaking with fright, he turned to look back, but the bushes hindered his vision. 'Harriet,' he sobbed.

'Hi there, are you all right?'

He looked up to see someone peering down through the gap made by Harriet's car. His mouth contorted, but before he could utter a word the ground beneath him shook as the car caught fire and exploded. Caught in the blast, he was flung to the ground, and lay with his hands covering his head.

It must have only been seconds, but it felt like forever before he raised his head and stared at the blaze. Flames engulfed the vehicle, and even from this safe distance the intense heat stung his face.

He stood up and clambered the rest of the way up to the embankment, away from the burning heat, his feet slipping on the mud-soaked grass. He reached the roadside and collapsed on the verge, his vision blurred, his breath coming in short hard gasps.

He felt a hand on his shoulder. 'Mr Pembroke?'

'What?' he muttered feeling bewildered and disorientated.

'Danny, are you okay?'

'Laura.' He recognised her now.

'What happened?' Her eyes were wide with shock as her gaze flicked from him to the burning car and back again.

'She hit the tree and spun off the road. I tried to get her out.' He felt embarrassed by the tears coursing down his face. He wiped them with his sleeve. 'I tried to save her.'

'There was someone still in the car!' Laura sounded incredulous.

He nodded.

'Who?'

'Harriet.'

'Oh, my God!'

'She must be dead, she can't have survived that. I couldn't get near the car.' He couldn't tear his gaze away from the flames. He staggered to his feet as he tried to marshal his thoughts. 'I must get help.'

He patted his pockets. 'Shit, I've left my mobile at home.'

Laura rummaged in her bag and retrieved hers. 'Oh my God there's no signal; must be the storm.'

'Fucking hell!' Danny sounded panicky.

'I'll go to the phone box,' Laura offered. 'You're in no state to drive.'

'Good idea. Thanks. There's one in the village, by the green.'

'I know.'

'Get the fire brigade and an ambulance.'

'Okay,' Laura's voice was shaky.

From inside the Jaguar the infant started crying. The baby! Christ! What was he going to do with it now that Harriet was dead? He stared blankly at Laura, his mind a fog.

Laura looked uncertain. 'I didn't know you had a baby?'

He said, without thinking of the consequences, 'it's Harriet's.'

'Right.' Laura looked puzzled.

'What am I going to do with her?'

'What do you mean?'

'I can't take her home. My wife will . . . '

Laura frowned. 'I don't understand.'

Danny started to shake. The horror of what had happened, the fear of Christine discovering the child, made him feel cold and dizzy.

'Christine . . .' he couldn't form the words.

Laura touched his hand. 'I think you're in shock,' she said. 'I'll get your wife.'

'No!' he almost screamed the word. 'Christine mustn't know.'

'What?'

'I'm the father,' he blurted out. He really must be in shock - he hadn't meant to say that.

Laura stared at him in concern. 'I'd better go and get the ambulance.'

'Yes.'

Laura ran towards her car. Danny looked at the Jaguar and then back down the embankment. Laura opened her car door and climbed in. 'Wait!' he shouted.

He saw her head turn in surprise. 'Can you take the baby to the phone box with you? I need to see if there's anything I can do,' he indicated back towards the burning car, 'and I don't want to leave her in the car.'

'Be quick then,' Laura agreed. She hurried back to the Jaguar.

He leant inside and lifted out the carrycot. Think. Concentrate. Laura could help him here. He straightened up.

'I need to hurry,' Laura reminded him.

'I know, I know, but it's about what I said, about me being the baby's father, I'd be grateful if you didn't tell anyone.'

'It's none of my business,' Laura said impatiently.

'Thanks.'

Laura grabbed the carrycot from him. 'What's her name?'

'Amy.'

'Right, well you get back down there, I'll take care of Amy and I'll be back as quick as I can.'

'Thanks.'

He followed her towards her car, thinking rapidly. 'Listen Laura, there's no way I can take her home – my wife – you understand – could you look after her for me until I sort something out.'

Laura looked shocked. 'Danny we've got to get help *now*. Sort the child out later.'

'It will be too late then.'

Laura was hurriedly strapping the carrycot into the front seat, not really paying attention. 'Well anyway, I'm not sure I can. I'm on my way to Devon, to my brother.'

He'd forgotten that. Even better.

'Please. A few days, that's all. I just need a bit of time and then I'll come and fetch her, I promise.'

She stared at him, clearly troubled.

'Please Laura, please. I'm in desperate trouble here.'

He felt her weakening. He took out this wallet and extracted a bundle of notes. 'Look take this, you'll need to get things, nappies and stuff.'

She looked at the money but made no move to take it.

'I'm begging you.' He could feel himself getting agitated.

'Okay, okay, calm down. I'll look after her.' She stuffed the money in her bag. 'You had better get down there to Harriet just in case . . . '

'I'm going.' He fumbled in his pocket and pulled out his diary. He tore out a page. 'Write down your mobile number on this.' He watched impatiently as she wrote.

He pocketed the note. 'Hang on, there's a bag.' He ran back to the car and retrieved a baby bag. 'Harriet left this, I guess it's baby things.'

'Right.' Laura took the bag from him.

'Listen, there's no need to come back after you've made the phone call. I'll wait here until they arrive.'

She looked down the embankment, at the fire, and then back to him. Her eyes were wide with concern. 'You take care, don't worry about Amy; she'll be fine with me.'

'Thanks, Laura, I owe you big time.'

She climbed into the car. He waited impatiently as she switched on the engine and began to reverse. Suddenly he lunged forward and banged his hand on the roof of the car.

She braked and opened her window. He looked at her intently; she seemed upset. 'You are still going to Devon now aren't you; you're not going back to Brett's?'

'Yeah.'

'Promise you won't tell anyone, anyone at all about this. Christine must never know.'

Laura nodded. 'You can trust me.'

'Thanks again. I'll ring you.'

'Okay.'

'Whatever you do don't ring me at the perfumery. I'll call you in a few days.' Without giving her time to respond, he stumbled away.

Engaging the clutch, Laura drove as fast as she could back

towards the village. She turned left at the crossroads and pulled up at the edge of the village green. Jumping out of the car, she ran to the phone box. She dialled 999 and asked for an ambulance and a fire engine, telling them there was an accident in Hunters Lane. When they asked for her name she hung up.

Outside the phone box she stared around. The place was deserted, thank goodness. She needed to leave the village quickly. She glanced at her watch: eight-thirty – she would be *really* late arriving at Terry's now.

Back inside the car again she glanced down at the baby. Amy turned her head and stared at her. The huge blue eyes were tear-filled, the dark lashes damp against her smooth cheeks; her bottom lip trembled. In that instant of eye contact Laura's heart contracted and she felt a surge of compassion for the child.

'You poor little thing. And you're so pretty.'

Amy started to whimper.

'Hey, don't be scared,' Laura said soothingly. 'I'll look after you.'

The whimpering continued and two large tears trickled down Amy's cheeks. Laura wiped them gently with her finger. She held the tiny hand, caressing the velvety skin, and the baby's grip tightened around her finger. She looked so tiny and helpless that Laura felt her own eyes fill with tears. It was tragic. Her mother was dead, and her father – fancy Danny Pembroke being her father – her father couldn't acknowledge her because his wife obviously knew nothing about the fact that her husband had fathered a child. What a mess.

The sound of an approaching fire engine spurred her into action. She couldn't go back down Hunters Lane, the road was blocked. She must take another route out of the village.

* * *

Danny stood on the grass verge staring down at the fire. It was spreading now, the bushes catching a light despite the wet. He cast a brief look across the undergrowth for any sign of movement, any indication that Harriet had managed to crawl to safety, but nothing stirred. He wondered vaguely if a braver man would attempt to go down there, but he knew he couldn't do it. The burning car was far too dangerous. It would be foolishly risky and futile. Harriet must be dead. He pushed from his mind a horrific image of Harriet's burning body. He consoled himself with the thought that she must have died before the fire started.

A shiver of panic made him fret. There was nothing he could do here. It would be better if he got away from the scene before the emergency services turned up and he had to explain his presence. Was the accident his fault? Was it because he was chasing her, nudging her car to make it stop? Guilt made his stomach churn. He hadn't wanted to hurt her and certainly he hadn't wanted her dead. Could he convince the police of that? Under questioning would he say more than he intended? It would be better not to put himself in that situation.

If he got back before Christine arrived home then he wouldn't have to account for his absence or the muddy state of his clothes.

As he climbed into his car he thought of Laura. What a Godsend her turning up. In a few days he would contact her, when he decided what was to be done about the child. But now he must hurry. He couldn't wait around; the emergency services would be here any minute.

He turned the car round and drove away at high speed. In the distance he heard the sirens of the fire engine and the ambulance. He had escaped just in time. He reached the crossroads and turned right, away from the village towards his home on the outskirts.

He opened his front door and stepped inside. The house was in darkness. Christine hadn't arrived home. He breathed a sigh of relief.

Chapter Eighteen

Laura felt worried as Amy's crying became distraught, her head rocking from side to side. She shouldn't have agreed to have her; she had no idea what to do. She didn't know a thing about babies, but she guessed Amy was hungry.

She was well away from the village now and on the A429 heading towards Cirencester.

Two miles further on, she came to a lay-by and pulled in. Climbing into the back seat, she opened the baby bag Danny had given her. Thankfully there was a bottle of milk inside a thermo-warmer.

Gently she lifted the child into her arms. Laura pushed the bottle teat into Amy's open mouth, and she began to suck hungrily. Laura relaxed in relief. The baby felt soft and warm in her arms; she kissed the top of her head and gazed down at her. Her tiny hands were clasping the bottle, as if to make sure it wouldn't be taken away. It made her smile; she looked so angelic.

Contented at last, the baby fell asleep, snuggling up against her. Rummaging in the bag again she found a packet of Pampers. 'Your mother must have been going somewhere,' Laura murmured, 'she came well prepared.' She changed the baby's nappy, fumbling in her ineptitude, but managing to do it without waking the sleeping child.

Her thoughts lingered on the accident. Although she hardly knew Harriet, the thought of her dying in that burning car sent a cold shiver through her; it was a horrible way to die. In her mind's eye she saw the flames leaping above the bushes and smelt the acrid smoke, and she shivered again.

She looked down at Amy and tears filled her eyes. The poor child was now without a mother. She would do her best to care for her until Danny came. What would happen to her after that, she dreaded to think.

Laura continued south, passing through towns she had never heard of, Trowbridge and Shepton Mallet and Honiton. She had been planning this journey for several days and although it seemed straightforward on the map, she had never been to Devon before. She had never driven anywhere other than to Cheltenham from the village, a distance of no more than five miles. Twice she got lost until finally, utterly exhausted, she reached Sidmouth in the early hours. She stopped the car on the seafront and searched in her bag for Terry's address. Willow Cottage. It sounded grand. Terry must have done really well for himself.

The front was deserted. She stared at the blackness of the sea, listened to the waves breaking against the rocks, and wondered if Terry's wife would mind her turning up with a baby. She thought of Danny Pembroke; she hadn't been able to refuse to help him, not after seeing the look of desperation in his eyes. So Zoe had been right, he had been having an affair with Harriet Malin. She hadn't believed her. She liked and respected Danny and couldn't believe that he would cheat on his wife. How wrong she had been. It just went to show you never really knew a person.

She thought of Christine Pembroke, who she had never spoken to. Zoe had said she was not friendly like Danny; you couldn't share a joke or make a personal remark with her. She'd heard rumours that it was her money that kept the business afloat. She could understand why Danny was afraid to tell her about Amy.

She gazed at Amy, sleeping peacefully, her long dark lashes fanning her delicate cheeks. She wondered what Danny was planning to do with her, and if he could do it without Christine finding out.

She shook her head slightly, it was not her problem; even so she felt concerned for the child. With a deep sigh she turned her attention to practicalities, and checked Terry's letter again.

Willow Cottage was in All Saints Road, near the town centre,

Terry had written. She started the engine again and turned back into the town. She found All Saint's Road without difficulty. However, Willow Cottage proved to be a disappointing two-up, two-down, mid-terraced house. Laura pulled up at the kerb and switched off the engine. Now that she was here, she felt nervous. She hadn't seen Terry for over three years. She had never met his wife, Alison. She hadn't planned to arrive here in the middle of the night, and with a baby.

A baby whose father must remain a secret.

Well she was here now and she longed for the comfort of a warm bed, and sleep; but most of all for the security of her brother's presence.

No lights were on in the house. Leaving the sleeping Amy in the car, she walked up to the door and pressed the bell.

Several minutes later an upstairs light came on, then the hallway light, and finally the door opened.

Terry blinked sleepily, his auburn hair was tousled and his face unshaven. He stared at her uncomprehendingly.

'Hi, Terry,' she said.

'Laura?'

She laughed nervously. 'Who else, don't you recognise me?'

'Only just, blimey, you look so grown up.'

'You are expecting me?'

'Yes, hours ago though.'

'Got held up. I'll explain later. Can I come in?'

'Sorry, of course.' He opened the door wider.

'There's someone else with me.'

Terry frowned and looked beyond her to the car. 'Who?' he asked suspiciously.

'I'll fetch her.' She turned to walk away and then turned back again. 'It is okay, isn't it? Me coming here, I mean.'

'Yes. Just hurry up though, it's bloody freezing standing here,' Terry said. 'I'll go and put the kettle on.'

More confident now, she fetched Amy, stepped into the house and closed the door softly. She wondered if she had woken Alison.

As she entered the kitchen Terry turned from the stove and

gasped. 'Jesus! You never said you had a *baby.*'

'She's not mine. She belongs to – to a friend,' Laura said quickly to reassure him as she placed the carrycot carefully on the floor. Amy was still sleeping soundly.

'What are you doing with her?'

'Taking care of her, it's only for a few days.'

'Where's the mother?'

At the simple question all her calm resolve of the past few hours crumbled. She began to tremble as she recalled the sight of the burning car. The horror of it came flooding back again and she burst into tears. 'She was killed in a car crash a few hours ago. It was horrible.'

'Bloody hell!'

Terry pulled her into a hug, holding her fiercely as she sobbed against his shoulder. 'Oh Terry, it was so awful.'

'Did you see it happen?' He was rubbing her back soothingly.

'Not the crash but I saw the car burning and . . .'she couldn't go on.

'You need a drink,' Terry muttered. 'I need a drink.' He poured the tea, then opened a cupboard, lifted out a bottle of whisky, and poured a measure into each cup.

Laura sipped the hot tea gratefully, although she usually hated the taste of whisky. Calmer now, she wiped her eyes and took her first proper look at her brother. Despite his dishevelled appearance he was handsome, his skin tanned and his gentle mouth wide and familiar, just like her own.

Terry was rubbing his hand over his face. 'I still can't work out why you have the child.'

'The father was in a terrible state. I had to help him. I knew him.'

'Was he injured as well?'

'No, he was in a different car with the baby. It's a bit complicated. I'll explain later.'

'Okay. Sorry sis. I'm not at my best this time of night.' He folded his arms around her again and she relaxed against his chest; the comfortable feeling of security, of affection still there despite their time apart. The reassurance of him sent the tears flowing again.

The door opened and a woman appeared in the doorway wearing a towelling bathrobe. She looked at first surprised, and then apprehensive, to see Laura crying in Terry's arms. 'What's happened?' she asked.

Terry turned. 'Alison, this is my sister, Laura.'

Laura moved out of Terry's embrace and swallowed nervously. As she stared at the older woman, who was taller than her but the same height as Terry, she understood how Terry had fallen in love with her. His letter describing Alison didn't do her justice. She was stunning; creamy skin and gorgeous long brunette hair that cascaded in waves to her shoulders.

Alison's face relaxed and her smile reached to her calm blue eyes. 'Laura, I've heard such a lot about you. It's great to meet you at last, but are you okay?'

'Yeah,' Laura gulped, 'sorry about the tears, it's just . . . '

She hadn't time to finish before Alison was hugging her. 'My goodness, you're cold, and you must be tired. Terry, go upstairs and run a hot bath. Explanations can wait.'

Terry pulled a face. 'Women,' he groaned, but he was smiling as he left the room.

Alison turned her attention to the baby, who was beginning to stir. 'Terry never told me you had a baby. Is your husband coming later?'

'I'm not married,' Laura said.

'Oh.' The small word spoke volumes. 'Sorry,' Alison looked embarrassed at her assumption.

'Amy's not my baby.'

Alison frowned. 'I see,' she said.

'No you don't.' Laura almost laughed at her expression. Once again, the words tumbling out, her voice shaking, she explained how she came to have Amy.

Alison bent and gently stroked Amy's face, her expression filled with tenderness. 'The poor little mite; what a tragedy. She's so beautiful, such thick black hair. How old is she?'

'Two months,' Laura made a calculated guess.

'The father must be distraught,' Alison said.

'He is.'

'He must be grateful to you for taking care of her,' Alison probed, 'but I'm surprised he wanted you to take her so far away.'

'It's only for a few days,' Laura reminded her. She had a feeling Alison didn't believe her story. After all it did sound a bit improbable.

'I guess so.' Alison still seemed uncertain and Laura prayed she wouldn't ask too many questions about Amy's parents. She was conscious of her promise to Danny that she wouldn't tell anyone. Before anything more could be said Terry returned to say the bath was ready.

Later that night, tucked up in the spare room with Amy asleep in her carrycot next to her, Laura re-lived the aftermath of the accident. Poor Harriet, to die so tragically was heartbreaking. She thought of how upset Danny had been; he must have loved her very much. She felt sorry for Christine and hoped she would never find out that her husband had betrayed her. And then she thought about Amy. How Danny was going to solve his problem without Christine finding out she couldn't begin to think. Poor man, what a dilemma he was in. Perhaps Harriet's husband would change his mind, now that Harriet was dead, and take care of Amy. If not then adoption seemed to be the only answer.

She wondered why she was worrying so much about Amy. The baby was not her problem and yet during the long journey, when Amy was awake, and she talked to her, she had felt a tugging at her heart. The child was so adorable, with such an endearing smile; it was difficult not to love her. The thought of her going into care, to strangers, was unbearable. She remembered her own childhood, the happy times before her father left. What kind of future would Amy have?

Chapter Nineteen

Laura woke the following morning to winter sunlight streaming through the window. She wondered what the time was but she didn't stir to find out. Instead she lay quietly, hearing movement downstairs. Uppermost in her mind was last night's accident and Amy. In the cold light of day she wondered if coming here was such a good idea. Terry and Alison were bound to ask more questions, and she was in no position to answer them without lying.

She turned her head and looked over to the carrycot, but it was empty. Slipping out of bed she dressed hurriedly and went downstairs to find Alison rocking the baby in her arms.

'I hope you don't mind I've given her a bottle. I was going to wake you but I hadn't the heart,' Alison said.

'Thanks,' Laura smiled in gratitude.

Alison handed her the baby. Amy had fallen asleep, her fist, small and white, rested sweetly against her cheek. It twitched occasionally as if she was dreaming. Laura smiled down at her tenderly.

Alison stood up. 'Would you like some breakfast?'

'Toast would be good, thanks.'

'It's so good to have you here,' Alison said with genuine warmth. 'Terry was always promising me we would visit you but he's so busy.'

Laura wondered how much Alison knew of Terry's past, if she was aware that he had been in prison, and resolved to ask him before she put her foot in it.

'How long have you lived here?' she asked.

'Just a few months. It belongs to Terry's boss, Kevin, we rent it from him.'

'Cool.'

'Terry's working this morning but he'll be home at lunch time and you can tell us all about yourself.'

Laura grimaced. 'Okay,' she said.

Alison pottered around her. 'You're the first person in Terry's family that I've met,' she said as she placed toast, butter, marmalade and a pot of tea on the table, before sitting down opposite Laura.

'Really,' Laura said warily.

'I'd hoped Terry would take me to meet your family, especially your Mum but he says she moved and he doesn't have her address.'

'We have no idea where she is.'

'That's sad.'

Laura wondered if Terry had told her about their father leaving them and Mum's new bloke. Once again she wondered if she knew about the prison sentence. 'What about your parents? Has Terry met them?'

'I never knew them. I was raised by foster parents but they died. That's why I'm so desperate to be part of a family.'

Laura thought she was going to be disappointed.

'What are your plans?' Alison asked. 'Terry said you're thinking of going to live in London.'

'Yeah, maybe. My friend Zoe is up for it but I'm not sure.'

'Well there's no rush. You can stay here for as long as you like.'

'Thanks.'

Later, when Alison went out, Laura turned on the TV to catch the morning news. She wondered if the accident would be mentioned, but nothing was reported.

Terry arrived home at two. They sat around the kitchen table drinking tea. Amy was fretful, and Alison offered to take her upstairs to settle her. Laura agreed with relief. Now she could have a private word with her brother.

'I'm so glad to see you. I've missed you so much.'

'Me too. Thanks for writing to me, your letters kept me going. I couldn't wait to get out and see you again.'

'But you didn't,' Laura said softly, remembering the letter that had upset her so much.

'I intended to, believe me.'

'What happened?'

Terry smiled. 'As I walked out of the prison gates, a mate, Kevin Richardson, was waiting for me. We shared a cell. He'd got out a month before me.'

'What had he done?'

'He was arrested for passing fraudulent money. I know everyone pleads their innocence, but he really was setup.'

'Right.'

'Anyway he got his conviction overruled.'

'Go on.'

'Kevin took me for a meal and told me about a garage he was buying in Sidmouth and how he was looking for a mechanic and wanted me to join him. Course I accepted right away, I mean I was flattered that he trusted me.'

'He sounds nice.'

'He is. I told him I wanted to come and see you first but there was no time. He had to be at the solicitors in Sidmouth by three that afternoon to sign the contract papers. Sorry, sis I feel bad that I neglected you.'

Laura touched his hand and smiled. 'That's all in the past. We're survivors you and me. Just tell me one thing, though. You said in court you did those things for money, what did you do with it? We were always broke.'

Terry flushed and looked sheepish. He took a few minutes to answer. 'I used to gamble, on the dogs. It became an obsession.'

'I was frightened it was drugs.'

'No way. Not ever.'

'Do you still gamble?'

'No. Being in prison was hell,' Terry said, 'but it made me realise what a fool I'd been. Made me aware of just how much gambling had ruled my life. I got help.'

They were silent for a moment then Terry said. 'So, you never found Mum then?'

'No. I guess you haven't either.'

'No. but then I haven't tried. I don't care if I never see her again.'

'That's a bit harsh,' Laura said, 'she was entitled to her life.'

'Not at our expense.'

'What do you mean?' Laura was surprised by the vehemence in his voice.

'Nothing, just stuff,' Terry shrugged, obviously no longer wanting to discuss it. Laura looked at him for a moment suddenly realising there was more to his leaving home than he had ever let on. She wanted to know more, but this was not the time to probe.

'Alison said you're going to stay for a bit,' Terry said.

'Yeah if that's okay. Just until I make my mind up what I want to do.'

'Of course it is. We have a lot of catching up to do.'

'I don't want to be in the way.'

'You're not, don't be silly. Besides you look as if you need feeding up. You're very thin. I hope you're not anorexic.'

Laura laughed. 'I'm okay, really. I've never been fat, you know that.'

'Hmm,' Terry grunted.

Alison returned before she had time to ask Terry if he had told her about prison.

They talked for the next hour or so. She told them about living in the squat, and how she had met Nancy and Brett, and her job as a waitress. She spoke light-heartedly, even making them laugh, although she noticed a protective worried look in her brother's eyes.

She learned that Alison was a midwife, that they had met when her mini had broken down, and it was love at first sight for both of them.

'I'm so happy you've found some one,' Laura turned to Terry. 'You seem to have done okay ever since you came out of . . .' she clamped her hand over her mouth. She looked at Alison.

'I know about Terry's past,' Alison said softly. 'We have no

114

secrets.'

Terry put an arm around Alison and hugged her. 'She's the best thing that ever happened to me,' he said nuzzling her neck.

'Stop it,' Alison giggled, 'you'll be embarrassing Laura.'

'Don't mind me, I think it's brill,' Laura said.

Chapter Twenty

Danny had a restless night. In the cold light of the morning mental images of Harriet's burnt body still haunted him. Guilt at his actions and fear of discovery battled for supremacy in his tormented mind. His head was aching.

He thought about Laura. What he would have done with the baby if she hadn't turned up he dreaded to think. He had a week to sort something out, but the task seemed impossible. Closing his eyes, he re-lived the previous night's trauma.

When he arrived home he had cleaned his muddy shoes and stuffed his clothes into the washing machine. He'd had a few anxious moments while he'd tried to fathom out how to use it.

He had just stepped out of the shower when he heard Christine enter the house. Trying to stay calm, he went downstairs into the kitchen and poured himself a large whisky.

Christine came to the doorway and stared at him with a worried expression. 'Are you all right? You look terrible; you're as white as a sheet.'

He turned and faced her. 'I'm fine,' he said weakly. He longed to tell her, to have her hold him, comfort him. The emotional and physical turmoil of last night had left him mentally bruised and battered. He wanted to pour out the details of the terrible scene, to explain how helpless he'd felt.

Of course he could do none of that.

'You really don't look well, you're shaking. I'm phoning Doctor Davies.'

'No!' he almost screamed. He took a deep breath. 'No,' he said again more calmly. 'It's only a chill.'

Christine turned back into the room. 'Why is the washing machine on?'

'Um – I – er – I was sick on my clothes. I must have a stomach bug as well.'

'Are you sure you don't need the doctor?'

'Positive.'

He had gone to bed early, taking the whisky bottle with him. By the time she had joined him he had turned out the light and lay on his side feigning sleep. Despite his exhaustion, sleep was difficult; flashbacks of the scene haunted his dreams and he tossed and turned most of the night, finally falling into a light slumber just before dawn.

He woke at ten, relieved to find that Christine had gone to the supermarket. Unshaven and unwashed, he sat in the kitchen nursing a cup of coffee. He felt dreadful, drained, his head pounding.

Slowly the hot black coffee revived him; he started to think more clearly.

He couldn't believe Harriet was dead. A deep sadness overwhelmed him, knowing he would never see her again. Perhaps he should have been kinder to her over the pregnancy. His love for her was a separate thing from his marriage and he had been so terrified that these two separate elements of his life would collide and destroy him.

Even now, even in his grief, he knew he must protect himself.

He began to tremble. Maybe he should phone Laura. Impress upon her how imperative it was to keep his secret. Her number was in his trouser pocket. *The trousers he had put in the washing machine last night.* Shit!!

He tried not to panic. He was probably worrying over nothing; nevertheless he would have to get hold of her somehow. Brett or Nancy would be sure to have her number or even Zoe. All he had to do was think up a reason why he needed to contact Laura.

Once more he thought of Harriet and wondered if it really had been his fault that she had crashed. If he hadn't chased after her she would have taken more care and seen the fallen tree. Then

117

again it wasn't his fault the tree was in the road. It had been an accident. In any case if she hadn't tried to force the child on him none of this would have happened.

He could have been more understanding though. She must have been at her wit's end to have left her baby with him.

He pushed the thought away. Stupid to feel guilty, it served no purpose. His thoughts turned to Harriet's husband. No doubt he would have been told of her death by now. Even though they no longer lived together he was still her husband, her next-of-kin. He wondered if it was true that Jeremy had found out about them, that he was the baby's father, or had Harriet just been winding him up. He hoped so. Either way he would deny everything.

He needed to get out of the house, be alone to think what to do about Amy. Christine would be home before long, asking questions, probing.

Hurriedly he showered, dressed and drove to the Montpellier flat in Cheltenham. He parked the car at the rear entrance and let himself in. The rooms were dusty and stale. It had been months since he had been here. He paused for a moment, feeling a sharp stab of regret.

It had all been so perfect, his secret life here. He thought back to the day he had first seen Harriet; she was so sexy, so vibrant and he had wanted her from that first moment. He had not expected to fall in love with her, yet he had. A different sort of love than he felt for Christine, a more physical passion, thrilling and dangerous. Harriet had been amazing in bed. He couldn't get enough of her; the uninhibited pleasure of Harriet's frenzied lust inspired and exhilarated him. The sheer joy of learning new ways to please her and to be pleasured by her made his life exciting. Christine would have been shocked with such goings on. He could almost see her look of distaste if he'd asked her to perform oral sex.

He'd had plenty of affairs before Harriet, but they had soon paled after the first buzz of the chase. His love for Christine had remained constant throughout these brief affairs, which were nothing more than a sexual diversion, a little stimulation to brighten his days. He had never been able to resist a pretty woman. Harriet had been different. Harriet had somehow got under his skin, he had loved her.

Yet despite his love, her pregnancy had appalled him. At first he had suspected it had been contrived in an attempt to force him to marry her. Eventually he had believed her when she told him it had been an accident. What he hadn't been able to understand was why she wouldn't have an abortion. It was obvious she didn't really want a child. Why make all their lives miserable?

His love for her changed a little, shifted in dimension. He no longer found pleasure in her company.

He sank into a chair and buried his head in his hands, overwhelmed by a deep sense of loss, of regret that it had all ended. That wonderful part of his life was over now.

After a moment he pulled himself together. He needed to move on. He must sell the flat, with its bittersweet memories. He didn't want it now, it was all too painful. Heartless as it might seem, the sooner he sold it the better. He would instruct the agent immediately. He arranged everything through Silverstone Properties. Christine had no idea he even owned the place. The mortgage and utility bills were paid for through a bank account Christine didn't even know he had.

First though, he needed to clear it out. Now was as good a time as any. Filled with a sudden need for action he hurried into the kitchen and found large black bin liners. He started in the bathroom, stuffing his shaving gear into the bag together with Harriet's toiletries; next the bedroom, where their dressing gowns hung behind the door; spare clothes from the drawers and wardrobe soon filled several bags. He found a box containing all the jewellery he had given her over the years. Necklaces, earrings, bracelets. Wondering what to do with them he pocketed them. In the living room he searched the drawers of her writing bureau. He found all the birthday and Christmas cards he'd sent her. He flicked them open, saw his bold handwriting. *With all my love, Danny.* He tore them to shreds. He rummaged further, to make sure there were no incriminating letters, and found Amy's birth certificate. Even though Harriet had forewarned him, it was still a shock to see his name on it. 'Bugger!' He muttered out loud. He pocketed the certificate and continued clearing up.

He bagged up all Harriet's clothes. There was a faint lingering of her perfume, a heady sensual scent with a hint of Jasmine. He had created it especially for her. He pressed a blue silk dress to his face, remembering her in it at a dinner in France, and a sob escaped him.

Why hadn't he done as she had asked? Why hadn't he let her move away, keep the child, he could have visited them, had a secret life with her. He had been such a coward.

Amy. What the hell was he going to do with her?

He only had a few days. A week at the most, before he had to fetch her from Laura. Then what? He had dug a hole for himself, a great big black pit. And he could see no way out.

With a resigned slump of his shoulders he took the bags out to the car. Sadly he would have to dispose of them at the tip; he could hardly take them home. He gave a final glance around to make sure nothing had been overlooked before he let himself out.

After visiting the tip, he drove to the perfumery and deposited the jewellery and the birth certificate in his private safe; a place where he hid anything he didn't want Christine to find.

When he arrived home Christine had been in and gone out again; there was a note for him in the kitchen that obliquely said *back soon*.

In the kitchen he switched on the radio and tuned into the local channel to see if there was anything on the news. As he listened to the broadcaster he went cold with shock.

"Last night's storm caused a series of disasters, not least to a woman lying seriously injured in hospital after her car hit a fallen tree in Hunters Lane, Upper Wyre. Police are appealing for any witnesses to the accident. . ."

Injured! Not dead.

Chapter Twenty-One

Danny passed a sweaty palm over his face. How could she have survived? It didn't seem possible. And yet, apparently, she had.

He paced the room, his thoughts in chaos.

Harriet was alive. Thank God, thank God. The guilt lifted from him.

He would go and visit her immediately. The report said she was in Cheltenham hospital. He would tell her how sorry he was. He might even suggest that as soon as she was well enough she should move away. Maybe to Devon, he could employ Laura as a nanny to help look after the baby. He would visit her.

This is what he should have done in the beginning. Well, no matter, it wasn't too late.

Incredibly he had been given a second chance.

Then a terrible thought struck him. His elation rapidly evaporated. The police were asking for witnesses. Surely there were none. He was certain of that. Well, almost certain, but suppose the police had already questioned Harriet. Suppose she had already told them he was with her, that he had been chasing her. He thought of explaining to the police why he had run away from the accident scene. He thought of Christine finding out. He shivered.

His thoughts ricocheted back to Harriet. He needed to see to her quickly. He needed to know what she had told the police; if it was not already too late.

Once more he drove to Cheltenham. He parked in the hospital car park, walked up the stone steps and entered reception through the pillared doors. His mouth was dry with nerves as he approached the reception desk.

The receptionist, busy with a demanding switchboard, glanced at him impatiently. 'Yes?'

'A woman was brought in last night after an accident in Hunters Lane, Upper Wyre.'

'Do you have a name?'

'Harriet Malin.'

The receptionist consulted her computer. 'Alexander House. Centre Block, down the corridor and the first door on the left will take you to the stairs for the first floor, and the ICU.'

He murmured his thanks and walked unsteadily down the corridor. Intensive Care Unit. Christ!

Reaching the unit, he was alarmed to see a red warning sign. No Visitors.

As he wondered whether to ignore it and slip inside anyway, an imperious voice said. 'Can I help you?'

Danny turned round sharply. A nurse, small and dumpy, was eyeing him with curiosity.

'I'm here to see Harriet Malin.' He felt a trickle of sweat between his shoulder blades. It was stupid to come here. Now he was going to be questioned.

'Are you a relative?'

'No I'm her employer. Can I see her?'

'No visitors I'm afraid, she's in a coma.'

Coma! Bloody hell!

He wanted to sit down, he felt shaken.

'Are you okay?' the nurse asked.

'Yes, bit of a shock. I thought – when I heard she was injured, I never . . .' He knew he sounded incoherent but he was struggling to get the words out.

'Mrs Malin is critically ill. Would you like to speak to a doctor?'

'Umm,' he had no idea what to say. He wished he hadn't come.

He heard the lift doors open and saw a man striding towards them.

'Ah here's Dr Kingsley now,' the nurse said with obvious relief.

'I'm afraid she's not really allowed any visitors, except her husband, she's too ill,' Doctor Andrew Kingsley said firmly.

'I understand. I only wanted to see her for a moment. I'm –we – are all very fond of her.' He swallowed nervously. He was making himself conspicuous.

Dr Kingsley seemed to be considering. 'All right you may have a brief moment,' he said.

'Thank you.' He wasn't sure he still wanted to. 'Is her husband with her now?'

'No he went home to get a change of clothes.'

'Poor man,' Danny tried to sound sympathetic. 'Will Harriet recover?'

'It's hard to tell. Her injuries are severe. She's lucky to be alive.'

'How – um – I mean I understood the car was ablaze – was she badly burned?'

'No, they found her in the undergrowth. She was thrown through the windscreen. Apparently she wasn't wearing a seat belt.'

'I see.'

'We'll know more when she regains consciousness.'

'Is there any hope of that?'

'Who knows, it's difficult to tell. And if she does there is the risk of brain damage.'

He was aghast. He tried to speak but his throat felt constricted.

Dr Kingsley left him, telling, yet again, he must only stay a few moments.

Inside the room the nurse checking the monitor ignored him. He waited until she had left the room before he turned towards the bed.

He felt so faint with shock that he had difficulty in breathing evenly. Moving closer he stared down at her. It was a frightening sight. Her head was swathed in bandages so that only her eyes were visible. Eyes that were black and swollen and giving no indication that she was even alive.

Her nose beneath the bandages seemed distorted. Tubes were coming out of every part of her; her nostrils, her hands; two drips hung above her head, a bank of monitors bleeped in the quietness. He shuddered. It was incredible she had survived that terrible crash.

His eyes filled with tears and he tried hard not to gasp out loud. He tore his gaze from the bed to the bleeping heart monitor, at the intravenous tubes feeding Harriet, and wondered how anyone in such a damaged state could ever recover.

This was his fault. Guilt and horror made him shake with remorse. 'Oh God, Harriet, I'm so sorry, so very sorry.' He desperately needed her forgiveness. That wasn't possible, not yet. Not until she woke. *If she woke.*

He didn't want her to die.

Gently he reached out to touch her poor broken face; then he pulled back afraid of hurting her. Instead he let his fingers trail lightly down the arm that lay completely still on the white sheet.

'Harriet, Harriet,' he said softly. He stepped back from the bed and left the room.

The nurse was still outside. 'Are you okay?' she asked seeing his obvious distress.

He nodded; his throat too full to answer. Swallowing hard he forced himself to walk calmly; he wanted to run, to escape the cruel mutilation inside that room.

Outside in the fresh air, he took a deep breath to calm his nerves. He mustn't distress himself.

He drove back to the village. He thought guiltily of how he had disposed of all Harriet's things. Of how he had left the accident and pretended he had never been there. If she recovered how would he explain that?

He sighed heavily, torn with emotion. He prayed fervently she would live; and yet if she regained consciousness she would tell the police of his involvement.

Whichever way you looked at it he was in trouble.

And there was still had the problem of the child.

Christine was in the living room standing by the window when he entered the house. By the straight tense line of her shoulders he knew something was wrong.

'Where have you been?' she asked coldly, 'I thought you were ill.'

'I feel better today and I had some business to attend to, nothing important.' He put his arm around her waist and attempted to nuzzle her neck. He needed a bit of comfort.

Christine moved from his embrace. 'Have you heard the news?' she asked.

'What?'

'Harriet's been in a terrible accident.'

'Really?' He feigned surprise.

'Here in the village. Hunters Lane.'

'Is she okay?'

'Apparently not. She's in a coma.'

'Good grief, poor girl.' He hoped he sounded genuine.

'I wonder if I should phone her husband, he must be terribly distressed.'

'I thought they were separated.'

'Are they? I didn't know that.'

'So I heard. The girls in the shop gossip, you know.'

He was uncomfortably aware of Christine's eyes boring into his back as he left the room. He wondered absently why Harriet's accident was bothering her. She had made it clear she didn't like her. If she was suspicious of his involvement with Harriet why didn't she just say so? But that was Christine all over; he never knew what she was thinking or feeling. She was a closed book to him.

He couldn't face going into the perfumery on Monday. He had spent the week-end pondering on the problem of how to contact Laura. Nagging at the back of his mind was the constant worry of what to do about Amy.

Even if Harriet regained consciousness it would be weeks, maybe months, before she could look after a baby. Assuming, of course, she wanted her. He hadn't forgotten that Harriet had tried to give her away. Meanwhile what was he supposed to do with Amy?

At ten he entered *Flamingo's*. Thankfully Brett was there.

'Hi,' he said, 'usual Cappuccino please.'

125

'Hi, Danny, how are you?'

'Okay.'

'Terrible news about Harriet; have you heard how she is?' Brett asked.

'Still in a coma I believe.'

'Poor woman. Her husband must be devastated. Was her baby with her, there was no mention in the local paper.'

'Not as far as I know,' Danny said casually.

Brett placed the coffee on the table before him. 'Thank God for that.'

'You must miss Laura,' Danny said as casually as he could.

'I do. She was a great kid.'

'Do you happen to have her mobile number, only she ordered some perfume from me and she forgot to take it? It's paid for and I want to send it to her. I think it was a present for someone.' It was a complete lie of course.

'I'm afraid not. Never had the need for it. I think Nancy might have a note of it somewhere but as you know she's moved to Scotland.'

'Can you contact her?'

'Yes but not at the moment, she's doing a tour.'

'How long for?'

'Three weeks.'

Three weeks! Christ!

'If you happen to come across it I'd appreciate it,' Danny said trying not to sound desperate.

'Sure. I'll have a look at home. And if I speak to Nancy I'll see if she has it.'

'Thanks. Now make sure you get another waitress as pretty as Laura.'

'I'll do my best,' Brett laughed as he moved to serve another customer.

Danny drank his coffee and wondered if he dare ask Zoe.

Chapter Twenty-Two

On Monday morning Laura had a text from Zoe. *Harriet in hospital in coma after car accident.*

Her hand shook as she switched it off. Harriet was alive. It seemed incredible after seeing that burning car. She needed to talk to Danny urgently.

Whatever you do don't ring me at the perfumery, Danny had said, but she hadn't a choice; he hadn't given her his mobile number.

Her throat dry with nerves she dialled the perfumery number. Luckily Zoe answered the call.

'Hi Laura how are doing?'

It was good to hear her friend's voice. 'I'm good. And you?'

'Yeah, good. Did you get my text?'

'Yeah, dreadful.'

'It was in Hunters Lane. I'm surprised you didn't see it, you must have passed that way.'

'Err – no – I went the back route.'

'Just as well, otherwise you might have been involved.'

'Yeah, lucky eh. So how bad is Harriet?'

'Well like I said she's in a coma, and her injuries are horrific. I heard she may *never* recover,' Zoe finished in a whisper.

Laura felt quite chilled by the thrill of horror in Zoe's voice. She chewed on her bottom lip as she said cautiously. 'Everyone must be upset.'

Zoe laughed. 'You mean like Danny?'

'Yeah.'

'I don't know. I guess so. He hasn't come in today. Christine's here. She's the one who told us about it. She has a face on her though.'

'Do you reckon she knows about Danny and Harriet then?'

'Course she does. You'd have to be blind not to have noticed.' Zoe giggled. 'Anyway I must go. Ring me when you've decided about London.'

'Okay.'

Laura hung up. She desperately needed to talk to Danny but she guessed she would just have to wait for him to call. He had said it would be only a few days.

Another text from Zoe on Tuesday. *Danny's acting weird, wanted your mobile number. Shall I give it him? Why does he want it?*

No idea, she text back, *but give it him anyway.*

Her mobile rang an hour later. Danny at last.

'I'm really sorry,' he apologised. 'I lost your number, had to get it off Zoe, who wasn't very helpful. I've been desperate to talk to you.'

Slightly mollified Laura said, 'is everything okay?'

'Yes and no. Harriet wasn't killed.'

'I know, Zoe told me.'

'Of course. Right. You haven't said anything, have you?'

'No.' Laura frowned at his worried tone. 'You must be so relieved about Harriet.'

'Well it's not that good, she's in a coma; has been since the accident. Doctors are hopeful but . . . '

'You mean she still might die,' Laura said.

'Yes,' Danny agreed.

'I'm so sorry. What are you going to do about Amy? When are you coming for her?'

'That's why I need to talk to you. Is she okay?'

'Yes, she's brilliant.'

'Could you keep her a bit longer?'

'Why?'

'I need a bit more time. I haven't been able to find anyone to have her. I'll send you some money.'

'How long for?'

'A couple of weeks.'

'I suppose so.' Laura said doubtfully.

'Great. Now give me your address and I'll post a cheque. There's one more thing.'

'What?'

'If any one ever asks you, I was never at the accident.'

'What do you mean?'

'After you left, I – I went home. I heard the police and ambulance arrive but I didn't wait around. I had done as much as I could, and help was on the way. I couldn't be involved, you understand?'

'I guess so.'

After making a note of Danny's mobile number, Laura hung up and hugged Amy to her. So that was why he had sounded so worried. 'Your daddy's in a lot of trouble,' she told the child.

That evening Laura told Terry the good news. That Amy's mother was alive and her father would be coming to collect her in a couple of weeks.

'Can't he come for her now; doesn't he want his child?' Terry said in disgust.

'He's not in a position to look after her.' Laura defended Danny.

'Hmm,' Terry shook his head in disbelief.

A week passed and then another. The promised cheque had arrived in the post. There was no call from Danny. It was just as well that she was enjoying looking after Amy. The baby was a delight. She was growing to love her so much. She cuddled the child all the time, talking to her and watching every tiny movement with awe. Every small development seemed like a miracle. She sighed deeply; she was becoming dangerously attached to the child.

As a third week came and went. Terry started to ask awkward questions. 'I thought you were only having her for another couple of weeks,' he said.

'That was the plan, perhaps something has happened,' Laura shrugged.

'I'm surprised he hasn't been in touch. What kind of a father is he anyway, if he doesn't care about his child?'

'I'm sure there's a good explanation,' Alison butted in, 'in any case it's no trouble having them here.'

'That's not the point,' Terry argued. 'It's not fair on Laura.'

'I don't mind,' Laura said.

'I'm worried you're getting too fond of her. Already I can see it's going to break your heart to part with her.'

Laura knew he was right, but it was too late. She had already fallen in love with Amy.

Danny's silence was worrying as well as annoying. She had been prepared to help him because she liked him, and she could see the predicament he was in. Even so, she hadn't expected it to be taken for granted that she would look after his baby indefinitely. Much as she wanted to, she couldn't afford to keep a baby. Anyway she had her own life to lead.

'You must telephone him again,' Terry insisted the following day.

Danny was not in at the perfumery and his mobile was switched off, when she tried the following morning. Laura started to fret. Where the hell was he? Why hadn't he been in touch? *He had promised.* She didn't know what to do, what to think. It was all so frustratingly uncertain. The longer she had Amy the harder it was going to be to part with her.

Her anxiety deepened with each passing day. Surely he hadn't abandoned his child?

Using the cash Danny had given her, Laura had bought a baby sling so that she could go out. With Amy snug against her chest she walked along the sea front and through the park. She talked to Amy, pointing out places of interest, even though she knew the child couldn't understand. Amy liked being outside, she was content and often fell asleep. She also bought clothes for Amy, even though she was worried about spending too much money.

Terry was getting agitated. Every night on his return from work he asked the same question. 'Has Amy's father been in touch?' Laura knew he couldn't understand why Danny hadn't rung.

At the end of the following week Laura decided to try once again. Maybe this time she would leave a message. This uncertainty was making her edgy.

Once again she phoned the perfumery, praying Mrs Pembroke didn't answer. It was going to be difficult to explain why she needed to talk to Danny.

Fortunately Danny came on the line. 'Ah, Laura, how are you?'

She wanted none of his small talk. 'Why haven't you come for Amy?' she said bluntly.

'Sorry. The thing is I still haven't found anyone to have her.'

Laura remained silent, wondering what to say.

'Harriet is still unconscious,' Danny was saying. 'The doctor said it could be months before she comes round. Could you keep Amy until she recovers?'

'I don't know,' Laura said, torn between relief at not having to part with her precious Amy just yet and prolonging the agony. 'I'm growing to love her and, well, the longer I keep her; the harder it will be to give her up.'

'There is another option,' Danny said guardedly.

'Oh.'

'First of all can I ask; are you planning to stay in Devon?'

'Not sure, I was thinking of maybe going to London, it all depends.'

'Do you ever intend to come back here?'

'I don't think so.'

'Would you like to keep Amy?'

For a few seconds Laura found it difficult to speak. 'Like a nanny you mean?' she managed to say. She had to be clear what he meant.

'I was thinking of something more permanent.'

'Adopt her you mean?'

'Sort of. Although it will be a private arrangement. You will have to swear never to tell anyone who Amy's real parents are. I will send you money, naturally.'

'What about Harriet. Surely when she recovers she will want her back?'

'I doubt it. No one knows how long that will be. She's very badly injured and even if she comes out of the coma it could be months before she'll be able to take care of Amy. Assuming that she wants her back.'

'Why wouldn't she?'

'There's something I didn't tell you. On the night of the accident she was trying to get me to have Amy. She actually dumped her on my doorstep. I was following her, that's why we were in Hunters Lane.'

'And Mrs Pembroke still knows nothing of this?'

'Nothing. You can see the fix I'm in.'

Laura was silent as she digested this. It really would scupper her plans to go to London with Zoe, not that she'd been keen on it anyway. The idea of keeping Amy filled her with excitement. Still she was cautious.

'I need to think about it,' she said, 'I mean what will I tell people? My brother for instance will think it very strange if I can't explain the real reason why I have her.'

'You must never do that,' Danny sounded alarmed.

'Can I ring you tomorrow when I've thought about it?'

'Of course. Thanks, Laura.'

Laura spent a sleepless night trying to think of a way to explain to Terry and Alison. They were already anxious and suspicious about Danny. She could just say she was being employed as a nanny but then they would wonder why she had to live so far away.

She had made up her mind to keep her. Her plans for an exciting life in London seemed superficial. This is what she wanted; a home, a baby. A husband would have been nice, but life didn't give you everything.

She wanted Amy so much, and the idea that it was now possible seemed so wonderful that she was almost afraid to believe it.

She would have to find a job of course, and a home. She would be responsible for Amy; she, who had never been responsible for anyone other than herself. It was scary. Then she thought of the past few weeks and of how much Amy had come to mean to her.

As she tossed and turned she had an idea. It was a bit risky, but she thought it worth it.

She phoned Danny the following morning as soon as Alison and Terry had left for work.

He was delighted she had agreed. 'Will this be a legal arrangement?' she asked when he mentioned the child maintenance.

'Not strictly,' he confessed, 'more of an understanding between you and me. You have my word, I will honour the payments.'

'I'm not worried about that, but what if Harriet changes her mind and decides she wants Amy back?'

'She won't, trust me.'

'Can't I legally adopt her?'

'That's a delightful thought, but you are too young, my dear, and it would be too complicated.'

'I guess I will have to trust you then,' she said.

'That's not a problem, believe me. I trusted you with my secret. You are the only one that knows.'

She felt flattered. 'Okay then I'll do it.'

'What will you tell your brother?'

'Don't worry about that. I have it all worked out.'

On Sunday morning after breakfast, when Alison had gone to the supermarket, she said to Terry. 'I want to tell you the truth about Amy.'

'What do you mean?' Terry looked startled.

'There is no friend. Amy is my baby.'

Terry thumped the table. 'I knew it!'

Laura's eyes widened. She was shocked.

Terry laughed. 'Come on sis, did you really expect me to believe that cock and bull story you gave us.'

She turned her head away, relieved at the absurdity of it. Terry had not believed the truth. 'No I guess not. I'm sorry I lied to you. I was scared.'

Terry's face softened. 'I understand.'

'Are you angry?'

'You should know me better than that. What about the father?'

Laura blinked rapidly to clear her thoughts. She would have to invent a boyfriend. 'We split up ages ago, before Amy was born.'

'Why?'

'I didn't love him.'

'Does he know about the baby?' Terry frowned anxiously.

Laura shook her head. 'No.'

'I assume Mum doesn't know.'

'Like I said, I couldn't find her.'

Alison returned loaded with grocery bags. Terry and Laura leapt up to help her.

Laura made coffee while Terry explained the situation to Alison.

The guilt at her lies made Laura tremble.

Later they discussed Laura's situation and agreed she could live with them until they needed the room for their own baby. As Alison was not even pregnant yet there was no rush.

'I'll have sorted out a place to live and got a job long before then,' Laura spoke confidently.

'How are you to get a job with the baby to look after?' Terry asked.

Laura looked from Alison to her brother. 'Perhaps I can get an evening job,' she suggested hopefully. 'That is if you'd look after Amy.'

'That's a great idea,' Alison said enthusiastically. 'I'll take great care of her, I promise.'

Terry said. 'I could ask at my local pub to see if they need an evening barmaid.'

'Wicked!'

'What about the rest of your belongings, you didn't bring much. No pram or cot for Amy,' Alison, ever practical, commented.

'I didn't know if I was staying. I'll buy some things this week,' she said thinking of the money Danny would be sending. 'I have some savings,' she added hastily.

Later that evening after Alison had gone to bed Terry said. 'I'm really glad you're here.'

'Thanks. It's great to be here. Are you really sure it's okay?' Laura said anxiously.

'Of course I am. I've been so worried about you.'

'There was no need. Well maybe in the beginning, but I survived.'

'I failed you though. An unmarried mother at nineteen. Good job Mum don't know. She said I'd get us both into trouble.'

'I thought you didn't care what she thinks.'

'I don't. I just hate the idea that she was right.'

'Oh Terry.' She held his hand, touched that he seemed so upset.

'Anyway, whatever she may think she can't make me feel any worse than I do already. I didn't take proper care of you.'

'It wasn't your fault.'

'Whatever, but I promise I'll look after you and Amy now.'

'Thanks.'

'Promise me just one thing.'

'What?'

'You're not in any trouble are you? I mean it was a bit odd turning up in the middle of the night. It's almost as if you're running away. You haven't done anything silly, got in trouble with the law.'

'No Terry, I promise everything is just fine.'

Chapter Twenty-Three

A week later over dinner Christine Pembroke said casually to her husband. 'I went to see Harriet today.'

'Did you, I thought you were meeting Diana for lunch?'

'I went before I met her.'

'Whatever for?' Danny looked uncomfortable, unable to meet her gaze.

Christine shrugged. 'I admit I was curious. I expect you know she and I didn't really get on. Having seen her though, I'm filled with shame that I wasn't more sympathetic. She looked terrible; I can't see any hope of her recovering.'

'Really.' Danny stopped eating and refilled his wine glass.

'I feel sorry for the child. Growing up without a mother. I wonder how Jeremy will cope.'

Danny stared at her, relieved that Christine, like everyone else, was assuming that Jeremy had the baby.

'I've no idea. Why are you concerned? It's nothing to do with us.'

'That's a bit heartless.'

Danny shrugged, painfully aware that his supposed indifference failed to ring true with her.

'You amaze me,' Christine continued coolly, confirming his suspicions. 'I can't believe your total lack of interest in someone you rated so highly, or have such blatant disregard for Harriet, who has suffered such terrible injuries that she may never recover. Where is your humanity?'

'What do think we can do?' Danny sounded alarmed.

'The very least is we could offer to help look after the child until Harriet recovers.'

Danny swallowed his wine the wrong way and spluttered. 'You have a business to run. How can you look after a baby, you have no experience of children.'

'It can't be difficult and I could take time off.'

Danny grimaced. 'I don't think that's a good idea, you would fret if you weren't at the perfumery.'

'I suppose so.'

'I mean you are always telling me that it's your life.'

Christine remained silent.

Danny risked a glance; her expression was closed, sad. He knew he had hurt her by denying them children. In the early years of their marriage he had insisted they wait until the business was profitable, even though Christine had been adamant that they could manage. By the time the perfumery was successful it was too late. A hysterectomy had made sure of that. He hadn't been too bothered, but he knew she had been devastated.

'How is Diana?' he said, to change the subject.

Christine and Diana had been at school together. Diana was one of the few women that he didn't get on with. For some reason she thought he was a womaniser and told him so. It might have been something to do with the fact that he had tried to kiss her during a dinner party. He'd had his face slapped for his trouble and a warning that if he tried it again she would tell Christine.

'She's fine,' Christine said now, 'her boys are growing up fast. Alistair is fifteen and Thomas is twelve. She's so lucky.'

Wrong subject to have started. He moved on.

'Stephen seems to be getting on okay?' he said now to change the uncomfortable tension.

They had replaced Harriet with Stephen Wyles, an eager young man, who also took over the role of buying the raw materials; the essential oils, the absolutes and aromatics that once compounded, made up the various perfumes.

'He's very good, I like him,' Christine smiled at last and Danny relaxed.

* * *

137

The call came late in the evening while he was watching television. Christine had gone to bed. He picked up the receiver with only half his attention as he watched a repeat of Dennis Waterman in *Minder.*

'Where is she?'

There had been no introduction, merely the stark sentence in a threatening tone.

'Who is this?' he snapped.

'What have you done with her?'

'Who?'

'The baby. What have you done with Harriet's baby?'

A cold sweat crept over Danny's skin. He swallowed hard before saying. 'I've no idea what you're talking about.'

'I could contact the police. They might look into the accident if I was to speak to them.'

'Accident?'

'Harriet's accident. I know more than you think about what happened.'

Danny's mouth went dry. He ran his tongue over his lips. 'Who are you?'

'Jeremy Malin, Harriet's husband.'

Danny groaned inwardly. This was all he needed, Harriet's husband wondering about the child. His thoughts raced. What did Jeremy mean that he knew about the accident? He couldn't possibly know. He would bluff it out.

'The accident had nothing to do with me.'

'Yes it had. You were there. Why did you run away? You were home even before the ambulance got there.'

Danny nearly choked. 'What are you talking about?'

'I was there that night. I followed Harriet to your house.' Resentment was evident in every nuance of his tone. 'I saw Harriet arrive, leave the child with you and drive off again. I saw you follow her. I was behind you, but when I reached the crossroads I didn't know which way you'd gone. I went back to wait for you. You arrived home just as I heard the sirens. I got to Hunters Lane as they were putting Harriet in the ambulance. There was no sign of Amy, so it stands to reason you must still

138

have her.'

'Well I haven't.'

'So where is she then?'

Danny was getting agitated. 'How the hell should I know?'

'She's your child.'

'Don't be ridiculous of course she isn't.' There was no way he was going to admit anything to Jeremy Malin.

'You stole Harriet from me. I loved her but she wouldn't have anything to do with me after she met you.'

'You're mistaken. Harriet was my employee, nothing more.'

'It's no use denying it. I know about the affair, I *know* you're the father of Harriet's baby.'

Danny was shocked. So Harriet hadn't been lying. He felt sick.

'What do you want?' he asked curtly.

'I've told you, I want to know where Amy is.'

'Why?'

'Have you killed her?'

'Now you are being ludicrous.'

'Am I? I don't think so.' Jeremy's tone was suddenly challenging. 'Amy must be an embarrassment for you. Especially as I suspect your wife has no idea you're the father.'

'I keep telling you, the child has nothing to do with me.'

'You're a liar. I'll find out the truth. I'll be in touch.'

The line suddenly went dead.

Danny replaced the receiver with a shaking hand. He walked to the window and looked out into the night. The streetlight reflected the empty driveway and the dark shadows of the trees. The wrought iron gates set in the high wall were securely locked. Even though there was no one in sight he shivered. Jeremy Malin had frightened him with his accusations.

Checking the security alarm, he turned out the lights and went to bed. He no longer felt like watching television.

Unable to get Jeremy's threats from his mind, Danny drove to Cheltenham police station.

The desk sergeant knew him and greeted him with a friendly smile. 'Don't often see you in here, Mr Pembroke.'

139

'Hello Tom. Is he in?' He didn't need to tell him he was enquiring for Detective Chief Inspector Robert Lloyd.

'Yes, I'll just buzz through.'

Less than five minutes later he looked up from where he was sitting browsing a Crimestop magazine to see Robert coming towards him.

He had known Robert since college. When Robert had gone to the University of Wales in Aberystwyth and later moved north for his first police posting they had lost touch until Robert was posted to Cheltenham and made contact again. Three years later, when Robert married Debbie, he was best man at their wedding.

'This is a surprise,' Robert said now, shaking his hand.

'Hello, Rob. I just need a minute if you can spare it,' Danny said.

'Of course. Come on through. Would you like a cup of tea?'

'No thanks. I'm not stopping.'

In his office Robert sat behind his desk and motioned him to take a chair opposite. Danny cleared his throat.

'No doubt you've heard about Harriet being in a terrible accident.' Robert knew Harriet as he knew all of the staff at the perfumery. He always bought perfume for his wife's birthday or their wedding anniversary.

'Yes shocking. Do you know how she is?'

'I went to the hospital she's – she's . . .' Danny shuddered. 'I can't see how she can survive her injuries.'

'Poor Harriet.'

Danny swallowed hard. 'Are you – are you investigating the accident?'

Robert looked surprised. 'No I don't think so. It was a straightforward accident. Her car hit a tree felled by the storm, and it spun off the road, out of control. We appealed for witnesses as a matter of routine. There were none anyway.'

'There were no suspicious circumstances at all.'

'None as far as I know. Why?'

'No reason. Just a thought.'

Danny rose. 'I must go, and leave you to get on. Thanks for seeing me.'

Robert rose. 'That's okay we must play golf again soon.'

'Look forward to that,' Danny agreed enthusiastically.

As he closed the door behind him he missed Robert's puzzled look and his low murmuring of, 'now what was that *really* all about?'

Chapter Twenty-Four

'Pint of bitter please.'

Laura barely glanced at the customer as she pulled the pint. She had started work in the bar of the Old Ship Inn. She had been nervous about leaving Amy.

'Stop fussing,' Alison had scolded lightly. 'I've never known anyone worry so much about a baby. She'll be fine.'

'If she frets please call me and I'll come home straightaway,' Laura said worriedly.

'Go! You'll be late.'

Laura kissed Amy's head. 'See you soon, sweetheart, be good.' She kissed her again and gave a rueful smile as Alison pushed her gently towards the door.

Colin, the landlord, was even-tempered and jovial. His round face was creased in a smile and his wisps of white hair beneath his balding head were neatly combed. Laura liked him immediately.

The pub had whitewashed walls, oak beams and dark wood furniture. Meals were served in a small room at the back by Julia, Colin's daughter. Food was cooked by Betty, Colin's wife, with casual labour hired during the busy times. Tonight the pub was quiet, with only a few locals in. Colin told her it would get busier nearer to Christmas and the summer months were always a mad rush. He showed her how to pull a pint and explained the optic measures. Then he went through the routine of the till and checking the stock of soft drinks. Laura's head was buzzing. She served her first pint under Colin's watchful eye. It was a total disaster, more froth than beer, but by the third attempt she had mastered it and as he praised her, she felt more confident.

She placed the pint on the counter. 'One pound sixty please.'

'Thanks.'

She made eye contact. Gentle, deep brown eyes, that reminded her of melted chocolate. What seemed like minutes later, but must have been only seconds, she found she was still staring. The heat rose to her cheeks as she took a deep breath. Her heart seemed to be racing at a hundred miles an hour. 'Hi,' she managed to stammer.

He didn't smile and her face felt hotter. 'My first night,' she confided trying to appear cool, yet friendly as Colin had suggested. 'Are you a regular?'

'Not really,' he answered with obvious reluctance.

'I'm Laura.'

He nodded and moved away to sit in a corner seat. She watched him unfold a newspaper and sip his beer as he read. He didn't once look up at her.

In between serving customers her eyes strayed to him. He was very thin she thought and his clothes were awful, brown corduroy trousers and a checked shirt, neither of which looked too clean. She guessed him to be in his mid-twenties. His dark brown hair was long and tangled, and judging by the stubble on his chin he hadn't shaved for days. His face looked strong and kind though. She noticed his hands were tanned and his fingers were long and slender. Not a manual worker then, despite his tan.

Despite his unfriendly attitude she was curious about him.

He left as soon as he had finished his pint. Tucking the newspaper under his arm he strode out without speaking.

'Who was that?' she asked Colin.

Colin laughed. 'Paul Adams, our local artist. He keeps himself to himself, bit of a strange character but he's pleasant enough, never causes any trouble.'

She turned to serve another customer and forgot about him.

The rest of the evening passed slowly. She spent much of the time reading the spirit labels and trying to memorise the prices. Her thoughts turned to the conversation she'd had with Alison last night. She had told her she must register Amy with a doctor as soon as possible and although the surgery she used was very busy she thought she might get them in.

She had tried not to show how frightened she'd been. She had no birth certificate, no maternity records. The doctor might become suspicious and send a social worker or even the police. The thought terrified her and she wondered what she going to do; she couldn't give Amy up, not now.

She jumped every time the phone rang behind the bar, convinced it was Alison and some disaster had befallen Amy. At last it was eleven o'clock and her shift ended.

'You did well,' Colin said, 'but try and relax a bit more.'

Laura asked Terry about Paul Adams the following evening.

'Paul. Yes I know him. I'm surprised you haven't commented on the picture over the fireplace.'

'Is that one of his?' she was impressed and went to have a closer look. It showed a background of rugged cliffs and the white foam of waves lapping against a shore. She instantly recognised it as Sidmouth. She saw his signature in the corner. 'It's very good, relaxing. Was it expensive?' she ventured.

Terry laughed. 'It was in payment for the service on his car. A couple of years ago, he was really broke. My boss, Kevin gave it to me as I'd done the work. I'm hoping one day it will increase in value and be worth a fortune.'

'Does he live in Sidmouth?'

'Yes he has a flat above his art gallery.'

'I'd like to go and see his paintings, but I can't afford to buy anything.'

'He wouldn't expect you to. A lot of people go and watch him paint. Usually he ignores them. I doubt if he would even notice you in there.'

'Great!'

Terry stared at her. 'Don't get any ideas. I know he's a good looking bloke but he's not interested in women.'

Laura laughed. 'Is he gay?'

'No. I didn't mean it like that. I'm just saying he was dumped, big time, and women are off the agenda.'

'Well that's fine because I'm not interested in him, just his paintings. I've never met an artist before.'

Paul came into the pub again a few days later. Once again he was polite but surly. Laura didn't bother to try and make conversation. Even so her curiosity increased. She wondered about the woman that had dumped him and why she had done it. Probably because he was so miserable, she giggled to herself.

Unable to get him off her mind she walked to his studio in Old Fore Street the following week. She had left Amy asleep in her pram with Alison keeping an eye on her. Alison had the day off.

She stood on the pavement looking in, suddenly feeling embarrassed about entering. A single painting on an easel stood prominent behind the panes of the bow window. *Sidmouth at Sunset* was the caption underneath. The vibrant red and orange colours were breathtaking. There was no price tag.

Taking a deep breath she finally entered the shop.

Paul glanced up from the oil he was working on. She was struck again at how handsome he was, well, apart from the scowl on his face as he recognised her.

Nervously she said. 'Hi.'

He stared at her. The silence became strained. 'Can I look around?'

'Sure.' He rose from his chair and, wiping his hands on a rag, disappeared into a back room.

She was the only customer. Feeling self-conscious, she wandered from picture to picture, looking at the displays covering the walls. There was a mixture of original watercolours and oils. A stand held a selection of greeting cards and small prints of Paul's work. A nearly finished painting balanced on an easel where Paul was obviously working. Laura looked closer. The pale colours depicted the shore at dawn, the water gently lapping against the deserted beach.

Paul returned with a mug of coffee. He began painting again, without as much as a glance at her.

'Wow. These are great,' she felt compelled to speak.

'Thanks.' His voice was marginally less surly.

'My brother, Terry has a picture of Sidmouth over his fireplace. I had no idea it was yours, it's amazing.'

'You're Terry's sister!'

'Yes.'

'Ah!'

'What's that supposed to mean?'

'He's always talking about you. He never said . . . '

'What.'

'Nothing, I got the impression you were just a kid.' His gaze was a mixture of irritation and confusion.

'I think I'm an embarrassment to him. Unwed mum and all that.'

'You have a baby?'

'Yep.'

'Hmm.'

He took a deep breath. 'I have to get this finished,' he said and turned his back on her.

A customer entered the shop and Laura left.

* * *

It was already dark when Laura returned home on Christmas Eve. She had been shopping in Exeter for Christmas presents. Alison had kindly offered to look after Amy. As she turned into All Saints Road her face broke into a wide grin. The house looked amazing. Terry had put Christmas lights round every window and the front door and even entwined some on a tall potted shrub. It looked like Santa's Grotto.

Christmas always reminded her of the happy times at home before their father left. She remembered hanging tinsel around the room, putting cheap baubles on the artificial tree, and the excitement of waking early on Christmas morning and unwrapping the presents. They hadn't much money but it hadn't mattered, they had been happy then, their parents talking to each other. Before it had all gone wrong and their father had found love elsewhere.

It still hurt that he had abandoned them. She could understand that he had fallen in love with someone else, but she could never forgive him for not keeping in touch with her and Terry. She was convinced that if her father had stayed with them, Terry would not have turned to crime.

However that was all in the past and she had to think now of her future. This was Amy's first Christmas and she had bought loads of presents for her; cuddly toys, a cot mobile, and lots of clothes. She had enjoyed every minute of shopping. Danny had been generous with the money he had sent.

Laura entered the house and found her brother in the kitchen peeling sprouts. It was such an ordinary thing to see that she felt her heart swell. She felt safe and happy here.

She stared at the mountain of vegetables and laughed. 'Are we expecting the army?'

Terry grimaced. 'No, but we are having guests.'

'You never said.'

'Last minute.'

'Will I know them?'

Terry shrugged. 'Yep, one of them is Paul.'

'Paul Adams?'

'Do you know another Paul?'

'Very funny. I just didn't realise he was such a close friend.'

'He's not really, it's Alison's idea, nothing to do with me. She collects lame ducks,' Terry laughed.

'Who else is coming?' she asked nervously.

'My boss, Kevin. Now he's single and a great bloke.' Terry smiled cheekily at her as he put the last sprout into the colander and dried his hands. 'Tomorrow's going to be great,' he said hugging her, 'the best Christmas since we were little.'

'I was thinking of that earlier,' Laura said, 'I was remembering how happy we were.'

'And we will be again, just as soon as I get you fixed up with a husband.'

'Stop it, Terry. I don't want a husband.'

'Course you do,' he replied. 'Now I must get changed otherwise Alison will blame me for being late.' They were going out for a drink with some friends, which would give her time to wrap their presents.

Terry was still laughing as he shut the door.

On Christmas morning, Paul arrived at midday.

He handed Alison a small square package. 'Sorry it's not much.' He looked embarrassed.

'You didn't have to,' Alison said, 'really.'

Another shrug and then he turned towards her. 'Hello, Laura. Hope you don't mind me intruding on your family day.'

It was the most civil his voice had ever been. 'Of course not,' she reassured him. She was holding Amy, who was wide-awake and gurgling, in her arms. At three months she was alert and her tiny fist grasped at the air.

'This is my daughter, Amy,' she said proudly, her face softening.

'She's lovely,' Paul said politely. 'She doesn't look a bit like you though.'

'Thanks.'

'Sorry, I didn't mean it like that, what I meant was . . .'

'Quit while you're ahead,' she laughed.

The doorbell rang and Terry rose to answer.

'Hi, everyone,' Kevin strode into the room; his arms piled high with presents, 'Happy Christmas.' He tried to lean over and kiss Alison's cheek but the parcels got in the way. Laughing, Alison helped him put them under the tree.

Laura had met Kevin on several occasions and liked his down-to-earth manner. She knew her judgement was biased because he had given Terry a chance, but even so he seemed a genuine honest bloke. In his early thirties, he was older than Terry but he acted and looked younger. His hair was cropped short, his face brown and weathered. She liked him a lot but she hoped Terry had been joking when he had suggested that Kevin might be interested in her.

By the time she had fed Amy and settled her in her pram Alison had returned with the carved meat on a platter, and Laura leapt up to help fetch the rest of the meal.

They all sat around the table. Watching Paul, Laura thought she had never seen anyone eat so much, so fast. He caught her staring and grinned shyly. 'Sorry I don't often remember to eat. This is great, Alison.'

Alison smiled. 'Thanks, I like to see a man with a good appetite.'

They pulled Christmas crackers; put on party hats and laughed at the awful jokes. Laura decided it was the best Christmas day since she was a child. After Dad had left, Mum was depressed at Christmas, and then when Nigel arrived it was awkward and uncomfortable. In Coventry and sharing rooms with Terry they'd had little money for celebrations. Christmas with Brett and Nancy had been good, but they were not family and she had missed Terry.

During the meal Kevin kept them amused with stories of his customers. Paul seemed to relax a bit and said how some people chose a painting so that the colour matched their décor and not for the picture itself. A groan of "philistines" from Kevin made Laura smile.

As the day progressed, and bottle after bottle of wine consumed, their laughter grew louder and more raucous.

It was only after Kevin and Paul left at midnight, that she realised how quiet Paul had been, how little he had given away of himself.

'Do you think Paul enjoyed himself?' she asked Alison as they watched him stagger down the road.

'I hope so. He's very drunk. We should have made him stay,' Alison said worriedly, 'he'll get run over.'

'He'll be all right,' Terry pulled her inside out of the cold. 'He only lives two streets away.'

* * *

Laura pushed the pram along the Esplanade, battling against the January wind. It was not sensible to be out today but she needed to think, to decide what to do about the letter.

She was already feeling stressed out having just come from the surgery. Under pressure from Alison she had taken Amy to the doctor because the cold she'd had for the last few days had gone to her chest. Filling in the registration form with the secretary had been scary, but she managed to convince the woman that she would get the replacement for the "lost" birth certificate soon.

Busy with a demanding surgery of patients with winter ailments, the doctor had checked over Amy and given her a prescription without too much probing. She was sure it was because he knew she was under Alison's care.

This was the second letter from Zoe, the first being after she had told her she had changed her mind about London.

Today's letter had started off bemoaning the fact that Laura didn't have a computer, because sending emails was so much easier. She had far too much to say in a text and it was too costly to phone. It made Laura smile.

Zoe had written pages about a man she had met and how she thought she was in love. The last paragraph was the one that worried Laura. *Harriet is still in a coma. I feel sorry for her poor husband. I asked Danny how Mr Malin was managing looking after the baby and he said the child was being taken care of by Harriet's parents. Danny was a bit snappy with me, but I expect that's because he's also worried about Harriet.*

I miss you and our nights out together. Hope you can visit soon. Love, Zoe.

Laura was puzzled. Why was Mr Malin telling everyone that Harriet's parents had the child? He must know that wasn't true. Perhaps he didn't care what had happened to it; after all, it wasn't his baby. Maybe he was just glad it wasn't around, a reminder of his wife's unfaithfulness.

A terrible thought suddenly occurred to her and she had to sit down on the nearest bench as her legs went suddenly wobbly.

Maybe he was quietly looking for it. It wouldn't be difficult for a private investigator to find her. Suppose they thought she had *stolen* Amy. After all it was only her word against Danny's and he wasn't even admitting to being at the accident scene, let alone being the father. Oh why hadn't she thought of these repercussions before?

Perhaps she was letting her imagination run away with her. None of it made any sense. Even so she longed to phone Danny, to reassure herself that she had nothing to worry about, but she knew he wouldn't speak to her.

She was so engrossed in her thoughts she took a wrong turning going home and found herself in Fore Street.

Paul was just about to unlock the shop. He stared at her.

He had been in the pub twice since Christmas Day and he still wasn't any friendlier with her. Alison had said it was because he was lonely. She said the girl that had dumped him and broken his heart had a lot to answer for, because now he was wary of women. Terry had scoffed at her, called her a romantic and said Paul was just a miserable bugger.

She was surprised now to see he was quite smartly dressed. His black trousers were neatly pressed and his shirt, although an unflattering shade of green was at least clean. He had even shaved.

Paul gave her a tight smile. 'You look frozen. Do you – er – want a cup of coffee?'

Startled by the invitation Laura nodded. 'Thanks.'

He helped her lift the pram up the three steps into the studio. 'Back in minute,' he said, 'I need to change. Had to look respectable for the bank manager.'

He was gone without explaining further. She looked around again. There was a new canvas on his easel with a finished painting of a sandy beach; a curve of footprints led to the sea. Laura studied it, and thought it was the most stunning painting she had ever seen; it was so tranquil and romantic. She read the title. *Footprints in the Sand,* and wondered if the two lovers at the shore's edge had any significance for Paul.

'This is beautiful,' she said when Paul returned carrying two mugs of coffee. He looked more relaxed in his faded jeans and a denim shirt rolled up at the sleeves.

'Thanks.'

His smile was warmer as they sipped the coffee and encouraged she said. 'Have you always lived in Sidmouth?'

'No.' Paul shook his head. 'I'm a Londoner, born and bred in West Ham.'

'Me too, born in Lewisham.'

'I know, Terry told me.'

'Oh right.' She wondered how much else Terry had confided. 'Do you miss London?' she asked.

'Sometimes, but I love it here.'

She thought he had a nice voice, warm and gentle, especially when, like now, he was being friendly. She was beginning to like him.

'Do you have any family?' she said.

'I'm not married, if that's what you mean.'

'No it isn't,' she frowned. 'I meant sisters or brothers.'

'No, there's only me; my parents died when I was a child. I grew up living with my uncle Harry.'

'I'm sorry.'

'Don't be. It was a long time ago.'

Later that afternoon she picked up Zoe's letter to reply. She must be careful in what she said.

She had thought she was safe here. Now she wasn't so sure. She was terrified someone would find her and take Amy away.

She missed the companionship of Zoe, but she could never visit of course. Amy had made that impossible. Having her had changed her life irrevocably.

Chapter Twenty-Five

It was getting dark as Danny prepared to lock the perfumery and make his way home.

There had been few customers; the icy January weather, with a threat of snow, had kept many people indoors. The front door was locked and the closed sign clearly in place, so it was annoying to hear someone banging on the door.

He walked through the darkness of the shop and peered through the window. Christ! It was Jeremy Malin. Danny felt his heart sink. There had been several calls over the past few weeks where there had been no one on the line when he answered. He had assumed it was Malin and had ignored them. He wasn't worried; if Malin had been going to the police he would have done so by now.

He unlocked the door. 'What do you want?' he snapped.

'I want to talk to you.'

'I fail to see . . . '

'Just hear me out.'

'You'd better come in then.'

He took him through the shop into his office. Switching on a desk lamp he was taken aback by the man's appearance. He looked gaunt and haggard, with sunken cheeks and an unshaven chin. His grey suit was creased and hung loosely on his bony frame.

Jeremy's eyes flitted nervously around the room, his hands were shaking. 'Do you have anything to drink?'

It was obvious that Jeremy had had quite a few already, but he decided to humour him until he found out what he wanted.

'Have a seat.' Danny gestured toward an armchair as he moved to a cabinet. 'Brandy okay?' he asked.

'Fine.'

Danny poured two large measures.

'So what do you want?' He asked when he was seated in his leather chair behind his desk.

Jeremy remained standing as he sniffed at the contents of the glass before swallowing the liquid. He wiped his mouth with the back of his hand. 'It's all such a fucking mess,' he muttered.

Danny sighed. 'What are you doing here?'

Jeremy didn't answer, just stared at him coldly. The silence lengthened until Danny felt obliged to speak. 'I don't know what you expect from me but if you don't stop harassing me I'm going to the police. I know it's you that's been making the silent phone calls.'

Jeremy sniggered. 'I don't think you'll go to the police. Not after what you've done.'

'Just say what you've come for and get out,' Danny snapped impatiently.

Jeremy slumped in the chair looking defeated. 'I've lost everything, my home, my wife. And now my job.'

'That's hardly my fault.'

Jeremy moved suddenly leaning across the desk and jabbing his finger at Danny. 'That's where you're wrong. It is your fault. Harriet is destroyed, you did that to her. You ruined her life and mine.'

Danny sighed. He was losing patience with the man. He looked pointedly at his watch. 'Can you get to the point?'

'Your wife still doesn't know does she?' Jeremy smirked.

'There's nothing for her to know. The affair is over, was over, long before the accident.'

'Maybe it is, but we have unfinished business.'

'What do you mean?'

'You owe me. I want compensation.'

'What! Don't be ridiculous.'

'Ten grand or I'll talk to your wife.'

'Go ahead! She won't believe you.'

'Oh, she will. I have proof you see. I have a copy of Amy's birth certificate.'

'You're lying.'

Jeremy fumbled in his jacket pocket and pulled out an envelope He threw it on the desk. Danny felt sick as he stared at it. He didn't open it; he knew Jeremy was telling the truth. He had the original locked here in his safe. He took a large swallow of the brandy and refilled his glass. He had no idea what to do.

'By the way, where is the child?' Jeremy's voice was calmer now.

Danny stared at him. Saw the arrogance in the bloodshot eyes and felt bile rise in his throat. God, he wanted to kill him, the smug bastard. 'Why ask me? You're the one that's been telling everyone she's in Canada, with Harriet's parents, so I assume that's where she is.'

'We both know that's a lie. I did it to protect Harriet from gossip.'

Danny shrugged.

'Guess I'll have to go to the police as well as Christine.' The calmness had slipped; the hysteria was edging in again.

The sound of his wife's name on Malin's lips infuriated Danny. He also realised that he was entirely in his power. He could not afford for Jeremy to talk to Christine. Even if he denied everything, said Harriet had lied on the registration, seeds of doubt would be set. He decided to give Jeremy some sort of explanation.

'The child has been adopted. Harriet didn't want it, that's why she was leaving it with me that night. I – we had already arranged it. I was taking the child to its new parents.'

Danny felt quite pleased with the inspirational lie but Jeremy looked doubtful.

'I need to check that out. Tell me who they are?'

'I can't without Harriet's permission. You'll have to take my word for it until she wakes up but it's the truth, trust me.'

Jeremy glowered. 'All right, but I still need some money if you want me to keep quiet.'

Danny reached inside the drawer and pulled out his cheque

book. 'I'll pay you just this once. Don't even think of coming back, okay?'

Jeremy ran his tongue over his lips. 'Better make it twenty then.'

'Don't push it. I'll pay you ten.'

After Jeremy had left Danny poured another brandy. He had a sinking feeling he had not heard the last of him.

Chapter Twenty-Six

Laura was polishing glasses when Paul came into the pub. It was early, not yet six o'clock, and the bar was almost empty. She looked at him in surprise.

'Just passing,' Paul said casually. 'It's freezing out there.'

'Right,' Laura said. She pulled his pint and watched him as he took a swallow. His manner towards her was becoming a lot friendlier lately. In the past few weeks she had gleaned a little more about him. She knew his uncle Harry was a bookie, and although he had been disappointed Paul didn't want to join the business, he had paid the fees for Paul to go to Art College. To keep himself out of debt, Paul had various jobs - waiter, courier, bar work - and still managed to find time to paint. He had left London and come to Sidmouth two years ago. His uncle had lent him the money for the deposit to buy the studio. He hoped one day he would sell enough paintings to pay him back.

'It must be hard juggling a job and bringing up a child on your own.' Paul said, breaking into her thoughts.

The question took her by surprise and she wondered what he was getting at. She stared at him, but his gaze was open and guileless. She realised she was overreacting. 'Terry and Alison have been brilliant. I couldn't have coped without them.'

'Does Amy's father not help?'

'No,' she said curtly.

'Sorry,' he apologised, 'that was out of order.'

She shrugged, 'that's okay.'

'You're not a bit like the mental picture I had of you from talking to Terry. He told me that you were a wildly uncontrollable teenager.'

Laura giggled. 'He was exaggerating. I wasn't that bad. I did dye my hair once, bright green.'

Paul laughed. 'I can't imagine it; you must have changed so much. Become . . . .'

'What, dull, boring?'

Paul shook his head. 'No, never that; you're gentle and caring. I see you with Amy and I'm full of admiration for the way you are with her. I guess being a mother changed you.'

Laura felt a slow flush reach up from her neck to her cheeks. 'Having Amy has made a difference in my life,' she agreed.

She feared the next question was going to be about Amy's father again, but fortunately a customer appeared and she was saved from answering. Paul left shortly afterwards. It was the most personal conversation she had ever had with him.

The April day was cloudless, the blue sky a welcome change after a week of rain. After she had put Amy down for her afternoon nap Laura went into the garden to hang out the washing. It wasn't much of a garden, long and narrow with grass full of brown patches, dandelions and moss. Even though Alison had made an attempt to brighten the place with pots of winter pansies, it didn't detract from the broken grey paving slabs stacked high together with junk that Terry kept promising to get rid of. Rusty parts of cars, an old lawn mower; an assortment of discarded household items; broken chairs and a lumpy mattress. Leaning against the wall were two blue and white striped deckchairs that she thought looked suspiciously like the ones lined up on the Esplanade. Alison complained constantly that it looked like a scrap merchant's yard. Incongruously amongst the junk, a magnolia tree, now in bud, had survived; soon its pink blossom would spread a little beauty.

Although it was Saturday, Laura was alone. Alison and Terry were both working. It was quiet and peaceful and the feel of the weak sun on her face evoked memories of her childhood and her mother telling her to watch her complexion, the sun was bad for her fair skin.

She wondered where her mother was now and how she could have discarded her, her only daughter. She thought of Harriet and how she didn't want Amy. *How could a mother do that?* It was the cruellest thing in the world to abandon your child. She knew she could never leave Amy, no matter what the circumstances, and she wasn't even her birth mother.

Laura pegged the last towel on the line to flap gently in the light breeze, and returned to the kitchen, her thoughts deep and troubled.

Ten minutes later a voice said. 'Any chance of a cuppa?'

Laura was startled to see Paul standing in the kitchen doorway. Paul had used the back entrance, but she had been so engrossed in her thoughts she hadn't heard the click of the gate latch or his footsteps on the path.

'Sorry if I startled you. Terry said it was all right to come over.'

'Terry's not here.'

'I know.'

Laura frowned.

'I came to see you.'

'Oh.'

'Do you mind?'

'No, of course not.' She rose and filled the kettle. 'Coffee?'

'Please.'

Laura concentrated on making the drink as Paul pulled out a chair and sat down. She felt curious. 'Was it about anything special?'

Paul lowered his gaze looking suddenly uncomfortable. 'I was wondering – well actually I have no right to ask but - well I was wondering if you would pose for me?'

'What!'

'I need a model. I want to try my hand at portraits. You have such wonderful hair and your bone structure is excellent. Only thing is I can't pay you much.'

Laura gasped. 'You want to paint *me*?' The question was so unexpected that Laura dropped her mug; the broken china shattered sending a pool of coffee over the floor.

'Sorry,' Paul apologised. He jumped up and began picking up the broken pieces. Laura fetched a dustpan and brush and a cloth.

'Bad idea, huh.'

'No I'm just surprised, well flattered really.'

'So will you do it?'

'Yeah, sure.'

'Great, shall I make you another coffee?'

Paul's studio was above the shop. She arrived the following week on Sunday afternoon. Terry and Alison had been excited when she told them.

'It's no big deal,' she had said casually. 'He's only using me to practise on.'

'Don't be so dismissive,' Alison scolded. 'He's very good. You should be thrilled he's asked you. I wish he'd ask me.'

'Nah you're far too ugly,' Terry grinned.

Alison threw a tea-towel at him and chased him round the kitchen. Amy, sitting in her high-chair, squealed with delight and clapped her hands.

Laura had a sudden thought. 'I hope he doesn't want me to take my clothes off.'

Terry guffawed. 'Don't be silly, he's not like that.'

Laura rang the shop door bell as he had instructed and waited. She was nervous. She had washed and brushed her hair until it gleamed. Even though he had told her not to wear any make-up, she had put foundation on her nose to cover her freckles, and green eye shadow to make her eyes look bigger. She wanted to look her best.

Paul's initial smile turned to a frown when he finally answered the door. He was wearing the awful brown corduroy trousers with a creased white shirt, hanging loose. She tried not to giggle at his terrible dress sense.

Silently he took her through the shop to the back, and up a flight of stairs.

The room surprised her. Large and square, with a big window that flooded the room with light, the studio was bright and sunny.

Canvases of various sizes were stacked against a wall and the stench of oil paint filled her nostrils.

Before she had time to take in any more, Paul indicated to a sink in the corner. 'Wash your face please.'

'What!'

'I said no make up. I need a natural look.'

Her hackles rose at his tone. She was about to refuse, to tell him to forget it, she didn't need this, but already he was setting up an easel.

Feeling childishly annoyed, she washed her face.

'There please.' He indicated a chair so that she was facing him with her back to the window.

'How many times will I have to come here?' she asked knowing her voice sounded churlish.

Paul didn't seem to notice. 'Just this once,' he said. He was busying sketching. 'Can you tilt your head a little to the left?'

She complied trying not to sigh. A please would have been nice.

It took an hour; an hour when she wasn't allowed to move or talk. She was dying for a coffee but she guessed that was out of the question.

She rose stiffly. 'Can I see?'

'Not until it's finished,' he said, throwing a paint-smeared cloth over it.

'I'd better go then.'

He looked at her, his brown eyes glinting with a sudden hint of amusement. 'Sorry,' he said. 'You're a good model.'

As an apology it was poor. Laura smiled. 'Thanks.'

'You must think I'm very rude.'

Laura shrugged. She wanted to deny it but somehow she couldn't get the words out.

He grinned suddenly and his whole face changed, making him look gentler, warmer. This time his smile was so infectious she thought it was a pity he didn't smile more often.

'It's okay,' she said, softening towards him.

'I don't talk to people much, I prefer it that way. It makes me forget the art of conversation, though.'

She saw a flicker of loneliness in his eyes that shook her. Without giving herself time to consider the wisdom of it, she said impulsively. 'Would you like to go out for a drink sometime?'

'With you?'

It was not the answer she was looking for. If he refused she would be mortified. 'No big deal, just a drink.'

'In The Ship?'

'No, not where I work, somewhere else, there are loads of pubs in Sidmouth.'

He seemed to be considering it. 'Okay,' he said at last.

'I have next Saturday night off.'

'Right.'

He turned back to his easel and she let herself out. As she walked back to Terry's she wondered if she had made the most awful mistake. It was going to be hard going next Saturday.

PART THREE

Chapter Twenty-Seven

Harriet felt the water closing in over her head. She tried to fight the blackness but the water was so heavy. Her legs wouldn't move in the direction she wanted them to. Fear engulfed her as she remembered she couldn't swim; she had always been terrified of water.

A huge shark with its jaws wide open was heading towards her. She could see white razor-like teeth in its great cavernous hole of a mouth. She tried to push it away but her arms felt leaden. The shark was enormous; a great bulk of shining silver, and it was getter closer. She struggled to breathe, to fight against the horror of being eaten alive. She had to get away but she couldn't move; her legs were pinned down. She was about to die and there was nothing she could do about it. If only she could scream for help.

'Harriet can you hear me. Harriet, wake up.'

Harriet opened her eyes slowly, the horror of the shark still so real that the fear was still with her. Where was she? Was she not in the sea?

'Thank God!' Someone was stroking the back of her hand. A face was hovering over hers.

Jeremy.

The terror receded. She stared blankly at him before her lids closed again. It was such an effort to stay awake.

'Harriet, Harriet,' Jeremy's voice had a desperate ring to it. He squeezed her hand. 'Wake up.'

She felt the waves lapping again. 'Danny,' she cried out in despair.

When she came round again she could hear them talking.

'She definitely spoke,' Jeremy was saying adamantly. 'I didn't dream it.'

'I'm sure you didn't.' A stranger's voice. 'And it was only one word, Danny?'

'Yes. It's so frustrating, doctor.' Jeremy sounded upset. 'I thought she was back with me and now she's gone again.'

'Hello, Harriet, this is Doctor Andrew Kingsley. Can you hear me?'

She wanted to respond but it was too much effort. She was so very, very tired.

Doctor Kingsley was saying curiously. 'Who is this Danny?'

Jeremy sounded angry now. 'Daniel Pembroke, her employer.'

'I seem to remember him coming to see her on the day after the accident.'

Danny had been to see her!

'I didn't know that,' Jeremy muttered sourly.

Kingsley touched his shoulder. 'You have to be patient,' he said, 'it's encouraging that the signs are there that she will eventually come out of this unless . . . '

'What?' Jeremy sounded worried.

Andrew Kingsley hesitated, sounding concerned. 'Unless there is some reason why she doesn't *want* to return to us; some private pain that she doesn't want to feel again, something that, if she returned, she would have to deal with.'

'Like what?'

'It could be anything. Was she in any kind of difficulty before the accident? Anything she was finding hard to cope with?'

'I've no idea; we were - um - separated as I told you.'

'But you did say it was amicable,' Andrew said tentatively.

'Oh yes, we're still good friends. In fact we were planning to get back together.'

Liar, liar, she wanted to scream.

'Good,' Andrew said. 'Keep talking to her; let her know how much you love her.'

Jesus!

'I will.'

'Is there still no chance of her parents coming?'

'No, like I said I telephoned her father, Bill, in Canada; her mother, Elaine, has Alzheimer's.'

Her mother! Oh God.

'Such a pity.'

'Yes.' Jeremy agreed. 'Bill really wanted to come but he couldn't leave his wife. There was no one else to look after her.'

She heard footsteps as the doctor left. Jeremy took hold of her hand. Someone else came into the room.

'Any news?'

Abigail.

'Not yet.' She felt Jeremy's grip tighten on her hand, she wanted to pull away.

'I'll forgive her everything if she will only wake up,' Jeremy was saying. 'It wasn't her fault, you know. Pembroke seduced her with his money, buying her jewellery, taking her abroad.'

Abigail sniffed. 'I can't believe you're prepared to take her back.'

'She's my wife.'

'You're a fool, Jeremy. If she does ever recover she won't come back to you.'

'She will. I'm all she's got now. Pembroke won't want her now, not with these injuries.'

'Any news on the child?'

'No,' Jeremy grunted.

'I can't believe that you lied about it, that you told everyone it was in Canada,' Abigail said. 'If something has happened to it you could be in trouble.'

Her baby. They were talking about her baby.

'Pembroke knows the truth, except he won't tell me.'

'You should have let me deal with him.' Abigail said.

'That wouldn't have done any good. Abby, why doesn't she wake up?'

Jeremy was crying.

Fuck, there was no way she was going to open her eyes.

Harriet moved her head very slowly. It hurt to move it. Her gaze gradually took in the pale blue curtains, the white walls; the strange looking machine at her bedside. At last her eyes focused on Doctor Kingsley.

Jeremy and Abigail had left ages ago and now the doctor was here again.

'Where am I?' Her mouth was dry and the words sounded rasping.

'In Cheltenham hospital.'

'What happened?'

'You crashed your car. Don't you remember?'

She raised her arm very slowly and touched her face. There were ridges on her cheeks. She explored further, felt the soft gauze of bandages around her head. 'I got hurt?'

'Yes. Don't worry about that, the main thing is you're alive.'

'How long have I been here?'

'Six months.'

'My God!'

She listened carefully as Andrew Kingsley explained about her injuries, about re-setting her jaw and her nose. He said that unfortunately her left knee had also suffered and she might be left with a limp, but until she was on her feet they couldn't assess the damage properly.

She was a cripple. Panic washed over her. She wanted to curl up and cry her heart out.

'I need to go to the loo,' she had said wanting him gone, wanting to be alone.

'Don't worry about that you have a catheter in.'

So there was no escape. Unable to meet his gaze, she stared down at her hands, clutched tightly together, and felt sick to the pit of her stomach.

Andrew's hand covered hers. 'You'll be fine, Harriet.'

She nodded numbly, not believing him. She was scarred for life. It would have been better if she'd died.

Andrew seemed determined to keep her positive. 'It could have been worse; at least you're alive. And your face can be repaired with reconstructive surgery.'

She wanted to scream. She closed her eyes, hoping it was a bad dream, a nightmare, but when she opened them again she was still in the hospital room.

'What about my knee, what if I can't walk? What if I'm confined to a wheelchair?'

'It won't come to that, a walking stick possibly. Stop worrying until we know the extent of the damage.'

A walking stick! It just got better and better.

She stared at him intently. 'Was anyone else injured in the accident?' She was almost too frightened to learn the answer.

'No. You were alone.'

She was about to say, what about Danny, what about my baby, but some instinct held her back. She frowned. 'There was no other car there?'

'Not as far as I know.'

Was her memory playing tricks? She struggled to clarify her thoughts. On the night of the crash Danny was chasing her – wasn't he? He had Amy with him.

'Are you sure?'

'Yes. I don't know much about the accident except you'd hit a tree. There was a bad storm that night, a tree had fallen across the road, it was suggested that you'd hit it before veering off the road. Your car plummeted down an embankment and burst into flames. You were flung clear and they found you unconscious in the undergrowth.'

Harriet touched her face again. 'How did I get so - so badly injured?'

'Apparently you'd gone through the windscreen with tremendous force.'

'And there was no other car involved?'

'No. Why, did you think there was?'

'It's a bit hazy,' Harriet said.

'Not surprising, you've been in a coma for months, you can't be expected to remember every detail immediately.'

Harriet nodded. She would leave it for now, wait until she felt stronger, but something was not right.

She felt the ridges of her scars. 'Do I look terrible?'

'We can concentrate on that later, when you're stronger, surgery perhaps on the nose . . . '

'Oh God, is it that bad?'

'Please relax. Our resident surgeon, Miles Haverstock, is excellent. And then later on perhaps skin grafting. We want to make you even more beautiful than you were,' Andrew smiled encouragingly.

'How do you know what I looked like?'

'Your husband showed me a photograph of you.'

Jeremy. Why had he persistently stayed at her bedside? Surely he didn't believe they had a future. She thought she had made it clear after Amy was born. She wanted Danny. He had been to see her; he must still care about her.

'Can I have a mirror? I want to see for myself,' she said dispiritedly.

'Later – we need to get some tests done.'

'What sort of tests?'

'Just routine, to make an assessment, nothing to worry about.'

The door opened and a nurse entered.

'Ah, Sally, Mrs Malin is to go to X-ray.'

'Yes, Doctor.'

Andrew turned to Harriet. 'I'll see you later,' he said.

Harriet watched the door for several seconds after he'd gone. Slowly she raised a hand to her face again, feeling the hard raised flesh. Why hadn't he let her have a mirror? She must look worse than she imagined. She turned her gaze to the nurse, searching for a sign of abhorrence; there was none.

'You're lucky having Andrew Kingsley,' Nurse Sally Pearson smiled as she pushed a wheelchair close to the bed. 'He's gorgeous isn't he?'

Harriet didn't answer. She was not interested in the gorgeous Doctor Kingsley; she had more important things to worry about. Six months she had been unconscious. Where was Danny now? Where was her baby?

The X-rays and tests tired her. She slept and woke later in the afternoon, to find Jeremy sitting by the window reading a

170

newspaper. As she stirred he lowered the paper immediately and came to her side, pulling up a chair. 'How are you feeling, love?' His smile was anxious as he caressed her hand.

'What are you doing here?'

'I'm your husband, where else would I be?'

Harriet removed her hand from his. 'I feel so weird, scared. Doctor Kingsley says I've been here for over six months, is that really true?'

'Yes. You've had everyone worried to death. You're back with us now and that's all that matters.'

'Dr Kingsley says you've been here all the time.'

'Of course I have.'

'I thought we were separated.'

'Only temporary,' Jeremy said, clearly hoping she wouldn't remember.

'Tell me the truth, how bad do I look?'

'Your face can be repaired, they can do wonders these days.' Jeremy said gallantly.

Harriet sighed. 'No one will let me have a mirror.'

'All in good time. You need to get well and strong first. Then I can take you home.'

'Home?'

Jeremy looked pleased with himself. 'I've moved back into the house. I cleaned up all the mess. You'd left it in a hell of a state. Never mind it's all clean and tidy now, ready for you. Now, you're not to worry about a thing. I'm going to take care of you.'

'How did you get into the house?'

He flushed. 'I – er – I kept a key.'

She was too dispirited to be angry but later she would make sure he gave it back. 'What about your job?' she asked listlessly.

'They let me go. I couldn't concentrate, not with you being so ill. Don't worry I'll soon get another, no problem.'

She wanted to tell him that she couldn't bear the thought of living with him again but this was not the time. Later, when she was stronger, she would make it clear that they had no future together. Instead she asked. 'Do you know where Amy is?'

'No.'

'Has Danny got her?'

Jeremy's face darkened. 'No.'

A sudden thought struck her. She leaned back against the pillow. 'She was killed wasn't she?'

'What are you talking about?' Jeremy frowned.

'She was killed in the crash and you're too afraid to say.'

Jeremy's voice was gentle. 'She wasn't killed, Danny has taken her somewhere. I've no idea where. I tried to find out, but he won't tell me.'

'You've spoken to him?'

'Just briefly, on the phone,' Jeremy's voice was scathing now. 'He denied he was Amy's father.'

Harriet's spirits sank. Of course Danny would not have admitted anything to Jeremy. Even so it was hard to hear him deny his child.

'I need to see Danny. I need to ask him about Amy,' she said.

Jeremy's eyes were full of jealousy. 'I don't like you having anything to do with that bastard. I'll find her.'

Harriet shook her head. 'Please let me deal with this.'

'You're not going back to him are you?' Jeremy glowered.

If only. 'No,' she said.

'Thank God. I have forgiven you, you know. We'll forget it ever happened, it will be a new beginning for us; maybe we can start a family. If we can't find Amy then we can have a baby of our own.'

'Jeremy I . . . '

'No, don't thank me now. You get some rest. We'll talk later.'

'Actually, I would like to sleep now, I'm really tired.' Harriet closed her eyes.

Jeremy rose. 'Of course, darling. I'll come back tomorrow. It's so wonderful you've recovered. It's been such – such a traumatic. . . ' Jeremy bent and kissed her closed eyelids.

As soon as he had left Harriet opened her eyes. Her shoulders slumped. She had so many questions and no one had the answers.

She slept badly that night. The flashes that came in her dreams seemed to have little to do with her. The scenes were a confusing mixture of bright flashing lights and deep dark woods and once she thought she heard a baby crying.

Chapter Twenty-Eight

Harriet studied the newspaper intently. At her request, Nurse Sally had bought her an old copy from the Gloucester Echo office. It told her little. The report only mentioned her. It was very strange. Her memory was a little fuzzy but she was certain Danny had been there that night. She remembered being outside Danny's house, and then being in her car, angry and tearful because he wouldn't help her. She closed her eyes, pushing herself to remember the drive home. In flashes of clarity she saw the dark lane, the windscreen wipers swishing against the torrential rain. Danny was chasing her – he had Amy with him – she heard herself screaming. And then nothing.

She was sitting up in bed the following day when Andrew Kingsley entered her room. Yesterday she had seen her face for the first time and nearly fainted with shock. The face in the mirror didn't seem to belong to her; more like something from a horror movie. She wondered how Jeremy; how the nurses and Andrew could look at her without flinching. Andrew had told her that her face could be repaired but she had grave doubts.

'How did you get on?' he asked now, indicating the newspaper.

'There's not much to go on. It merely mentions a storm and the accident caused by a fallen tree.'

'I did warn you,' Andrew agreed, 'but you seem to think there should be more to it.'

It was tempting to confide in him, but she held back. Somehow she had to find out about her baby, but not this way. Only Danny could tell her that.

The nurse brought a telephone to her bedside. She dialled the perfumery number quickly before she lost her nerve. 'Mr Pembroke please,' she said when it was answered.

'Who shall I say is calling?'

'A customer.'

Danny came on the line. 'Good afternoon, how can I help you?'

To hear his voice made her want to cry. She steeled herself to stay calm. 'Hello, Danny,' she said huskily.

'Harriet.'

'Yes.'

'You're awake. That's wonderful, wonderful. Are you okay?'

'Not really. Danny we need to talk. Come and see me tomorrow, in the afternoon, Jeremy won't be here then.'

'Is that wise?' A wariness had crept into his voice and she gritted her teeth in frustration.

'You were my employer, you have a right to visit me.'

'I realise that but . . . '

'Tomorrow, Danny. *Be here.*'

Harriet raised her eyes from the magazine she was reading as the door opened. Danny edged sheepishly into the room.

'Is it okay to come in?'

'Danny!' Relief made her cry out his name. It was nearly five o'clock and she had given up hope that he would come.

Danny moved slowly towards the bed. He bent and kissed the top of her head. 'How are you?'

The tender gesture, the obvious concern surprised her.

'Not good,' she managed a weak smile as she touched her face, 'this hurts like hell. My knee is smashed. I might be crippled for life.'

'I'm so sorry. The main thing is that you're alive, though.' He pulled up a chair and sat down.

'Are you glad about that, that I'm alive?' Her voice trembled.

'Of course I am,' he looked genuinely shocked, 'what a thing to say.'

'You weren't hurt at all?'

'No I was lucky.'

'You *were* at the accident, though, I hadn't imagined it.'

'Umm yes I was there.'

Harriet watched his uneasiness. 'I can't remember much about that night. Flashbacks now and then. I remember that I was driving too fast because I was trying to get away from you.'

'You'd dumped the kid on me, remember.'

'My mind's still a bit muddled.'

'Understandable.'

'What I don't understand is why there was no mention of you or Amy in the newspaper report?' she asked.

Danny ran his hand over his face. 'I left before anyone arrived. I had the child to sort out.' He sounded defensive.

'You didn't wait for the ambulance? *You left me to die!*'

'I thought you were already dead.'

'Even so, you could have waited.'

'Don't be like this, Harriet. What good would it have done to get our names linked in the papers?'

Harriet sighed and let it go.

A silence lay uncomfortably for several seconds.

'Danny, where - where is our daughter?' She held her breath, dreading the answer.

Danny shifted on the chair. 'I was distraught. I didn't know what to do.'

'What do you mean?'

'I did it for the best, you have to believe that. I had to act quickly.'

'*Just tell me.*'

'She's being taken care of. I couldn't take her home, you have to understand that.'

'Was she hurt?'

'Of course not, what makes you think that?'

'When Jeremy said no one knew what had happened to her and that you wouldn't tell him anything, what was I supposed to think? I thought maybe your car had crashed as well and she was injured.'

'I didn't crash. I wasn't driving as fast as you.'

'Thank God for that.' Harriet took a deep breath. 'Where is she then?'

Danny hesitated for a moment. 'With someone I know in Devon.'

'Right. I suppose they'll want me to have her back when I get out of here. I hope they realise that it won't be for some time. I couldn't cope with her, not yet.' Harriet felt herself growing agitated. Her relief that Amy was okay was overshadowed by the thought of having to care for her.

'Actually I've had her adopted.'

'*Adopted!* How did you do that? - I mean surely . . .'

Danny interrupted. 'No one thought you'd recover. I did what I thought was best. I suppose I could have approached Jeremy, although I doubt very much he would have wanted her, or I could have had her taken into care. I didn't think either option was appropriate.'

Harriet winced at the slight sarcasm in his tone.

'I had to make a decision and quickly.' Danny sounded defensive now, obviously misinterpreting her reaction and trying to justify what he has done.

'I'm sorry,' Harriet apologised. 'I can see that you only acted for the best. You did right. I can't understand how you managed it without my permission though?'

Danny moved uncomfortably. 'I forged your signature on the papers.'

Harriet was silent as she digested this. She was sure the adoption process was more complicated then signing some papers. It seemed strange that Danny could give away her child without any consultation from her. Something was not quite right. Still, she supposed, in the circumstances, if they really thought she was going to die . . . she wouldn't dwell on it.

She felt a twinge of guilt that she was so relieved. Briefly she wondered if Amy would ever learn about her. What would her new parents tell her when she grew up? Would she feel abandoned and unloved that her mother had not wanted her?

She sighed heavily. 'You were quite right, it was the only way. It was fortunate you found someone willing to take her so quickly.'

'Yes it was.'

She looked at him, saw his discomfort and wondered what he was hiding. Well, she wouldn't question him. She couldn't deal with it right now. Maybe later when she was stronger, she would probe deeper and get the truth.

'What will you do when you leave here?' Danny steered the conversation to safer ground.

Harriet gave a derisive laugh. 'Jeremy has promised to look after me. Apparently, despite what I've done, he still loves me.'

'That's good isn't it?'

'I suppose so.'

Harriet touched his hand. 'What about you? Do you still love me?'

'Of course I do.'

He sounded sincere but she couldn't be sure. 'After I get out of here can we be together again? I mean without the baby it should – well we could - I mean . . .' she floundered as she saw the look in Danny's eyes.

'Let's wait and see shall we? It's a bit awkward.' Danny looked regretful. 'You concentrate on getting better. Now I must go.' Danny rose to leave with obvious relief.

Harriet looked at him, desperately wanting him to hug her. He said he loved her and she clung to that small comfort.

'Take care, Harriet.' Danny reached over to kiss her again. It was only a fleeting brush of his lips against her hair.

'Will you come again?'

'Of course.'

'Bye, Danny,' Harriet closed her eyes and waited until she heard the door softly shut before opening them again. Tears squeezed out from under her eyelids and she buried her head in her hands and sobbed.

Harriet had another visitor later that day. She did not, at first, recognise the woman, who seemed ill-at-ease.

'Hello, Harriet.'

Harriet groaned inwardly. 'Hello, Abigail.'

'I'm sorry about your face; it's a terrible mess.'

Harriet laughed mirthlessly. 'Subtlety was never your strong point.'

'I say what I think,' Abigail snapped, 'I always have done. No point in doing anything else.'

Harriet stared at her, unable to think of an answer.

Abigail fiddled with the wooden handles of her handbag, a huge tapestry affair that Harriet remembered.

'Jeremy tells me that you two are getting back together.'

'Does he?' Harriet shrugged diffidently.

'I've come to ask you a favour.'

'Oh.' This was a surprise. Abigail was not usually prone to putting herself under anyone's obligation.

Abigail's gaze was firm. 'I want you to tell him that you've changed your mind; that you want a separation. If it was at all possible I would suggest a divorce but I can't encourage him to commit such a sin.'

It was tempting to tell her that a divorce was exactly what she had in mind, yet perversely she said. 'Why would I do that?'

'You don't love him, you never have. It broke his heart when you split up.'

'You were happy though that we parted, I mean you never liked me.'

Abigail flushed. 'That was because I knew you were never right for him. I knew you'd hurt him, and you did. I couldn't bear to see him so miserable.'

Harriet sighed. She had forgotten how possessive Abigail was about her brother. It always annoyed her. She thought Abigail's adoration of Jeremy was unhealthy.

Abigail said earnestly. 'He still thinks he loves you, but it's only pity. He feels sorry for you, he thinks that you'll need him now that your fancy man has ditched you, but it won't last. In a few months you'll be off again with someone else and I'll have to pick up the pieces all over again.'

Harriet said crossly. 'I don't think I'll be off with someone else as you so crudely put it, not in my state. Who'll give me a second glance with a face like this?'

'What are you saying, that you intend staying with Jeremy for the rest of your life?'

'I might.'

'Don't make me laugh.'

'Whether I stay with Jeremy or not, that's my business, it's nothing to do with you.'

'Yes it has, he's my brother. I care about him. I won't stand by and see you destroy him.'

'That's a bit melodramatic. He's a grown man, he doesn't need you as his nursemaid.'

'You're a callous, unfeeling, wicked woman.' Abigail's face was white with anger. 'And one day you'll pay for what you're doing, you mark my words.'

'Please go, Abigail, I'm tired, I need to sleep.'

'You're making a big mistake if you don't leave Jeremy alone.' Abigail rose. 'A big mistake.'

Harriet watched her leave the room; she could almost feel the air bristling with her rage. She closed her eyes. Bloody hell, hadn't she enough to contend with without Jeremy's batty sister pestering her.

Chapter Twenty-Nine

'I passed Paul's shop yesterday and it was closed,' Alison said. 'Is everything okay?'

They were sitting on deckchairs in the garden enjoying the warmth of the May sunshine. Terry had gone with Kevin to a football match, Amy was asleep upstairs. Alison had her eyes closed so Laura was surprised when she spoke.

'Yeah, he's gone to London to exhibit some of his paintings.'

'Including the one of you?' Alison sat up in excitement.

'He says so,' Laura blushed.

'Wow. You could be famous.'

'Hardly.'

'Well, it was a lovely portrait.'

'Yeah,' Laura agreed. She had been thrilled with the finished portrait. He had made her look beautiful. When she had challenged him on it he had looked surprised. 'You are beautiful,' he had stated in a matter-of-fact voice.

Her heart had lurched with pleasure. Especially when he said he wanted it to be part of his exhibition so that he might get commissions to do other portraits. *Fancy her portrait being in a London gallery!*

Somehow he had managed to make her hair look like burnished gold and her eyes the deepest green. She had always hated her hair, mainly because she had suffered the usual sneers at school, carrot-top and ginger-nut. She had once suggested to Alison that she should colour it, but Alison had been horrified. 'It's a gorgeous colour,' she had said, 'never, ever change it. Be proud of it.' After that she had felt better about it. Now seeing it as Paul had painted it made her think that Alison was right. She was proud of it.

After that first evening when they had gone for a drink, she had seen little of him. He had been busy getting his canvases ready for the exhibition.

Contrary to her expectations the evening had been pleasant. He asked her lots of questions about herself and she told him about the café and Brett and Nancy, taking care not to mention Danny or the perfumery.

He said little about himself. She had wanted to hear about the woman who had dumped him but she was afraid to ask. They were getting on really well and she didn't want to risk annoying him.

'You do like him don't you?' Alison probed now.

'Mmm,' she answered distractedly. She did like him, it was true, liked him a lot actually.

He might be infuriating and sometimes downright rude, but he was never boring or shallow. She suspected if she ever got to really know him, she could fall in love with him. It worried her. How could she possibly start a relationship, it would be unfair. She might long for love, but marriage was out of the question. She couldn't admit that Amy was not her child and she couldn't tell the truth without betraying Danny.

Even so she was happier than she ever thought possible. Amy was her life, the centre of everything she did, the pivot on which she existed, and if being in love with Paul put that in jeopardy, then she must curb her feelings.

She laughed to herself. Who was she kidding? The idea of Paul falling in love with her was just ridiculous.

Laura turned now to see Alison watching her, waiting for an answer.

'Yeah okay,' she admitted. 'I like him, but we're just friends.'

'Sure, right,' Alison grinned. 'Perhaps if you gave him a little more encouragement.'

'Don't start,' Laura warned.

'It's only that you seem to get on really well and he'd be a great dad for Amy.'

'Shut up!' Laura said.

'Still, early days yet …' Alison rose, laughing. 'I'll make some tea.'

Laura didn't move as she thought about Alison telling her how Paul would make a great father for Amy and for a moment she let herself dwell on the pleasure of the three of them being together as a family; then common-sense returned. It could never happen.

Laura eagerly opened her letter from Zoe. As always it was full of gossip about the village. However today's letter had some startling news that filled her with fear.

'Harriet has finally recovered from her coma after all this time.'

Laura was shaking so much she couldn't finish the letter.

It took her an hour to pluck up courage to phone Danny. He sounded annoyed when he answered.

'Harriet's recovered hasn't she?' Laura said.

'Yes'.

'Why didn't you tell me?'

'What for?'

'She'll want Amy back now, won't she? I'm going to lose her,' Laura started to cry.

'Listen to me,' Danny said firmly. 'I've spoken to Harriet, I told her the child was adopted, she's fine with that, she can't care for her, she's too badly injured. There's nothing to worry about, believe me.'

Laura sniffed. 'Does she know it's me that has Amy?'

'She wasn't interested in who has got her.'

'Are you sure?'

'Positive. Laura, please don't worry.'

'Okay.'

'Are you receiving the money all right?'

'Yes, thank you.'

'Good. Goodbye then. And no more phone calls please.'

'Wait, there's something I need to know.'

'What's that?'

'Amy's birthday.'

'I can't remember.'

'Please Danny it's important.'

'September. It's September 10th.' The line went dead.

Laura replaced the receiver. She was not comforted by the call.

* * *

Laura reached Jacob's Ladder Beach and began to climb the zigzag walkway upwards. Small white clouds scudded across the sky, occasionally giving respite to the summer heat as they momentarily obscured the sun. The path was steep and she was out of breath pushing the pram. Her thoughts were troubled. She wasn't sure whether to believe Danny. Maybe she should contact Harriet, make sure she really didn't want Amy back. The danger in that was that Harriet might say she did. Then what would she do.

When she reached the top a welcome breeze lifted her hair. Raising her hand she shaded her eyes from the heat of the sun, and saw Paul in the distance. Sitting on the grass he was sketching the view of the ocean across to Ladram bay.

'Hi, Paul.'

Paul had returned from London yesterday, full of his exhibition, especially her portrait, which he said had caused a lot of interest and even some possible commissions.

'Laura.' He smiled at her. 'This is a nice surprise.'

'Am I disturbing you?'

'Not at all. I've finished.' He showed her the sketch.

'It's amazing how you get it so life-like.'

'Thanks.' He tucked the pad away and bent to Amy, who smiled at him broadly, showing her first tooth.

'I was hoping to see you,' he said. 'I wondered if I could take you out to dinner.'

Laura bit down on her lip. Dinner. That would move their friendship onto a more personal level. Much as she wanted that she knew she must refuse.

'I'm sorry,' she said regretfully, steeling herself. 'I don't think that's a good idea.'

Paul looked shocked. 'Why not?'

'I'm not interested in a serious relationship.'

'Hey, who said anything about a serious relationship? I only want to take you out to dinner to thank you for sitting for me.'

Laura flushed. She didn't know what to think now. Feeling foolish she said. 'Sorry.'

'So will you?'

'Okay yeah, fine, that will be cool.'

'Next Saturday?'

'Yeah.'

'Can I pick her up,' Paul said.

'What?'

'Can I pick Amy up and give her a cuddle.'

'Yes of course.'

She watched him jiggling Amy on his knee making her laugh. *He'll make a great dad,* Alison had said. She thought so too. She hadn't expected him to be interested in Amy, but he was a slave to her just like everyone else. This tender side to him bewildered her; what a contradiction he was.

'I'm moving into a flat,' she said.

'Are you, where?'

'Above Kevin's garage, he's letting me have it cheap if I do it up.'

'Fantastic.'

'I need my own space, need some privacy.'

Paul grinned. 'Right,' he said.

Oh hell, she must have given him the wrong impression. 'I mean Terry and Alison have been brill but it's time I moved out.'

'Of course,' Paul agreed, still smiling.

Her cheeks flushed. She turned to the picnic basket.

'They look good, I'm starving,' Paul said eyeing the sandwiches. 'I don't suppose you have any spare.'

'These *are* for you,' Laura grinned, handing him a plastic plate piled high.

'Thanks,' he bit hungrily. 'How did you know I'd be here?'

'Saw you pass the house earlier.'

'Ah so you're stalking me.'

'Do it all the time,' Laura laughed, taking Amy from him so he could enjoy his lunch.

'So when do you move?' he asked reaching for another sandwich.

'As soon as I've got it ready.'

'Need a hand?'

'Yeah, thanks, that'd be great.'

They walked back together, passing the Methodist church in the High Street. The doors opened and a flood of people spilt out followed by a bride and groom. They stopped to watch for a few moments.

'The bride looks gorgeous doesn't she,' Laura said chattily.

'Hmm,' Paul grunted.

She glanced at him, saw the sudden scowl on his face and wondered if the sight of the bride had upset him. He was obviously still harbouring feelings for the woman that had dumped him.

* * *

Thackeray's was in the village of Woodbury, twenty minutes drive away. With Paul's erratic driving, and the speed in which he took the bends on the country lane, Laura wondered if they would actually get there.

The grade 2 listed coach house had been internally modernised into a sophisticated French restaurant. Paul parked the Vauxhall Astra, taking up two spaces, and climbed out oblivious to her shattered nerves.

The restaurant was busy. 'Good job I booked,' Paul grinned as they were shown to a secluded table.

'I've never been here before, it looks dead expensive,' Laura whispered.

'Only the best for you, you are, after all, my star model.'

'I'm your only model,' Laura reminded him.

Paul grinned. 'Good point. Anyway, if I do ever get any more models none will be as good as you.'

'Stop it,' Laura giggled, and flushed with pleasure. 'I thought you had more commissions anyway.'

Paul pulled a face. 'I did but I turned them down.'

'No way! Why?'

'They weren't really subjects I wanted to do.'

Before she had time to question him further a waiter approached, handing them menus. Laura's heart sank. It was all in French. She was going to make a right fool of herself.

'Would you like a drink?' Paul asked.

Laura nodded. 'Coke please.'

'Wouldn't you prefer some wine?'

'Is that what you're having?'

'Yes. A nice Beaujolais I think.'

'Okay then.'

The waiter took the order and left. Paul studied the menu. Laura's eyes wandered around the glamorous room. Elegant and intimate, with red silk full-length drapes at the windows, the room was softly lit with single candles on every table. Red velvet walls held a mixture of Toulouse Lautrec paintings of the Moulin Rouge, and gilt-edged mirrors. Crystal chandeliers hanging from the ceiling enhanced the ambience of 19th century Parisian decadence. She was pleased Alison had lent her a black dress.

'Shall I order for us?' Paul said.

'Yes please,' she said gratefully.

She watched him as he ordered. His French was fluent, flawless. Another surprise.

'Where did you learn to speak French so well?' she asked after the waiter had departed.

'I spent a year in Paris after college.'

'Did you go there to paint? Were you a penniless artist living in an attic?'

Paul laughed. 'You've been watching too many movies. No, I went with a fellow student from the art academy. His parents owned a house over there. I went one summer . . .' Paul lifted his glass and took a large swallow. He suddenly looked sad.

'Go on,' Laura prompted.

'You don't want to hear about my boring life.'

'Oh I do,' Laura said earnestly, leaning across the table. 'I want
. . .'

She was interrupted by their starter arriving; a seafood platter
to share. They ate in silence, with only Laura giving occasional
gasps of delight at the food.

'Is it okay?' Paul looked anxious.

'Delicious,' Laura nodded.

Suspecting that the subject of France was painful to him Laura
said. 'Tell me more about your uncle Harry.'

Paul smiled. 'He was a character. I'd never met him until –
until my parents died.' Once again a shadow of sadness crossed
his face.

'Sorry, is it painful to remember that time.'

'Sometimes. I was only seven. They died in a house fire while
I was away on a school holiday in Hayling Island. Harry was my
mother's brother; they didn't approve of his lifestyle and I suspect
they would not have wanted me to live with him, but there was no
one else, both sets of grandparents were dead.'

'How awful for you.'

Paul gave a wry smile. 'The first time I saw him was at the
funeral. Harry was a huge man, six foot two with massive
shoulders. He seemed like a giant to me and I was so scared. He
took me home with him without saying a word. That first night
when he cooked the tea; sausages, bacon, eggs, fried bread and
black pudding, all swimming in grease, my stomach had heaved
and I couldn't eat it. I was sure Harry would be angry but he just
shrugged and ate it himself. "Waste not, want not," he had
grunted.'

The waiter came and cleared the plates and brought the main
course. Tender slices of duckling in an orange sauce, a tiny
mound of mashed potatoes with a sprig of mint and an artistically
arranged selection of mange tout and baby carrots.

'Good job we're not starving,' Paul leaned across and
whispered.

Laura grinned. She forked a slice of duck into her mouth.
'Umm it's yummy.'

Paul grunted and spread butter on his roll.

'Go on,' she said fascinated by his story.

'Later,' he said, 'otherwise this food will get cold.'

Caramelised pear *tartine* with ice cream followed and minuscule cups of strong black coffee. Paul paid the bill and tried not to appear shocked. 'Shall I pay half?' Laura asked.

'Certainly not.' Paul looked offended.

They drove back to Sidmouth and Paul stopped the car on the sea front. 'Fancy a walk and a bag of chips,' he suggested, 'I'm still hungry.'

Laura wasn't hungry at all but she liked the idea of a walk. They found a chip shop and headed for the promenade.

'You promised to tell me the rest,' Laura reminded him as she watched him pop a hot chip into his mouth.

Paul stopped and leaned on the railings, looking out to the sea. 'It's such a long time ago but I remember that night so vividly. Lying in that strange, unfamiliar bed it seemed to me my world had ended. I had tried all day to be brave, but in the dark I couldn't stop crying. Uncle Harry must have heard me sobbing my heart out. He came into my room and the bed had groaned under his weight. The smell of whisky on his breath had been overpowering. Harry had put a hand on my head and said gruffly. "Don't fret lad, we'll be okay, you and me." I could see he was as upset as I was and that helped a bit.'

'And were you all right?' Laura said, tears beginning to well up as she pictured the little lonely boy.

'Eventually. It was hard going. Harry hadn't a clue how to look after me. He was, after all, a bachelor in his fifties. To be fair he could have handed me over to social services, yet he didn't. He did his best. Mind you at the time I didn't appreciate it. I had to get myself up for school, cook my own tea and generally look after the both of us. Harry was so busy at the bookies, although he did take me to the football. He was an ardent West Ham supporter and we went to all the home games. Only now do I appreciate how hard it must have been for him and how generous to take on the responsibility of a small boy. Harry's kindness and patience have been limitless.'

'That's a wonderful story,' Laura said, 'sad but still wonderful.'

'Tell me about your childhood,' Paul said as they began to walk again.

'Not as interesting as yours,' Laura said, and told him about their father leaving and Nigel.

'Will you try again to find your mother?' Paul asked.

'Dunno. Maybe one day.'

'She doesn't know she's a grandmother, I take it?'

'No,' Laura shook her head and was glad of the dusk to hide her face.

'Terry said that you no longer see Amy's father, is that right?'

'I left him before Amy was born.'

Paul looked deep in thought. Laura watched him anxiously. 'What's the matter?' she asked eventually.

'Will he ever come back for Amy?'

'No. Why all these questions?'

'No reason. I wasn't sure if you were still involved with him, that's all.'

Laura swallowed hard. 'Well, I'm not,' she said uneasily.

They walked back to the car. 'I've enjoyed tonight,' Paul said.

'Me too.'

'Do you want to do it again sometime?'

'Umm, maybe.'

Paul gave her a puzzled look as he unlocked the car and started the engine. They drove in silence back to Terry's house. She got out, expecting him to drive off, but he cut the engine and walked with her to the door.

'Would you like to come in,' Laura said, 'I expect Terry and Alison will still be up.'

'I'd better not, it's late.'

'Thanks for a great evening.'

It seemed to her, as she remembered later, that what happened next was inevitable. She had no power to stop it. She watched nervously as Paul moved closer. Her whole body tensed at the sudden nearness of him, but she couldn't move away. He touched her cheek, letting his finger slide gently down to her mouth. He lifted her hand and pressed it to his chest. She felt his heart beating through his cotton shirt. He kissed her very softly, very briefly; then tilted his head back as if to gauge her reaction.

She raised her hand to his neck, to the base of his skull, letting her fingers stroke the fine hairs on his neck. Closing her eyes she let out a long quivering sigh. In the instant before they kissed again she felt an urge to say, I can't do this, I can't get involved with you, then she opened her eyes, saw Paul's tender gaze and her resolve slipped.

This time the kiss was long and lingering. When they moved apart she felt bereft.

'So will you?' he said.

'What?'

'Come out with me again.'

Chapter Thirty

Harriet took a last look around the hospital room that had been her home for the past eight months. Her belongings had been packed for hours and she was now waiting for an ambulance. Today she was going home and the idea scared her. She felt safe here where everyone was used to the sight of her. Her broken nose had been re-set and her jaw was now healed. The swelling on her face had gone, only an ugly scar remained. She felt vulnerable, especially as, until her knee was strong enough, she couldn't walk without the aid of a crutch. It humiliated her, struggling down the corridors like some old woman. The pitying glances, the offers of help, which she rejected abruptly, did nothing for her self-esteem.

Sometimes, in her own room, where no mirrors were allowed, she tried to forget her disfigurement and feel normal. She thought constantly of Danny; of his visit when he told her that he loved her. Even though he had not come again she clung on to that, replaying the scene in her head over and over.

She was glad her parents weren't here to see her. Jeremy had told her about her mother's illness and she felt sad that they had not been reconciled. No chance of that now with her mother ill. Harriet blinked back tears. She thought back to that last day she had seen them. That awful row.

It had been the night before she was to go to uni when they told her they were selling up their house in Worthing and moving to Canada. It was the first she had heard of it.

'But it's my home,' she had cried, 'where will I go in the holidays?'

'You can come to Canada.'

'As if I can afford that on my student loan.'

'Surely you have friends you can stay with?' It was their cold-hearted attitude that had upset her. She knew why of course; they had never been the same with her since that business with Uncle Cyril.

'Why are you going?' she had demanded angrily.

'Cyril has started his own company out there. He wants your Dad to be his partner.' Elaine sounded proud that her brother had requested Bill to join him.

'I can't believe you're going with him after . . . '

'Harriet! Don't start all that again.'

'You won't admit it, will you? You take his word against mine, your own daughter.'

Elaine had turned away, refusing to discuss it. Harriet had been so angry with her. It had been so unfair. Why couldn't they see what he was like, what he tried to do to her?

She had been thirteen and had tried to tell them that for months Cyril had been leering at her, putting his hand on her bottom, brushing against her breasts at every opportunity. Then one night he had come into her bedroom and tried to force himself on her. Terrified, she had managed to fight him off. The following morning she had told her mother, expecting outrage. Elaine had not believed her.

'Don't be ridiculous, you're making it up.' Elaine had been angry.

'I'm not. Why won't you believe me?'

'Because I know my brother and he would never do that.'

'Well he did.'

Nothing more was ever said. Harriet knew it was useless to try and make them see she was telling the truth. Fortunately Cyril emigrated shortly afterwards.

Harriet sighed now at the memory.

Nurse Sally Pearson entered to tell her the ambulance was waiting. Nodding her thanks she bent to pick up her bags. 'Do you want a hand?' Sally asked.

She was about to automatically refuse but she knew she

couldn't manage everything. 'Please,' she smiled. She had said goodbye yesterday to Andrew and the rest of the nurses. She would have to come back for physio and check-ups, but now she was going home.

Harriet sat on the sofa in the lounge and stared at the wall. She let her thoughts drift to the future.

Somehow she had to get Danny back. It was only the thought of them being together that had kept her from total despair over the past few weeks. Danny loved her, he had said so. Even though she was a cripple, disfigured, he loved her. And she loved him. She wanted him and she was determined to have him.

First she had to deal with Jeremy. He would be here soon, rambling on about how wonderful the future was going to be, and how he would get Amy back for her. 'Amy's been adopted,' she had told him. He had smiled, a strange knowing smile, and said he knew how to get her back when she was ready. She couldn't seem to convince him that she didn't want Amy. Not ever. She was glad Danny had given her away. She didn't think she could bear to look at the child and not hate her for the pain she had caused.

She needed Danny. She missed him so much. She ached to see him. Now that she was home, and the problem of Amy taken care of, there was nothing to stop them being together. She intended to make sure that they were. Danny wanted that as much as she did, it was just that he was too weak to make it happen. She wasn't though, she was strong, and she would do whatever it took, and soon.

Meanwhile, she had a few hours alone before Jeremy got back, to make her plans.

The house was clean and tidy, which surprised her. Jeremy was not usually a tidy person. His efforts didn't please her. She had wandered into the room that had been Amy's, saw the nursery furniture exactly as she had left it and went out again, closing the door firmly. As soon as she could she would get rid of it all; perhaps then Jeremy would stop trying to find her daughter.

It was good to be home. In the sideboard she found just what

194

she was looking for. A half bottle of gin. She grabbed the bottle and a glass and returned to the sofa.

The hammering seemed to be in her head. As she roused herself she realised someone was banging on the front door. She opened her eyes wider; the room was in darkness and she wondered how long she had slept. Groaning, she staggered to her feet and slowly made her way through to the hallway.

'Who is it?'

'Jeremy.'

She let him in. 'Forget your key?'

'No, the safety catch was down on the lock. I've been trying to get in for ages.'

'Sorry, force of habit,' she smiled weakly.

He struggled into the kitchen clutching several bags of shopping. He stared at her, taking in her dishevelled appearance, and shook his head. 'You look terrible,' he commented, 'have you been drinking?'

'So what!' she growled.

'Do you think you should?'

'Don't preach; you're not my mother.'

Jeremy looked hurt, but she didn't care. 'I'm going to have a shower,' she said.

'Shall I help you upstairs?'

'For Christ's sake!' she snapped irritably. 'I can manage.'

When she returned downstairs Jeremy had cooked the dinner. Pushing the food around her plate she said. 'I'm going to look for a new job.'

The idea scared her to death and she knew it was going to take all her courage to face people, but she wasn't about to admit that to Jeremy. Her face bore a terrible scar down the left side; the skin puckered and ugly. It made her self-conscious and nervous of meeting people. The surgeon had suggested having skin grafting done, but she wasn't quite ready for the trauma of that.

'A job,' Jeremy looked horrified. 'It's far too soon. Besides there's no need, I told you I'll look after you.'

'I don't need looking after,' Harriet snapped. She knew she

195

sounded ungrateful, she couldn't help it; he was already irritating her.

'I want to.'

They ate in silence for a while. 'Do you want me to sleep in the spare bedroom?' Jeremy said.

'Yes.'

'Okay, no problem, I guess you need time to adjust.'

'Thanks. Actually I think I'll go up now, I'm shattered.'

'You've had a long day. Get some rest, I'll clear away.'

Jeremy rose and came to her side. He kissed her good cheek. 'Goodnight, darling. Don't worry about anything.'

Harriet made her way upstairs, trying to stem the tide of exasperation. Jeremy being helpful was almost as annoying as when he used to be carelessly untidy. 'I'm a bitch,' she thought to herself, 'an ungrateful bitch.'

'How did you sleep?' Jeremy asked at breakfast.

'Not bad,' she lied. She didn't want to confess she had lain awake for hours, remembering the happy times before her life had gone so drastically wrong.

Jeremy seemed cheerful. 'So what do you want to do today? Shall we have lunch out?'

'Okay.' After a moment she added thoughtfully. 'Would you take me somewhere first?'

'Anywhere,' he seemed pleased that he was needed.

'Thanks. There's a problem though, I'm not sure if I can get into a car again.'

'I can understand that. I promise I'll drive very slowly and carefully. Where do you want to go?'

'Hunters Lane.'

'Are you sure that's a good idea?'

'I need to go there.'

'Okay. We can have lunch somewhere nearby.'

'Fine,' she said distractedly.

Later, outside on the pavement, she leaned heavily on her crutch as they walked to where his new Ford Mondeo was parked close by.

'Nice car,' she commented. 'I'm surprised you can afford it though, without a job.'

'I had savings,' Jeremy said, turning away as she looked disbelievingly.

This was not the time to question it. As she stepped towards the car she felt her knees buckle. It was only Jeremy's supporting arm that saved her from falling. She was shaking badly.

'You don't have to do this,' he said worriedly.

'Yes I do, I must.'

It took every ounce of her self-control to slide into the front seat. Aware of Jeremy's worried glance she gritted her teeth and smiled at him. 'I'm fine, really I'm fine.'

Jeremy drove slowly and carefully, even so she felt the cold sweat of panic prickle at her skin and her mouth was dry.

They reached Hunters Lane half-an-hour later and as the car turned into the road, vivid flashes of that terrible evening came flooding back. Her heart began to race and she folded her arms around her body, hugging the panic to her.

'We can go back,' Jeremy said anxiously. 'You look terrible.'

'We're here now; it's round the next bend.'

Jeremy brought the car to a halt and Harriet eased herself out. Grabbing her crutch from the back seat, she hobbled slowly to the side of the road and stared down the embankment. Somehow she expected to see something, some evidence that her life had nearly ended here, but all she saw was a huge hollow in the ground where the lightning-struck tree had once been.

She wondered whether if she went down the embankment there would be some sign, some broken sapling or gouged bush, but she couldn't bring herself to venture down the slippery grass slope. From where she stood, there was no trace of the terrifying descent that had nearly cost her her life. She closed her eyes and felt again that frightening moment as the car plunged through the air, saw again the copse, illuminated by the headlight beams as they pierced the darkness, and remembered how her scream had ended suddenly as she was hurtled through the windscreen into blackness.

She opened her eyes, wiped her moist palms on the side of her trousers and took a deep breath.

Returning to the car she said. 'I can't face having lunch out, take me home.'

Later that afternoon Jeremy left to visit Abigail. The moment his car was out of sight, Harriet telephoned for a taxi. There was somewhere she needed to go, on her own.

Chapter Thirty-One

Harriet reached the house in Upper Wyre and asked the taxi driver to return in an hour. She walked slowly up the drive and knocked on the door.

Christine Pembroke answered almost immediately.

She faced the woman calmly. 'Is Danny in?'

Christine's eyes narrowed. 'No he's not.'

'Good. It's you I've come to see.'

Christine hesitated and then opened the door wider. 'You'd better come in.'

Harriet followed her through the wide hallway into a spacious lounge, beautifully furnished with dark brown leather sofas and chairs set against cream walls and a thick cream carpet. Christine indicated for her to sit on a low sofa. She ignored the gesture; she wanted to stand. She hobbled to the patio doors that led to a large conservatory. Turning slowly, she deliberately pulled back her headscarf, exposing her damaged face clearly and showing the ugly scar. She waited for Christine's reaction, for the look of revulsion or a horrified gasp, but Christine remained unmoved.

'What do you want?' Christine said coldly.

'Are you not repulsed by the way I look?' Harriet said ignoring the question.

Christine held her gaze. 'You look better than when I saw you last,' she said calmly.

Harriet was taken aback. 'Oh, when was that?'

'I visited you in the hospital,' Christine confessed, 'before you regained consciousness.'

'No one told me. Why did you come?'

'I was your employer. I needed to know the extent of your injuries. You were on maternity leave. I wondered what the likelihood of you returning would be before I asked Stephen to stay on permanently. I'm so very sorry about the accident.'

Harriet didn't believe her. The words were cold and unfeeling. 'That's why I'm here. I came to see if I can have my old job back?'

Christine looked startled. 'I hardly think under the circumstances . . . '

'You mean because of the way I look?'

'No. Because you have been having an affair with my husband.'

Christine's tone was harsh even though she remained calm. The woman's cool demeanour was unnerving. She had always suspected that Christine must have been aware, or at least had some suspicion. It was a shock to hear the words spoken out loud, to have her adultery flung in her face. No matter, it made what she had to say easier.

'How long have you known?' she asked quietly.

'Since the beginning.'

'Why did you never say anything?'

'I have my reasons. Besides you were only one of his many mistresses.'

Harriet flushed. 'I'm more than that to him. We love each other.'

Christine gave a derisive laugh.

Annoyed, Harriet held her gaze. 'It's true. We want to be together, and we could be if you would divorce Danny.'

Christine gasped. 'Why should I do that?'

'Danny and I are meant for each other. It's not as if you love him. I mean Danny said you only stayed married because of the business.'

'Is that what he told you?'

'Yes, and I could see for myself when I worked for you that you weren't close.'

'We are professional people; we don't bring our marriage into the business place. In any case, that gave you no right to have an affair. He was married to me, regardless of whatever way we choose to live.'

'You can't love him, not really, not like I do?' Harriet cried passionately.

Christine gave her a tired smile. 'He's my husband. I won't divorce him, not now, not ever.'

Harriet became annoyed. 'How can you still love him after what he's done to you?'

'What do you mean?'

'If you knew about our affair then you must have realised that Danny is the father of my baby.'

Christine's laugh was incredulous. 'You're lying. I know Danny. I know he would have made sure he never got you pregnant. He was always careful with his other mistresses. You were no different.'

Harriet guffawed. 'Believe me he did.'

The cool demeanour slipped a little. 'I don't believe you.'

'It's true. His name is on Amy's birth certificate.' There was no need to clarify it, to say that Danny had been shocked and angry when she had told him. Suffice to let Christine believe he had agreed.

Harriet was surprised to see how utterly shaken the other woman was. She faltered for a moment. Christine's pain was so palpable that she felt a tug of remorse, no longer certain that she should have told her. Danny had said that Christine would be devastated but she hadn't believed him, she thought it had just been an excuse.

'Oh God!' Christine sat down suddenly on a sofa.

'When I was pregnant did it not occur to you that Danny might be the father, you've already said you knew about our affair?'

'Maybe fleetingly, but I trusted Danny to honour his promise.' Christine's mouth trembled. 'Sorry. It's just that I can't believe Danny would he be so cruel, he knew how badly I always wanted a baby.'

'If it's any consolation he didn't want mine; he wanted me to have an abortion.'

'That doesn't surprise me. It's true he didn't want children. I never understood that. I'd hoped he'd want a son, someone to inherit the business, but Danny said he didn't care what happened after he was dead.'

Their eyes met and for a fleeting moment a look of empathy passed between them. Christine rose. 'Please excuse me for a moment.'

There was no time to reply before Christine hurried from the room. Feeling uncomfortable with Christine's distress, Harriet finally sat down, waiting for her to return. She had come here full of determination that she could persuade Christine to let Danny go. She had truly believed she didn't love him. That their marriage was one of convenience as Danny had led her to believe. However, according to Christine, they were still very much man and wife. The jealous feeling was all-consuming.

Five minutes passed before Christine came back. Her composure regained, Christine said calmly. 'Where is the child now?'

It wasn't the question Harriet had been expecting. 'According to your husband, Amy's been adopted.'

'Danny had her adopted!'

Harriet nodded. 'He came to see me after I'd recovered. I asked him where Amy was. I thought she might have died in the accident. He said he forged the adoption papers.'

'So your baby *was* with you when you crashed?'

'Not in my car, in Danny's.'

Christine's face was pale and strained. 'You had better tell me what happened,' she said.

Harriet's voice trembled as she recalled the details of that night. The confrontation, the chase and then the hazy recollection of the crash. Lowering her head she suddenly felt defeated and she started to cry. The emotional turmoil of reliving that night had left her feeling bruised. The knowledge that Danny had lied to her about his marriage was hard to accept.

She sensed Christine leave the room again. She stayed with her head buried in her hands until she could control her sobbing.

'Here drink this, it's camomile tea, it will soothe you.'

She hadn't been aware of Christine returning and she raised her head and took the cup, sipping gratefully. 'I'm sorry,' she said after a few moments.

'What you have told me explains a lot. But if Danny was at the accident, why didn't he get questioned by the police?'

'He left before they arrived,' Harriet shrugged.

'Before the ambulance came?'

'Yes.'

'My God!'

'He thought I was dead. He didn't want our affair to be made public.'

'Even so.'

'I don't blame him,' Harriet said stoutly.

Christine still looked pale. 'This has been such a shock. I had no idea of any of this.'

'Why do you stay with him?' Harriet asked curiously.

'That's my business.'

'I'm sorry, that was impertinent.'

Christine sighed heavily. 'It's not that easy for me to end our marriage. There's the business you see. I love it. I'm so proud of what we've achieved. It's become my life,' she gave a wry smile, 'my compensation for being childless. I tolerate Danny's indiscretions because divorce is unthinkable. Pembroke Perfumery would suffer. One of us would have to relinquish the partnership. I am not prepared to do that and neither is Danny. It would get very messy. You see I'm as much tied to the business as I am to Danny.'

Harriet took a tissue from her handbag and wiped her eyes. 'When I told him about the baby I thought he would marry me. I know he loves me. I thought he was just being weak in not asking you for a divorce. Danny doesn't like confrontation, he prefers the easy life. I expect you know that.'

'I know Danny loves women, he always has. His affairs have never worried me, it's just sex. I do feel betrayed though that I have missed out on being a mother.'

'You must hate me.'

Christine shrugged. 'Not really. Tell me, did you start the affair with him before you came to work for us?'

'Yes. We met in Bath. At first it was just a bit of fun. Then I fell in love with him. I didn't mean to, it just happened.'

They sat in silence sipping their tea.

'Aren't you angry that Danny gave away your baby?' Christine asked after a few moments.

With a very slight slump of her shoulders, Harriet said. 'It's for the best.'

Christine's eyes clouded with sadness. 'I don't think I could have done that. Why don't you want her?'

Harriet gave a harsh laugh. 'I can barely look after myself let alone a baby.'

'Is there no one to help you, what about your husband?'

'Jeremy left me when he knew about the baby.'

Christine gave her a puzzled look. 'I thought he was with you at the hospital.'

'He wants us to get back together.'

'And will you?

'No.'

'What about your parents?'

'They live in Canada, my mother has senile dementia. In fact they're not even aware of Amy's existence. We don't actually get on.'

'I see.'

The sound of the taxi car horn startled them. Harriet rose. 'I'd better leave. Please think about my job, I really need it.'

Christine looked at her coolly. 'And Danny, are you prepared to stop seeing him?'

The question shook her. She bit down on her lip. Was she prepared to give him up? Could she give him up? There seemed little hope of them ever being together and yet the thought of never seeing him again filled her with despair.

'I'm not sure I can,' she said honestly, 'but I'll try.'

Christine escorted her to the door. Neither spoke until Harriet was on the doorstep, when Christine said. 'If you see Danny, please don't tell him that I know about you and the child.'

Harriet looked into Christine's eyes, saw unbearable pain there, and for a moment regretted she had come here. 'All right,' she agreed.

'I want to be the one to confront him,' Christine explained, 'in my own time.'

Chapter Thirty-Two

The door bell rang unexpectedly one afternoon in August. Amy was having her afternoon nap, and Laura was grabbing a few moments to read her *Hello* magazine. The sweltering heat was unbearable, and even though she was only wearing a thin tee-shirt and shorts she felt the sweat trickling down her back.

She had moved into the flat a month ago, and still couldn't believe her luck in getting it. Although it was above the garage it had its own private front entrance.

She smiled to herself as she remembered how embarrassed Kevin had been about the state of the place. All it had needed was a good clean and a coat of paint.

'So what do you think?' Kevin had asked.

'It's perfect, if I can afford the rent.'

'The rent is minimal, you're Terry's sister. Just pay the utility bills, can you afford those?'

'Yes, of course. Wow! Thanks, but I'd like to pay you something.'

'It's really not necessary.'

'I don't want charity,' Laura bristled. She could easily afford the rent from the money Danny sent, not that she could admit that to anyone.

'Laura!' Kevin looked hurt. 'I thought we were friends.'

'Sorry. Thanks again. I'm really grateful.'

Kevin shuffled his feet and looked embarrassed. His face turned pink. 'Maybe we could go out for a meal sometime.'

Laura was startled. Kevin had never so much as hinted that he was interested in her. She wondered how to let him down gently; he was such a nice man she didn't want to hurt his feelings.

'That would be good,' she said, 'but there's someone else.'

'Your artist friend, Paul?'

God, how did he know that? 'Yes,' she blushed, suspecting Terry having had a hand in this.

'Sorry I didn't realise it was serious.'

'It's early days,' Laura muttered uncomfortable with the lie.

When the door bell rang again Laura reluctantly put down her magazine and went to answer it.

'This is a nice surprise,' she said, letting Terry in. 'Alison not with you?'

'No she's got a home birth. I just thought I'd come for a chat.'

'I'll put the kettle on.' Laura was always pleased to see her brother, but she wondered if he had an ulterior motive for this sudden visit.

Terry chatted about work and the alterations he was making to the house. Laura put mugs of tea and a plate of biscuits on the table and sat down.

'Are you still trying to find Mum?'

The question took her by surprise. 'Not for ages,' she said. 'Why?'

'I bumped into an old school mate last week - Adrian Marshall, do you remember him? He was always at our house, tall lanky lad.'

'Vaguely.'

'He was down here on holiday. He said he'd heard that Nigel had died of a heart attack.'

'My God! Poor Mum.'

Terry shrugged carelessly.

'Does Adrian know where Mum is living now?'

'Unfortunately not. He said he'd try and find out though. I gave him my phone number.'

'I hope she's okay,' Laura said frowning.

When Terry didn't respond she said. 'I know you didn't get on, but she is our mother.'

'She shouldn't have done what she did,' Terry muttered.

'What was that?' Laura asked curiously. She had always felt there was more to Terry leaving home than he let on.

'Shacking up with that loser for one thing, and then . . . .'

'Go on,' Laura prompted.

'Nothing.'

'Terry you can't stop now. *Tell me.*'

'He was a druggie. He got Mum hooked on heroin. She was spaced out most of the time.'

Laura stared at him in disbelief. 'Are you sure?'

'Course I am, you don't imagine things like that. I bet you any money they got kicked out of the house because they were in debt. No doubt that was the reason she left without a word.'

Laura thought back to the last few weeks of living at home, her mother's irrational behaviour, and knew Terry was right. 'Why didn't you tell me before?'

Terry shrugged. 'I didn't want you to worry.'

'Thanks for telling me now.' She wondered if this was the reason he had come round but his next question made her realise her mistake.

'Why have you stopped seeing Paul?'

'I was never *seeing* him. We had dinner once. End of.'

'I thought you liked him.'

'So?'

'He certainly smitten with you.' Terry helped himself to a biscuit.

Laura continued to stare at him in sullen silence.

'What's the matter with you? He's a great guy and he'll make a great dad for Amy. What's your problem?'

Laura said flippantly. 'You're determined to get me married.'

'Are you telling me you don't want to?' Terry asked quirking an eyebrow.

'That's right.'

'I don't believe you.'

Laura sighed deeply, remembering that evening back in June, Paul's kiss that had her senses racing, then the realisation that she must stop before they got in any deeper. The hurt bewilderment in his eyes when she had told him she wouldn't see him again because she didn't want a serious relationship.

It had sounded such a put down that she felt really awful. The worse thing was that she did really like him. She'd had to steel herself to walk away. She missed Paul more than she thought possible. She hadn't seen him or spoken to him since. He had not even come into the pub.

'Is this because of Amy's father?' Terry said, breaking into her thoughts.

'No. I'm just not ready for marriage.'

Terry pulled a wry face. 'I don't understand you. Paul's such a decent bloke.'

'Mummy, mummy,' Amy cried from the bedroom.

'I'll go,' Terry offered, 'you make us another cuppa.'

When Laura returned to the living room, Terry was bouncing Amy on his knee, tickling her, making her giggle. He, like everyone else, adored the child. At eleven months, Amy was beautiful, with ebony-black hair, huge blue eyes and the most endearing smile. Laura couldn't imagine life without her. Amy's lively and precocious nature gave her many hours of pleasure. Even when she was asleep, her very presence made Laura contented. Sometimes at night she lay awake staring at her, grateful for her, praying that she would never lose her.

She smiled at the sight of them as she put the mugs of tea on the coffee table. Terry tore his loving gaze from Amy and glanced up at her. His face was suddenly solemn. 'You know, sis, I'm worried about you.'

'How do you mean?'

'I still think there's something you're not telling me.'

'I don't understand.'

Terry sat Amy down on the floor. He reached for his tea. 'Are you sure you're not in trouble with the law. I've always felt, ever since you turned up late that night, and those lies you first told about Amy, that you were in some sort of trouble. That maybe Amy's father was violent and you're so terrified of him you're hiding from him. There is *something,* I know it.'

Laura stared at her brother; her eyes were level with his. His gaze, beneath thick unruly eyebrows, was clearly worried. She felt terrible that all these months he had been unnecessarily anxious on her behalf. What could she tell him to put his mind at rest? She had always trusted him, ever since she was a child and he had never let her down, but this was such a big thing, such an important secret.

She lowered her gaze. 'I'm sorry, Terry, sorry I've caused you to worry.'

Terry's arm came across her shoulder in a gesture of comfort and she watched the corner of his gentle mouth tightening.

He leaned closer and pressed his forehead against hers. 'Confide in me, sis, trust me, you always used to.'

Dare she? It would be such a relief to talk to someone. The strain of always being on her guard was getting her down. She took a deep breath. 'Can I tell you something in *complete* confidence?'

'You know you can.'

Terry's face paled as she told of the car accident and the way Amy had been thrust into her life.

'Christ!' He shook his head in disbelief. 'Why did you agree to this? This man – what's his name – Pembroke, has broken the law and you're a party to it. Not only has he illegally given away his child, he left an accident scene. Don't you see how this implicates you?'

'It was his baby; surely he could give it to whoever he wants.'

'It was also Harriet's baby. He would need her consent.'

'He thought she was dead,' Laura argued.

'But she wasn't.'

Laura shoulders slumped, knowing that Terry was right. She had closed her mind to the legalities of having Amy because she had been so desperate to keep her. Danny had been so convincing that Harriet didn't want her child, and she had believed him. She still believed him. He wouldn't lie to her.

'What was I supposed to do? I couldn't refuse to help him. He's such a lovely man; he's not a criminal, just desperate to keep his wife from finding out about his affair and anyway, Harriet didn't want the baby, so who are we hurting?'

Terry didn't answer. Laura rose from her chair and knelt on the floor in front of him.

'Please,' she begged, 'don't tell me I have to give her up. It would break my heart.'

'I'm not saying that. I just don't like the sound of this at all.' Terry looked worried. 'Can't you contact Harriet and persuade her to make it legal?'

Laura's face had dropped. 'You're kidding, right?'

'No I'm deadly serious.'

'I can't do that. It would be betraying Danny, he trusted me to keep quiet about this.'

Terry looked annoyed. 'You seem to admire this Danny, but what I can't get my head around is, what is there to like about a bloke that had no time for his own child, and clears off leaving the mother for dead?'

'You make him sound so cruel; but it wasn't like that.'

'It just seems wrong,' Terry said.

'Anyway I asked Danny once about adoption, but apparently that's not possible,' Laura said. 'Not without his wife finding out.'

'To hell with Danny, go and see Harriet.'

'I can't, not without telling him. He's been sending money all this time. It wouldn't be right to go behind his back.'

'Hmmm,' Terry grunted unconvinced.

They sat in silence for a moment until Terry said. 'This is the real reason you won't see Paul isn't it?'

'Yes.'

'And you haven't told him?'

'What do you think?'

'Well I agree with that, the fewer people that know the better.'

'What does that mean?'

'Well he might talk, not intentionally, don't get me wrong, but a casual remark. You could be in serious trouble.'

'Paul wouldn't tell anyone, not if I told him not to.'

'Even so, better not to say anything.' Terry sighed deeply. 'It seems such a shame when you two are so right for each other.'

Laura shrugged. 'It can never happen.'

'There must be a way round this,' Terry said, reaching down and lifting Amy up onto his knee again.

'Like?'

'I wish I knew. I need to think about it.'

'Will you tell Alison?'

'No,' Terry said reluctantly.

'You don't sound very sure.'

'I hate keeping anything from her.'

'Oh Terry I'm sorry . . .' Laura couldn't finish the sentence, her throat felt too constricted.

'Don't cry, Laura. We'll sort it out somehow. I don't want to lose Amy any more than you do.'

'Thanks.' Laura wiped her wet face with her sleeve.

That night Laura lay awake in the darkness. She couldn't sleep. She almost wished she hadn't told Terry. The burden of her secret would weigh heavily on him. He had suggested that he contact Danny and have it out with him. But she begged him not to.

Her mind ached from all her confusing emotions. Her thoughts switched to Paul; she really missed him. Would there ever come a day when she could explain about Amy? She suspected not. Not unless she could figure out a way to admit to the truth without jeopardising Danny.

She was in an impossible situation and she couldn't begin to find an answer to it all.

As she finally drifted off to sleep, she knew she had to accept that she and Paul had no future together.

Chapter Thirty-Three

Alighting from the taxi, Harriet stared at the light in the upper window of the perfumery and breathed a sigh of relief. Danny was working late.

She had to see him. She couldn't get him out of her head. The need for him grew more obsessive every day. He wouldn't answer her calls, which made her more determined than ever. She was not going to let him shut her out of his life, not after all she had been through. Despite promising Christine that she would try and end the affair, she knew for her part, it would never be over. Even if she couldn't marry him, she wanted to spend the rest of her life with Danny.

Jeremy had moved out a week after she had returned home from the hospital. She hadn't been able to stand living with him. There had been a massive argument, where he had accused her of being heartless after all he'd done. She had been impervious to his threats and tears. In the end he'd had no option when she reminded him that he had no legal right to be there. The house was hers.

She had phoned the perfumery earlier in the day and Pauline had told her that Christine was abroad, in Brussels with Stephen Wyles, the man that Christine had employed to replace her.

Harriet was disappointed that Christine had refused to let her have her job back but she could hardly blame her. What use was she? Although she had changed her crutch for a walking stick she still had difficulty in getting around.

Ever since her visit to Christine, a month ago, she had been expecting Danny to call her. Surely he must be furious with her because she had told his wife about Amy. It puzzled her that he hadn't been in touch. It could only mean that Christine had not confronted her husband. Well that suited her.

The September evening was warm. After several days of rain the weather had changed at last. Even so, crossing the cobbled street was hazardous and she walked carefully. She approached the wrought iron gates; they were shut, although thankfully not locked. Danny's car was in the courtyard.

She pushed open the gates and made her way to the rear entrance, which led directly into the compound room. She rapped sharply on the door. It took several knocks before it was opened.

'We're closed . . . ,' Danny began before recognition dawned. 'Harriet.' He looked nervous.

'Hello, Danny, can I come in, I need to talk to you?'

'This is not a good time.'

'It's important.'

Looking disgruntled he moved aside to let her in, closing the door behind him.

'How are you?'

She had combed her hair forward, to hide her face, but now she lifted it aside so that he could see the ugly lacerations.

Danny looked upset. 'Can't they do anything about your scars?'

'I'm having surgery in two months. The doctors are confident I will look normal again,' she said.

'Great.' Danny turned away. 'What do you want to talk about? I'm really busy, I haven't much time. I have an urgent order to get ready, Stephen is away and I'm behind schedule.'

'I'll come and help while I'm talking to you.'

'You being here is not a good idea. If Christine . . . '

'Christine's in Brussels.'

Caught out, Danny merely shrugged. 'Even so . . . .'

His tone was not very friendly. Harriet ignored it. The sight of him made her heart race. She wanted so much to reach out and touch him, to have him wrap his arms around her, to hear him say that he still loved her. She recalled the first heady days of their affair; surely all that passion could not be lost; surely in time it could be regained? She had been so happy then. Despite her injuries she was still the same person inside, could Danny not see that? She had given him four years of her life. *Given birth to his child.* She deserved something better than the cold mask of irritation on his face.

She wandered around the room, feeling a deep sadness as her fingers lingered over the equipment, the gas chromatographer, the weighing scales; the coldness of the stainless steel table. She still thought of this as her room and felt an unnatural resentment at Stephen Wyles for intruding into her space.

Ignoring Danny's sour expression she walked through the adjoining door to his laboratory. Propping her walking stick against the Formica table she sat down on a plastic chair. Her eyes strayed to the shelves that held hundreds of little brown bottles containing highly concentrated essential oils. She knew them off by heart; patchouli, ambergris, ylang-ylang, musk, jasmine, linalool, bergamot, sandalwood . . .

Danny was behind her. She lifted a phial from its rack on the table and sniffed the contents. 'Who's the customer?'

Obviously uncomfortable with her being there Danny said curtly. 'Sir Michael Westbury.'

'I thought we kept his special fragrance in stock, are you designing a new one?' Harriet remembered it well; she'd helped to formulate it. It had been a prestigious order, Westbury's chain of perfumery stores were countrywide.

Danny shrugged. 'It's not for Sir Michael's retail shops.'

'Ah.' Harriet smiled knowingly, understanding and remembering how Danny had once designed a special fragrance for her at the beginning of their affair.

'He must be paying you well if you're doing a special order.'

'I'm only doing a modification. He wants something a little more musky.'

'And?' She knew him well; he would have an ulterior motive.

'He's a member of my golf club and Grand Master of the local Freemason's lodge. I'm hoping he will put my name forward to be balloted for membership this year.' Danny proceeded to fill a new pipette. 'Now will you please tell me what it is you want?'

'My goodness, you are grumpy.'

Danny didn't answer and she said. 'I expect it's because you don't want to be here, not on such a perfect evening, especially with Christine being away. No doubt you have someone waiting for you. A new mistress perhaps?'

'The only thing waiting for me is my evening paper and a large whisky. But you're right, I don't want to be here.'

Harriet gave a derisive laugh. She placed the phial back in its holder. 'You should try a touch of sandalwood,' she advised.

'I was about to.'

She watched him as he carefully counted the drops of sandalwood into the phial. 'I want my job back.'

Danny's hand shook. He swore as he spilled the liquid. 'You are joking!'

'No, I'm very serious. I'm good at what I do.'

'I know you are, that's not . . . '

'Please Danny you owe me that much.'

'We have employed Stephen now.'

'There must be something I can do.'

'Let me think about it.' Danny mopped up the spillage and threw the paper towel in the bin.

'Thanks.' She touched his arm gently. 'I want to work with you again, be close to you. I miss you.'

'I miss you too,' Danny said. The insincerity in his voice hurt, 'but my hands are tied. I can't invent a job for you; Christine might get suspicious about us.'

Harriet looked at him in amazement. It seemed incredible that he had no idea that Christine knew. Well, she wasn't about to enlighten him.

'I'm sure you'll think of something,' she said carefully. 'You have a bit of time. I don't want to start until after I've had my operation.'

Once her face was healed she was determined to win him back. Now that the child had been taken care of there was nothing to stop them rekindling their affair.

'One last thing before I go. I want you to tell me about the people who adopted Amy.'

Danny raised his head. 'Why?'

Harriet shrugged. She was tempted to say that she couldn't stop thinking about her, that she felt guilty, that she wanted her back. Danny would know she was lying. 'I need to know who her new parents are,' she hesitated knowing she was about to seem cold-hearted, yet she had to tell him the truth. 'I want to make sure that they don't contact me.'

'Why are you asking me now after all these months?'

'There's been no opportunity before. You never come to see me.'

Danny gazed solemnly at her; he seemed to be considering what to say. He held the pipette to his nose and sniffed. 'Perfect,' he said with a satisfied smile.

'Danny!'

'All right! It was Laura.'

'Laura?'

'The waitress from the café.'

'She's just a kid.'

'No, she's nineteen and very capable.'

'Why her?'

Danny cleared his throat. 'She was there, on the night of the accident. I thought you were dead. I didn't know what to do. She was a godsend; she took the baby with her, there and then. It was only supposed to be for a week, but in the end she agreed to keep her.'

'It wasn't a proper adoption then, you didn't forge my signature like you told me?'

'No.'

'I knew you were lying when you told me you'd had Amy adopted. I thought it was probably an illegal adoption, I didn't realise it wasn't an adoption *at all*. Why did you lie to me?'

'I didn't want to be cross-examined about my actions. You'd have given me the third degree and, well quite frankly, what I did was for the best for all of us.'

Harriet swallowed nervously. If Amy wasn't officially adopted . . . what if Laura got fed up with her and tried to return her . . .

216

she couldn't have her back … she just couldn't cope with her.

'Where does Laura live?'

'She went to her brother in Devon, I don't know where. We don't keep in touch. I send her child maintenance through the bank.'

'You pay for the upkeep of Amy?' Harriet was astounded.

'Yes.'

'Does Laura know that I'm alive?'

'Yes, I told her. I also told her that you wouldn't want Amy back. You don't do you?' Danny looked worried.

'No. But perhaps I should talk to her.'

'Why?'

'I was hoping she might like to legally adopt her.'

Danny looked horrified. 'To do that you would have to go through the proper channels, explain what happened, tell them I'm the father. Bloody hell, Harriet you can't do that.'

'Perhaps you're right. As long as she's being cared for properly,' Harriet said, thinking that a little bit of concern would put her in a good light.

'I'm sure she is. Laura is a good person.'

'I'd better go now. Promise me you'll think about the job.'

'I will.' Danny smiled for the first time as he escorted her back to the compound room.

Reluctant to leave him, she moved closer and put her arms around his neck. She pressed the good side of her face to his cheek. 'I love you Danny. I'll always love you.'

Danny stroked her hair. 'I never meant for you to get hurt,' he said softly.

Tentatively she pressed her lips to his, desperate for his kiss, yet nervous in case he found her face repulsive. He didn't pull away as she feared, but closed his eyes as he returned the pressure of her mouth. She relaxed into him, confident now that the love between them was as strong as ever.

'This is all very cosy.'

Harriet spun round. They had been so engrossed they had not heard the door open. 'Jeremy, what the hell are you doing here?'

'I knew you were lying when you said you'd finished with

217

him,' Jeremy glared from Harriet to Danny and back again.

'Whether I have or not, it's nothing to do with you?' Harriet snapped.

Jeremy moved further into the room. As he got close to Harriet, she could smell the whisky on his breath. His words slurred as he said. 'You're still my wife, I have a right to know what you're up to.'

'Don't be so pathetic,' Harriet moved back from him. 'You don't own me and besides I've already filed for divorce.'

'I don't believe you,' Jeremy looked shocked. 'You said it was only a trial separation.'

'I had to say something to make you move out,' Harriet sneered.

'You bitch,' Jeremy raised his hand as if to strike her, but Danny grabbed his arm. 'Harriet's just leaving and I suggest you go home.'

Jeremy shrugged off Danny's restraining hand. 'Home, what home? I've got no bloody home thanks to you. You've ruined my life. She would never have left me if you hadn't seduced her.'

'Oh *please!*' Danny scoffed, 'not that again.'

'Well it's true.'

'How did you know I was here?' Harriet interrupted, 'have you been following me.'

'Just as well I did. Abigail told me I was stupid to trust you. She said it was obvious you would go back to *him*. I didn't believe her. I came to see you tonight to ask you to reconsider. When I saw you get into a taxi I just knew this is where I'd find you. Abigail was right about you.'

'Do you follow her everywhere,' Danny said with slight amusement.

'She is my *wife,*' Jeremy growled. 'I want her back. I'm even prepared to bring up your kid. Not like you, you've no intention of leaving your wife and you want fuck all to do with your brat.'

Harriet saw the strained expression on Jeremy's face; saw the pulse beating in his neck and felt a burning hatred. *The sanctimonious prick!* How could he even *think* that she would go back to him?

Danny chose not to retaliate to Jeremy's caustic remark. Instead he looked pointedly at his watch. 'I really do need to get this order finished,' he said.

Jeremy's face twitched in agitation at the dismissal. 'Don't take that attitude with me. I know what you did and I'll never forget it.'

Danny began to lose patience. 'Harriet and I had an affair. Big deal. Now it's over. Go away and leave me alone.'

'Will you two stop discussing me as if I'm not here,' Harriet shouted.

The remark fell on deaf ears.

'You are evil!' Jeremy said. 'You take what you want without any thought of the consequences. What does your wife make of this? I might still have to tell her.'

'Leave her out of this,' Danny's voice was dangerously quiet. 'I paid you enough.'

'What does that mean?' Harriet frowned.

'Nothing,' Danny said, regretting his remark.

Jeremy smirked. 'Your precious lover paid me to keep your sordid little affair from his wife's ears.'

Harriet turned to Danny. 'Is this true?'

'He has a copy of Amy's birth certificate; he threatened to show it to Christine. He didn't give me a choice.'

'Jesus Christ!' Harriet wasn't sure who she was the angriest with; Danny, for being willing to pay to protect Christine; or Jeremy for his sordid blackmailing.

'How much?' she screamed at Jeremy.

'Ten thousand pounds.' The reply came quietly from Danny.

Too humiliated to look at Danny she fumed at Jeremy. 'You really have shown your true colours now. I didn't think even you would stoop this low, you bastard.'

Trying to restore some resemblance of calm Danny turned to Jeremy. 'There is no point in pursuing this. Now please go!'

Jeremy seemed not to hear him. He was becoming more agitated. He began to move about, muttering under his breath. He moved towards the corner of the room where a row of 45 gallon drums of compound were neatly stacked.

Danny looked alarmed as he watched Jeremy lurch towards the far wall where boxes of perfume stood ready for delivery. 'If you don't leave now, I'm phoning the police.'

Jeremy laughed; a high girlish giggle. 'And tell them what exactly?'

'That you are causing a disturbance. The chief inspector is a friend of mine. I could say you threatened me.'

'Go on then. Ring them. I have a few things I'd like to tell them. Like how you caused Harriet to drive recklessly. That you did nothing to save her. That you fled the scene.'

Danny almost smiled. 'You can't prove any of this. In any case I didn't flee the scene, I went to get help.'

'Bullshit!' Jeremy sneered, clearly not believing him. His face was full of malice as he said. 'Giving away her baby is against the law.'

'The baby was adopted.' Danny moved towards the door. 'Whatever you say, no one will believe you. It's your word against mine. I'm a respectable businessman and you're a nutcase. Look at yourself, the state you're in. Get out, Jeremy, get out!'

Jeremy gave him a murderous look and then he lunged at him. Caught off guard, the punch caught Danny square on the jaw with ruthless accuracy. Stunned, Danny reeled back against the doorframe.

Danny, his face livid with rage, clenched his fist and retaliated; two swift punches to Jeremy's stomach.

Jeremy, gasping for air, staggered backwards, bumping into the stainless steel compound table. His eyes took on a manic gaze as once more he lunged towards Danny.

Harriet screamed. 'Stop it! Both of you stop it!'

Locked in a grip, the two men struggled together, crashing first against the stack of boxed perfume bottles before lurching back towards the table. The force of their combined weight rocked the table. The chromatographer looked in danger of falling over.

Danny aimed a vicious blow at Jeremy's head but missed. Jeremy laughed and kicked out. His foot landed in Danny's groin. With a cry of pain, Danny doubled over. His hand grasped the cold steel leg of the table as he tried to stop himself falling, but his feet encountered a small patch of spilled oil. He landed on his back with a groan. In an instant Jeremy was on top of him, his hands around his throat, pressing on his windpipe.

Harriet saw Danny's eyes bulge, saw his face distort as he tried to draw breath. *Dear God, Jeremy was killing him.* Frantically she looked round for something to stop him.

A drum spanner was lying on top of one of the 45 gallon drums. It was heavy, made of solid steel. Grabbing it she swung it with all her strength. It caught Jeremy on the shoulder and he cried out. Rolling off Danny, he made to stand up, but Harriet lashed out again, savagely this time, tears of rage and frustration blinding her. She caught his face and he screamed in agony. He tried once more to get to his feet, but his legs buckled and he fell forward, striking his head on the corner of the steel table. As if in slow motion, she watched him slither to the floor and lay still.

She lowered the drum lever, gazed down at the inert figure of her husband and fainted.

Chapter Thirty-Four

It was Amy's first birthday party. There were no children to invite; Laura had not made friends with any other mothers, fearing questions about childbirth. She spent the morning making a birthday cake. When Terry and Alison arrived at four she was hot and flustered and nearly in tears. The sponge had not risen and the pink icing was too vivid.

Terry scolded her for getting upset. 'It'll taste great and Amy won't criticize it,' he grinned.

Laura laughed, realising how silly she was being and poured them all a glass of wine. Later, as she watched Alison help Amy unwrap the presents they had brought, she saw how fond Alison was of Amy. She told everyone that Amy was her niece even though her and Terry were not married. She wondered what she would say if she knew the truth. She felt a surge of guilt at the secret she was keeping from her.

After they had eaten, Amy, with the help of Terry blew out the one candle on the cake and they all sang, Happy Birthday.

Later, after they had left, Laura sank onto the sofa. Colin had given her the evening off.

Amy was in bed and she poured herself another glass of wine. She wondered if Harriet was thinking of Amy on her first birthday or if she had even remembered it. She looked down the years, at all the birthdays to come, and wondered if there would come a time when she would have to tell Amy that she was not her real mother.

Pushing the frightening thought away, she rose to begin to clear up, when the doorbell rang.

It was a shock to see Paul on the doorstep. He was a holding a huge package. 'I guess I'm too late for the birthday party. I was at Jacob's Ladder and forgot the time.'

'I'm afraid Terry and Alison have gone and Amy is asleep.' She felt nervous of being so close to him, worried of betraying her feelings.

'Sorry.'

He looked so crestfallen she relented. 'Would you like to come in for a glass of wine anyway?'

'Please.'

Laura poured the drink. 'I had no idea you knew it was Amy's birthday.'

Paul looked sheepish. 'Alison told me.'

'Ah.' She knew Alison was always hoping they would get together. But then Alison didn't know the truth.

'Would you like something to eat?' she offered.

'I'm okay thanks.'

'Can I tempt you to a slice of birthday cake, I made it myself so I'll understand if you refuse.'

'Cake would be great,' he laughed.

Paul sat on the sofa, his eyes following her as she circled the room, tidying up the tea cups and empty plates. She was wearing a very short skirt and she was conscience of Paul's eyes constantly on her. He seemed tense.

They chatted about nothing in particular. He rose and moved to her side where she was piling dishes into the sink. 'Laura, can we at least be friends. I miss you.'

Laura turned. Her face was inches from his. 'Oh Paul, I've missed you too.'

The passion of his kiss took her breath away. He caressed the nape of her neck, her skin felt hot against his fingers. They were so close she could feel his erection.

'Sorry,' he apologised.

Her hand went down and touched him. He groaned. 'Don't,' he whispered against her neck. 'This is hard enough.'

'I know,' she giggled.

There was no turning back; she couldn't even if she had

223

wanted to. It was wrong, so wrong to deceive him but she couldn't stop, not now.

'You are so beautiful.' Paul was raised on one elbow looking down at her.

She reached up and caressed his face, letting her gaze travel over the surprisingly clean-shaven chin, the thick arch of his eyebrows and the long, long dark eyelashes. Raising her head she kissed his mouth lightly. 'That was amazing.'

'You were amazing,' he teased. 'I had no idea you were so wanton.'

She giggled and snuggled up to him.

'Have you had many boyfriends – sorry I shouldn't ask,' Paul said seriously.

Laura hesitated before replying. There had only been Mark on the night of the disco and he could hardly be classed as a lover. She didn't want to tell him that she'd had a one night stand it sounded so cheap. 'Just one,' she murmured.

'Presumably that was Amy's father?'

Oh God, what a tangled web.

'Now it's your turn,' she said not answering his assumption.

'What do you want to know?

'Alison said a woman broke your heart? Tell me about her,' she said softly.

'Why?'

'Because I want to know everything about you.'

Paul was silent for so long that she was prompted to say 'Is it too painful to talk about?'

'No, not any more. I thought it would be, but suddenly I find it isn't.'

'Did you love her very much?'

'Yes. First love and all that,' Paul grinned. 'We met at Art College. Emma was exquisite, so beautiful she took my breath away. It was incredibly romantic, well I thought so. She was wild and passionate and I adored her. She was the first girl I ever made love to and she taught me so much. We were both twenty, but she seemed so much wiser, so mature. I wasn't her first love and that disappointed me, but I got over it. I proposed after six months and we became engaged. There was no hurry to get married; we had all our lives before us. I needed to finish college and get work. I bought her a ring, quite a cheap thing because I hadn't any money. I promised her I would get her the real thing as soon as I became famous.

The summer of my second year, my friend, Jules invited me to spend the summer in Paris. His parents owned a house there. It was such a wonderful opportunity, and although it would be a wrench being apart from Emma for three months, I wanted to go. She said she understood. When I returned in September there was a letter waiting for me. A "Dear John" letter. She was on her way to America with her college tutor. They were getting married in Mexico and going to live in California. She was sorry. *Sorry!* She hadn't even had the decency to tell me to my face or phone me.'

Laura squeezed his hand, hearing the bitterness in his voice.

'What did you do?' she asked.

'I got drunk, completely smashed. I stayed drunk for a week until Uncle Harry came and hauled me home.

I was determined never to fall in love again. I told myself it wasn't worth the pain. After a few months of feeling utterly miserable and sorry for myself, I wanted to paint again. I had come to Sidmouth with my parents one summer holiday when I was about five and I never forgot it. I decided I needed a fresh start so I moved here.'

'I'm so glad you did,' Laura said, kissing him tenderly.

'Me too,' Paul said softly. 'I'm glad I told you, I don't want there to be any secrets between us.'

Laura wriggled free from his embrace. On the pretext of getting a drink she moved into the kitchen. *No secrets.* Fuck, what was she going to do?

Chapter Thirty-Five

'Is he dead?'

Harriet had come round to find Danny bending over Jeremy's body.

'I think so. I can't find a pulse.'

'Oh God, I've killed him.' Harriet began to cry hysterically. 'I only wanted him to stop, he was strangling you. I never meant . . . Christ! I've murdered him.'

'Be quiet a minute I have to think,' Danny said.

'What's there to think about? He's dead.'

'We have to decide what to do with him.'

The unexpected remark stopped Harriet's tears. 'Surely that's up to the police?'

Danny looked at her oddly. He walked into his lab and returned with a brandy bottle and two plastic tumblers. Pouring a generous amount in each he handed her one. 'You want to call the police?' he said quietly.

'We have to.'

'Go on then.'

Harriet struggled to her feet. She had drunk the brandy in one swallow and although it had a calming effect she was still shaking badly; her stomach churning and her whole body shivering with shock. 'What shall I say? They will believe it was an accident, won't they?'

'I don't know. You hit him several times, remember.'

'He hit his head on the table, that's what killed him,' Harriet whimpered.

'Perhaps.'

'I'll say it was self-defence, I'll say he attacked me.'

'You have no injury to prove that.'

'Danny, help me, please help me.' Hysteria made her voice screech.

'Calm down. We're not phoning the police.'

Harriet was shocked. 'We must, we have to report it.'

'You'll go to prison and I'll be implicated. I'll be finished, ruined. After all the trouble I've gone to, to keep my name out of all this, I can't let that happen.'

'What are you going to do then?' Harriet asked incredulously.

'I don't know. I have to think.' As he was talking, Danny walked across the room and leaned against the sink, his hands splayed on the white edge, his head lowered. He gazed at his knuckles, the skin broken and cut where he had hit Jeremy. After a moment he said. 'We have to dispose of the body.'

'For Christ's sake, Danny!'

'There's no other way.'

'But how, where?'

Danny didn't answer as he paced the floor. He began to mutter out loud. 'In the woods, at the end of the lane. No, no that's no good, we can't risk being seen taking him anywhere, we have to do it here. In the garden, we'll bury him in the perfumery garden.'

Harriet started to cry again. 'I can't believe we're doing this.'

'Harriet, get a grip. It's not as if you cared for him. Stop playing the grieving widow. Now I need you to help me. I can't do this alone.'

'I c - c - can't.'

'You have to.' Danny removed his white laboratory coat. 'Come on, we need to cover his head, otherwise the blood will trail all over the floor.'

'I can't touch him,' Harriet sobbed.

'Harriet!' Danny shouted.

Slowly and with difficulty she knelt down beside Jeremy's body. Danny had put on plastic gloves and as he lifted Jeremy's head she wrapped the white coat round it.

'Now open the door,' Danny ordered.

She did as he asked, trying not to look as Danny dragged the body across the floor and out into the garden. It was dark now, the light fading. She peered fearfully into the gloom. The garden was well screened with a high wall and mature trees; it seemed safe.

'Go back inside,' Danny hissed. 'Clean up, and make sure the floor is washed of all traces. There's some bleach under the sink. I may be some time.'

Harriet closed the door on him, thankful he had not asked her to help bury Jeremy. She found bleach and a few cleaning cloths. Suddenly her stomach heaved and she was violently sick in the sink.

Harriet was in Danny's laboratory, her head resting on his desk, when she heard him return. She walked back into the compound room. It was spotless. She had scrubbed the stone floor, a slow arduous task, and disposed of the cloths in the incinerator. She had swept up the broken glass from a carton of perfume bottles damaged in the scuffle, but the spilt scent still lingered heavily in the air.

'Where have you buried him?' she asked.

'Better that you don't know,' he said. He was sweating and filthy. Moving to the sink he began to scrub his hands.

'What shall we do with his car?' Harriet asked.

'I've been thinking about that. We need to leave it at an airport, make out he's gone abroad. Did he have a passport?'

'Yes it's at home with mine.'

'Good, destroy it.'

'Then what?'

'The police will eventually find the car and assume his disappearing act was planned.'

'Are you sure that will work?' Harriet asked doubtfully.

'No, of course I'm not bloody sure, but do you have a better idea.' Danny snapped angrily.

'Sorry.'

'How will we get the car to the airport?'

'You can drive it there. I'll follow and bring you back.'

'I can't drive,' Harriet said in panic. 'My knee is not properly healed yet.'

'Bloody hell! I'd forgotten that.' He was thoughtful for a moment. 'It's your left knee isn't it?'

'Yes.'

'You can drive my car, it's an automatic.'

Danny locked up and they stepped into the street. It was now after midnight and the place deserted. Jeremy's car was parked at the kerb.

'Where are the keys?' Harriet whispered. 'Shit, don't say you buried them with him.'

'I'm not that stupid. I took the keys and his wallet out of his coat.'

She watched nervously as Danny got into the Mondeo and then she reluctantly climbed into the Jaguar. It was difficult manoeuvring her leg into the low coupe and panic filled her every pore. Taking a deep breath she clipped the seat belt into place and started the engine. When Danny said they were going to Birmingham airport she had been terrified. 'I can't drive all that way. Can't we leave it somewhere nearer?'

'We could go to Bristol but Birmingham is quicker. You'll be fine if you follow me. I'll take it steady. Now come on, we must get going.'

Harriet stayed close as Danny followed the signs for the M40. Convinced that they would be stopped by the police, she was surprised when they reached the motorway without incident. The minor roads on the Fosse were quiet, but every time a car passed them Harriet's heart lurched in fear. They reached Birmingham International Airport just over an hour later. As Danny had instructed, she waited in the Jaguar while he parked Jeremy's car in the multi-storey car park.

It freaked her out when she saw him returning wearing Jeremy's hat.

'Found it on the front seat,' he said, 'thought it was a good idea, in case I'm caught on the CCTV camera.'

She nodded, feeling too sick to reply.

Harriet slumped in the passenger seat as Danny drove them home. He'd thrown the car keys down a drain and made sure he'd wiped the car clean of his fingerprints.

'You seemed to have thought of everything,' she muttered almost resentfully.

'One of us has to.'

Her arms were wrapped protectively around her body, as she tried to stop thinking about the enormity of what they had done. They must have covered several miles in silence before Danny spoke again. 'Has Jeremy got any relatives, any one that will miss him?'

'Just his sister. His parents died when he was a child.'

'That's good.'

'No it isn't. You don't know Abigail; she's never going to believe that he went abroad without telling her.'

'Don't worry about her; she's the least of our problems.'

'I'm frightened, Danny. Terrified of what I've done.'

'Stop it, Harriet. I've made sure no one will find him.'

'Are you certain?'

'Positive.'

Harriet lapsed into silence again, only slightly comforted by Danny's reassurance.

Danny pulled into her driveway just after three-thirty. It was still dark.

'Will you come in for a minute,' Harriet asked, reluctant to go into the house alone.

'I'd better not.'

'Please, just for a few moments.'

'Okay, but I can't stay long.'

In the kitchen Harriet lifted the kettle and took it to the tap. Her hands were shaking as she made coffee. 'I'm not sure I can go through with this.'

'Yes you can, you have to. The alternative is prison.'

Harriet handed him a black coffee. 'I'm so scared, Danny.'

'Try to stay calm and everything will be okay. Lots of people disappear and are never heard of again.'

'Abigail will never believe her brother has left without telling her.'

'It's irrelevant whether she believes it or not. She can't prove anything.'

'Do you really think we can get away with this?'

'Yes, if we keep a cool head and don't panic.'

'What will you do?'

'Carry on as normal. Christine and Stephen are not due back for a few more days, so I'll make sure I haven't overlooked anything. Check over the lab again.'

'When will I see you?' Harriet moved towards him, aching for him to hold her, to take away this feeling of terror. He took both her hands in his and she leaned against his chest.

'Listen Harriet, we mustn't have any contact whatsoever for a while. We must pretend we have not met since you left work.'

'But Danny . . . '

'I mean it, Harriet, don't phone me, or come to the house or the perfumery. Do you understand me?'

'I can't do this alone.'

'It's only for a while, just until we know we're safe.' He pulled his hands away. 'Now I really must go.' He walked to the door and stopped. 'Take this and destroy it.' He handed her Jeremy's wallet. He stepped out into the night without looking back.

'Danny,' she called softly.

He turned clearly annoyed. 'What?'

'Thank you.'

His face softened for a fraction of a second. She caught a fleeting glimpse of the love they once shared, and then he was gone.

She locked the door and stood for a moment in the silence. Although she felt exhausted, she knew she wouldn't sleep. She fingered Jeremy's wallet, stroking the expensive brown leather cover. She had bought it for him a few Christmas's ago. Inside there was a photograph of herself, taken just after they had first met. The photo was creased, as if taken out and studied many times.

She sat in the living room and thought over the night's travesty and wondered what the day would bring.

Chapter Thirty-Six

Laura paced the flat nervously. Paul had been due to arrive half-an-hour ago.

The table was set for a romantic meal, with candles and flowers. Amy was having a sleep-over at Terry and Alison's. Where the hell was he?

She pulled back the curtain and looked out at the wet November night. Her nerves were stretched to the limit.

Last week she had made a decision. She had changed her mind; she was going to tell Paul the truth about Amy. She was going to do it this evening. She had been on the brink of telling him so many times, ever since they had become lovers in September, but always her nerve failed her. She had to do it though if she wanted any kind of a future with Paul. And she did, she loved him. This was the first step to being honest with him.

When she had told Terry that she was planning to tell Paul she had thought he would be pleased. Things had been strained between them since Amy's birthday. He had been shocked with her for becoming involved with Paul.

'It's not right,' he had said angrily 'You are deceiving him by not telling him and yet if you do you are putting yourself at risk.'

'What do you want me to do?' she snapped.

'You know what you have to do. Go and see Harriet.'

'It's not that simple.'

'Yes it is.'

But she didn't agree. She could not, would not betray Danny.

Last week he had annoyed her by asking yet again if she intended going to see Harriet. When she had said she had no intention of doing so he had turned on her angrily. 'I won't keep lying to Alison,' he snapped, 'go and see Harriet or I'll tell her the truth.'

'I'll see,' she had said to pacify him but she knew she wouldn't have the courage to go. She was bothered though that she was deceiving Paul and tonight she wanted to put that right.

Tonight she was going to tell him. If he ever turned up!

She was on her second glass of red wine when the doorbell rang an hour later.

Paul was looking unusually serious as she let him in.

'Sorry I'm late. I've had some bad news,' he said, without preamble.

'What's happened?'

'Uncle Harry has died.'

'Oh Paul, I'm so sorry.'

'It's a bit of a shock,' Paul confided. 'I had a call from the London Metropolitan Police. He was found dead this morning. I need to go to London, they want me to go and formally identify him.'

'How awful for you.'

'I'm not looking forward to it, I admit,' Paul said shakily.

'How did he die?'

'I'm not sure. They'll give me the details when I get there.'

'Is there anything I can do?'

Paul shook his head. 'No, but thanks anyway.'

Laura saw that he was trying to hide his feelings and she put her arms around him. 'I know he meant a lot to you,' she said softly. 'Are you okay?'

'I'm fine,' Paul said. 'A drink would be good.' He glanced at the table. 'Sorry I've ruined your meal.'

'It doesn't matter,' Laura poured him a glass of wine. Paul drank quickly. 'How long will you be gone?'

'A few days I expect.'

'I love you,' Laura said impulsively as they sat side by side on the sofa.

Paul face lightened. 'Do you, really?'

'Yes,' Laura laughed softly.

'I love you too. I was so looking forward to tonight. I had something to say to you.'

'So had I,' Laura said nervously.

They smiled at each other, sharing a moment of intimacy. He lifted a strand of her hair and kissed her earlobe. He moved closer and she felt her heart thumping. It was always the same, they only had to be together a few moments and she was aching with desire for him. The look in his eyes deepened as his mouth came closer. His lips were sensuously warm and soft and she seemed to melt into him.

Paul looked into her upturned face. His hand around her waist drew her closer still. He kissed her again, tenderly this time. 'I had plans for this evening,' he said softly. 'I was going to propose to you tonight over our romantic meal. Now it will have to wait until I get back.'

'Oh.' Her heart gave a little leap of joy. She wanted so much to say yes but first she had to be honest with him. It was too important to keep hiding it from him. She had to tell him the truth about Amy, she had to be sure he would understand and keep her secret. But not now, this wasn't the right time, he had enough to contend with. She tilted her head and gave him a sad smile.

Paul pulled away; saw the troubled look in her eyes and totally misunderstood it. 'You don't look overjoyed,' he said bleakly.

'Of course I am but. . . '

'But?'

Laura hesitated unsure what to say.

'Is this to do with Amy's father?' Paul said quietly.

'In a way.'

'You still love him?'

'*No!* No it's not like that. It's more complicated. I'm sorry Paul, I . . . '

Paul rose quickly not giving her time to finish. 'I shouldn't have started this conversation. This is not the right time. I have to go. I'll see you when I get back.'

Upset at the pain in his voice she put her hand out to stop him leaving. 'Paul, wait!'

But he was gone. She heard the front door slam down in the hallway. For some reason it sounded so final.

'Have you seen Paul?' Terry asked her early the following morning as he brought Amy home. 'Only I can't get hold of him and we are supposed to be going to the match this afternoon.'

Laura lifted Amy and hugged her tight. 'Sorry, I was supposed to tell you. He's gone to London for a few days, his uncle died.'

'Crikey. They were very close, weren't they?'

'Yeah. Have you time for a coffee?'

'Just a quick one. I have to open the garage; Kevin is out on a call.'

Laura put Amy in her baby-walker and switched on the kettle.

'Are you okay, sis,' Terry said suddenly noticing that her eyes were red-rimmed.

'I'm fine, think I might have a cold coming,' she said.

'Bullshit,' Terry said, 'something's up.'

Laura sniffed. 'Paul asked me to marry him before he left for London.'

'Ah.'

'I was going to tell him about Amy but I never got a chance. Now he thinks I've rejected him.'

'Maybe it's for the best. If you can't bring yourself to go and see Amy's mother then you can't have a future with Paul.'

'That's a bit harsh.'

'Sorry, it's the way I feel.'

'Have you told Alison yet?'

'No.'

'Thanks.'

Terry frowned at her. 'It's only because I don't want her to be troubled by what you've done. She loves you like a sister and she thinks the world of Amy. But I hate keeping secrets from her.'

'I'm sorry, Terry.'

'I wish I understood you, sis. You are hurting so many people, including yourself and for what? A selfish womaniser.'

'Stop it, Terry. Don't say things like that about Danny.'

Without a word Terry turned from her and slammed out of the flat.

She threw his coffee down the sink, upset that Terry was still angry with her. Once again she wished fervently she had never told him. Far from it being a relief to have confided in him, it had made it ten times worse.

Hearing the rattle of the post being delivered, Laura went downstairs. Amongst the usual junk mail was a letter from Zoe.

Returning to the kitchen she read the letter avidly. Apparently Harriet's husband was missing. *The general opinion is that he has left Harriet and buggered off abroad,* Zoe wrote, *and who can blame him, but Jeremy's sister, Abigail has been wandering around with pictures of him asking if anyone has seen him. Most people think she's mental, but it's strange all the same.*

Zoe went on to tell her that she was now engaged and hoping to marry next year and trusted that Laura would come to her wedding.

Laura folded the letter away. She wondered how Harriet was feeling. First she loses her child and now her husband.

Chapter Thirty-Seven

Harriet gazed at the woman opposite her with a mixture of impatience and fear.

Abigail wasn't attractive in any sense; her cropped brown hair looked as if it had been hacked by kitchen scissors, and her black-framed glasses with thick lenses did nothing to improve her hawkish features.

She hadn't wanted to let Abigail in, but she had pushed passed her in her usual aggressive manner.

'What's going on?' Abigail asked curtly.

'What do you mean?'

'There's a For Sale sign outside. You can't sell this place, it belongs to Jeremy.'

'No it doesn't. It belongs to me. I bought out Jeremy's share.'

Abigail looked shocked. 'Jeremy never said. Why are you leaving anyway?'

'I can't afford the mortgage payments now I'm no longer working.'

'Can't you get a job?'

'Do you think I haven't tried? Every time I get an interview I see the revulsion on people's faces and then the polite rejection letters. I don't blame them. Beauty products is all I know, I'm hardly an advert for them, am I?'

'Where are you going? I'll need your address.'

'Will you, why?'

'When Jeremy comes back he will want to know where you are.'

'I can't see the need for that. We were separated remember.'

Abigail's eyes narrowed. 'As if I could forget what you did to him.'

'Is there a reason for this visit?' Harriet's said wanting her gone.

This wasn't Abigail's first visit by any means and she was getting impatient with the constant repetitive questioning. She was also afraid that if Abigail persisted in her quest to find her brother, the police would try harder to find him. Jeremy had only been gone two days before Abigail was round to see if she knew where he was. Harriet's stomach had churned at the sight of her on the doorstep and it had taken all her self-control to stay calm and pretend she was as mystified as anyone. Since that first visit she had been round every week. It was getting on her nerves.

'I've been to see DCI Lloyd again,' Abigail said now, 'the police are useless. They haven't done a thing since I last visited them. No one is doing *anything* to find him.'

Harriet guessed that Robert Lloyd was getting as impatient with Abigail as she was. He had been to interview her after Abigail had reported Jeremy missing. The interview had been nerve-racking, but she thought she had convinced Robert that Jeremy's disappearance was not entirely a surprise. She had looked suitably concerned as she had explained that her husband had been depressed after losing his job, and the fact that they had split up. Robert had been sympathetic and told her not to worry.

'What did he say?' she asked Abigail, curbing her irritation.

'I reminded him that Jeremy has been missing for over two months. *Two months.*'

'And?'

'I don't think they are taking me seriously. He tells me the same thing, that Jeremy is recorded as a missing person, but there are no suspicious circumstances to suggest any foul play. That they found his car at Birmingham airport, although there was no record of him being on any flight. He tried to make me believe that Jeremy disappeared of his own free will, that maybe he used an assumed name. Apparently a lot of people do that and he will come home when he's ready.'

Harriet remained silent. She had heard this so many times, she almost knew it off by heart.

'I told him that Jeremy would never go abroad without telling me. We were very close you know.'

'I know.'

'They wanted to know if Jeremy was anxious or depressed, trying to insinuate that he might have committed suicide. I was furious.' Abigail stared at her with ill-concealed dislike. 'If he had been depressed it was your fault.'

Harriet sighed heavily. Her nerves were at stretching point. 'If there's nothing else . . . ' she began

'He was devastated when you left him. How could you get pregnant by another man?' Abigail glared.

'Abigail, it's none of your business.'

'Yes it is. I virtually brought him up.'

Harriet had heard the story before, how they had lived together ever since their parents had died when they were children, Jeremy twelve then, and Abigail sixteen. After a long battle with the social services they had finally been allowed to stay in the council house that had been the family home. Abigail had left school and got a job in the Co-op so that she could look after Jeremy.

Jeremy had told her, as if she hadn't already guessed, that Abigail had taken an instant dislike to her. 'She thinks you're too bossy,' Jeremy had laughed in the early days of their marriage. 'She's just upset because she's now on her own, she'll come round.'

Abigail hadn't, of course.

They had even bought a house close to her so that Jeremy could be near her. What a mistake that was. No sooner had they married when Abigail was constantly wanting Jeremy at her beck and call, demanding he fix a broken shelf, or repair a dripping tap, mow her lawn, decorate the house; any excuse to get him over there. It had annoyed Harriet.

It had been a relief when Abigail married Reg Weston, who also worked in the Co-op, in menswear. Harriet had thought that they would get some peace. Unfortunately they had only been married nine months when Reg died suddenly of a brain tumour. Abigail hadn't mourned his death; in fact she had returned to work the day after the funeral. Jeremy had said that she hadn't liked marriage, not the bedroom bit of it, as Abigail had referred to it, and was secretly pleased that the whole sorry episode of marriage was over.

Harriet realised that Abigail was speaking again. 'Jeremy never stopped loving you, you know. He talked about you for hours. He used to follow you, coming home silent and morose. You didn't deserve a kind sensitive man like my brother.'

She really wanted to tell Abigail to piss off, she'd had enough of her sanctimonious twittering, but she held her tongue. It would be too dangerous to openly antagonise her.

'You couldn't have wished for a better husband, even after what you did to him, what you put him through, he spent every day at the hospital after your accident. It nearly destroyed him thinking that you were going to die.'

Harriet had had enough. She rose. 'You must excuse me,' she said, 'but I have potential buyers coming to view the house in an hour and I need to tidy up.'

Abigail glanced around the immaculate room and sighed, it was obvious she was being got rid of. 'When are you moving?'

'As soon as the house is sold.'

'Make sure you tell me where you are.'

Harriet didn't answer. She had no intention of telling her.

Harriet closed the door after her and breathed a sigh of relief. The sooner she sold the house and moved away, the safer she would feel.

It was true what she had told Abigail, she couldn't afford to stay here, not that she wanted to. There were too many memories of Jeremy. She was haunted by what she had done, seeing his face in her dreams. Over and over she re-lived that night; seeing the blood; the nightmare drive to the airport. She knew Abigail was suspicious of her; she was surprised she hadn't come right out and accused her.

She poured herself a gin and tonic and turned on the television. There had been a time when she would never have watched daytime TV, but now she needed the sound of someone's voice. The house was empty, lonely.

Danny was conspicuous by his absence. Not once had he tried to call her. She needed him, she needed to know that she was not going through this alone. That was another reason to sell; she wanted to be nearer to him.

What a surprise he was going to get when he discovered where she intended to live.

Chapter Thirty-Eight

Danny heard the front door slam and looked up in surprise. He was not expecting Christine home so early. She had gone out for lunch at the Park Hotel in Cheltenham with her friend, Diana. They met once a month and she usually took all afternoon. She never came home early. He was enjoying a quiet read of the newspaper in the conservatory, the April sun filtering through the windows felt quite warm.

Worried, he rose and went into the hall to greet her.

She looked furious.

'What's the matter?' he asked.

Christine removed her coat and hung it in the cloakroom. Without speaking she moved passed him and into living room. He followed her.

'Christine love, what on earth is it?'

She seemed to be having difficulty in controlling herself. Her face was white with anger.

'I saw – I saw Edna Cooksley, from the post office today. We met in the lounge of the Park hotel.'

Puzzled, Danny raised an eyebrow.

'She said wasn't it great that the old cottage down Mill Lane had been sold at last.'

'About time too, it's been empty for years. Hate to see places like that not lived in, causes vandalism or squatters.'

'Danny!'

'Sorry, am I missing something here?'

'Don't pretend you don't know who has bought it?'

Danny was surprised by her tone. 'What do you mean?'

Christine glared at him. 'I don't believe you don't know that the new owner is Harriet.'

Danny's mouth opened and closed, but no words were uttered. Jesus Christ! Harriet was here in the village? What on earth was she playing at?

He fought to keep his voice neutral, hoping Christine hadn't noticed his shock. 'No I didn't know. What has it got to do with us anyway?'

Ignoring his question she said. 'Apparently she moved in three weeks ago, I'm amazed we haven't seen her around.'

'Is there any reason why we should?'

'I want to know why she's moved here of all places.'

'No idea.'

His cheerful tone seemed to rile her.

'Have you no regard for my feelings?' she said coldly. 'Don't you care at all that you are hurting me?'

'Christine what are you blabbering on about?'

'Can you honestly tell me that you and she are no longer lovers?' she spat.

There was a moment of total silence. He found his voice at last. 'What are you talking about?'

'Harriet came to see me after she came out of hospital. She wanted her old job back. I thought she had a damned cheek, so I confronted her. She didn't deny it.'

'Christine, sweetheart we had a brief fling, nothing more.'

'She said you are the father of her child.'

'She's lying, I can't be. I'm sterile.'

'Are you?' she looked shocked. 'When did you find that out?'

'A few years ago, before your hysterectomy. Why do you think we've never had children?'

'I thought it was because you never wanted any.'

'It's true I didn't, but I knew you did. I would have given you a baby if I could have.'

He moved closer, his arms outstretched to hug her. It was a mistake; she lashed out, snarling at him. 'Don't touch me, don't you dare touch me.'

Danny dropped his arms to his side. 'Christine, sweetheart, the affair meant nothing. I love you.'

'I want you to leave. I want you out today!'

'No. It's over, I promise, it is over.'

'You're a liar, a damned liar, I don't believe you. Why has she come to live here in the village then if it's over?'

'I have no idea. I promise you it has nothing to do with me.'

Her voice quivered. 'Do you intend to see her?'

'No!'

'I'll never forgive you if you do.'

'I'm sorry. I never meant to hurt you. The affair meant nothing, it's just sex.'

It took him by surprise when she hit him. Punching his chest and shoulders and sobbing. 'Why Danny, why do always do this to me? I can't stand it any more. I never have a moment's peace.'

He took her in his arms; her shoulders sagged as the rage left her. He held her as she sobbed, murmuring that he loved her and kissing her hair. Suddenly the warmth of her body, the almost forgotten familiar feel of her, stirred him. He reached for her mouth, pushed his tongue against her teeth and she gave a little moan. Her cheeks were wet against his and he tightened his embrace.

He felt himself harden and then they were pulling off each other's clothes. It had been a long time since they had made love.

'I promise you,' he said later, 'I promise the affair is over. I never want to see Harriet again.'

He wondered is she believed him. If she believed his lie about the child.

Damn Harriet. He wished she wasn't going to be living so close. Her presence in the village was going to be a constant thorn in his flesh, a reminder that somewhere there was a child. Harriet's daughter. *His daughter.*

PART FOUR

Chapter Thirty-Nine

2006

Laura wiped her forehead with the back of her hand. The heat was sweltering, and the pub full to capacity. Customers overflowed into the tiny rear courtyard, where white wrought iron tables and chairs stood underneath the brewery's green and red striped umbrellas. Summer changed the quiet days; there was now a steady stream of holidaymakers, all wanting to be served yesterday. This week, and especially today, Saturday, was particularly busy, with the International Music Festival swelling the number of visitors. During the summer months, she worked lunchtimes as well as evenings. Alison and Terry, who now had their own baby daughter, Chloe, were happy to look after Amy, taking her to and from Stepping Stones pre-school that she attended part-time.

Amy loved her little cousin. It brought a lump to Laura's throat to see her mothering the baby. At eighteen months, Chloe was gorgeously chubby, with blonde hair and huge blue eyes, a complete contrast to Amy's dark looks. Laura had worried that looking after the two of them would be too much for Alison; she wasn't strong and she'd had a terrible time giving birth.

'Stop worrying,' Terry had said, 'she's loving every minute. You know she adores Amy, we all do.'

'I know,' Laura smiled, thanking him once again. She was so lucky to have him and Alison, and if at times she felt lonely and unloved, she only had to think of how much she owed to them both. They had supported her through those first dark months when she'd realised Paul was not coming back and that it was her own fault that she'd lost him.

Terry was waiting for her when she finally left at three. Sitting on a low stone wall, he had Amy with him.

'This is a nice surprise,' she said. Terry rarely came to the pub. 'Where's Alison?'

'At home, I fancied a walk.'

Laura looked surprised. Terry was usually working. 'Nothing wrong is there?'

'Not really, it's only that – well I need a word.'

'Go on.'

'I had a phone call last night.'

'Who from?' Laura bent to kiss her daughter who smiled and wound her arms around her neck. 'Mummy, can I have an ice cream?' Amy gave her a wide grin.

Laura raised her eyebrows. 'And the magic word is?'

'Sorry Mummy, *please* can I have an ice cream?'

'I expect so. I think I might even have one myself, how about you Terry?'

'What?'

'You haven't been listening. Do you want an ice cream?'

'Er – no – thanks.'

Laura turned, surprised at the seriousness of his voice. 'What's the matter?'

'I said I had a phone call last night.'

'Oh sorry, so you did, was it important?'

'Paul's coming back,' Terry said.

Laura stopped walking. 'Coming back, as in to live here again?'

'I believe so.'

'Why now?'

'He didn't say.'

She felt shocked and anxious. She forced herself to walk on. 'When?' she asked.

'Not sure, next month I think.'

She gazed at her brother, knowing he would be fully aware of what that meant to her.

That evening after Amy had gone to bed, she stood in the living room looking at the picture Paul had given her when she had first moved into the flat. She loved the scene of the dawn in Sidmouth bay, with the sun just rising.

She ran her fingers over his signature and sighed.

She had missed Paul so much. Four years he had been away. At first when she hadn't heard from him, she had assumed he was busy sorting out his uncle's estate. She had sent him a text on her mobile to ask if he was okay but he hadn't replied. When the second week passed without a word, she was alternately worried and confused. He had stormed off angrily, but she didn't think he had been so upset as not to contact her at all.

When Terry had told her that Paul had phoned him to tell him he wasn't returning to Sidmouth, she had been devastated. Then she had been angry. He could have phoned, written, sent an email, well maybe not an email as she didn't have a computer, but he could have texted, anything, but to leave her in limbo was cruel. It showed how little he had really loved her. He had never returned from London, never contacted her, and his silence had hurt. So many times she had been tempted to phone him, but pride held her back.

Over the years she got the occasional snippet of information about him from Terry. His uncle had left him a lot of money in his will and he had bought himself a house in London. He had also opened a gallery in Mayfair and was making a success of his paintings. There was no mention of any woman in his life, but she was sure he must have found someone else by now.

She thought Paul had settled in London and had no plans to return.

But he was coming home apparently.

She wondered if he was bringing anyone with him. She wanted to ask, but was afraid of the answer. She told herself she wasn't bothered.

Pouring herself a glass of wine, she curled up on the sofa and thought back over the past four years, and how much had changed. Zoe had finally married and had written that she was really disappointed Laura couldn't get to her wedding. Her friend no longer lived in Upper Wyre but had moved to Cardiff. *'Not quite London,'* Zoe had said, *'but a great place.'* Her letters were still fairly regular. Brett had married. Another wedding invitation she'd had to refuse. Nancy and Angus had given birth to twins. She felt sad that she couldn't get to see them, that all the contact they'd had since she'd moved to Devon had been Christmas cards.

There had been no contact from Danny apart from his monthly amount into her building society account. Not once had he faltered in his payments. She hadn't heard anything more about Harriet either and she tried not to think about her, to wonder if she ever regretted giving up Amy. Despite pressure from Terry she had refused to go to see Harriet. Anyway, there seemed no point now that Paul was no longer around. She wasn't going to risk Harriet claiming Amy back.

She couldn't imagine being without Amy, she was her life. Amy came before anything. She'd had a few dates, but if anyone got serious she ended the relationship. She couldn't bear to put herself through what had happened with Paul.

* * *

Laura held Amy's hand tightly as they walked towards the school. The September morning was glorious, warm with a gentle breeze that cooled the air. Amy would be five on Sunday and today was her first day at All Saints Primary School. Laura gazed down at her daughter, looking adorable in her pink school dress and red cardigan. Her hair had been tied into bunches with pink ribbons and her face was alive with excitement.

As they reached the school gates and gazed around the playground, thronging with children, a frown appeared on Amy's face. 'I can't see Megan.' she whispered, her grip on Laura's hand tightening.

Megan was Amy's best friend and lived next door to Terry and Alison. They had started at Stepping Stones together.

'She'll be there, don't worry,' Laura reassured her.

A bell sounded loud and clear.

'Shall I come to the classroom with you?' Laura offered.

'No,' Amy looked horrified, 'everyone will think I'm a baby.'

'See you later then, sweetheart,' Laura bent and hugged her tight. 'Have a nice day.'

As Laura watched her walk away, tears filled her eyes. She looked so little and yet so grown up. Her backpack was nearly as big as her, but she had insisted on having the Bratz one.

For the rest of the day it was hard to concentrate. She thought of Amy constantly. At three-o'clock she was the first mother outside the school gates.

Amy was almost the last child out. She shuffled across the school yard head down. Even at a distance Laura could see there was something wrong.

When she finally reached her side Laura bent down so that her face was level with hers. Amy had obviously been crying and her knees were scraped. 'Did you fall over?' Laura said gently.

Amy shook her head. 'I had a fight.'

Laura tried not to smile. 'Who with?'

Amy's shoulders heaved. 'Megan.' Her eyes were pools of tear-filled wretchedness. Her bottom lip trembled.

'Why did you fight her?'

'She told everyone that I was a bastard, that I had no daddy.'

Laura's heart lurched. The comment from Megan could only have come from her parents. Terry's neighbours had made cruel remarks before. Laura had wanted to discourage the friendship, frightened of her daughter getting hurt but the girls had formed a close attachment at pre-school. Today's remark however, showed just how fickle children's friendships were.

'Why haven't I got a daddy?' Amy raised her tear-filled eyes.

This was not the first time Amy had asked about her father and she had told her that her daddy had moved away. Amy had seemed to accept it at the time.

'I explained to you before, of course you have a daddy, he – he works abroad.' Terry had warned her that this lie would backfire on her one day, but she hadn't listened.

'Megan said I can't have because even daddies that live away come and see their kids sometimes.'

'Don't believe everything Megan tells you,' Laura said annoyed.

'So will he come one day?'

'Possibly.' What else could she say? It was breaking her heart to see Amy so upset.

Amy's face brightened slightly. 'Maybe he'll come for my birthday on Sunday.'

'Paul's coming to the house tomorrow,' Alison told Laura when she collected Amy the following Saturday.

Laura looked cross. 'It's Amy's birthday party.' They were having the party at Terry's house because Amy had invited her whole class and there wasn't enough room at the flat.

'I know. I told him that. He said he'd remembered and was it still okay to come.'

'What did you say?'

'I said yes.'

'I really wish you hadn't.'

'Sorry. I just thought your first meeting with him might be easier if there were lots of people around.'

'I don't need protecting from him; he means nothing to me now, nothing at all.'

'Aren't you just a little bit curious about him?'

'No,' Laura said stubbornly, 'why would I be?' It was a complete lie of course. She wanted to see him very much.

Paul arrived at Terry's house at two, an hour before the party was due to start. Her stomach had been fluttering with nerves all day.

As he entered the living room, she stopped talking to Terry and stared at him. Despite the well-cut suit with an open neck shirt he looked exactly as she remembered him. His dark brown hair was still long and unruly, and his eyes soft and gentle. She was disconcerted to feel a great surge of longing for him that was so intense it took her breath away. She remembered the first night they had spent together, ironically on Amy's first birthday. She remembered his kisses and the feel of his naked body. She wanted to rush into his arms and tell him that she loved him and would marry him, now, today. She so wanted to kiss his face and rip off his clothes. She wanted to hate him for ignoring her for four years and then coming back.

She tried to remain indifferent, to put on an air of detached coolness, but the longing for his touch unsettled her. She seemed unable to think or act coherently, so she remained silent.

His eyes were wary, as if unsure of his welcome.

She smiled at last, in spite of all the jumbled emotions surging through her. It took a tremendous effort, but she managed to say, 'It's great to see you.'

He relaxed. 'You too. I like the hair.'

She flushed with pleasure. Her tangled curls had been cut off and her hair re-styled. 'Thanks.'

Paul turned towards Amy. 'Look at you, all grown up,' he said, 'and you are so beautiful, like a princess. Happy birthday.' Paul handed her a large parcel.

Amy said solemnly. 'Thanks. Are you my daddy?'

Paul looked stunned for a moment and then he gave her a gentle smile. 'What makes you think that?'

'Mummy said my daddy was away, but that he would come back one day and I prayed really hard last night for him to come on my birthday.'

An awkward silence followed.

'Open your present,' Alison said.

Amy ripped off the paper. Her eyes widened. 'Roller skates,' she squealed, 'Bratz roller skates. How did you know these were what I wanted more than anything? Bratz is my favourite.' She was jumping up and down in delight. Amy turned to her mother, her face flushed with excitement. 'See I said he would come for my birthday didn't I.'

She had taken the silence as confirmation that Paul was her father. Nobody had the heart to disillusion her. Laura knew she would have to speak to her later. It was going to break her heart.

Amy was on the floor struggling to take off her shoes to try on her skates. Laura bent down to help her, her face was crimson.

How on earth was she going to explain this to Paul?

'You're becoming quite the wealthy entrepreneur,' Terry remarked to ease the tension. 'A house in London; a Mayfair art gallery, and a bookmaking business, are you a millionaire yet?'

'Hardly,' Paul laughed, 'anyway I sold the bookies years ago and now I'm selling the London house. Today I signed a contract for an art gallery here in Sidmouth. I love London, but it's too commercialised.'

'So you really are coming back for good then?' Alison said.

'Absolutely.'

'Thank you for the present and for remembering,' Laura said quietly when Amy had persuaded Terry to take her into the garden to try out her skates and Alison had tactfully moved to the kitchen on the pretext of checking that there was enough food for the party.

'I remember a lot of things,' Paul's gaze was intense. 'But I don't remember being her father.'

'Sorry about that.' Laura flushed.

Paul looked at her quizzically, but she wasn't prepared to explain. 'What made you decide to come back here?' she said instead.

Paul hunched his shoulders. 'I missed the place.' His eyes held hers steadily, telling her more than his words did that it wasn't just the place that he missed.

'Where are you living?' she asked politely, refusing to be drawn into any admission, 'are you back in your old studio?'

'No. I bought a house.'

'Really!'

'I'd like to show it to you sometime.'

'I'm rather busy.'

'Please Laura, let me explain.'

'There's no need.'

'But there is. I need to talk to you.'

'We haven't anything to say to each other.'

'You're wrong, we do. I do. Please Laura, just a couple of hours.'

When she didn't answer he handed her a piece of paper.
'Here's my address, I'll be there tomorrow afternoon about two.'

'I really don't think I can make it.'

'I'll be there anyway.'

He turned and went to Alison to say goodbye and then he was
gone.

Chapter Forty

She wouldn't go of course.

Even though Monday was her day off she still had no intention of going.

She took Amy to school. She was upset over the fact that Paul was not her daddy. It had been a difficult conversation and she was sure Amy was still unconvinced.

Terry and Alison had been awestruck when she had told them where Paul now intended to live.

'It's a beautiful valley,' Alison said. 'You must tell me all about it when you get back.'

'I'm not going,' Laura said emphatically.

'I'd go just out of curiosity,' Alison said.

'That's because you're nosy,' Terry laughed at her.

Laura busied herself all morning, washing, shopping, cleaning. At two o'clock she made herself a sandwich. She couldn't eat it, she felt sick. At two-thirty she phoned Alison. 'Would you be able to pick Amy up from school?'

Tactfully Alison agreed without asking the reason why.

She drove through the tiny village of Sidbury and followed the narrow country road down into the valley. The view was stunning, right down to the sea.

She parked in the newly block-paved driveway, next to a brand new Mercedes. She remembered the old Vauxhall Astra he'd driven so erratically and hoped his driving had improved. Climbing out, she studied the building. A recently converted barn, the first floor frontage of exposed oak beams and white stucco offset the deep red brick of the ground floor, and the leaded bay windows contrasted beautifully with the oak door nestling under a slate roofed porch.

As she raised her hand to the knocker, the door was flung open. 'I'd given up hope,' Paul said grinning.

'I can't stay long.' Laura shifted from one foot to the other. The closeness of him was making her uncomfortable.

'Come on in, I'll show you around,' Paul opened the door wider and she stepped inside.

The phone was ringing as they entered the hallway. Laura got an impression of space and light. The cream walls held a few watercolours. 'Look around while I get this,' Paul said indicating that she should go into the lounge.

The room was long and wide, with French doors opening out to a paved patio. She stepped outside; a copse obscured her view of the sea but she could hear the waves, smell the salty air. Beyond a walled garden she could glimpse fields reaching out to the undulating hills in the distance. It was very peaceful.

She returned to the room. Natural oak beams supported the high ceiling. A log fire was laid but not lit in an open fireplace of red brick with a slate hearth.

The furniture was minimal, just two soft, black leather couches, and a low glass table standing on a cream rug. The solid oak floor looked expensive.

Laura moved into the designer kitchen. It was big and square with a central island; white distressed oak units under granite work surfaces, and a profusion of stainless steel. She glanced through the glass door of the eye-level oven to see a leg of lamb roasting. It smelt delicious. Stainless steel pans stood on the cooker and she lifted a lid and peeped inside to find neatly cut vegetables ready prepared for steaming. She wondered who he was having to dinner.

'Sorry about that,' Paul said coming in and switching on the kettle. 'Tea or coffee?'

'Tea please. This is a kitchen to die for.'

'Glad you like it,' Paul said, 'the place has just been revamped by a builder. I haven't had to do much except furnish it.'

'It's great,' Laura acknowledged, wishing she hadn't come; she was beginning to feel nervous.

'While the tea is brewing let me show you the rest of the place,' Paul said.

Reluctantly, she followed him up an open-plan staircase to the floor above. 'Wow' she exclaimed at the marble tiled bathroom with a sunken bath, and remained silent in the bedroom at the sight of the king-size bed. Obviously Paul was not intending to live here alone. There were two further bedrooms and then another smaller flight of stairs to a converted loft. The room was large and amazingly light, with glass sliding doors opening out onto a large veranda with a glorious panoramic view of the valley. Various sized canvases were stacked along the walls. She recalled the familiar stench of oil paint.

Back downstairs Paul placed the cups of tea on the glass table and indicated for Laura to sit down.

'So you like the place then?'

'Yes, it's fabulous. I'm wondering though, what on earth are you going to do with a house this big?'

'I intend to get married and have a large family,' Paul grinned.

Her throat tightened. She felt sick. So he had met someone else. She didn't want to hear it. It had been a mistake to come here. His expression was unfathomable as she gazed into his eyes, waiting, knowing how much it was going to hurt.

She found her voice at last. 'Right,' she said.

'Is that all you can say?'

He really was turning the knife. She really should wish him good luck, but the words stuck in her throat. She turned away, before he could see her tears, before she made a fool of herself.

'Laura?'

She felt agitated, every nerve end seemed alive. 'I really must go.'

'Go! But you've only just got here,' Paul looked stunned.

She shrugged. 'Sorry.' She reached for her bag and stood up. 'Bye Paul.'

Paul spoke softly. 'I've missed you so much.'

Laura bristled. 'Not enough to phone or write. You didn't even reply to my text.'

'What text?' Paul looked genuinely puzzled.

'I sent you a text that first week I was worried about you.'

'I'm sorry I never got it. I wish I had, it might have made a difference.'

'Would it?' Laura said sceptically.

'Maybe, knowing that you cared, I don't honestly know.'

'So why didn't you get in touch?'

Paul rose. 'Shall we go for walk?'

'A *walk?*'

He held out his hand. 'Come on.'

Ignoring the outstretched hand, Laura followed him, she wasn't sure she was going to like what he had to say, but she had to find out.

They left the house by the rear garden. A coastal bridle path led steeply down to a private cove. Stepping onto the soft sands they walked in silence. She couldn't look at him; instead she stared out at the ocean, at the waves gently lapping at the shore's edge. She was very aware of Paul's presence next to her. They reached a secluded recess under an overhanging cliff. He touched her arm and they stopped.

Paul took hold of her face in his hands. For a long moment their eyes held one another. She felt frozen unable to move. 'You are so beautiful,' he whispered softly.

He kissed her gently, almost reverently. The remembered feel of his lips made her heart race. Her hand caressed his cheek as the kiss deepened. Lost in the wonder of the moment she gave into the pleasure of him. The warmth of his body, the smell of his skin.

A seagull screeched overhead. She broke away.

'Don't, Paul, this isn't helping.'

'What's that matter?' He sounded confused.

'You said you would explain why I never heard from you.'

He moved to sit on a boulder. 'I wanted to. You have no idea how much.'

'And?'

He shrugged. 'That last evening you made it clear you didn't want to marry me. I assumed we had no future.'

She had no defence against that. It was her fault. Even so, he could have tried. Four years of silence, of hurt and bewilderment could not be erased that easily.

She swallowed hard. Her throat felt constricted. When she couldn't speak he took her hand and pulled her down onto the sand. 'I'd like to try and explain, to make you understand how I felt.'

'Go on,' she shrugged. There was nothing he could say to put it right, no excuse would be good enough.

'That first week when I was in London I hadn't time to think about how hurt I was over your rejection. I was upset at my uncle's death and the manner in which he died. Then there was so much to do sorting out his estate. When I could think straight, I got it into my head that you were probably waiting for Amy's dad to return. You must have loved him to have had Amy with him. You probably still loved him. I convinced myself that I was just someone to pass the time with until you got back together. I realise that my assumption was based on what Emma did to me. I cursed myself for trusting a woman again.'

'It wasn't like that,' Laura said stunned by what he was saying.

Paul put up his hand. 'Hear me out please. I had fallen so much in love with you. I bought you an engagement ring, and was convinced you loved me until that last night. You have no idea how devastated I felt, it was like a repeat performance of Emma's rejection.

I didn't come back because I didn't want to see you, I didn't want to feel that sort of pain again. I threw myself into my work. Painting has always been a kind of solace for me.

But even though I was in bits, I couldn't forget you. You have no idea how many evenings I spent looking out of the window in my house in London. Evenings spent alone, wondering what you were doing at that precise moment, bringing your image into my mind. Or I would lounge in front of the fire picturing you curled up next to me. The images tortured me. I walked the streets at night aching with loneliness. I dated a few women, but I couldn't seem to find the inclination to pursue a relationship. I measured every one against you. But you didn't want me; you were in love with Amy's father.' He took a deep breath. 'But I know now that I was wrong.'

'Yes you were,' Laura said quietly. 'Very wrong, but what made you realise it.'

'When I decided I'd had enough of London and wanted to come back I wasn't sure I could face you. I rang Terry to ask him about you.'

'I didn't know any of this.'

'I told him not to tell you.'

'What did Terry say?'

'He said it was never a question of you and Amy's father. It was complicated and he couldn't explain but that you would.'

'Right.'

'I asked him if I stood a chance with you if I came back.'

'And?'

'He said a strange thing.'

'What?' Laura's heart thudded.

'He said there was something I needed to know but it was up to you to tell me.'

'Terry had no right to interfere.'

'What's the big secret?'

She lifted her shoulders, not answering.

'Is it about Amy's father?'

'Yes, but not in the way you think.' Laura stood up. Damn Terry for putting her in this position. Damn Paul for coming back. She failed to keep the bitterness from her tone as she said. 'Well it doesn't matter now, we've both moved on.'

Paul's eyes clouded. 'I see.'

The obvious bewilderment in his voice surprised her, but she didn't question it. 'I think we should go back.'

Paul didn't move.

'Like I said, it's water under the bridge.'

'I guess I can't blame you for feeling like this but can we at least be friends?' Paul said softly.

Friends. Was that what this was all about? He had eased his conscience and now he wanted to be *friends!*

'I suppose so,' she said stiffly. She made a point of looking at her watch. 'I really must go. I have to pick up Amy.'

Paul looked disappointed. 'Oh, I was hoping . . . '

'What?'

'Nothing. Of course you must go.'

They walked in silence back to the house. Refusing his invitation to go inside, she unlocked her car. 'Thanks for showing me the house,' she said politely.

'I cooked dinner for you.' He reached for her hand. She pulled away.

She looked at him uncertainly. 'I'm not hungry,' she shrugged.

'Are you still angry with me?'

'No, it's just . . . '

'What?'

She wanted to ask him how he felt now. He had explained how he felt four years ago but had those feelings changed. He had kissed her, but he had not said he loved her. He had indicated he was getting married so where did his future wife fit in all this. She wanted to ask lots of questions but she wasn't sure she wanted the answers. It was better to leave before she made a complete fool of herself. He wanted to be friends but she knew he could never be just that.

'Nothing. I'll see you around,' she said lamely.

'I thought I'd explained.' Paul looked bewildered and miserable.

'I'm sorry.' She opened the car and got in, switched on the engine and reversed out of the drive, down the road back towards the village. Tears filled her eyes and spilled down her cheeks. God help her, but she loved him.

Chapter Forty-One

A week passed. She felt bad-tempered and miserable. Amy sensed it and was being difficult. Amy was also sulking because Paul was not her father and demanding to know when she was going to meet her real daddy.

Laura grew impatient with her constant moaning and snapped at her, something she had never done. Amy had flown to her bedroom and sobbed herself to sleep. Later, when she had calmed down, she looked in on her. She was curled up, the duvet thrown aside, her thumb in her mouth, the dried-up tears streaked on her face. Laura's heart constricted. She loved this child so much.

Terry called at the flat. 'How did it go with Paul?' he asked tentatively.

'Not good,' she admitted.

'Oh.'

'He kissed me and then said he just wanted us to be friends.'

Terry frowned. 'Are you sure, only . . . '

'What!' she snapped.

Terry looked sheepish. 'Actually I've been talking to him and he says he got the impression it was you that didn't want *him.*'

'You had no right discussing me with Paul,' she said furiously.

'Sorry I was only trying to help.'

'Well don't; keep your nose out of it.'

Terry held up his hands is a gesture of supplication. 'Hey, hey don't take it out on me.'

Her shoulders slumped dispiritedly. 'I don't know what to do,' she admitted.

'You do love him?'

'Yeah. Like crazy,' she grinned at last.

'Then go and see him. Tell him.'

'It's not that easy.'

'Yes it is. Just do it.'

'I'd feel awkward; as if - as if I only want him now he has money.'

'Don't be daft. The guy's crazy about you.'

'I told you, he just wants us to be friends.'

'Bollocks. You misunderstood.'

'I didn't.' Laura insisted. 'It's what he said.'

'Even so, you got it wrong. He was just being cautious.'

'I don't think so.'

Terry shrugged, knowing he wasn't going to convince her. 'Did you tell him about Amy?'

Laura shook her head.

'Why not, you were going to before he went away.'

'There's no point now.'

'Of course there is. For God's sake tell him the truth.'

'I'll think about it.'

She called at Paul's new studio on Friday afternoon. The double-fronted shop was twice the size of his old one and in a prime location on the High Street.

Paul was sitting at an easel, painting. He was wearing faded jeans and a washed-out black tee-shirt. He hadn't changed that much, Laura thought with a grin.

Paul glanced up and his face creased into a smile as he saw her. Putting down his brush, he wiped his hands down his jeans. 'Hi.'

'Hi.' She felt awkward now she was here.

Two customers came in and he moved away to serve them. She wandered around looking at the pictures conscious of his eyes on her. He came over to her after they had gone. 'Can we talk?' she said.

'Sure. Do you fancy going for a drink tonight?'

'Yeah. I'll get Alison to look after Amy.'

Paul took her to Browns Bistro in Fore Street. After he had bought drinks and they had sat down, she said. 'Tell me about your uncle.'

'It was awful,' he said, his face saddening, 'the identification at the mortuary freaked me out. Apparently Harry had been dead several days before they found him. The police told me that he had died from carbon monoxide poisoning because the gas boiler in his flat had been faulty.'

'Oh Paul that's dreadful.'

'It was hard going back to the flat. It had once been my home. It was in a terrible mess, and filthy. I sat on his lumpy sofa, remembering the first time I had gone there, and cried my eyes out. I couldn't face clearing it out; it was too painful so I got a house removal firm to do it. I felt bad about that afterwards.'

Laura reached across and touched his hand. Paul didn't seem to notice as he carried on talking. 'I couldn't stay at the flat, so I booked into a hotel. I couldn't sleep. I was haunted by the fact that I should have visited him more, seen that he was okay, given him money to repair the boiler. After all he had done for me I'd neglected him. I felt so guilty.'

Laura eyes filled as she heard the sadness and remorse in his voice. She had no idea how to comfort him. As she tried to find the words, Paul was speaking again. 'Course all of this was before I went to see the solicitor. The meeting with Uncle Harry's lawyer knocked me for six. I was the sole beneficiary of Harry's Will, which included his bookmaking business. Harry had been a wealthy man, there had been no need for him to have lived in that terrible flat; he could have afforded a luxury detached house. It was such a shock.

I remember clearly that night taking a bottle of brandy to my room. I felt restless, my head full of memories. I decided to go out, I wanted to think.

I walked along Green Street, passed the football ground, remembering all the times Harry had taken me to watch West Ham play, and trying to feel excited about the fact that I was now rich. All I could think of was you. I couldn't get my head around why you wouldn't marry me. I don't think I have ever known such a sense of despair. I felt crushed. One thing I knew for certain was that none of this new wealth meant anything without you.

Still, I had to accept that you didn't want me, so I had to get on with my life. My despair turned to anger that evening. Anger at you, mostly anger at myself, for allowing you into my life. For lowering my guard.

I made a decision. I would stay in London. That way I didn't have to see you, didn't have to suffer the pain of knowing I couldn't have you.'

'I'm sorry, Paul,' Laura said gently. 'I never meant to hurt you.'

Paul looked at her seriously. 'I know now that it must be something serious. I should have trusted you, believed in you. I'm the one that should apologise.'

Now was the time to tell him. It was what she had come here to do. Paul rose and went to fetch more drinks. As she waited doubts set in again. What if he was angry that she had lied to him all this time? She felt sick at the thought of losing him again.

Paul came back and began to tell her about his galleries.

Later he drove her home.

'Goodnight, Laura.' He kissed her cheek. It took every ounce of her will-power to stop herself from inviting him in. She wanted him so much. He had touched her heart tonight and she knew now he obviously loved her as much as she loved her. Yet still she hesitated.

She let another week pass. Every day she was filled with conflicting, desperate emotions, feelings that swayed from wanting to tell him and the fear that he would not condone the fact that she had taken Amy illegally. She only had Danny's word that Harriet didn't want her daughter, and if she was honest with herself she knew she should contact her. She persuaded herself that Harriet would, through Danny, be aware of where she lived, and if she really wanted Amy she would come for her.

Much as she wanted to be honest with Paul, she let the week pass, still nervous of committing her secret to him. Terry plagued her every day. She knew he was right in everything he said.

Laura pulled up outside the house. Locking the car, she shivered inside her jacket. The October evening was feeling cool, but she knew the chill that went through her was more to do with nerves than the weather. Although it was gone ten she was relieved to see lights in the window.

Paul had been at the London gallery for the last two days, but she knew he had arrived back this afternoon.

She rang the bell. After a few moments she saw the hallway light come on through the opaque glass panels in the door. She heard his tread and the door opened.

He looked as if she had woken him up. His hair was ruffled and his eyes drowsy. She thought he had never looked so sexy.

'Hi,' she said casually as if her being here was the most natural thing to do.

A smile lit his face. He opened the door wider. 'Laura, what a lovely surprise; come in.'

She followed him into the lounge, where the remains of a Chinese take-away littered the coffee table A half empty glass of red wine stood on the floor. Logs were burning in the fireplace.

'Sorry about the mess. I've not long got back from London. I dozed off.'

'It's okay. I should have rung first but. . . '

'No problem, glass of wine?'

'Yes please.' She needed something.

She waited while he fetched a glass and poured the wine. She took a huge gulp.

'I need to talk to you.'

Paul looked suddenly alert. 'Am I going to like this?'

'Depends.'

'Come and sit on the sofa, it sounds like I might need to be sitting down.'

She sat down next to him. Her heart was hammering so loud she was sure he must hear it. 'I want to say that I love you and I have never stopped. Okay, I was angry with you, but I know it was partly my fault.'

He took her hand. 'Does this mean you'll marry me now?'

She had expected this, had been prepared, but still the words stuck in her throat. 'First I need to tell you something and then you must decide if you still want me to be your wife.'

'You're scaring me.'

She took a deep breath. 'This is hard for me. I have kept this secret for so long, but the thing is, it's not only – not only me that's involved.'

'I don't pretend to understand, but if you don't want to tell me, it's okay.'

'I need to. I can't marry you if I don't.' She dropped her gaze down to the oak floor. Her palms were sweating and she wished for a moment she hadn't started this conversation.

Paul said lightly, trying to lighten the atmosphere. 'You had better hurry up and tell me then.'

'Amy is not my child.'

'Is that it? I thought it was something terrible. So you adopted her, no big deal.'

'I didn't adopt her exactly.'

Paul reached across and grasped her hands. 'I think you had better start at the beginning. I'm completely confused.'

In halting tearful words she told Paul of the accident and the subsequent events. Although it was so long ago, the memory of it all was etched forever in her mind. When she had finished, Paul was silent for a few moments.

'Let me get this straight. Are you telling me that Amy's father gave her to you, *illegally?*'

Laura bristled. 'It wasn't like that. I was only meant to look after her for a week or so and then I fell in love with her and because of his circumstances we agreed that I would keep her.'

'Christ!'

Laura saw the shocked look of disbelief on his face and her heart sank.

'And he expected you to raise her!'

'He sends me money every month.'

'I should hope so. That's not the point though; you could be in serious trouble. Why did you agree to it?'

'Because I *love* Amy, I wanted her. Can't you see it's as much my fault as Danny's? Sure he wanted her out of his life, but I *needed* her. It would have broken my heart to give her back.'

'Could you not have adopted her properly?'

Laura shook her head. 'Not without his wife finding out.'

'Did you ever speak to Amy's mother, made sure that was what she wanted?'

'No. Danny said . . . '

'How do you know he wasn't lying? How can you be certain that even now she is not pining for her child?'

'I trust Danny.' Laura said in a small voice, not wanting to hear what Paul was saying because deep in her heart she had always feared this. Feared it and hidden it from herself. She had convinced herself over and over that Harriet would have found her, come for Amy if she really, really wanted her. But supposing Danny had refused to tell Harriet where she lived.

She couldn't look at Paul, a small sob escaped her. She should have kept her secret. He was as horrified at what she had done as Terry had been. 'I'm so – s-sorry,' she hiccupped.

Paul rose and pulled her in his arms. 'There is nothing to be sorry for. It wasn't your fault. This Danny put you in an impossible situation.'

'I couldn't tell you before. I really shouldn't be telling you now, I promised Danny, and well I – I was so afraid of losing you.'

Paul kissed her gently. 'I can see the dilemma you were in. And for the record you can never lose me.'

Laura leaned against his shoulder and sobbed, relief and love for this man overwhelmed her.

Paul refilled their glasses. 'I think you should go and see this Harriet, I'll come with you.'

'Would you?' She was touched.

'Of course.'

'Terry keeps telling me I should go.'

'He's right. You can't spend the rest of your life like this, always worried, always afraid. If the woman really doesn't want Amy, then I'm sure she'll be willing to let you adopt her.'

'And if she wants her back?'

'It's a risk we'll have to take.'

Laura lay in Paul's arms in his huge comfortable bed. It was two o'clock and Paul was fast asleep. Making love with him had been as fantastic as she remembered it. She had been nervous at first, wondering if he still found her body attractive. She had put on a few pounds, even though she still only weighed eight stone. But the moment they were in bed her fears dissolved. He started by caressing her, his touch sending erotic shivers right down to the tips of her toes. Then he had kissed every inch of her, his lips hungry and insistent, while murmuring how beautiful she was. His body had not changed; it was still as thin as ever, but she loved the softness of his skin and the hardness of his muscles. Running her hand along his taut thighs she had breathed in the clean fresh smell of him and when at last they had come together she knew she would never let him go again.

Now, however, she was wide-awake and fretting, torn between doing the right thing and seeing Harriet and terrified that she would lose her beloved Amy.

Her thoughts were filled with Amy. She loved this child so much. From the first moment she had seen her, she had loved her, cared for her, watched her take her first steps, comforted her when she had cut her first tooth, taught her to read and write her name before she started school, and now to think that she might lose her. It was unbearable.

'What about Danny?' she had asked Paul last night.

'He's not your problem. So what if his wife finds out, tough. You can't ruin your life because of his indiscretions.'

'I guess not.'

'Have you thought about what you're going to tell Amy when she's older?'

Laura looked startled. 'I – er – I wasn't planning to tell her.'

'There will come a day when you have no choice.'

'Will there? Why?'

'Think about it. Presumably her birth certificate is not registered with your name as her mother?'

'Obviously.'

'There will come a point in her life when she will need it. What will you do then?'

'I've never given it much thought.'

'When she's older she will need it to get a passport, get married. I'm amazed you've got away without it for so long.'

Laura remembered the surgery and how she never did get the replacement. She had been lucky they had never pursued it.

'Amy is already asking where her daddy is. She will want answers. She will need to know who her real mother is.'

It was an echo of a conversation she'd had with Terry a long time ago. She had pushed the problem away, hoping she would never have to deal with it. How stupid was that.

'I've no idea. Actually I haven't even got her birth certificate.'

'See what I mean. What happens when she needs it? Go and see her, darling. It might not be as bad as you fear.'

But it might be. It might be worse.

Chapter Forty-Two

Harriet crossed the churchyard and followed the sunken footpath to the ornamental low bridge that spanned the River Windrush. She continued walking, head down, the Canon camera on her shoulder weighing heavily. She turned left at the kissing gate, then along the lane flanked by drystone walls and high hedges. Her long black wool cape flowed around her, brushing against the overgrown grass.

She passed a cluster of white stone cottages until she came to a field gate. Skirting round the edge of the pasture, keeping away from the grazing cows, she climbed a stile and made her way down the muddy incline until she reached the river edge. Most villagers or tourists reached the river by the tarmac lane, but she preferred this route. She walked slowly along the tow path. It was her favourite place, chosen because of its solitude. It was used very little; mostly by people walking their dogs. There wasn't a great deal to attract visitors in this quiet section of the river, except an occasional boat moored in the summer, but the river was deserted on this cold December day.

She loved this river bank, and had spent many hours here taking pictures, the narrow boats, the swans. Winter pictures were the best, a robin on a naked tree branch, frost on the hedges, the river shrouded in fog.

Carefully placing her bag on the ground, she settled herself on a wooden bench and removed the camera.

Her venture into photography had happened almost by accident, not long after she had arrived in the village. She had visited a small gallery in search of pictures for the cottage. A local artist had been holding an exhibition of his black and white photographs and she had been fascinated by them.

She found to her surprise she had an aptitude for capturing interesting subjects. Intuitively she knew what would work and what would not. She bought loads of books on the subject and after several initial mistakes finally processed her first sepia print. Two years later, her black and white pictures went on sale in the *Flamingo* café. Brett had been impressed with her work and was more than willing to display them on his walls.

She found photography both relaxing and therapeutic; it got her through the bad days. She also found it rewarding that people actually paid money for her work. It wasn't to everyone's taste, the starkness of some of her pictures did not appeal to every customer, but they sold well.

An hour later she switched off her camera without having taken a single shot. She couldn't concentrate today. She sat gazing along the river, to where a mist was rising. A package had arrived for her this morning and it had upset her. On top of which Danny was supposed to have called, but he hadn't shown up.

She scrubbed her eyes with the back of her hand, horrified to feel tears threatening. She never cried. *Never.* Tears would weaken her and she had to stay strong.

She had stayed strong throughout the years of living with her guilt. Throughout all the dark days of despair she had stayed resolute, determined never to look back, never to dwell on what she had done.

Not that it always worked. There were times when her guilt overwhelmed her and she thought she would go insane remembering the horror of it all.

Her love for Danny had remained constant. She had long forgiven him for abandoning her, for not wanting their child. She no longer blamed him for the accident, for her injuries. He had saved her from imprisonment and for that she would always be grateful. If it hadn't been for his quick thinking that night . . .

She put up with her isolated life just to be near him. The rest of the world could go hang, she didn't care; being with Danny was all that mattered. She had never loved anyone as much as she loved him. She just wished he would leave Christine and be with her. It galled her that she had to be content with the short time they had together. Now even that was changing. She had noticed a difference in him lately; his visits were becoming strained, and today he hadn't turned up at all.

Despite everything he still had the power to make her want him, need him. She was tied to him forever, sharing their guilty secret.

Six months after Jeremy's death she sold her house in Charlton Kings and bought a cottage in Upper Wyre.

She had been in the cottage three weeks when Danny called to see her. His presence filled the small room. She was so happy to see him, until she saw the anger in his eyes.

'Harriet,' he had said coldly, 'what the devil are you doing here? Christine said you had bought this old cottage, but I didn't believe her. Are you mad?'

'Nice to see you too, Danny,' she said sarcastically.

'Why have you moved here?'

She shrugged. 'Is there any reason why I shouldn't live here?'

'I thought we'd agreed not to see each other until it was safe.'

'But it's been months . . . '

'Harriet, you committed a murder. We can't take any chances.'

She didn't need reminding. Her pleasure at seeing him deflated, she felt overwrought. 'I can't handle this. I can't forget what I've done. Sometimes I think I'll just go to the police and confess, get it over with. It would be such a relief.'

He glowered. 'That would be very silly. Do you want to spend the rest of your life in prison?'

'I don't care. If we can't be together there's no point to my life . . . I *need* you Danny.' Her voice became hysterical.

'All right, all right,' Danny said soothingly. 'Calm down. Maybe in a week or two . . .'

'Promise,' she pleaded.

'Yes. Now actually there's another reason why I'm here. Christine said you told her about us and the child.'

'Yes I did, months ago.'

Danny ran his hand through his hair. 'I can't believe you did

274

that. I thought she was going to leave me, she was so devastated.'

'Would it have been so awful if she left you? It would mean we could be together.'

'You don't get it do you? I don't want her to go. I like my marriage.'

Harriet lowered her gaze so that he couldn't see how much his words hurt her. 'What did you say to her?' she asked.

'I promised her that it was over between us. I told her the child couldn't be mine, that I was infertile.'

Harriet smirked. 'She believed you!'

'Yes, I think so.'

She moved closer to him, needing the comfort of his arms around her. 'I can't live without you Danny, please don't say it's over.'

'Harriet . . . '

'I'll be discreet,' she promised, 'but don't abandon me again.' She pressed her lips to his mouth, and tightened her arms around him, rubbing her body against his.

He groaned and responded as she knew he would.

Since that visit Danny came to the cottage once a month, on the day Christine met her friend in Cheltenham for lunch. These visits were all that kept her from total despair. Without them she had nothing to look forward to; they gave her life a tiny fragment of meaning. It was pathetic, but she couldn't let go of her need of Danny.

The years had dulled the guilt as loneliness crept in. Danny's infrequent and unsatisfactory visits gradually turned her gratitude to bitterness. Sometimes she tried to goad him into visiting her more often, but he always reminded her of what she had done. She resented the hold he had over her, the knowledge that he knew she was a murderess.

It was impossible not to believe that one day Jeremy's body would be found. She wondered if she could convince a court of law that it had been an accident. It had always amazed her that the police had not suspected her, especially as Abigail continued her relentless search for her brother. At least, thank God, she no longer came to the cottage. In the weeks after Jeremy's "disappearance" Abigail had hounded her, poking and prying, trying to get answers. She had not informed Abigail of her new address, but somehow the woman had found her. For a while she called regularly. She would drink a cup of tea, sitting stiffly on a chair, without taking off her coat and hat. The conversation was always about Jeremy. Now she only sent Christmas cards with a cryptic message that said. *I will never forget you.* She knew it was a threat rather than an endearment.

She looked back across the fields to the village church. When she had first come here to live, she had sat in a cold empty pew in St Peter's and prayed for forgiveness. It hadn't helped. The guilt, the horror of what had happened never left her. She had no idea where in the perfumery garden Danny had concealed the body. She didn't want to know. She never went to the perfumery.

She was aware that her presence in the village had been greeted with undisguised curiosity. She hated their sympathy and soon made it clear that she would not tolerate their intrusion. They took offence at her cold, unfriendly attitude and now no one talked to her. The vicar had called once, but she had been so rude to him he hadn't repeated the visit. She didn't care, she preferred it that way.

Harriet sighed as the afternoon light faded and the cold penetrated through her cloak. From the bend in the river, the dark hulk of a narrow boat came into view. She could see a figure at the helm waiting to throw the rope to the mooring stake. With no desire to be sociable, she collected up her bag and started back. The fresh air had not cleared her head, which had ached unbearably all day from the large amount of gin she had drunk the previous night. She had only meant to drink one glass to take the edge of her loneliness. She ended up finishing the bottle.

She limped slowly home. As she reached the cottage, Satan, her black cat, was mewing on the doorstep. She unlocked the door and the cat bolted inside. Satan had appeared the day after she had moved in. She had tried to ignore it, but it persisted in mewing outside her door until at last she fed it. Now she found its presence a comfort.

She closed the curtains and switched on the lights before going into the kitchen to make a coffee. After filling the kettle she looked around for a clean mug, but the sink was full of dirty dishes. She rinsed one under the cold tap and made a drink.

Back in the living room, she settled into her chair and retrieved the package that had arrived that morning by registered post. She could look at it now without being upset. It was from her father. Her mother had died. "It was a blessed release for her", Bill had written. Inside the package were several pieces of her mother's jewellery.

Although the short letter mentioned the day and time of the funeral, the day had passed. There was no mention of her father returning home or any invitation to join him now that he was alone, not that she would consider going, but it would have been nice to have been asked.

It had been a long time since she had seen her mother and now, of course, she never would. The realisation was upsetting. She should have made the effort to go to Canada, made up the awful row and now it was too late.

Harriet fingered the bracelets and necklaces, they were all made from eighteen carat gold and the stones were genuine sapphires and emeralds. There was a pair of diamond earrings and an eternity ring with a solitaire diamond. She remembered Dad buying her mother the ring for their twenty-fifth wedding anniversary.

At five, she fed Satan and poured herself a drink as she mulled over what to do about her father. She sat in her chair and lifted her feet up on the footstool.

Maybe it was time to heal the rift; maybe she should go out to Canada and see him. What was there to keep her here now? Four years she had lived this miserable existence, living for the once-a-month visits from Danny. Dear God, why was she so pathetic?

She knew why of course. She had totally lost it after killing Jeremy. Haunted by what she had done, she had shut herself away. Shunning the outside world, afraid of people, she had weaved a cocoon of loneliness around herself which was her solace and her downfall. Sometimes she thought she was going mad. She closed her eyes, trying to shut out the past.

Her rest was short-lived, interrupted by the sudden rattle of the door-knocker. Satan shot out of the chair and arched his back. She bent down and stroked him. 'Now, who on earth can that be?' she muttered. It was too late in the day for it to be Danny, and anyway he had his own key.

She moved to the window and carefully lifted the curtain aside, trying to see who was there, but it was too dark to see properly.

The silence was broken by another knock, louder this time. With an irritated curse she made her way to the front door and opened it with a swift movement. 'What do you want?' she snapped ungraciously.

'Excuse me, are you Harriet Malin?'

'Who wants to know?'

'My name is . . .'

'I don't want whatever it is you're selling.'

'I'm not selling anything. My name is Laura . . . '

Chapter Forty-Three

Earlier that day Laura had stood outside the perfumery glancing through the bow windows to see if she could see Danny.

She had arrived in the village late the previous evening. She had travelled by train to Cheltenham and then the local bus. Terry had advised her against driving, said her car was not reliable. He had been relieved when she had told him that Paul had talked her into going to see Harriet.

Paul had wanted to come with her but in the end she had decided against it. It had been a wrench leaving Amy but she hadn't wanted to take her. Paul had offered to look after her, said he wanted to get to know her. They had moved into Paul's house last month and their wedding was arranged for next May. Amy was excited at the thought of being a bridesmaid.

She had booked into the Stag Hotel, a character hotel built of Cotswold Stone with ivy covering the front walls. The hotel had been modernised since she lived here and the new owners were strangers to her. Too anxious to eat breakfast, she hurried to the perfumery.

She moved to the side archway leading to the rear gardens and peered through the black wrought iron railings. She felt nervous of going in, of confronting him. She wanted to see him, to explain that she couldn't keep his secret any more, and to find out if he knew where Harriet lived.

There was no sign of Danny, so she entered the shop before she lost her nerve and approached the assistant, a middle-aged woman with a friendly smile. Not someone she knew. That was good.

'Can I help you?'

'May I speak to Mr Pembroke, please?'

'He hasn't arrived yet. Can I help?'

'It's really Mr Pembroke I need to speak to, can I wait?'

'He'll probably be about half and hour.'

'That's okay.'

'There's a nice café, next door, *Flamingo,* if you sit by the window you will see him arrive. You can't miss him; he always wears a black overcoat and carries a brown brief case.'

'Thanks,' Laura turned away, hiding a smile.

Laura sat in the café's window seat, drinking coffee as she watched people passing by. No one in the café was familiar. The waitress looked no more than sixteen, too young to have been here five years ago. She wondered if Brett still owned it. The place had changed, looked more modern. No frilled aprons on the waitress or lace cloths on the tables. Several framed black and white and sepia photos adorned the whitewashed walls. She wondered if it was a local artist but she didn't go closer to find out.

Every time someone came into view she looked up expectantly, but it was over half-an-hour before Danny arrived. His stride was purposeful, his black pin-striped suit hanging perfectly underneath an overcoat draped loosely on his broad shoulders. The breeze had ruffled his hair and he smoothed it down before entering the building.

She glanced at her watch. It was nearly ten, she wondered if he still came into the café for his morning coffee.

Another half-an-hour passed. She was just about to leave when Danny entered. The place was full now and he didn't notice her. She watched him order, flirting with the waitress and then unfolding his newspaper.

She waited until his coffee had arrived before she rose and approached the table, sitting down uninvited.

Danny glanced up, frowned and then, as recognition dawned, his eyes changed. The colour left his face. 'What on earth are you doing here? Is something wrong?'

'No nothing like that. I need to talk to you.'

'You made me a promise, you said you've never contact me, never come here. Thank God Christine's in Cheltenham.'

'Please Danny, I must speak to you.'

Danny seemed to hesitate, and she thought he was going to refuse. 'All right,' he said, 'come to the perfumery, we can't talk here.'

He gulped the rest of his coffee and rose.

She followed him out and into the perfumery. 'Jenny, hold any calls, I don't want to be disturbed,' he snapped at the assistant.

'Okay.'

Jenny smiled at her with eyes alive with curiosity.

'Follow me.' He strode across the floor and Laura hurried after him, manoeuvring around the display shelves of delicate glass perfume bottles.

In the laboratory, he laid his briefcase on the table and flung his overcoat over the back of a chair before sitting down. He indicated for her to sit opposite. 'Well?'

'Things have changed.'

'How?' he sounded angry.

'I'm getting married.'

'Congratulations,' his tone was dismissive. 'What has that got to do with our arrangement?'

'I told Paul, my fiancé, the truth. He's worried that I have Amy illegally. He says I should never have let you talk me into it.'

'I thought you'd promised never to tell anyone.'

'I had to tell Paul. I couldn't marry him and keep such a secret. I couldn't make him an accessory to our illegal . . .'

Danny raised his hand to stop her. 'I seem to remember you were more than willing; that you *wanted* her.'

'I did – I do,' Laura stammered, 'it's just that it's been really difficult lying to everyone and now I want to make it right. I - we want to adopt her legally.'

Danny ran his hand through his hair. 'That's not possible.'

'Please, Danny there must be a way. I'll go and see Harriet, see if she agrees, maybe we can do it without involving you.'

Danny remained silent. There was no telling what he was thinking behind his inscrutable expression. The silence stretched interminably. His gaze seemed to go out of focus. After a moment he pulled himself together.

'I can't take the risk.'

Laura felt anger surging. 'I'm going to see Harriet anyway. This is important to me.'

He shrugged. 'That's up to you, but I warn you now, I'll deny everything.'

'Fine. I really don't want to make any trouble for you. Now please, can you tell me where Harriet lives?'

Danny ran his hand over his face. There was another long silence. At last he sighed heavily. 'She lives here, in the village, Lilac Cottage at the end of Mill Lane. You can't miss it; it's the only building. I should warn you though; she won't want to see you.'

'Why?'

Danny gave a wry laugh. 'It's going to be a shock to her, you turning up out of the blue. She won't want to be reminded. . . '

'I'll take my chance.'

Danny rose. 'I'm sorry to rush you, but I do have a busy morning.' Danny walked to the door, opened it, and waited for her to leave.

After Laura had left, Danny went to the window, lifting one of the slats of the Venetian blinds slightly, so that he could see her as she left the building. He watched her walk across the tarmac yard and out through the gates. He returned to his chair and sat down thoughtfully. His heart was still racing from the shock. Even now it was hard to think straight, to decide what to do.

He needed some air. He went through the rear entrance and out into the gardens.

The grounds, although walled and private, were not large. When they had first bought the premises, Christine had designed the garden so that visitors could enjoy a few moments on the rustic seats and admire her rose garden and rockery. The rose garden was especially beautiful, as were the borders of pale blue forget-me-not and delicate white lily-of-the-valley. Beyond that was a mimosa tree with pretty yellow flowers and a climbing jasmine. Now, twenty years on, the garden was looking decidedly neglected. The grass was full of moss and the paths were cracked and discoloured. Ted, the old gardener, came once a week in the summer to cut the grass and do a little light weeding. Now, however, it really needed more than that. Christine had wanted to renovate it but he dissuaded her. He couldn't risk anyone messing around here.

He walked slowly along the brick-paved pathway, surveying the flowers beds. In the summer months the roses grew in abundance, their sweet fragrance filling the air. English Rose was one of the fastest sellers, as was the lavender that grew in purple and white clumps in the rockery. Not that the perfumes were made from these plants, he imported his compounds, nevertheless the visitors enjoyed the gardens, it gave them a taste of what the flowers smelt like. He snipped off a late yellow rose bud and inserted it into his jacket lapel.

He passed the wishing-well and shivered. He rarely came down here; it gave him the creeps to think of Jeremy . . . it had been a long time since he'd thought about that catastrophic night.

Harriet. She was interminably woven into his life because of that night. Jeremy's death had bound them together, even though the love he once felt for her had diminished over the years. She was too needy, too demanding and even sex was no longer exciting.

He wished he could end the affair. He dreaded Christine finding out that he was still seeing Harriet, but he feared the consequences of what Harriet would do even more.

He had hurt Christine deeply and for that, he felt remorse. He had vowed to her that he would never leave her, never ask for a divorce and although their marriage was not ideal, at least they had some semblance of normality. He loved Christine; she was his rock, constant and faithful. He didn't deserve her loyalty, not after what he had done; nevertheless, he was determined not to lose her.

He was so deep in thought that he was startled to find Jenny at his elbow. 'Are you all right, sir?'

'Yes, yes,' he answered impatiently, 'I needed a bit of fresh air.'

'Is that girl okay, only she looked a bit upset when she left?'
Jenny was prying, dying to find out what his visitor wanted.
Danny gave a wry smile. 'She used to work in the café.'
'What did she want?'
'She was after a job,' he said with a forced laugh.
'Ah.' Jenny turned with a nod, leaving him alone.

He waited for another few moments before following her, and
then re-entered the building and strode into his laboratory. He
was supposed to be seeing Harriet this morning, but there was no
way he was going there today, not with Laura turning up. In fact,
he needed to work, take his mind off his problem. He needed to
think what to do if, God forbid, Christine found out the truth.

His mobile rang. He checked the screen, saw it was Harriet and
switched it off.

Chapter Forty-Four

Everything about Lilac Cottage looked old and forbidding. Tiny panes in square windows, honey-coloured limestone walls covered in lichen beneath a slate roof. Laura hesitated by the gate, suddenly terrified of confronting Harriet.

After leaving the perfumery, she had wandered around the village, lingered in the shops and had lunch back in the café, anything to delay going to see Harriet.

She was nervous of meeting her, especially as Danny seemed to think she wouldn't be welcome. Now, as the late afternoon was growing dark, and a light drizzle of rain had started, she reached Mill Lane, which was nothing more than a track; the thin layer of tarmac, old and cracked, with many pot-holes. The road was long and winding, twisting down towards a river.

She had almost turned back, thinking that she was on the wrong path; there seemed to be no sign of habitation, when she saw a thin spiral of smoke through the trees.

With a resigned shrug she pushed open the gate, and walked up the short path. There was no bell, so she banged the black wrought iron knocker set in the white wooden door. She waited a few moments and when there was no response, knocked again. A curtain twitched in the downstairs window and after a few minutes the door was flung open. A soft yellow light illuminated the narrow hallway and a black cat streaked passed her.

The woman was very thin. Was this Harriet? She barely recognised her. Her angular face was partly hidden by her black shoulder length hair, which was combed straight down, hiding one side of her face. The black skirt that reached her ankles was splattered with mud at the edges and the several jumpers of various lengths were grubby. Her gaze was cold and unfriendly.

'What do you want?' she snapped ungraciously.

Laura swallowed hard. 'Excuse me, but are you Harriet Malin?'

'Who wants to know?'

'My name is . . .'

'I don't want whatever it is you're selling.'

'I'm not selling anything. My name is Laura Armstrong. I've come about Amy, your daughter.'

Harriet's eyes flickered for a moment; she seemed shaken.

'Rubbish, I don't have daughter, go away.' As Harriet made to close the door, Laura said quickly. 'Please let me explain.'

'Certainly not.' The door slammed shut.

Laura walked back down the path, her shoulders slumped with defeat. Closing the gate she stood looking back at the cottage, feeling frustrated with disappointment. Danny had warned her, but she had not expected such a curt, blunt denial.

She walked back down the lane, feeling angry again. First Danny, and now Harriet dismissing her as if it had nothing to do with them. Treating Amy as if she didn't matter, almost denying her existence even. *How dare they!*

She returned to the hotel. She wasn't going to give up, she would go back tomorrow.

* * *

Harriet poured herself a large gin and tonic. After draining the glass, she felt less shaky. The appearance of Laura had been a tremendous shock. Danny had sworn that Laura would never contact her, would never want to return the child to her. It had been an instinctive reaction to send her away, to deny everything. She poured another drink. She had to think. Was Laura here to make her take the child back? Well she wouldn't, she couldn't. Her life was settled, there was no room in it for a child. There never had been. She knew she lacked any maternal instincts. Over the years she had hardly given her baby a thought. There had been no desire to discover where Amy was or even to know what she was like. She didn't want to be reminded about the baby she had given away. The baby, whose face she couldn't remember; an anonymous child. The cause of all her problems.

The gin eased her anxiety, helped her to recover from the shock. And it had been a shock, the unexpected confrontation. She justified her actions, as she re-enacted the scene on the doorstep, in her head. Bloody hell, what did Laura expect? How was she supposed to react? Turning up, out of the blue, without any warning.

Laura would be back, of that she was certain. She poured yet another drink, feeling the panic rise again, the dry mouth; the sweating palms. She needed to talk to Danny, to warn him. She reached for her mobile phone and punched in his home number. He wasn't going to like her ringing him at home; it was something they had agreed she would never do. He was going to like it even less when he listened to what she was going to say to him.

However his phone was on answer message. She tried his mobile, but that was still switched off.

* * *

Laura phoned Paul's mobile. 'Hi, it's me.'

'How did you get on, did you meet her?'

'Briefly.'

'And?'

'She slammed the door in my face.'

'Huh. Guess you were the last person she expected to see. What are you going to do now?'

'Go back tomorrow, and then the day after and the day after that until she talks to me. I'm not giving up.'

'Shall I drive up?'

'Thanks, but I need to do this on my own. How is Amy?'

'Great. Missing you, though.'

'Give her a hug for me.'

287

Laura sat on the wall outside Harriet's cottage. She had spent a solitary evening in the hotel. The only other resident in the dining room had been a dowdy woman carrying a large tapestry handbag. The woman had not spoken or looked at her and had spent the entire meal reading a book.

Now she had come to try again with Harriet. She had knocked several times, but there had been no answer. The black cat mewed at her feet and she bent and lifted it up, stroking it. 'Hello cat.'

Half an hour later Laura looked down the lane and saw Harriet walking towards her, her gait was awkward beneath the black hooded cloak that flowed around her. Laura stood up and waited. The cat was wriggling to be set free, but she held it tight.

'What's its name?' Laura said when Harriet was within hearing distance.

'Satan. Put him down, he doesn't like to be fussed.'

She let the cat down. It immediately rushed to the front door mewing loudly. Harriet followed and inserted her key into the lock. Laura waited, half expecting the door to slam shut again.

'You'd better come in,' Harriet said.

Hardly believing that Harriet had relented, she stepped inside before she could change her mind.

In the dimly lit hallway, she took off her coat and when Harriet made no move to take it from her she hung it over the newel post at the foot of the stairs. Harriet had turned and was moving into the living room. Laura followed her.

The room was a surprise. Despite all the mess and dust, the large square room was beautiful, with a low beamed ceiling and mellow stone walls. A black cast iron wood burner set in a recessed chimney breast gave off enough heat to make the room warm and cosy.

Laura looked around, noticing the oak dresser, the plush sofa and armchairs and the thick carpet. No shortage of cash then. Poverty was obviously not the reason she had abandoned her child.

Harriet lowered herself into one of the armchairs by the fireplace and indicated for Laura to sit opposite in the other. The cat had already beaten her to it and swished his tail, hissing angrily, when she lifted him off. She sat on the edge of the chair, trying not to mind the profusion of cat hairs.

'What do you want?' Harriet snapped imperiously.

Laura hesitated; she wished she could see her face properly. Harriet's long hair was pulled forward partly obscuring her features. She decided to come straight to the point; she suspected Harriet would not tolerate prevarication.

'I don't want to cause any trouble.'

'Good.'

'I've come to talk about your daughter.'

'You've made a mistake. I don't have a daughter.'

Laura sighed in exasperation. 'Danny gave her to me when you had the car crash. I was there when it happened. I know Danny is Amy's father.'

'I think you had better leave, I can't help you.'

Laura stood up. She looked at her for a few moments, trying to stem a really dreadful thought. Was she really not Amy's mother, had Danny been lying to her? Did the baby belong to someone else?

No, that was absurd.

'I spoke to Danny yesterday . . . '

'You spoke to Danny?' Harriet interrupted, her voice shocked, 'what about?'

Laura shifted her weight from one foot to the other. 'That was what I want to talk to you about.'

Harriet stared at her. 'You had better sit down again. I'll make a drink.'

Laura returned to the chair, lifted the cat onto her knee and stroked it while she waited for Harriet to return. It was disconcerting to think that this strange cold woman was Amy's mother. Amy was such a happy, sunny child. She wondered what sort of life she would have had if Harriet had not given her away. She thought it would have been awful. Harriet was no mother figure.

Laura gazed around the room again, noticing several framed black and white and sepia photos on the walls that looked similar to the ones in the café. She wondered if Harriet had done them.

Harriet returned with two mugs of coffee. Once more she sat facing Laura.

'Does your husband live here?' Laura asked.

Harriet looks startled. 'My husband?'

'I thought you were married.' Laura was probing, trying to find out if Jeremy Malin had returned. Zoe had said he had mysteriously gone missing some time ago.

'He left me. I don't know where he is and I don't care, abroad somewhere for all I know.'

'I'm sorry.'

Harriet shrugged.

There was silence for a few moments. 'Okay, Amy is mine but I can't take her back,' Harriet suddenly blurted out.

Laura's eyes widened. 'That's not why I'm here, just the opposite in fact. I want to adopt Amy. Danny is okay with it, so long as we can keep it from his wife. I'm getting married soon and, well, I want it all to be legal.'

Harriet's face relaxed. 'What does that involve?'

'Going to an adoption agency, I think.'

'Oh no, I can't be doing with that. People poking into my life; asking questions. No definitely not. It would cause too many problems and it would be worse for you; they'll want to know why you've had Amy all this time without my permission.'

Laura blanched. Terry and Paul had been right; she could be in serious trouble. 'So what can I do?' she asked bleakly.

'Keep her. I promise you I don't want her. Danny certainly doesn't want her. I can't see what your problem is.'

'But I need something to make it legal,' Laura said, desperately. 'Maybe we don't need to go to an agency, maybe a letter of consent will suffice.'

'I'm not sure.' Harriet sipped her drink and looked away. 'I can't be doing with any hassle.'

'It's just a letter,' Laura pleaded.

'Let me think about it.'

'There's something else.'

'What?' Harriet glared.

'When Amy is older she will want her birth certificate.'

290

'Oh, you can have that.'

'Can I? Thanks.' Laura smiled uncertainly. She had not expected it to be so easy. 'And you are sure you don't want her back.'

Harriet snorted. She raised the curtain of dark hair from her face. It was hard not to gasp at the puckered scar that ran from her left eye down to her mouth. Her skin was creased, making her look older than her thirty-four years. 'I have enough to contend with. I couldn't cope with a child.'

Harriet let her hair fall loose again. 'Not a pretty sight is it? I was beautiful until – until the accident.' She stopped talking, her eyes bleak as if the memory was too painful to continue.

Laura wanted to ask why she suffered the scar when surely plastic surgery would help, but she wasn't sure how to phrase the sentence; it seemed too personal a question. Harriet, however, seemed to read her thoughts.

'I had skin grafting done once, but I got an infection, made the bloody thing worse.'

'I'm so sorry,' Laura murmured.

Harriet lifted the edge of her long skirt and tapped her knee. 'See that, my knee was smashed. Never properly healed. I'll always walk with a limp.'

'I'm so sorry.' Laura repeated, appalled at the sight of the twisted knee.

Harriet grunted. 'I was beautiful once, now I can't bear to look in the mirror.'

'I know you were. I remember you from the perfumery.'

Harriet shrugged indifferently.

Laura said impulsively. 'Would you like me to bring Amy to see you? She's five now, and so cute.'

'That won't be necessary.' Once more, the cold tone was in her voice.

'Right, well then, if you can give me Amy's birth certificate I'll get out of your way.'

'I don't know where it is. I think Danny has it.'

Not so easy after all.

Laura bit down on her lip. 'Would you do me a favour and ask him for me.'

'For pity's sake!'

'Please.'

A shrug. 'Come back tomorrow, not too early.'

Laura finished her coffee and rose. 'Thanks.' She placed an envelope on the table. 'Photos of Amy if you're interested.'

Laura let herself out.

Long after Laura had left, Harriet sat smoking by the firelight. She opened the envelope. A dozen or so photos spilled out. Her hand shook as she gazed at them. There had not been many occasions when she had allowed herself to think of Amy. The baby Danny had given away. The little girl in the photo was adorable, but she felt no connection with her, no recognition that this was her child.

She shuffled the photos back into the envelope. Far too late to feel any guilt, any remorse for her lack of maternal care. Tomorrow she would ask Danny for the birth certificate, then perhaps Laura would go home and leave her in peace.

Stubbing out her cigarette, she poured herself a gin and tonic and made her way upstairs.

Chapter Forty-Five

Laura woke early the following morning. Far too early to visit Harriet, who had told her not to call before midday.

After breakfast she went for a walk, remembering the time she had lived here. Zoe and Nancy had both moved away of course. She had no idea whether Brett and his wife still lived in the village. Later she would call at the house and see.

Hunched in her thick wool coat, gloved hands deep into her pockets, she tramped down the lane of frozen pot-holes. The day was raw; a biting wind stung her cheeks. Reaching the end, she climbed over a stile gate. A crisp frost covered the ground, making the fields look picturesque. It was peaceful in the early morning air, the weather too cold for most people to venture out. She reached a bridleway and followed the river bank, thinking of Harriet. She felt a twinge of guilt, wondering if she had been too traumatised by the accident to appreciate what she had given up. Surely, as Amy's mother, she must have regrets.

It had been a rash impulsive suggestion, the offer to bring Amy here. Supposing she had wanted to see her. Once Harriet had met Amy she was bound to have feelings for her; it was only natural.

A shiver of anxiety coursed through her. The fear of losing Amy was irrational, yet real.

How would she bear it if Harriet changed her mind? Maybe now that Amy had grown into a sweet little girl – quite different from coping with a screaming baby – Harriet would claim her right to have her daughter in her life – where would that leave her, the occasional visit like a distant aunt? Or not even a visit.

She had poured out her troubled thoughts to Paul on the phone last night. He told her she was being silly. 'I thought Harriet said she wanted nothing to do with her?' he reminded her.

'I know, but what if she changes her mind after she's looked at the photos. Oh I wish I hadn't given them to her.'

'Stop fretting. From what you have told me about Harriet I would think it's highly unlikely she wants her.'

Harriet answered the door almost immediately when Laura returned to the cottage. She didn't greet her or acknowledge her, merely stood aside to let her in.

Laura decided to come straight to the point. 'Did you to see Danny,' she said, shrugging out of her coat. 'Did you get the certificate?'

'Apparently Danny went to Scotland this morning,' Harriet said, sounding annoyed. 'He won't be back for a couple of days. I'd go and see Christine, but I doubt she will know where he keeps it.'

Laura looked puzzled. 'Danny's wife doesn't know about Amy.'

Harriet smirked. 'Oh yes she does. I told her.'

'But Danny – Danny has always been afraid of Christine finding out, even now he's worried sick.'

'I know.' Harriet chortled. 'That's the beauty of it. She has always known about us, right from the beginning. Danny went to such great lengths to hide our affair from her and she knew all the time.'

Laura frowned. 'I don't understand.'

'When Christine told me that she knew about us, I assumed she also knew that Danny was Amy's father. Apparently she didn't. That came as a shock to her. Of course Danny denied it when Christine confronted him. He told her I was lying and he said she believed him, but I doubt it.'

'This all sounds a bit complicated.'

Harriet shrugged her shoulders.

'Why doesn't she leave him?'

'I think it's her pride, and the fact that, despite whatever he has done, she still loves him, wants to stay married to him. I know he won't leave her. I've tried, God knows, to make him.'

'Why?' Laura was shocked.

'Because I love him.'

'But he's married to Christine.'

'So!'

Laura was silent, unsure what to say.

Harriet looked annoyed. 'People divorce every day. He won't though. He's such a coward, can't face confrontation.'

Laura said quietly. 'Maybe he loves Christine.'

'No he doesn't,' Harriet was scornful. 'He's just weak and selfish. If he'd had the balls to leave Christine years ago, I wouldn't be in this mess. I wouldn't be alone.'

'Does he love you?'

'Of course he does. Do you think I'd put myself through all this if we weren't in love. I didn't *choose* to love him. Believe me I would stop if I could, but it's not that easy to switch off your feelings.'

Ignoring the sudden self-pitying tone, Laura said. 'Loving him obviously doesn't make you happy.'

Harriet raised her eyebrows. 'Oh, an expert on love are you?'

'Of course not. I just feel that Danny has gone to great lengths to protect Christine from the truth. That must mean something. If he didn't care about her, he would have just told her about Amy.'

'Bullshit.' Harriet glared and reached for a cigarette.

'Do you know he has been sending me money for Amy's upbringing, he's never missed a month? At least he has a sense of responsibility towards Amy. Not like you.'

Harriet's eyes narrowed. 'Sending money is not because he cares about Amy, it's guilt. He knows he should never have abandoned me and his daughter.'

When Laura didn't reply, Harriet rose and went to the dresser. She poured herself a large gin without offering anything to Laura.

'I'll post the certificate on to you when I get it.' Harriet's tone was sharp now.

'Will you also do me a letter of consent?'

'Yes, yes that as well.'

'I'd rather stay on a few days until Danny comes back.'

'Please yourself.'

Laura approached the reception desk at the Stag Hotel.

The receptionist, a young leggy girl with long blonde hair smiled. 'Can I help you?'

'Yes please. I'm in room twenty. Can I book a further two nights please?'

'Oh dear, I'm sorry, we have a wedding party coming tomorrow. All the rooms are booked.'

'Is there nothing at all?' Laura said in dismay.

''fraid not.'

'Is there any other hotel in the village?'

'There's a couple of B&B's, although I think they close for the winter. Don't get much call you see.'

Laura thanked her and turned away. There was no option but to go home unless . . .

For the second time that day, Laura knocked on Harriet's door. It seemed a bit of a cheek what she was about to ask but what better way to get to know Harriet. And she needed to know as much as she could about her. One day Amy would ask all sorts of questions and she wanted to be ready with the answers.

She was greeted by a cold stare, a surprised lift of the eyebrows. The invitation to come in was less than friendly.

'I was wondering if maybe I could stay here until Danny gets back.'

'Stay here, with me. Why?'

'The hotel's fully booked for a wedding.'

Harriet continued to frown, not answering.

'It would just be a couple of days,' Laura prompted.

'I'm not sure, I like my privacy.'

'I'd keep out of your way. Please, I'd be no trouble.'

'There's only the spare room up in the eaves, you'd have to see to it yourself. I have trouble getting up the stairs.'

'That would great.'

Laura followed her into the living room. Harriet sat down. Laura moved to the wall displaying the photographs. 'Did you take these?' she asked.

'Yes.'

'I saw some in *Flamingo's*. They're very eye-catching. Do you print them yourself?'

'Yes.'

'Here at the cottage?' Laura asked, struggling to maintain a conversation with Harriet's monosyllabic answers.

'I have a studio in the garden, converted a summer house into a darkroom. Why are you asking?'

'I'm interested. My fiancé, Paul is an artist. Not photography, he paints. He has a gallery in London. You may have heard of him, Paul Adams.'

'No. Now do you want to see the attic room?'

The curt dismissal hurt. 'I'm sure it will be fine.'

'I could just post the certificate you know?' Harriet reiterated.

'I'd rather stay.' Laura insisted. She knew that if she left there was no way Harriet would remember or bother to get it.

'Suit yourself.'

'I'd better go, you must be busy.'

'Don't come too early in the morning.'

'I know, you told me before.' Laura turned. 'Don't get up I'll let myself out.'

With time to kill, Laura wandered around the village again. She wished she could understand Harriet. The woman was obviously lonely and yet she shunned any attempt at friendship. She was strange, that was for sure. She worried Laura. What did she *really* feel about her daughter? Harriet had professed not to care, but she was convinced that under that careless shrug of disinterest, that she *must* want to see Amy. She was her mother for God's sake!!

Was the affair with Danny still going on? She suspected it was. She wondered why Danny's wife tolerated it. It was a small village, prone to gossip.

She hoped Danny would be back soon; she didn't think she would be able to stomach staying with Harriet for too long.

She entered the village store-cum-post office. There were no customers and the woman behind the counter was reading. Laura bought a magazine and walked over to the café and ordered tea and cream scones. She needed cheering up.

A different waitress today.

'Does Brett still own this café?' she asked her.

'Yes. He's away on holiday in Malta with his wife and baby.'

Laura was disappointed. She had been looking forward to seeing him, and explaining why she hadn't been to visit after all they had done for her. Perhaps, when this was all sorted out, she would bring Paul and Amy here.

Laura arrived at Harriet's the following day at two. There was no answer to her knock. Thinking she might be in her studio, she left her case on the doorstep and walked to the side gate. It squeaked as she opened it. Uneven paving stones covered in moss led to a brick-built summerhouse. The garden was a mass of overgrown shrubs, buddleia and rhododendron fought for space.

She knocked tentatively, fearing Harriet's anger at her trespassing.

Again no answer. She tried the handle, a black latch. To her surprise it opened. She hesitated, reluctant to enter, then curiosity won.

Inside was a surprise. No dust or untidiness here; the room was clinically clean, the whitewashed walls almost sterile. A bewildering array of equipment filled the room, tanks and spools, graduates and bottles of chemicals. A large flat-bed dryer filled most of the space. Cautiously, Laura moved to the side wall, where a line stretched across one end of the room on which several prints were pegged to dry. Pictures of canals and barges and the curves of a river all depicted in black and white.

'What the hell are you doing in here?'

Laura spun round. Harriet, looking furious, stood in the doorway. 'Sorry. I was looking for you.'

'This is private. You have no right to be in here.'

Embarrassed Laura said. 'I was only admiring your photos. Sorry.'

Harriet put down the camera slung round her neck. 'You had

better come into the house and unpack.'

Laura retrieved her case from the doorstep. The stairs were narrow and curved and she banged her case against her shin several times.

The room had obviously not been used for some time, the air felt musty and damp. She tried to open the tiny window but it was stuck. With a grimace she noticed cobwebs hanging across the panes of glass and the sill thick with dust. Ducking her head to avoid the sloping roof, she put her case on the bed and started to unpack. The room wasn't big enough for a wardrobe, so she hung her clothes on a hook behind the door. Next she made up the single bed with sheets and a duvet she had collected from the airing cupboard in the bathroom. At least they were clean and dry. She had slept in worse, she thought, thinking back to the squat.

That evening, she offered to cook dinner. Harriet accepted with her usual offhanded shrug.

Earlier she had found a few cleaning materials in the kitchen and had done her best to clean her room, hoping she hadn't offended Harriet, although by the state of the rest of the place she doubted it.

'I remember the accident,' Laura said. They were sitting at the pine kitchen table eating scrambled eggs. It was all she could find in the fridge. 'Seeing the burning car and feeling appalled to think you were trapped in it. It must have been horrific for you.'

'I don't remember much about it. I was in a coma for months.' Harriet was smoking a cigarette and drinking black coffee, her food hardly touched.

Laura ate in silence for a while. 'When you recovered, didn't you want Amy back?'

'How could I have looked after her? I could barely look after myself.'

'I guess not,' Laura admitted.

'You see, you know nothing about me, you have no idea about my life.'

'Sorry,' Laura mumbled, ashamed that she was judging her.

'I knew she would be all right.' Harriet said.

'How?'

Harriet gave deep sigh. 'Because I knew she was with you.'

Laura was shocked. 'You knew! All this time you have known where she was?'

'Not exactly, just that you lived somewhere in Devon.'

'It wouldn't have taken much effort to find us.'

'There you go again, being judgemental. She was better off not knowing about me. I assumed you would never tell her.'

'I don't want to,' Laura admitted, 'but she will need her birth certificate when she's older.'

Harriet stubbed out her cigarette and remained silent. After a few moments Laura said. 'Before the accident, you must have loved her, wanted her.'

'Not really. I wasn't ready for motherhood. I couldn't face bringing her up on my own. She got on my nerves, always crying, forever demanding. I couldn't cope.'

'If you didn't want a baby why didn't you have an abortion?'

'I wish now that I had, but I couldn't get rid of Danny's child.'

'Instead you just abandoned her.' Laura hadn't meant to sound angry but the words just came out. She thought of how she was going to explain all this to Amy and it broke her heart.

'I was depressed, alone. Oh for fuck's sake, I don't have to explain. I didn't want her, all right!'

The following morning Laura woke early. Her thoughts would not let her rest. She had not slept well, the mattress was hard and lumpy, and although she had laid her coat over the duvet for extra warmth she had still felt frozen during the night.

She slipped out of bed, feeling the cold wooden floorboards beneath her feet, and looked out of the window. It was hard to see much through the tiny leaded attic panes. She watched two starlings chirping in the wizened lilac tree that shadowed the cottage, and from which it got its name. Shivering, she dressed quickly and went downstairs. In the kitchen she made herself some tea, and carried it into the living room. Harriet had told her not to wake her, so she made herself useful by reviving the fire and opening the curtains. A sharp frost gave the morning a fresh clean look. Satan mewed around her feet, so she returned to the kitchen to feed him.

The atmosphere last night had been awful. Harriet sullenly getting more and more drunk. Laura sinking into her angry thoughts. She loved Amy, unconditionally. It upset her that neither Danny nor Harriet cared about their daughter. It seemed so callous. She was angry that they had made her lie to Terry, to Paul, to cover up their sordid affair. She had lived in fear of discovery, keeping their secret, breaking the law, and even now they were not brave enough to let her legally adopt Amy. Christine *knew* for fuck's sake! What was their problem?

She would wait until Danny got back. If it wasn't resolved then she would personally go and see Christine. Her loyalty had been stretched too far.

Chapter Forty-Six

Laura knocked on the door and waited. Three days had passed and Danny had returned at last, but Harriet had not approached him. Yesterday, she had told her it was up to her to see him if she wanted the birth certificate. She had been shocked by the wicked gleam in Harriet's eyes, as if she was enjoying the fact that Danny would be totally fazed by her visit.

And he would, she knew that, but they left her no alternative. If they thought she would quietly go away they were mistaken.

Despite her determination, she felt nervous as she waited for the door to be answered. If Danny dismissed her request she was stumped. She had no real power to make him give the birth certificate to her. If she wasn't careful, this visit could go so very wrong. Before she had time to dwell on the problem the door was opened.

Christine Pembroke smiled politely. She was elegantly dressed, in a blue cashmere jumper with a silk scarf at her neck, and a navy pleated skirt. Two white Yorkshire terriers snapped at her feet. 'Quiet,' the woman commanded sternly and they stopped barking.

'Is – er – is Mr Pembroke in?' Laura was almost stammering in her nervousness.

'And you are?'

'My name is Laura Armstrong.'

The polite smile turned to a frown. 'Is my husband expecting you?'

'Not exactly, but I really need to speak to him.'

'You'd better come in, then.' Christine said.

302

Laura stepped over the threshold. She bent and fussed the dogs. 'They're cute,' she said. 'What are their names?'

'Snowball and Casper; a present from my husband last year.'

Laura thought she could detect a note of exasperation in her tone, as if she hadn't really wanted the dogs.

She followed her along the hallway and into a sitting room, shutting the dogs out. They walked the length of the long room to the French doors and stepped into the conservatory.

'Danny, you have a visitor.' Christine said.

Danny was reclining on a brown leather sofa reading a newspaper. He raised his head and gave Laura a startled look. For a moment he looked panic-stricken.

'Hello.' His tone was less than friendly, but she hadn't expected it to be otherwise.

Now she was here, she had no idea what to say. She didn't want to antagonise him. She wished Christine would leave the room, but she had settled down into an adjoining chair.

Her gaze was drawn to Danny's eyes, an amazing bright blue, so like Amy's. She tensed her shoulders rigidly, unable to speak.

The silence filled the room. Christine raised perfectly arched eyebrows then indicated for her to sit down. Laura moved automatically towards a chair. Her mouth felt dry and she wondered if, after all, she has done the right thing in coming here. She glanced nervously at Christine.

'I'm staying with Harriet and . . .'

'Harriet!' Christine snapped sharply.

'Yes I . . .' Laura shifted uncomfortably. She was aware that Danny was watching her nervously. 'I – er – um – Harriet says that Danny has some papers he was looking after for her and she wondered if I could collect them.'

'What sort of papers?' Christine frowned.

Danny had leapt to his feet. 'I'll get them, they're in my study, come with me,' he instructed Laura. He turned to Christine. 'Sorry love, won't be a moment; it's nothing important.'

Laura glanced quickly at Christine before she followed Danny from the room. Christine's face was like thunder.

In the study Danny glared at her. 'What the hell are you

playing at?'

'I'm sorry if I've caused an upset, but I'm desperate.' Laura swallowed her nervousness 'I need Amy's birth certificate. Harriet said you had it. I tried to get it discreetly, but I'm tired of playing these games between you. If you give it to me now I'll be gone and you won't ever hear from me again.'

'It's locked in the safe at the perfumery. I'll get it tomorrow. Now go and I'll try and think of a plausible excuse to give Christine.' Danny ushered her from the room, down the hall.

'Tomorrow, I'll contact you tomorrow,' he said in an undertone and then the front door was closed on her and she was alone in the driveway.

Christine glared at Danny. 'Don't take me for a fool, this is to do with the child isn't it? *Your daughter.'*

'Of course not. Don't be ridiculous. I've told you I'm not the father.'

'Oh for God's sake Danny, did you really believe I swallowed all those lies.'

Danny flushed at her derision. He slumped down on a chair and buried his head in his hands. He knew it was no use pretending any longer. 'I'm sorry, I'm so sorry,' his voice was low, defeated.

'Sorry you've been found out you mean,' Christine snapped.

'No! Of course not.' Danny raised his head; his eyes were blurred with tears. 'Sorry I've hurt you.'

Christine glared at him and left the room, slamming the door.

Danny stared at the closed door and took a deep breath to calm his ragged nerves. Now that the truth was out in the open he had a feeling nothing was going to be the same again.

* * *

Laura walked slowly back to Harriet's. It was peaceful in the growing dusk of the late afternoon and she thought about Amy. She was missing her so much. She hoped Danny would keep his promise. She wanted to get home as soon as possible.

She felt a twinge of guilt imagining what must be going on back at Danny's house. She doubted he would be able to talk his way out if it this time.

Passing *Flamingo's* she went inside and ordered a pot of tea. Anything to delay going back to Harriet.

She punched in Paul's number on her mobile. He answered instantly.

'Hi, darling, how's it going?'

She told him about the morning's confrontation. 'Hopefully I'll get it tomorrow morning and then I'll get the train. I can't wait to get home.'

'Are you okay, you sound stressed?'

'I'm fine, don't worry.'

Harriet seemed cheerful at dinner that evening and produced two bottles of red wine. Laura had bought a chicken and vegetables and cooked the meal.

Seeing Harriet was in a more receptive mood, Laura tried to discover more about her. She badly wanted to understand how she could have abandoned Amy.

'Were your parents not around to help you when you had Amy?'

Harriet waved her fork dismissively. 'Haven't seen them in years.'

'They do know about her, right?'

'No. Hardly the thing to tell them that their only daughter was shagging a married man and had managed to get herself pregnant.'

'I guess not.' Laura said. She tried to picture herself giving away her baby and couldn't begin to imagine how distressing that would be. It was hard to believe that Harriet had done it, without as much as a tear, apparently.

Harriet looked up and caught her gaze. She pushed her plate away, her food barely touched, and lit a cigarette.

'Have you no regrets at all,' Laura probed.

'Oh for pity's sake!'

'Sorry.'

Harriet ignored her and refilled their wine glass.

Undeterred Laura said. 'When Amy is older what shall I tell her about you?' She had agonised about it for hours, trying to image the conversation, what she would say. It didn't bear thinking about. How could she tell her that neither of her parents wanted her, that they had abandoned her? She remembered how unloved she had felt when her father had left her and Terry. That awful feeling of unworthiness would be part of her for the rest of her life. How much worse it will be for Amy. There would be little consolation that Laura loved her with all her heart. She was not even a blood relation.

'Tell her anything you like.' Harriet said coldly.

'Shall I tell her that you didn't want her?' Laura felt angry at the indifference Harriet was showing.

'It's up to you.'

'I'll say you gave her away without a second thought,' Laura snapped trying to get a reaction, some feeling of remorse.

'Whatever.'

It was hopeless. 'Why are you so rude and uncaring?'

'Why should I be anything else?'

Laura washed the dishes and cleared up the kitchen, wondering why she was doing it, but unable to leave it in a mess. Harriet had disappeared upstairs. When she had finished, she picked up her glass of wine and went into the front room. Turning the radio on low she sat down in the armchair and closed her eyes listening to the music.

She was surprised when Harriet entered the room half-an-hour later. Even more surprised when she handed her a small velvet box. Laura lifted the lid. A pair of diamond earrings twinkled in the soft light.

'Give them to Amy whenever you feel is the right time,' Harriet said.

'They're beautiful,' Laura said. These were not the usual costume jewellery she bought from Claire's Accessories, but real diamonds.

'They belonged to my mother,' Harriet said indifferently.

'Actually she died quite recently.'

'I'm sorry,' Laura said shocked at Harriet's apparent lack of feeling.

They sat in silence for a while.

'What about your father?' Laura said finally.

Harriet poured herself a gin and tonic. 'He still lives in Canada.'

Laura strolled around the village the following afternoon. The morning had been miserable, Harriet moody and drinking heavily. She was getting racked off with her. Harriet was making no effort at all to be pleasant. Despite aching to go home, she stubbornly refused to go until she had the birth certificate. She prayed Danny would show up today as promised.

Unable to stand the atmosphere any longer, she had come out.

She skirted St Peter's church and took a sunken path flanked by dry-stone walls until she came to a field. Leaning on the gate she remembered summers here with Zoe, lying in the grass, dreaming of love. It seemed a different lifetime. She wondered what her friend would make of how her life had become entwined with Harriet's. She could almost see her shocked look.

She returned the way she had come, crossing the stone bridge that spanned the tranquil flowing waters of the river Windrush. It was getting towards dusk as she let herself into the house - Harriet had given her a key - and was surprised to find it in complete darkness. A quick search confirmed that Harriet was neither in the cottage or her studio.

She wondered where on earth Harriet could be; she had not said she was going out. Unsure of what to do next, she prepared the vegetables for dinner and put the chicken pie she had made that morning in the oven. An hour passed. She was starving, but she didn't want to eat until Harriet returned.

Her mobile rang.

'Laura, this is Christine.'

'Hi,' Laura said warily.

'Danny has what you want. Can you please come and get it and while you're here talk some sense into that bloody woman.

She's driving me mad.'

'Harriet's with you?' Laura gasped.

'She's standing under the willow tree in the front garden. Just standing watching the house, she's drunk, completely inebriated. I don't know what the hell she thinks she's doing, the stupid, stupid woman. I've been out and asked her to leave, but she just stares at me. We have important dinner guests. I could kill Danny.'

'I'll come now.' Laura said.

'Actually don't bother. I'm phoning the police.' The phone disconnected immediately.

Chapter Forty-Seven

Harriet tried to smile at Danny. Her face felt frozen in a silly grin. His image swayed before her as she tried to focus.

Today had been bad. She'd drunk several gin and tonics to take the edge of her depression. It hadn't worked. Laura's attempts to be friendly were beginning to irritate. She wished she'd bugger off home, and leave her in peace.

As dusk settled, she put on her cloak and went out. Her steps had taken her to Danny's house. The curtains of the front window were open and she stared at the huge dining table set for dinner guests. The flames of beautiful white candles flickered, casting shadows against the silverware and crystal. In the background, she could see Danny and Christine moving around the room and she been so overwhelmed with misery that she had stood and stared and couldn't seem to move. Christine had finally spotted her and had come out and shouted at her.

Now Danny was standing in front of her.

'What the hell are you playing at Harriet?'

'Come home with me,' she implored him, slurring her words.

'Don't be stupid. What's got into you? You're making a fool of yourself.'

'Come with me, just for an hour, *please.*' She reached out to touch his arm, but he took a step back.

'Out of the question. We are expecting friends to dinner at any moment.'

'Tomorrow then. You haven't been to see me for weeks. You've got someone else haven't you?'

'No, of course not.'

'I love you Danny, I want to be with you. Leave Christine, let's go away together.' She knew she sounded pathetically maudlin, but her need for him overshadowed everything, even her pride.

'Stop this. Go home, you're drunk.'

She clung to his hand. 'Danny, Danny, don't abandon me, I'll die if you leave me.'

'I've called the police.' Christine was at Danny's side, glaring at her.

Danny turned. 'You shouldn't have done that. I'm dealing with this.'

Harriet sank to the ground and started to sob. 'Danny you're all I've got. I need you.'

Christine snorted in disgust. 'Dealing with it are you?' she snapped, as she turned and walked back to the house.

'Harriet, get up,' Danny grabbed her hands and tried to pull her to her feet. 'Come on, get up.'

Harriet refused to move. As Danny bent and tried to lift her up, she flung her arms around his neck. Straining with the effort, he finally got her to her feet. 'I'm taking you home,' he said.

'I'm not going home unless you stay with me.'

'You know I can't.'

Harriet pushed herself away from him. Swaying erratically she headed towards the house. 'I'm going to tell your fancy friends about you. I'm telling them what you did.'

As Harriet reached the French doors, a figure blocked her path. Her eyes, unfocused, did not recognise, DCI Robert Lloyd. He took her arm and said gently, 'Come on, Harriet come with me.'

She tried to release his grip. 'Bugger off, whoever you are,' she snarled.

* * *

Laura entered the police station feeling worried. Earlier she had arrived at Danny's house to see Harriet being taken off in the police car. Christine had shoved an envelope into her hand and told her brusquely to leave.

'Can I see Harriet Malin?' Laura asked the duty officer.

'Are you a relative?'

'I'm her friend.'

Behind the desk sergeant a man replaced the phone receiver, turned and looked across. 'I'll deal with this, Tom,' he said.

The man lifted the desk flap and walked into the reception area. He ushered her into an interview room and indicated for her to sit down. 'Hello Laura, how are you?'

Laura smiled at DCI Robert Lloyd. 'Hi, I'm fine. Is Harriet okay?'

Robert grimaced. 'She will be when she's sobered up.'

Laura nodded wondering what to say.

'I understand you are staying with her,' Robert said.

'Yes.'

'Is there a reason for that?'

'I was -um - I was just back to see my friends and the hotel was full and Harriet kindly offered to let me stay.' She stumbled over the words.

Robert looked serious. 'I had a long conversation with Christine last night. She tells me you have been looking after Harriet's baby since her accident.'

Laura began to shake. It was all going to come out now about her illegally having Amy. Was he going to arrest her? 'Yes,' she managed to utter, her mouth was dry with nerves.

'That's very kind of you.'

Was this a trick? Did he know or was he trying to get her to confess? She swallowed hard. 'Harriet couldn't look after her and Danny . . .' Shit, she hadn't meant to mention him.

Robert's expression softened. 'It's okay, I know all about it. Just be careful with Harriet.'

'Why?'

'She's – er - not very stable - this is not the first time she has been arrested for disorderly behaviour.'

'She's okay with me. Can I see her?'

'Not a good time. We'll release her in the morning. Come back then.'

'Okay, thanks.'

'Are you staying with her for very long?'

'I'm going home tomorrow.'

Laura was woken early the following morning by a loud and insistent banging on the door. She slipped out of bed, tugging on her sweatshirt and jeans. It was freezing as she made her way downstairs and opened the door.

'Sorry, did I wake you?' DCI Robert Lloyd said.

Laura glanced worriedly at him as she stood back to let him in.

'I came to tell you that Harriet has been taken into hospital.'

'Oh God, what's wrong with her?'

'She collapsed last night.'

'Is it serious?'

'I don't think so; she was in a bad way but I don't think it's life threatening.' Robert sounded more annoyed with Harriet than concerned. She suspected he was, like everyone else, intolerant of Harriet's continued drunkenness.

'Thanks, Robert, for telling me.'

'That's okay. And just a quick word of advice, as a friend, not a policeman. If you want to keep the child, get her adopted legally.'

'Oh, Robert if only I could.'

After he had left, Laura went into the warm kitchen where the AGA stove churned out heat. She switched on the kettle and fed Satan. She had planned to go home today, now she didn't know what to do. She could hardly leave while Harriet was in hospital.

She switched on her mobile to ring Paul. She had spoken to him yesterday evening, but now she needed the comfort of his voice. Bugger it, she was out of credit. Grabbing her coat, she left the cottage.

There was a thick white frost as she made her way through the village. It lay on the hedges and fields, making a chocolate box scene, which would have delighted her if she hadn't been so worried.

In the general store, Edna Cooksley was speaking to a customer, her face animated. Glancing up as Laura entered, she stopped talking.

'Do you have top-up cards for Orange?' Laura asked.

'Yes love, ten pound or twenty five?'

'Ten please.'

Edna said, 'You're staying with Mrs Malin aren't you?'

'Yes.'

'Is she okay, only I saw the police were at her house?'

Laura shrugged. 'It was nothing.'

'Really! I thought they'd arrested her, last night.'

'It was a mistake.'

'She was outside Mr Pembroke's house, completely drunk. I saw her with my own eyes. I was coming back from my bridge evening. It was her all right; no mistaking her with that limp and the black hooded cloak she always wears to hide her poor damaged face. She needs to be locked up. Making a nuisance of herself with a married man. I told that to DCI Lloyd this morning.'

I bet you did, Laura thought, but she said nothing. She left the shop more worried than ever.

She rang Paul.

'Laura, is everything all right? You sound a bit upset,' he said.

'Harriet's been arrested.'

'Crikey, what happened?'

Laura blurted everything out. The scene in Danny's garden, Harriet's drunken behaviour and now her being in hospital.

Paul sounded anxious. 'Is there no one to look after her?'

'No she's alone.'

'I take it you're not coming home today after all?'

'I thought I'd stay a bit longer just until she's out of hospital. I want one last attempt to see if she will agree to an adoption. The good news is that I have Amy's birth certificate.'

'That's great, so when do you think you'll be home?'

'I don't know. I'm on my way to visit her, see how bad she is.'

Laura knew he was thinking of Christmas, just a week away.

Paul was silent for a moment. 'Okay love, do what you think is best.'

'Can I speak to Amy?'

'Of course. Talk to you tomorrow. I love you.'

'Love you too.'

Laura waited excitedly for Amy to come on the phone.

'Hi mummy?'

'Hello sweetheart are you being a good girl for Paul?'

'Yep.'

'What are doing?'

There was a slight pause then she said. 'Talking to you on the phone.'

Laura laughed. 'I know, I meant, oh never mind.'

'When are you coming home, Mummy?'

'Soon, darling. Do you miss me?'

'Yep. But I'm *desperate* to put the fairy on the Christmas tree, only Paul says we have to wait until you come home.'

Laura felt a choking lump. She knew her daughter missed her, but the Christmas tree held priority. After reassuring her daughter she would be home in a couple of days, she flicked her mobile shut and headed for the bus stop to take her to Cheltenham.

'Why do you drink so much?' Laura asked. She was sitting on a plastic chair by Harriet's bed in Cheltenham general hospital.

Harriet shrugged. 'Because of everything, because of what I've done.'

'Danny?'

'Partly.'

'Do you want to tell me?'

Harriet shook her head. 'You wouldn't want to know.'

'That wasn't very clever was it, getting yourself arrested outside Danny's house? I thought you loved him.'

Harriet snorted. 'How dare Christine have me arrested? And Danny didn't make any attempt to stop her.'

'I don't think he had a choice.'

Harriet turned her head away, but not before Laura had seen the look of despair in her eyes. She held her hand. 'The doctor says you have to stay in until they get the results of your blood tests and then you can come home. It probably won't be until tomorrow. I'll come and fetch you.'

'I thought you were going back to Devon.' Harriet pulled her hand away and slid it under the sheet.

'I can stay a couple more days.'

'Don't stay on my account. I thought you'd want to be with your family.'

'Of course I do, but I …'

'But you feel that you have to look after me,' Harriet snapped.

'No – well, yes.'

'Don't bother.'

Laura seethed at her angry tone. It was tempting to walk out, go home and leave her to it. She rose and pulled a wry face. 'I'll see you later, hopefully in a better frame of mind.'

Laura shopped in Sainsbury's for milk and bread before she went back to the cottage, not wanting to visit the village store again. The fire had gone out in the living room so she relit the burner, piling on plenty of logs. Then she made herself a sandwich with the last of the chicken and sat by the fire thinking about Harriet. She wondered what would happen after she had gone home. Harriet didn't seem to have anyone in her life. Probably not even Danny now, after her appalling behaviour outside his home. She wished there was something she could do to help her.

A loud knock on the door interrupted her thoughts. Probably Robert Lloyd again she thought as she rose to answer it.

She was so certain it would be him that she was momentarily nonplussed to see an elderly stranger on the doorstep. He was tall, with pure white hair that enhanced his tanned face. Dressed immaculately in a light grey suit, his clear blue-grey eyes held a puzzled expression.

'Hello, I was actually looking for Harriet Malin, has she moved away?'

'No, no this is her home, she – er – she's not in at the moment though.'

'And you are?'

Not willing to explain the details to a perfect stranger Laura said. 'I'm a friend.'

The man's face creased into a friendly smile. 'Will she be back today?' he asked.

'No, she's away until tomorrow. Umm, sorry, but can I ask

who you are?'

'I'm so sorry, how rude of me. I'm Bill Malin, Harriet's father.'

Chapter Forty-Eight

Laura's eyes widened. Amy's grandfather! Her grandfather, who had no idea the child existed. *A relative that might lay claim to the child.*

How on earth was she going to handle this?

Pulling herself together, she opened the door wider, 'Please come in,' she offered. 'Was Harriet expecting you?'

'No, I wanted to surprise her.' Bill wiped his feet vigorously before stepping into the hallway. 'I've retired from my business in Canada and have time on my hands at last. I came to visit my daughter because – well, to be honest, we haven't spoken for some time.'

'Right,' Laura said, not quite knowing what to say.

Bill followed her into the living room. He looked at her intently. 'Where exactly is Harriet?'

'Err, she's is hospital, nothing serious, she'll be home tomorrow.'

'I see. Is her husband, Jeremy, with her?'

'No he - um - they separated, he went abroad, I think.'

'Good Lord. I had no idea. I spoke to him a few times when Harriet was in a coma. He seemed to care for her a great deal.'

Seeing that he was upset, Laura offered to make him a cup of tea.

'Thank you, that's kind.' He followed her into the kitchen and sat at the pine table while she filled the kettle and lifted mugs down from the dresser.

'Are you looking after the house for her?' Bill asked.

'Sort of.' It sounded vague, but she was unsure what to tell him.

He seemed to sense her unease. 'Is anything wrong?' He waited, not speaking, just looking at her and when the silence became heavy, she blurted the words out.

'Harriet was arrested last night because - well she was drunk and making a nuisance of herself at Danny's house.'

'Oh Lord, and Danny is?'

'Um -oh dear, this is so awkward, I'm not sure I should be telling you this.'

'Then don't my dear. I'll wait until I see Harriet.'

Grateful for his understanding, Laura placed the tea and a plate of biscuits on the table and sat down.

She listened attentively as Bill told her about his life in Canada. Of the successful advertising business he owned with his brother-in-law and the sad years of his wife's Alzheimer's. Of his devastation that he hadn't able to visit Harriet when she was ill and the need to see her now. He was a lovely man.

'How long are you staying here?' he asked suddenly.

'Just until I get Harriet's consent,' Laura said without thinking.

'Consent for what?'

Christ! Now she'd done it.

She had no choice, but to tell him. He was a good listener even so, it took a while. The tea went cold.

Bill's eyes widened with incredulity. It was a moment before he spoke. 'Bloody hell!' he said.

'I guess it's a bit of a shock,' Laura said nervously.

Bill's gaze wavered. 'A granddaughter, eh,' he seemed to be fighting back tears. 'What a lovely surprise.' The words were choked with emotion. Bill wiped his eyes that had become watery.

'Shall I make some fresh tea?' Laura offered, feeling that she too wanted to cry.

'Good idea,' he smiled tremulously. 'Good idea.'

Laura made the tea and they went into the living room.

'I can't believe Harriet never told us,' Bill said as he settled into an armchair. 'That's the saddest part; that she never felt we would stand by her. I guess that reflects on us really. Thank God her mother's no longer alive; she would never have forgiven her.'

Laura reached inside her handbag. She handed the photo she always carried. Bill gazed at it intently, running his finger across Amy's face. 'She's the image of Harriet at that age. Same hair, same eyes. She's adorable.'

'Are you pleased to find out that you have a granddaughter?'

'I'm thrilled.'

Laura felt a sinking feeling. 'I guess you'll want to take care of her now.'

'Good Lord no. I'm far too old to have the responsibility of a - how old did you say Amy is?'

'Five.'

'Please don't worry. I won't take her away from you. Although I would like to meet her.'

'Of course you can.' Relief flooded through her.

'I can't believe Harriet gave her away.' Bill lowered his head.

'Please don't be upset. I've taken good care of her.'

'I can see that you're a caring person, but it could have been a very different story. I shudder to think what could have happened. To give a child away to a total stranger, it beggars belief.'

'I wasn't a complete stranger. I did know Harriet and Danny.' She felt defensive.

Bill laid his hand over hers. 'Sorry, that was insensitive.' He smiled suddenly. 'I came here today to try and make amends with Harriet. I never dreamt I would find a granddaughter.'

'Harriet will be angry that I've told you.'

'Don't worry about that. Now tell me, do you have other children?'

Before she could answer, the sound of the front door slamming made them both jump.

Harriet's head was lowered as she entered the room so she did not see her father at first. Her gaze became startled and then wary. 'What the hell are you doing here?'

Bill didn't respond immediately, he just looked at her, his eyes clouded in hurt. Then he rose, and slowly moving towards her, gently touched the scar on her face. 'Hello Harriet, love, I've missed you.'

Harriet brushed passed him and made for her chair.

'You are supposed to be in hospital,' Laura said.

'Discharged myself. Damned doctors, trying to tell me how to run my life.'

Bill gave Laura a resigned look, which didn't go unnoticed by Harriet. 'I suppose she's told you I got arrested,' she snapped, glaring at Laura.

'Yes and about the child and quite frankly I'm shocked.'

'I knew you would be.'

'Not about the fact that you had a child, but the terrible way you have kept her from us. You knew how much we would have loved a grandchild.'

'Even a bastard child? I doubt it.'

'Harriet!' Bill gasped.

Ignoring him, Harriet lowered herself into her chair. Satan immediately jumped down from the window-sill and sprung onto her lap. She stroked the cat's fur and Satan purred loudly. Harriet buried her face into the cat's neck.

Bill's face softened. 'What's wrong with you, that you had to go to hospital?'

'Don't you start,' Harriet barked, 'it's none of your damned business.'

'It is my business. I'm your father. I care about you.'

Harriet flinched. 'Taken you a long time to realise that,' she said. 'How long has it been? How many years?'

'Be fair, Harriet, you could have come to see us?'

'I - I'll leave you alone,' Laura said. Neither of them seemed to notice her departure as they glared at each other.

In the kitchen, she paced the floor, sick with worry. Would this make a difference, would Harriet not give consent now she had her father back in her life to help? She could hear the murmur of voices, angry and then pleading from Bill, sarcastic and cold from Harriet.

She waited, wondering whether to return to the living room, when she heard the front door open and close. She returned to the living room to find Harriet alone, standing by the window.

'Where's Bill?'

'He's gone.'

'Why?'

Harriet shrugged.

'That was horrible what you said, calling Amy a bastard.'

Another shrug.

She hesitated, waiting for Harriet to say something, maybe even apologise, but when it was obvious she wasn't going to Laura went up to her room.

Laura waited at the stop for the bus into Cheltenham. She had tried once again to get Harriet to talk about the adoption, but Harriet stormed out of the house without replying. It was hopeless. She packed her bags and left. She was close to tears. She felt terrible leaving, but she couldn't stay with her another day. She didn't actually like her. Despite the occasional softening, she knew she would *never* like her. Harriet's bitterness and hostility would never change.

'Are you leaving?'

Laura looked up to see Bill at her side. She had been so engrossed in her thoughts that she hadn't heard him approach.

She nodded, too upset to speak. He seemed really nice and she felt sad that Harriet had been so awful to him, he didn't deserve her scorn.

'I'd like to talk to you.'

'I have to get the bus to Cheltenham station. I'm going home.'

'If you could spare me an hour, I'll drive you there later.'

She could see it was important to him. 'Okay,' she agreed.

'Come on, it's too cold for my old bones to be out here any longer. There's a nice café just across the road called *Flamingo.*'

'I know,' Laura smiled. 'I used to work there.'

Bill ordered a pot of tea and homemade scones.

'I had no idea my daughter had grown into such an embittered woman,' Bill said.

'She drinks too much,' Laura said carefully. 'She's fast becoming an alcoholic.'

'I guessed as much. Is that why you're leaving?'

'Not really. She won't give her consent. She was so angry when you left. There's no point in staying. She'll never agree . . .' Laura stopped as tears threatened. 'I need to be home for Christmas to be with Amy and Paul.'

Bill covered her hand with his. 'I'm so sorry. Don't give up. Give me time, I'll try and persuade her. Let me have your address, I want to come and see Amy anyway, that is, if you don't mind.'

Laura smiled. 'Of course not. That would be wonderful.'

'Thank you.'

'Have you returned to England for good?' Laura asked.

'That depends on Harriet.'

'You must miss your wife.'

'Yes, but I've also missed Harriet all these years.' Bill paused and looked at her directly. 'I'm glad you have Amy. I probably shouldn't say this, but I doubt Harriet would have made a good mother. She was always a difficult child, stubborn and uncompromising. You seem to me to be a very special young woman; caring and kind.'

'Thank you,' Laura said in a soft voice, feeling embarrassed.

Bill looked at his watch. 'I guess I'd better get you to Cheltenham,' he said. 'Don't want you missing the train.'

At Cheltenham station, Laura gave him her mobile number. He hugged her and she kissed his cheek, feeling a rush of affection for him.

Once on the train, she found a seat and closed her eyes. She was so glad to be going home. It had been a traumatic few days, but she had what she came for. Amy's birth certificate and Bill's promise that he would persuade Harriet to give her consent.

Despite Harriet's caustic behaviour, she couldn't help feeling sorry for her. Maybe now Bill was there to look after her, she would find some peace.

Chapter Forty-Nine

Danny was awake in a small hotel in Scotland, chosen for its discretion. He was awake and fretting. Cheryl, his latest mistress, was fast asleep at his side.

Danny was fretting because, despite all his efforts, he had, for the first time in his life, failed to get an erection. It terrified him. It must be stress, he decided, and it wasn't surprising since that visit from Laura before Christmas.

Christmas had been tense, with Christine hardly speaking to him. New Year had been even worse, so now, this second week in January, he had decided to come to Scotland for a week, playing golf and seeing Cheryl.

Even now it was hard to credit that Christine had pretended to believe him when he had sworn he wasn't Amy's father. *Devious bitch!* He'd tried so hard to protect her, keep the truth from hurting her, worrying himself stupid in case she found out and she had *known* all the time. How ridiculous did that make him feel!

Raising himself up on his elbow, he looked down at Cheryl, her dark hair fanning the pillow, her pretty young face serene and peaceful. But then why should she have any worries, she was only twenty-two, in the prime of her life. Why she was interested in him, he had no idea, but she seemed to like him and sex with her was great. Just like it had been when he first knew Harriet.

Harriet no longer made him happy; in fact, she was infuriating. Her constant drunkenness was a worry, especially after that stunt she pulled before Christmas. She was a liability.

His gaze lingered on Cheryl and he wondered whether to wake

her and try again, but he suddenly felt weary, so he closed his eyes and tried to sleep.

He had met Cheryl several months ago at the Liberty Golf club, where she was a new recruit serving behind the bar. He had long since given up seeking a new mistress; Harriet and Christine were enough to contend with. However, when she started flirting with him, he had been unable to resist. He had been flattered and a little proud that he could still attract a pretty young woman. The temptation was too strong and he had taken her out to dinner and slept with her. Scotland was far enough away from home to keep her a secret from Christine and Harriet.

It seemed he had hardly drifted off before a knocking on his door woke him. 'What the devil – what time is it?' He switched on the light and glared at the bedside clock. One-thirty.

Climbing out of bed, he shrugged on his dressing gown and opened the door. George, the night porter, looked anxious.

'Phone call for you, it's your wife, says it's an emergency.'

'Did she say what emergency?' he asked as he followed George down the stairs to the lobby.

'No, but she sounded agitated. She called earlier, but I said you were out.' George winked at him.

Picking up the receiver on the desk he said anxiously. 'Christine, what's happened?'

'Where have you been? I've been trying to get hold of you for hours.'

'Sorry, dear. Dining with clients, what's the matter?'

'You have to come home, Danny. Something terrible has happened.'

'What?' He envisaged all sorts, house burgled, perfumery broken into, a fire . . .

'A body - found in the perfumery garden - the police have been here.' Christine sounded hysterical.

The air seemed to be sucked from his lungs. He couldn't speak. He drew a deep breath as a cold clammy sweat spread over his skin. 'What do you mean a body in the garden? Whereabouts in the garden?' He knew, of course, but he had to give himself time to think.

'Down the disused well.'

'Who has been poking around the well, it's dangerous.'

'An engineer came this morning from Cheltenham Water Board. He lowered a bucket down to get a sample of water. It must have dislodged the - the body. He got such a fright. He was only a young lad.'

'What was the water board doing here?' Danny said puzzled.

'I want to restore the garden, make a feature of the well,' Christine was calmer now. 'I thought it would attract visitors. I arranged for the water board to analyse the water to see if it still held healing properties.'

'I thought we'd agreed not to do that. It was too costly.'

'No *you* decided. I want it done.'

'Jesus Christ! Without telling me,' he snapped.

'It doesn't matter now. You have to come home, Danny. The police are coming back in the morning to question us.'

'Question *us!* Why?'

'It's on our premises. Of course they want to talk to us.'

'Oh, right. Um - have they identified the body yet?'

'If they have, they haven't told me.'

'I can't drive home tonight, I've been drinking, I'll leave first thing in the morning.' He replaced the receiver. He felt sick. George was watching him curiously. 'Bad news?' he asked.

Danny nodded absently. Bad news hardly covered it. 'I need to check out early tomorrow,' he said. 'I have to get home.'

He left before seven the following morning. Cheryl, unused to being dragged out of bed so early, was sullen and silent. He was thankful, being in no mood for conversation. He dropped her at her flat in Edinburgh with a vague promise to call. His mind was in turmoil, trying to figure a way out of this disaster. He ran a hand over his sweaty face. He needed to stay calm. He would emphatically deny all knowledge. This had nothing to do with him. If he said it often enough, it would sound convincing.

He thought of Harriet and wondered if he should tell her before the police did. He decided against it. He couldn't be seen talking to her. He shivered; he had thought his secret would lay undiscovered forever, and now because his wife wanted to restore the fucking wishing well . . .

The police were waiting for him as he pulled into the driveway. The place was swarming with reporters. He swore under his breath. As soon as he stepped from his car, they descended on him, bombarding him with questions. He bowed his head against the flash of cameras and ignored the requests for a statement. Hurrying to his front door, he stepped inside, slamming the door behind him. In the hallway, he took a deep breath. He had been hoping for a few words with Christine before the police arrived, to make sure she didn't say anything to implicate him. But it was too late. They were already there, waiting for him.

He walked into the lounge, where two plain-clothed officers were standing by the fireplace. He smiled with relief when he saw that one of them was Robert Lloyd. Christine was seated on the sofa looking pale and strained.

'Hello Rob,' Danny smiled affably.

'Danny.' Robert Lloyd acknowledged him without smiling. 'This is my sergeant, Mark Walker. I'm afraid this is not a social call, Danny.'

'So I gather. I understand you've had a gruesome finding on our premises. Incredible.' Danny glanced briefly at Walker before moving to sit next to Christine. He took her hand. 'This must have been a terrible shock for you, darling,' he said.

She nodded, not looking at him.

Danny turned his attention back to Robert. 'How can I help? I've been in Scotland for a few days. Have you any idea who it is? Was it a man or a woman?'

'A male definitely, we have established that much. Forensics are still working, it shouldn't be too long before we know who he is, but a list of all your employees and ex-employees from you would be helpful.'

'Good heavens, are you suggesting it might be someone who worked here?'

'Not necessarily. The list will be purely for elimination purposes.'

'Right. How long has the body been there do you think?'

'Hard to tell, a few years certainly.'

Danny looked thoughtful. 'I suppose it could even have been a customer, we do allow them to visit the garden, but how did he end up down the well? We always keep it boarded up and there's a notice telling people of the danger.'

Robert remained silent and Danny shifted, uncomfortable with his scrutiny. 'I presume it was an accident?'

'We are waiting for the forensic report to establish the cause of death,' Robert said. 'I assume you can't shed any light on who it might be?'

'None at all. I'm sorry.'

Robert nodded. 'Well, if you could just get that list.'

'Christine will sort that out, won't you darling? She deals with the administration of the place, and excellent she is too.'
'Thank you for your help, we'll be in touch.'

He followed them into the hallway. 'Any chance you can get rid of that hoard of reporters outside?'

'I'll do my best.'

'Thanks, Rob.'

As he closed the front door on them, Christine appeared in the hallway. 'Who on earth do you think it can be?'

'I've no idea,' he shrugged.

'Do you think it could be someone we know?'

'Like who? I mean have any of our friends disappeared?'

'No, except . . .'

'What?'

'Harriet's husband went missing a few years ago.'

Danny felt as though he'd been punched. He took a sharp intake of breath. 'Why on earth should it be him?'

'I don't know, I'm just guessing.'

'I thought he went abroad.'

'That was always a bit suspect.' Christine gave him a hard look.

'Anyway, I can't see how he could have accidentally fallen down our well.'

'I suppose you're right. We will just have to wait and see what the police find out. It's all very terrifying though.'

He watched her enter the small sitting room, closing the door. He stayed for a moment, his heart still hammering in his chest. He wondered whether to follow her, to probe further into why she thought it was Jeremy, but decided against it. If she was suspicious of him, surely she would have said so.

* * *

Abigail Weston sat watching the local lunch time news whilst knitting a cardigan in a bright shade of green wool. She had picked up the skeins at a boot fair for the ridiculous price of fifty pence. It wasn't a particularly nice shade of green, but it was too good a bargain to miss. Her attention to the programme was half-hearted as she struggled with her poor eyesight to read the knitting pattern, so that she nearly missed hearing the newsreader.

" . . *human remains . . . have been found in the gardens of Pembroke Perfumery in the village of Upper Wyre yesterday. Police have not yet identified the remains, which are thought to be male, but a spokesman said it may have been buried for several years. The gruesome finding was discovered when the owner decided to . . .*"

Abigail dropped her knitting as her hands flew to her mouth. Jeremy, it had to be Jeremy.

She just knew it. She'd had her suspicions that Harriet and Danny were somehow involved ever since he had gone missing. She often visited the village, watching Harriet, noting how many times Pembroke visited her. It was so obvious to her that they were responsible, but she could never convince the police.

Oh God, after all this time, to find him like this.

Robert Lloyd was reading the pathologist's report on the skeleton. Although it was gone eight o'clock, he was still in his office trying to make sense of it all. It was only a preliminary report; the cause of death had still to be established.

A sharp knock on the door interrupted his thoughts. The door opened and Sergeant Walker entered. 'Sorry to interrupt, guv, any news on the body?'

'Just reading the report now.'

'Do we have any idea who it is?'

'Yes. It's a Jeremy Malin.'

'That was quick.'

'We had a stroke of luck. Do you remember Abigail Weston?'

'Oh God, not her, she was a nutcase.'

'Don't knock it. She's saved us a lot of time. She was here earlier and gave us the name of her brother's dentist and fortunately they had kept his records. It's Malin all right.'

'Right,' Walker looked suitably chastised. 'Has Mrs Malin been notified?'

'Not yet. I intend to go there shortly.'

'Shall I come with you?'

'No, you get off, I'll update you in the morning,' Robert said.

'Thanks, goodnight guv.'

'Goodnight, Mark.' Robert had already returned to the report before Walker left the room.

Judging by the condition of the skeleton it would appear Malin had been dead about five years, which was corroborated by his sister's statement as the time he went missing. He wondered if Malin was killed on the premises. And had either Danny or Harriet killed him?

He must make sure he didn't let his friendship with Danny cloud his judgement. Even so he couldn't quite believe Danny was capable of murder. Maybe it was Harriet. She was cold-hearted enough. Had she wanted Jeremy out of the way because of her affair with Danny? It seemed a bit drastic, besides could she have physically done it? He thought it unlikely considering her disability. It would have taken a great deal of physical strength to push Jeremy down the well.

None of it made sense.

He needed to wait until he had the forensic report showing the exact cause of death. That would help. He needed a lot more evidence before he could make an arrest.

As Robert drove to Harriet's cottage three-quarters of an hour later, he wondered, as he had many times before, if he had done the right thing in not going for promotion to Superintendent when he'd had the chance. He had not applied because he hadn't wanted to spend any more time than he did already at his desk. His wife, Debbie, had not agreed, saying it could mean he would be home earlier. Now of course it was too late to consider her wishes; she had died of cancer two years ago. He was glad he was still a DCI. He loved his job, liked the people he worked with and although some thought him a bit unorthodox, he usually got results. His job had got him through the difficult year of Debbie's illness and her painful death. He missed Debbie so much.

He sighed heavily, thinking this would probably be his last major case. He was being pensioned off due to ill-health. He had angina. Nothing too serious, but he was fifty-five and he had plans. He wanted to enjoy life while he still could. He wanted to finish renovating a *gite* he owned in France.

Tonight's decision to come alone to see Harriet would be frowned upon by his boss, Chief Superintendent Ted Wilkinson, but he thought Harriet would respond better to an informal visit.

He stepped out of the car and looked towards the cottage. He hunched his shoulders as he walked up the path and wondered if Harriet was sober for once.

* * *

Danny was dismayed to see Robert so soon, the following day. Unable to go to the perfumery because the premises had been closed and cordoned off, they had not long finished breakfast. Christine showed Robert into the study.

'We have identified the man as Jeremy Malin,' Robert informed them.

'Oh my God I was right,' Christine gasped.

Robert looked surprised. 'Why did you think it was him?'

'Just a guess,' Christine flushed.

Danny tried to look suitably shocked. 'Does Harriet know?'

'Yes.'

'Must have been a terrible shock for her. She always assumed he went abroad. How on earth did he end up in the well? What a tragic accident.'

330

'It hasn't been confirmed yet that it was an accident.'

'Really, you mean - you mean he might have been *pushed* in?'

'Not exactly.'

'What then?'

'That's what we're trying to establish.'

'I see.'

Robert consulted his notebook, clearly uncomfortable. 'I interviewed Harriet last night. She said something very interesting.'

'Oh.'

'She said that Jeremy surprised you both one evening at the perfumery. You and Jeremy were in a fight and he fell and accidentally hit his head on the compound table, killing him. She claims that you got rid of Jeremy's body. That she had no part in it.'

'What! That's a damned lie. The woman's demented. Why would I have a fight with him? I hardly knew the man.'

'Harriet claims that Jeremy threatened to tell Christine that you are the father of her child.'

'Rubbish.' Danny was panicking. He kept his fear under control with difficulty. 'That's a slanderous accusation.'

'It's no use denying it. Robert knows you're Amy's father,' Christine said wearily.

Danny stared at his wife. He was shocked that she had told Robert. He felt the sweat creeping over his skin as he saw a glance pass between them. What was going on here? What else did she know?

'Danny?'

He dragged his mind back as Christine's voice penetrated his thoughts.

'Okay, maybe I am the father. But that doesn't mean I had anything to do with Jeremy's death.'

'And you didn't dispose of his body in the well?'

'Of course not.'

Robert snapped his notebook closed. 'I'd like you to accompany me down to the station,' he said to Danny.

'Are you arresting me?' Danny gasped.

'No. I just need you to answer some more questions.'

'Shall I come with him,' Christine asked.

Robert shook his head.

Danny felt Christine's eyes on his back as he walked calmly from the room. Despite his outward appearance he felt anything but calm. He needed to think up a plausible story, convince the police he had nothing to do with it, he wasn't there. He mustn't look or feel guilty. It was not his fault. He must keep telling himself that over and over. *Bloody Harriet. Damn the woman.*

Chapter Fifty

Harriet poured herself a large gin and tonic, even though it was only ten in the morning. She hadn't slept all night.

Robert Lloyd's visit had terrified her. She had been taken to the police station last night, questioned and then released. She had no idea if he believed her story of it being an accident. When he had questioned her on how the body had got down the well she had panicked. She had not meant to involve Danny, but Robert had frightened her with his interrogation, asking her if she needed legal advice even though he had insisted he was not charging her or making an arrest.

Finishing her drink, she put on her coat. A walk by the river might calm her nerves.

She hadn't gone far before she met her father.

'I thought I'd find you here,' Bill said. 'I called last night, but you were out.'

Harriet gave him a surly look. She had thought he would have gone back to Canada by now. She hadn't exactly been pleasant to him. He had taken her out for a meal at his hotel on Christmas day and invited himself to her cottage on New Year's Eve, but on each occasion she had struggled to be civil. His questioning her at length on why she had given Amy away, and why she hadn't asked for his help, had annoyed her. Since then he had called every day, no doubt wanting to make up for his neglect, trying to be a loving, caring father, but she didn't want him around. It was too late for him to be involved in her life. Far too late.

'Where were you last night?' he probed. 'I was worried.'

Harriet glared at him in silence. She took a deep breath.

'There's something you need to know.'

'Go on.'

'The police came to see me last night. Jeremy – Jeremy's body has been found in a disused well in Danny's perfumery.'

'Bloody hell, I thought you told me he'd gone abroad.'

'That was a lie.'

'What do you mean?'

Harriet shrugged not looking at her father. 'It was an accident.'

'I don't like the sound of this. Go on.'

'There was a fight. I - I hit him. He stumbled and hit his head. Danny put him in the well.'

Bill's mouth dropped open. 'Bloody hell!' he said again.

'I was questioned last night at the station and allowed to come home, but I'll have to go back.'

Bill's face paled. 'I need to get you a good lawyer. I know someone. Leave it with me.'

'I'm guilty, Dad. I killed him. It was an accident but I still killed him.'

'The police will have to try and prove it was intentional. Now don't say anything else until you've spoken to a lawyer. Don't admit to *anything.*'

'Don't worry, I don't intend to. I only told you because I wanted you to know the truth.'

'Have the police questioned Daniel Pembroke?'

'I've no idea. I haven't spoken to him.'

Harriet needed a drink. 'Can we go back?' she said.

'Of course,' Bill took her arm; he could feel her shaking and his grip tightened in comfort.

As they walked, she wondered if Danny had been arrested yet and what he would say to the police.

At the cottage she made her father a coffee and poured herself another large gin and tonic. Bill raised his eyebrows, but he refrained from his usual comment that she drank too much.

Sitting at the kitchen table, Bill covered her hand with his. 'Harriet love, let's forget our differences. I'm here for you now.'

'Perhaps,' Harriet said.

* * *

Sergeant Walker knocked on Robert Lloyd's office door and entered the room.

'You wanted me?'

'Ah yes. I want Harriet Malin brought in for questioning again. Take PC Hopkins with you, and be careful; make sure Harriet understands it's only for further questioning - it's not a formal arrest. Harriet might panic, so be clear in what you say. She might want a solicitor, but I'd prefer to get just a few more satisfactory answers from her before she discovers she has the right to say nothing.'

Walker looked worried.

'Just do it,' Robert snapped, 'and don't tell Karen Hopkins about this conversation.'

'Right, Guv.'

Robert Lloyd was already waiting in the interview room at Cheltenham police station, when PC Hopkins ushered Harriet in. 'Thank you for coming in, Harriet,' he said pleasantly.

'I didn't have much choice,' Harriet snapped. 'Why have you brought me here again?'

'I need to go over again the questions from last night. I've arranged for the duty solicitor to be present, he should be here in about and hour, but we can have an informal, off the record, chat now if you agree.'

Harriet shrugged. 'Yes, just get on with it.'

'Of course,' Robert smiled. 'Would you like a cup of tea?'

'I'd prefer coffee, black no sugar.'

Karen Hopkins hurried off to get it.'

Robert cleared his throat. 'I spoke to Daniel Pembroke earlier this morning. At first he denied everything, but later, at the station, he finally confessed to disposing of Jeremy's body in the well.'

Robert looked down at his notes. 'He said your husband's death was no accident, that you hit him with a drum spanner, several times. Danny says you killed him deliberately.'

'He's lying.'

'He said that you blackmailed him into helping you.

Otherwise you would tell his wife about your affair.'

'Rubbish.'

'He claims you both engineered an elaborate plot to make everyone believe your husband had gone abroad.'

'It's a pack of lies, all of it.'

'From our records your husband was reported missing, by his sister, six years ago.'

'So.'

'*You* didn't report it though?'

'No. Why should I? We were separated,' Harriet shrugged.

'What was the argument about?'

'What?'

'You said your husband and Daniel Pembroke had an argument.'

'Jeremy accused Danny of deliberately running my car off the road. He also thought I was still seeing him.'

'Were you?'

Harriet shrugged again.

'What happened to your child?'

'What?' Harriet felt confused by the sudden switch in questioning.

'Your baby.'

Harriet lowered her gaze. She began to feel frightened. Robert Lloyd had done his homework. 'I had it adopted.'

'Why was that?'

'I wasn't ready for motherhood. Look, what has this got to do with my husband's death?'

'Just trying to build a picture. You see, I know the child wasn't adopted. I know that young Laura Armstrong has her illegally. Do you see where I'm coming from?'

'No.'

'You are not telling me the complete truth on any of this.'

'I have told you the truth, exactly how it happened. Jeremy fell and hit his head on the compound table. The blow must have killed him.'

Robert Lloyd leaned across the table and stared at her intently. 'I now have a full forensic report and I find it puzzling. Your husband didn't die from a blow to his head. *He died from a stab wound.* Part of a stake was found lodged in his ribcage. There is no doubt that was the cause of death. How could that possibly be an accident?'

Harriet paled. 'I don't understand. Okay, I admit I did hit him with a drum spanner. Danny was lying on the floor and Jeffrey was kneeling on him with his hands around Danny's throat, strangling him, and I had to stop him, so I grabbed the drum spanner and I hit him on his shoulder but it didn't stop him so I hit him again on the side of his face. He fell and hit his head on the compound table. I didn't *stab* him.'

'Forensic tells us a different story.'

'It doesn't make sense.'

'So you can't explain how Jeremy came to get that fatal wound.'

'No, I can't, but I didn't stab him.'

Bill was waiting for her when she got home. He made tea and sat down opposite her at the kitchen table. He looked as pale and shaken as she was.

'I've contacted my lawyer friend, Henry Whittaker, he'll be arriving tomorrow.'

'Thanks Dad, I think I'm going to need him.'

'What happened with the police this morning?'

'Robert Lloyd said that Jeremy was stabbed to death, with a garden stake. I didn't do it.'

Harriet bent her head into her hands. 'It must have been Danny. That's the only explanation. But why? Why stab him when he was already dead?'

Bill looked thoughtful. 'He obviously wasn't dead.'

'What do you mean?'

'Did you make certain? After you'd hit him, did you feel for a pulse?'

'Danny did that.'

'But you didn't check?'

Harriet shook her head; her eyes narrowed in anger. 'All these years he has let me believe I killed Jeremy when all the time. . . '

Bill touched her hand. 'We'll get some answers, don't fret.'

'The bastard! I need to see him.'

'Not yet. Wait until you have spoken to Henry and got some advice. We'll pull through this, just keep calm.'

'*Calm!* How can I keep calm?'

'Why don't you go and lie down for bit. You look exhausted. I'll see to dinner. And I think I should move in.'

'Whatever.'

Chapter Fifty-One

'Harriet, why the hell are you phoning me?'

'I need to talk to you, Danny.' It was the following morning and she hadn't slept again. Her father had stayed overnight and had only just gone out to fetch his morning paper. She didn't want him to know that she was ringing Danny; that she couldn't wait for his lawyer to arrive before she spoke to him. This was nothing to do with legal advice, this was personal.

'What about?' Danny snapped.

'What the fuck do you think it's about?'

'Don't take that attitude with me.'

Harriet gasped at his arrogance. 'I'm not taking the blame for Jeremy's death when you were the one that killed him.'

'What!'

'Robert Lloyd told me Jeremy died from a stab wound. We both know I didn't inflict that.'

Harriet could hear Danny's sharp intake of breath, then silence.

'I can't discuss this with you,' he said after a moment.

'Yes you can. Meet me on the canal tow path.'

'Are you completely mad? We can't be seen together.'

'Danny, I *have* to talk to you.' Her voice rose hysterically. 'Five o'clock. It will be dark by then.'

Harriet replaced the receiver, before he had time to refuse.

Harriet paced up and down the tow path. Where the hell was he? She had been waiting for over an hour.

She still couldn't get her head around Robert Lloyd telling her that Jeremy had been stabbed. Danny must have done it after he'd dragged Jeremy out into the garden. And the bastard had put all the blame on her!

At last, she saw him striding over the bridge. She waited, glancing nervously about to see if there were any people around, but the stretch of river was empty. He was at her side in minutes.

'This is madness, meeting like this,' he said coldly.

'It won't take long and there's no one here.'

'What do you want?'

'I want to know what happened that night, why you stabbed Jeremy.'

With furtive glance around, Danny sat down on the wooden bench. 'I had no choice.'

Harriet flared but she kept her temper under control. She wouldn't learn the truth if she let her anger show.

Lowering herself down beside him she said calmly. 'Tell me what happened.'

Danny stared silently towards the river as he told her about that night.

He had dragged Jeremy into the perfumery garden with no clear idea of what he was going to do. Bumping the body over the uneven path he found himself in the small arbour, rear of the rose garden. Secluded by the garden's high walls and screened from the perfumery by the arched privet hedges, he paused to get his breath. He looked around for a suitable place. The wooden arbour seat would be easy to move, but the patio slabs would take a lot of lifting. Old Ted, the gardener would be bound to notice they had been uplifted.

It was then he remembered the well. He had forgotten about it, it had been boarded up and disused for years because the crumbling masonry made it dangerous. A century ago it had been a wishing well, and a source of local attraction for the healing properties of the spring water. Now it was hidden by overgrown bushes and a dilapidated notice telling people to stay clear.

It had taken quite an effort to pull out the metal garden stakes and remove the protective wire mesh before prising up the wooden boards. He stared down the shaft, where he could just see the dark shiny surface of water. He remembered that the well was very, very deep. Perfect.

It was then he heard Jeremy groan. It had scared the shit out of him. He had been convinced that he was dead.

Jeremy had turned his head and stared at him, his eyes bulging with recognition and fear. His reaction had been instinctive, he had grabbed the first thing to hand, a metal stake and plunged it into Jeremy's inert body, aiming for his heart. His death had been instant, a low gurgle and then silence.

He resumed his gruesome task. The weight of him was so heavy that it took an immense effort to ease the body over the edge and tip it down the shaft. He watched it fall, heard the resounding splash as it hit the water. Shaking with exhaustion, he had carefully replaced the boards.

It was only later when he returned to the perfumery, after abandoning Jeremy's car and taking Harriet home, that the full impact of what he had done hit him. He had hurried to the toilet and been violently sick.

Even though Harriet had cleaned up the blood, he scrubbed the lab floor again, his whole body shaking, not only with the physical exertion, but with the horror of it all. He washed the drum spanner again with a cleaning solvent. He had been tempted to bury it with Jeremy's body, but someone would be bound to question why it was missing.

'I had to kill him. I could see in his eyes that he knew what I was about to do,' Danny said finally. 'You have no idea what's it been like all these years. I have nightmares about it, every time I close my eyes I see his bulging eyes, see the fear in them; hear that last sigh. But I did it for us.'

Harriet was silent when he finished. She stared at him in disbelief. 'All these years you let me believe that it was me that killed him.'

Danny shrugged. 'I'm sorry.'

'*Sorry!* Is that all you can say.'

'None of it matters now. It's all too late.'

'Why are telling me this now? Are you going to the police; are you going to tell them the truth?'

Danny laughed wryly. 'No darling. I'm going away.'

'Where?'

'Not sure yet. Somewhere where I can't be found.'

'You can't escape the law. You won't get away with what you have done.'

'Maybe not, but I'm going to try.'

'Take me with you?' she pleaded suddenly.

'Sorry, I can't.'

'Are you taking Christine?'

His eyes clouded. 'No. I have done her enough harm over the years. I won't make her a fugitive. She deserves to have a better life.'

'How heroic,' Harriet said scathingly. 'And what about me, what do I deserve?'

He laid his hand gently on her arm as he turned to look at her. 'Harriet darling, we deserve each other, but that won't happen. I'm sorry love, sorrier than you'll ever know. I hope in time you will forgive me.'

He leaned and kissed her on the mouth. Then he rose and strode down the path.

'Danny!' she screamed after him.

Harriet slumped on the bench, sobbing. It was over. She was never going to see him again. How would she live without him? He was the only man she had ever truly loved and he was gone.

She rose stiffly and walked to the river's edge. Her life had no purpose any more; she might as well end it. Staring bleakly into the water she thought of all the lonely, desperate years she had endured hoping that one day he would finally leave Christine and come to her. That was never going to happen now. Even if she avoided a prison sentence there was nothing to live for. It was unbearable.

As she brushed the tears from her cheeks she heard the crunch of footsteps. Danny. He had changed his mind; he had come back for her. She turned, her face alight with expectation, but it was not Danny.

'Oh it's you,' she said, her whole body sagging with disappointment. 'What on earth are you doing here?'

It was a moment before she understood the intention and then it was too late. As she hit the water her scream died in her mouth.

Chapter Fifty-Two

DCI Robert Lloyd sat with his feet up on his desk, his chair tilted, as he stared out of the window. It was now twenty-four hours since he had requested Danny come to the station for a DNA test. As yet no one had seen or heard from him. He wondered how much Christine was protecting him.

It was frustrating. He needed Danny to take the test, primarily to at least eliminate him, even though his gut feeling was that Danny was guilty. It was highly suspicious that he was not co-operating.

He had spoken to Abigail Weston again, had established yet again, that her brother had told her he was going to see Danny on the day Jeremy disappeared. She had no idea what it was about, but she said that her brother was upset by Harriet continuing to be involved with Danny. Abigail had said that Jeremy knew something about Danny, something damaging, but she didn't know what. He guessed now it would have been about the baby, Jeremy must have known that Danny had arranged for its supposed adoption.

It had been an oversight on his part that he had not questioned Danny back then; that he had been dismissive of Abigail's accusations. It was as well he was leaving the police force soon, he suspected he would be severely reprimanded for that.

He shouted for Mark Walker. 'Come on, we're off to Daniel Pembroke's home again,' he said sharply.

'Right Guv,' Mark started to follow and then stopped to answer the telephone.

Robert strode the length of the outer office towards the door.

'Guv,' Mark called after him.

He turned with irritation. Saw him waving the phone in the air. 'Not now, Mark.'

'But, Guv, this is urgent.'

Knowing Mark would not have called him unless it really was important he strode back to his desk and snatched the receiver. 'Lloyd.' he snapped.

He listened for a moment and then swore. 'Okay, on my way.' He replaced the receiver.

Mark was waiting patiently. 'What's up?'

'Harriet Malin has been found dead, drowned in the river apparently.'

'Jesus!'

'Come on,' Robert urged, 'we'd better get over there.'

'What about Daniel Pembroke?'

'That can wait. This might change things.'

The banging on the door woke Christine from a fitful sleep. Slipping on her dressing gown, she glanced at the clock before going downstairs. Nine o'clock. She didn't usually sleep in so late, even on a Saturday. Then she remembered; she had taken sleeping pills last night.

Unlocking the door, Christine stared from Robert to Mark Walker and knew something had happened. She stepped back and they followed her into the kitchen. She switched on the kettle before turning to face them. 'Have you found him?'

'What? Found who?' Robert said.

'Danny. Isn't that why you're here?'

'Yes, we've come to question him.'

Christine burst into tears. 'He's gone,' she sobbed.

'What do you mean?' Robert moved to where she was leaning against the sink and put his hand on her shoulder; a comforting gesture.

'A lot of clothes have gone and when I checked, his passport is missing.'

'How long ago was this?'

'I haven't seen him since yesterday morning. I've tried ringing his mobile, a dozen times, but it's always switched off. I think he's run off with Harriet. I heard him arranging to meet her.'

'I don't think so. Harriet's body was recovered from the river this morning.'

Christine's hand flew to her mouth. 'Oh my God!'

'Listen Christine, we need to find Danny, urgently. You said he was arranging to meet Harriet. Was it by the river?'

'I don't know, but Danny couldn't have had anything to do with her death. He wouldn't. It must have been an accident.'

'You have been loyal to Danny long enough. It's time to face the truth. Two deaths and Danny was very much involved with both victims.'

'I can't believe it.'

'Have you any idea where Danny might have gone.'

Christine shook her head. 'He didn't come home last night. I thought he'd - I thought he'd finally left me for her.'

'Look, I have to go. Will you be okay? I'll come back later.'

Christine nodded.

After they had left, she made a coffee and sat down. Harriet dead. She couldn't believe it. And all the time she had been imagining them together. She had even cancelled her Friday WI meeting, she had been so upset. Where was Danny? Had he really killed her? If he was innocent why hadn't he come home?

Chapter Fifty-Three

'Have you seen this morning's newspaper?' Paul said to Laura as she returned from taking Amy to school.

'No. What's happened now?'

Only last week they had read of the gruesome discovery of Harriet's husband. They had debated whether Harriet could have killed him, but she had been reluctant to believe it.

Paul handed her a copy of the Daily Mail.

Suspicious Death Of Woman Drowned In River Linked To Murder Enquiry.

A second murder enquiry has been launched after a woman was found dead at the river bank in the Gloucestershire village of Upper Wyre. At this time the identity of the victim cannot be named but it is believed to be Harriet Malin, a local resident. The police are linking this death to the body of Mrs Malin's husband discovered last week.

A post-mortem is taking place on Wednesday. Detective Chief Inspector Robert Lloyd heading the investigation said, "We are still at the very early stages of the investigation and would ask anyone with information that could assist our inquiries to contact the police immediately."

The report continued with a statement to say that the police were very keen to trace Daniel Pembroke, owner of the local perfumery, in connection with the recent findings of a skeleton discovered in a disused well in the grounds of the perfumery, now identified as Jeremy Malin.

Laura raised her head, her face drained of colour. 'Oh my God! Poor Harriet, who would kill her? I know she wasn't well liked, but to kill her . . .'

'What about this Danny, sounds like she gave him a hard time from what you were telling me,' Paul said.

Laura laughed incredulously. 'Danny! Never! Not in a million years.'

'Well the police are linking him to her husband's death. And why has he done a runner?'

'I don't believe that either.'

'Perhaps Harriet killed her husband after all.'

'No!'

'It was just a thought. I mean you did say she was a bit unbalanced.'

'I never said that.'

'Maybe not unbalanced, but a bit strange.'

Laura shook her head, clearly distressed. 'Perhaps, but even so, I can't see her as a murderess.'

'I wonder why the police are looking for Danny then,' Paul mused reading the article again. 'They must suspect he had something to do with Mr Malin's death.'

'I don't know, but it doesn't say it's in connection with *Harriet's* murder.'

'Not outright but reading between the lines I'd say it's a strong possibility.'

'You're wrong, Paul. I know you're wrong.'

Paul looked at her warily. Laura had been a bit spiky since returning home, not speaking much about her visit. She'd answered his questions with short monosyllabic answers, and volunteered little information. He knew the visit had not been successful, and that Harriet's cold behaviour had obviously upset her.

The sound was a choked whisper and he saw that she was crying. Going to her side he wrapped his arms around her, rocking her and stroking her head as he murmured soothing words of comfort. 'I love you so much.'

'And I love you, but I'm so scared. Harriet's death and this publicity, they'll find out I have Amy and take her away from me, I know it.'

'You can't be sure of that. They will see she has a good home here, no one else wants her. And you did say her grandfather, Bill would help.'

'I'm glad there are no secrets any more but I wish - I wish I had never gone to see Harriet.'

Laura sobbed, tears streaming down her face.

'I know, sweetheart I know, but you did the right thing.' He kissed her hair and pushed it back from her face. Searching in his pocket he found a tissue and wiped her wet face with a tender gesture. Laura sniffed. 'I feel like I'm two years old again,' she said.

Paul handed her the tissue. 'Here, blow your nose. I'm not doing that for you.'

Despite being upset she couldn't help but smile.

Later as they sat together drinking coffee she thought of Bill. 'Poor man,' she said, 'do you think I should go and see him, he must be devastated. He had only just made contact with Harriet after all these years.'

'I'd leave it a few days and see what happens. There's a murder enquiry going on, you don't want to get involved. Not with the situation with Amy. You could ring Bill though, and tell him how sorry you are.'

'Okay, I'll do that.'

Laura was silent for a moment. 'I think I'll ring Robert Lloyd first. See if he can tell me anything.'

'Good idea.'

Robert was unavailable so Laura rang Bill's mobile. It took a while to answer and the voice was not the well-assured one she remembered but a cautious, 'hello.'

'Bill, it's Laura. I've just read the news. I'm so sorry.'

'Thanks love. It's been awful. I've just been to identify her body.'

She could hear him fighting for control and she gave him a moment before she said gently. 'Do the police have any idea what happened?'

'They think she was pushed in, and . . .' his voice broke, 'and they are looking for Pembroke. He's disappeared.'

'Danny! They really think *Danny* did it?'

'They are not saying that, but they do want to question him and about Jeremy's death.'

She was shocked. 'They must have made a mistake. I can't believe it.'

'Before Harriet died she - she told me that she and Danny killed Jeremy.'

'What!'

'Harriet confessed to it. It's a bit complicated. I can't tell you on the phone, but both of them were under suspicion.'

'Oh Bill!'

After she had hung up, she sat in stunned silence. She thought of all the anger Harriet had displayed, of her obsession with Danny and wondered how much more she didn't know.

Chapter Fifty-Four

Laura climbed out of the Mercedes and turned her gaze away from the curious onlookers, a small group of local villagers gathered by the open church door.

She opened the rear door to let Amy out. Paul had been against bringing the child to Harriet's funeral, saying she was too young, but Laura said that when the time came for them to explain to Amy who her birth mother was, then she would have a memory of today and hopefully feel some connection with her. She also thought meeting his granddaughter might help Bill in his grief. She had no qualms about bringing Amy here. With the help of Bill's solicitor she had already started the process of legally adopting Amy.

She waited for Paul and they each held Amy's hand as they walked through the lych-gate and up the mossy path into the church.

The dark cold interior smelt musty. They made their way slowly towards the front and settled themselves in the second pew. Laura was surprised to see the church was packed. She surmised, rightly, that most of the congregation were there purely out of morbid curiosity, so that later they could gossip about the day's proceedings, and comment on Harriet's untimely death. She noticed Brett and his wife, and made a mental note to speak to them later. She was surprised to see Christine sitting with DCI Robert Lloyd.

Bill sat in the front pew. He turned his head and smiled sadly at Laura. She felt an overwhelming pity for him. To bury your only child must be the worst nightmare imaginable, particularly in these circumstances.

Bill's glance moved to Amy and he smiled at her. Earlier that day the introduction had been emotional. Bill had been overcome that Laura had brought her to meet him.

A few minutes later the coffin, with a simply bouquet of white roses, was carried in. The six pall bearers were strangers to Laura.

As the vicar arrived and the service started, Laura turned her thoughts to Harriet. What a tragic end to her life. A month since her death and apparently the police were no nearer to finding her killer, if indeed she had been murdered at all. Suicide had been suggested and although there had been no note left, it couldn't be ruled out. There were no marks on her body, or anything found from the post-mortem, to suggest foul play, but apparently the police were still suspicious. Harriet was familiar with the river tow path; she had walked it every day and because of her fear of water she never went too close to the edge, so it seemed unlikely she would have fallen in accidentally, which prompted questions. Had she been pushed? Pushed in by someone who knew that she couldn't swim?

She wondered if she would get a chance to talk to Robert Lloyd. She was curious to know what he thought about Harriet's death. Had she really been murdered by Danny, and did he have any clues as to where Danny might be? She remembered that Robert and Danny had been friends.

Laura turned her head as Bill rose shakily to his feet. She watched him walk to the lectern and her heart went out to him. Bill's face was tight with the effort of control. She saw his gaze sweep across the congregation. He met her eyes briefly before lowering his gaze. Bill cleared his throat and began to speak.

'Today's reading is from Corinthians 2. *The God of all comfort. . .*'

Bill returned to his seat and the first hymn began. Laura felt herself shaking, tears falling freely down her cheeks.

She paid attention as the Rev John Forbes started his eulogy. He tried to give a positive address, but it was obvious he hardly knew Harriet. But then, had anyone?

And then it was over. Laura watched sadly as the bearers lifted the coffin and she lowered her head as it passed.

They emerged and shook hands with the vicar. People began to walk away. Laura hung back when she saw Christine approaching. Christine stopped and looked down at Amy. Her mouth tightened. 'Is this Harriet's daughter?'

'Yes, this is Amy.'

'She has Danny's eyes.'

Laura wondered what Christine was thinking. She had been shocked to see her here; surely she must hate Harriet for what she'd done. 'I'm sorry,' Laura murmured, 'this must be hard for you.'

Christine gave a tight smile. 'She's gorgeous.'

Amy pulled at Laura's hand. 'Come on Mummy, Paul is going without us.'

Laura saw Christine was having difficulty in controlling her emotions. 'We have to go I'm afraid.'

Christine nodded. Laura turned to walk away but then said. 'Have you heard from Mr Pembroke?' she asked tentatively, feeling the question was an intrusion, but anxious to know the answer. She couldn't believe he had killed Harriet.

Christine shook her head, her voice wobbled. 'No.'

Leaving Amy with Paul, she followed Bill as he made his way along the side path towards the graveyard. Enclosed by a dry-stone wall, wild flowers grew here in the spring underneath the overhanging willows. It was very peaceful.

The vicar finished his prayer and Bill threw a single white rose onto the coffin.

They moved away and she took hold of Bill's arm to steady him, he seemed so frail; she walked slowly down the gravel path between the gravestones. Bowed with sorrow, he clung to her for comfort.

Laura thought back to the few short days she had spent with Harriet. It seemed strange that someone she hardly knew could have had such a profound involvement in her life.

At the cottage Laura made tea and sandwiches. Bill seemed comfortable in Paul's presence and spoke of the past, of his wife, and how he regretted the rift that had caused so many wasted years apart from his child. His gaze constantly strayed to where Amy was playing on the floor with Satan. She had been pestering for a cat for ages and so far Laura had resisted.

'Thank you for bringing Amy,' Bill said in a low tone. 'Does she know it's her mother we buried today?'

Laura shook her head shocked at the question. 'Amy thinks I'm her mother,' she reminded him. 'It's too soon yet to tell her the truth.'

'Yes of course, sorry.'

'I promise I will tell her about Harriet.'

'Thank you.'

'What are you whispering about?' Amy said coming to her side.

'I was telling your granddad what a clever girl you are,' Laura smiled.

Amy grinned at Bill and when he held out his arms she went and sat on his knee. 'I'm so glad I have a granddad,' she whispered in his ear. 'Megan hasn't got one, only a grandma. Will I get a grandma soon?'

Bill chuckled. 'I don't think that will be likely. Will I not do?'

'Oh yes,' Amy nodded vigorously, then wriggled down and returned to the cat.

'What will you do, will you live here now?' she asked Bill.

'Live here?' he said surprised, accepting a mug of tea.

'The cottage is lovely, I thought maybe – but perhaps it will be too painful.'

'I only want to stay until everything is settled, but I don't want to live here permanently. In any case I doubt very much that the cottage belongs to me. I can't find Harriet's will, assuming she made one. If not then the courts will have to decide on her estate, but I should imagine it will go to Amy. I'm more than happy for her to have it.'

Laura wondered if Amy would want it. This had not been a happy place for Harriet. She kept her thoughts to herself.

353

'Where do you intend to live?' Paul asked.

'I'm not sure. I haven't anywhere in mind really.'

'Perhaps you could come and live in Sidmouth,' Laura said. 'It's a great place on the coast. You'd love it. And you would be near Amy.'

Bill looked from one to the other and laid down his mug. He reached over and held Laura's hand. 'I'd like that. I'd like it a lot, if you wouldn't mind. I mean my daughter wasn't exactly, well - she didn't do very well by you. I wouldn't blame you if you didn't want anything to do with me.'

'Oh Bill,' Laura said upset that he could think that way. 'None of this was your fault. We'd love you to be near us, for Amy to get to know her grandfather properly.'

Bill squeezed Laura's hand as tears ran down his cheeks.

Laura went upstairs to pack Harriet's clothes into boxes for the charity shop. It was a sad, arduous task, but she couldn't leave it for Bill to do. The bedroom must have been beautiful once, but now the whitewashed walls were stained yellow and the room dusty and unkempt. The bed was unmade and clothes littered the floor. Laura moved to the little leaded window and looked out, her gaze falling across the meadow to feast her eyes on the church spire and a row of thatched cottages, and thought how pretty the village was even in winter.

Her hand rested lightly on her abdomen and for a moment her eyes shone with happiness. She was expecting a baby. At first, when her period was late, she had thought it was the stress of the past few weeks, but yesterday the doctor had confirmed she was three months. She had told no-one, not even Paul yet. She wanted to get today over with first.

Turning back into the room she began lifting out clothes from the wardrobe and carefully folding them. She started on the chest of drawers. Underneath a pile of underwear she found an envelope. Opening it carefully she discovered a photograph of a new born baby. Tears welled up in her eyes and for a moment she couldn't read the writing on the back. Amy – 10th September 2001.

So Harriet had kept Amy's baby photo all these years, had pretended not to care, but she must have done, she must have cared a little. She slipped the photo into her jacket pocket; she would show it to Amy when she was older.

She had decided, since Harriet's death, that she would never tell Amy that her mother had abandoned her, and that her father had gone to great lengths to deny her existence. She would fabricate a story that Harriet had never recovered from her coma and had eventually died and that her father, stricken with grief, had died of a broken heart.

What was one more lie if it would save her precious child from knowing the heartbreaking truth?

Her thoughts turned to Harriet again and how dismissive she had been, and she wondered yet again how a mother could give away her child. Laura sighed heavily; she would never understand it.

She thought of her own mother, the mother she had never found. Maybe she would try again one day.

Chapter Fifty-Five

Robert Lloyd walked beside Christine as they left the church. By mutual agreement they decided not to attend the grave.

'Will you come back to the house for lunch?' Christine said.

Robert thought of the stack of paperwork on his desk. *Bugger it!*

'Yes,' he replied, smiling, as he took her arm, 'thank you.'

He had always admired Christine, thought she had a raw deal with Danny even though Danny had been his friend. She had been a great support to him during his wife, Debbie's, illness and he would never forget that. He felt sorry for her now, she seemed lost, broken.

'There's something I want to ask you.'

'Oh dear, not more questions,' Christine smiled tightly.

'It's not about Danny this time.'

Christine glanced at him, but his face remained inscrutable.

Deciding she would not get an answer until they were home, she walked in silence with him to his car.

'Can I help?' Robert asked, watching her move expertly round the kitchen preparing toasted panini for their lunch. Christine handed him a bottle of wine to open.

'What are your plans?' Robert asked.

They were both aware that the chance of Danny returning was remote. Although trying to find him now involved Interpol, Robert was not hopeful. He seemed to have vanished into thin air. Without the DNA test, all he had was circumstantial evidence that Danny was involved in either or both of the crimes.

Christine looked downcast. 'I'm selling the perfumery.'

'You're selling!' Robert looked shocked. He knew how much it meant to her.

'It was a hard decision, but I can't carry on there, not after all that's happened. A rival company have made me a good offer.'

'What will you do?'

'I'm not sure. I shall certainly leave the village.'

'I can understand that, but where will you go?'

'I haven't decided yet. I can't bear to stay here any longer, though. It holds too many bad memories.' She placed the toasted ham and cheese panini's on the table with a bowl of salad. They sat down.

Christine gulped down half a glass of wine.

'You look as if you needed that,' Robert smiled.

'I did. Today was difficult. Especially seeing – seeing Danny's child.'

'That was a shock I agree. I must admit I was surprised that you went to the funeral, that you asked me to accompany you.'

Christine said sadly. 'I went today to pay my respects to Harriet. Even though I disliked her, hated what she did to us, she didn't deserve to die. And if Danny was responsible, well, I just felt I owed it to her.'

Robert reached across the table and laid his hand on hers. 'Don't look back, move on.'

'I want to, I hope I can. The perfumery has been my whole life. It would be different if I'd had children. . . ' She sounded defeated.

He was not a man given to impulsive gestures. He surprised himself when he said carefully. 'I have a place in France. I plan to retire there. It's deep in the countryside, beautiful, but lonely for a person to be on their own.' He looked at her tentatively, wondering if she would pick up on what he was trying clumsily to say.

Christine smiled. 'Are you asking me to come with you?'

'Does it appeal?'

'I think it might.'

Epilogue

Danny sat in a bar drinking lukewarm lager. His suit was crumpled from the heat and his shoes dusty. Idly he picked up a discarded week-old copy of an English newspaper. His hand shook as he read the article. Outraged that the police were looking for him in connection with Harriet's death made him shake with anger.

He held his hand up to killing Jeremy, but that had been unpremeditated, an act of self-preservation. But he would never have killed Harriet. She had infuriated him over the years, but he had loved her. He had genuinely meant what he had said that last evening. He was sorry for the hurt he had caused her.

He tried to think of anyone who had a grudge against her, enough to push her in the river but no one sprang to mind.

He signalled the barman and ordered another Stella. He drank it quickly. then picking up the newspaper left the bar. He walked slowly towards his hotel. He would move on tomorrow, he decided, this heat didn't suit him. Cairo didn't suit him. Where to next? South America maybe, Brazil appealed. He would decide later. Money was not a problem. Christine had bought out his share of the perfumery when her parents had died, leaving her a large inheritance. He hadn't wanted to accept the money; he told her it was half hers anyway, but she had insisted that she had complete control. He suspected she needed the security since finding out he was still involved with Harriet. He knew she was always afraid he would leave her, but that had never even remotely been his intention. He had deposited the money in an

358

offshore account and now it had saved his life. He would travel extensively until he found somewhere he would be safe.

He couldn't return to England to clear his name of the accusation that he had killed Harriet because he would be arrested for Jeremy's murder. There was nothing for him back there anyway. His marriage to Christine was over. It was a sad fact, but he was on his own.

Poor Harriet. He couldn't believe she was dead.

* * *

Several thousand miles away, back in England, in a small terraced house, Abigail Weston sat and waited for the police to come and arrest her. She was ready to confess to Harriet's murder, to explain that she had no choice but to kill her. It wasn't right that Harriet should live and carry on with that Daniel Pembroke after what she had done. She had seen them together, sitting on the bench. She had seen them kissing. The sight of it had incensed her. It wasn't fair. She had to have justice for her brother's death because the police had refused to see the truth.

She couldn't understand what was keeping them. She had been waiting for days. But no one came.

Coming Soon

If you have enjoyed Harriet's Daughter don't miss

A STEP TOO FAR

Sarah Turner

2007

November

Martin Burrows pushed the dilapidated pram along the towpath of the Grand Union Canal. It was an old style carriage pram, a Silver Cross, black and cream, with a wobbly wheel. He walked slowly because it was dark and because the pram was heavy, filled with all his possessions. He wore a filthy, grey army coat, fastened at his waist with string. His hair hung in a tangled dirty brown mass as did the growth covering his weather-beaten face.

The evening was cold and the air filled with the threat of rain. The path was muddy and several times he almost slipped and fell.

As he ambled along he contemplated his life, something he rarely did, but for some reason tonight he felt despondent. How had everything gone so wrong in such a short space of time? One minute he was a successful lawyer, married to a beautiful woman, with a wonderful son, then in a split second, a moment of distraction, and his life had shattered into a million pieces.

He sniffed and wondered if he was catching a cold. His coat was damp and crusted with mud and his shoes were lined with cardboard so it wouldn't be surprising.

Reaching Kingswood Junction where the Grand Union linked up with the Stratford-on-Avon canal he struggled over the bridge humping the pram across the steep uneven concrete path and headed towards the lock basin.

Passing under an iron bridge as a train thundered overhead he paused to look at the narrow boats moored alongside, their tiny lights glowed and he wished he was sitting inside, feeling the warmth and comfort, with a hot meal and perhaps a glass of wine. There was a time when he took such things for granted, never believing for one moment that they were fragile things, ready to be snatched away in the blink of an eye.

Spotting a cigarette butt he bent down to pick it up. From the depths of his deep pockets he found a book of matches and lit up, savouring the pleasure. He coughed as the smoke hit his lungs and his eyes watered, but he continued to puff away until it was all gone.

A clap of thunder made him jump and before he had time to seek shelter the rain hit him in large heavy drops. 'Bugger it.' He began to hurry as the rain came down in earnest and he looked around for a suitable place to shelter before he got completely drenched.

With a sigh of relief he spotted a red and blue narrow boat, *Morning Dew.* The boat belonged to Kirsty Ellis; he had forgotten she was moored here. He hadn't seen her for over two years and was surprised she was still here. She would give him shelter, even in his present state. It hadn't bothered her last time.

Even so, he still hesitated. Things might have changed, she might not be alone.

A flash of lightning and another clap of thunder made the decision for him. Hurriedly he crossed to the picnic area and pushed his pram into the bushes, praying no one would pinch it. As he turned back towards the narrow boat a figure stepped off the short plank onto the towpath.

His eyes widened in surprise. Andrea Merrick. What on earth had she been doing on Kirsty's boat? He had thought they had fallen out years ago. It had been ages since he'd seen her too but he knew her instantly. She was not someone you forgot easily.

He watched her as she turned and cast a furtive glance back at the barge.

'Andrea?'

She screamed. Backing away she stared at him clearly not recognising him.

'Andrea it's Martin. Are you okay?'

She gazed at him as if he wasn't there.

'Has something happened?' Martin probed, reaching out his hand to her.

She flinched and stepped back. His breath caught in his throat as he watched her raise her hands to her face, hands that were covered in blood. As he stared she lowered them, gazing down in horror, and giving a small cry of distress. Before he could stop her she had fled, disappearing into the darkness.

'Andrea, wait.'

Even in the dim light the terrified expression on her face had been clear to see. Something had scared her. He made to go after her, to find out how badly she was injured, but self preservation halted his step. *Don't get involved.* The voice in his head was loud and clear. He looked towards Kirsty's narrow boat again. He scratched his beard, pondering. Should he still seek shelter, was Kirsty also injured? Much as his instincts told him otherwise he knew he couldn't walk away.

The rain intensified as he made a dash for the boat and jumped on board. Hindered by his overcoat he stumbled and fell heavily rocking the boat. 'Shit!' He swore as he heaved himself to his feet. Discovering the cabin door open he called out.

'Hello, hello, Kirsty, are you there?'

Silence.

Strange. He bent his head and stepped inside. The galley and saloon were tidy with no sign of habitation. He chewed on his bottom lip as he decided what to do next. If Kirsty wasn't here what had Andrea been up to?

He made his way towards the front cabin and pushed open the door. In the darkness he could just about make out the shape of someone on the bed. His hand searched along the wall until he reached the light switch. As light illuminated the prone figure the sight made him gasp and his hand flew to his mouth. 'Oh God, oh God!' he staggered backwards, crashing against the door frame. He hesitated just a few seconds longer. This was none of his business. He couldn't get involved.

He was off the boat in a flash; grabbing his pram, heedless now of the lashing rain, he began to run, run faster than he had ever run in his life.